Praise for
BEDTIME STORY

"Creative and well-written." *Winnipeg Free Press*

"About a good book, we say we 'devoured it.' But what if a book devoured us? . . . In Robert Wiersema's *Bedtime Story*, it does."
The Vancouver Sun

"An all-consuming love story to books." *Edmonton Journal*

"A fun read. . . . Serpentine and clever in structure."
The Globe and Mail

"Powerful. . . . Wiersema's most ambitious work to date. . . . *Bedtime Story* is all that it should be. More. It is frightening. It is fabulous entertainment. It is intensely thought-provoking. Above all, it is a hint and a tickle of things to come." *January Magazine*

"A well-crafted story, one that really works through the fantasy novel cliches and looks at the darkness lurking behind them. . . . Wiersema's a fine storyteller, and once he gets his hooks into you, you won't want to stop reading." *Boing Boing*

"An absorbing excursion. . . . [*Bedtime Story*] . . . is a genre unto itself, a hybrid of supernatural thriller and sword-and-sorcery fantasy." *Times Colonist*

BEDTIME STORY

A NOVEL

ROBERT J WIERSEMA

VINTAGE CANADA

Published in Canada by Vintage Canada, a division of Random House of Canada Limited, Toronto, in 2010. Originally published in hardcover in Canada by Random House Canada, a division of Random House of Canada Limited, in 2010. Distributed by Random House of Canada Limited.

Vintage Canada with colophon is a registered trademark.

www.randomhouse.ca

Library and Archives Canada Cataloguing in Publication

Wiersema, Robert J.
    Bedtime story / Robert J. Wiersema.

Issued also in electronic format.

ISBN 978-0-679-31376-2

    I. Title.

PS8645.I33B42 2011   C813'.6   C2011-902043-X

Book design by Leah Springate

Printed and bound in the United States of America

10 9 8 7 6 5 4 3 2 1

For Xander, as promised.
And for Cori, the heart of magic.

The Child is father of the Man.
—William Wordsworth

HE COULD HEAR the sirens.

Brent Corvin looked out the apartment window, craning his neck to see down the block.

Lights flashing, the ambulance manoeuvred up the narrow street, hedging its way past the parked cars, through several groups of kids headed toward the beach, carrying coolers, waving flags.

"They're coming," he called to Matt's bedroom. "They're almost here."

"Brent." Carol's voice was faint.

He ran through the living room, knocking a stack of books and papers off the coffee table, not even pausing to glance at them.

The apartment was stifling, the fans just pushing the hot air around. Matt's room was the worst. With his door always closed, the blinds always pulled, it was unbearable. Stepping inside was like walking into an oven.

"They're coming," he repeated. "How's he doing?"

He could barely see his wife in the gloom. Matt's reading lamp was smashed against the wall. It seemed more evening than afternoon.

It didn't occur to Brent that he could reach over and flick a switch.

Carol was slumped on the floor, pressed into the corner between the bed and the wall, her arms wrapped tight around Matt. "It's okay, honey," she whispered, her face close to his. "The doctors are coming. You're gonna be okay."

She looked up at Brent, her lips split and bleeding.

"Is he . . .?" Brent began.

Cautiously, Carol loosened her grip on Matt. She didn't completely relax her arms, in case he started again. Without his mother's restraint, Matt slid back toward the bed, his eyes wide.

"Matt? Matt?" Squinting in the dimness, Brent remembered the light.

Carol flinched and closed her eyes against the sudden brightness. Matt didn't react at all. He didn't even blink.

Brent kneeled beside him. His son's face was slack, expressionless. A thin string of drool escaped from his lips, trailed across his cheek.

"Matty?"

If the boy heard his father, he gave no sign. Clad only in undershorts, Matt was covered in goosebumps. His chest rose and fell, but he looked . . . Brent couldn't bring himself to even think the word.

Only Matt's eyes moved, flicking ceaselessly from side to side. Brent watched his green eyes for several long seconds, waiting for his son to blink.

He didn't.

The buzz of the intercom shattered the still of the apartment.

"The ambulance," he said.

It had started less than fifteen minutes before.

Their Fourth of July had been quiet so far, everyone busy with their own projects as the temperature inside the apartment rose. Brent had stripped down to his cut-offs and angled the fan so it blew near him without sending his papers across the room. He had spent the morning at his desk, pressing through yet another proofread of his thesis. If not for the clattering of his calculator, his wife and son might have forgotten he was home.

He looked up from the pages and glanced at the clock when he heard Carol's steps behind him. 12:30. Where had the morning gone?

"I brought you some lemonade," she said, careful not to startle him.

Brent turned in his chair. "That'd be—"

He stopped.

She smiled at his reaction.

She was wearing cut-offs that rode high on her slim thighs, and a top that was tied off well above the belt-line. She'd pulled her hair back in a ponytail and her eyes were dancing.

Carol touched his shoulder as she passed him the glass. "You're sticky," she said.

She looked cool and soft and she smelled of baby powder.

He sipped his lemonade. "This is nice," he said, unable to take his eyes off her.

"A special treat," she said, her smile widening. "It's not every day I've got both my boys home. Between teaching and your thesis, you haven't had a day off in weeks." She looked meaningfully at the desk, with its chaos of yellow pads and calculations. "If you call this a day off."

"I'm sorry."

"I know," she said. "The sooner you finish, the better it is for all of us. I can't wait to be the math professor's wife."

She tousled his hair, and he wondered if they could get away with sneaking into their bedroom and locking the door for a while. Probably. Matt wouldn't even notice. Even talk of the Blue Angels doing an air show over Lake Union for the Bicentennial hadn't been enough to tear him away from his reading.

"But it *is* a holiday," Carol continued. "And I'm not going to let my boys miss out on all the fun."

Brent laid his pencil across his thesis. It was clear from her tone that he wasn't going to get any more work done.

"So what did you have in mind?" he asked, slipping his fingertips into one of the back pockets of her cut-offs.

She spun playfully away. "Not that. Not now, anyway. Right now we're going to have a bite of lunch—the three of us—and then we're going to take the cooler I've packed out to the lake and have a real holiday. You know, the kind with real people and real jet planes and real sunburns." She kept a tantalizing distance, and swayed a little as she spoke. "And if you're lucky, you might even discover that there's a very cold six-pack tucked under the ice and the potato salad, just for you." She danced back into arm's reach and trailed a finger down his chest. "And if you're really lucky—" The finger stopped tantalizingly close to the top of Brent's cut-offs. "You might finish off the day with some fireworks."

She moved away again, turning to say, "Wish me luck. I'm going to bring Matty some lemonade and break the bad news to him."

"Luck," he said, watching her walk away, the gentle, hypnotic sway of her back pockets.

He had only just turned back to straighten his desk when he heard the sound of smashing glass, and Carol's scream.

The paramedics each carried battered red medical kits that looked like toolboxes.

"Where's the patient?" asked the one with the shaggy blond hair and moustache.

"Through here." Brent led them to Matthew's bedroom. "Be careful, there's—"

But the paramedic, who looked like a surfer just past his prime, was already kicking broken glass out of their way. Brent followed the second paramedic, whose close-cropped hair made him look older, like something off a military recruiting poster.

By the time they reached the bedroom, the surfer was lifting Matt away from Carol. The boy's body drooped in the man's arms, limp and somehow empty.

He laid Matt on the bed and opened his kit.

"Can you tell me what happened?" the older medic asked, pressing his fingers against the artery in Matt's neck.

"I came into the bedroom," Carol said, standing up uneasily. "I was bringing him some lemonade."

The older medic was listening to Matt's chest with a stethoscope while the younger wrote on a clipboard.

Carol's face was flushed, wet with sweat and tears. Her hair had come out of its ponytail and was messy and sticking to her skin. Wherever Brent could see bare flesh, there were red marks where Matt had hit her.

"Was he in distress when you came into the room?" the older medic asked.

Carol took a moment to answer. "Yes. Yes, he was lying on his bed, and he was . . . he was kicking and his arms were . . ." She struggled for the words. "His whole body was jerking."

Brent had raced to the bedroom after hearing Carol scream. At first he assumed something was wrong with her—with the broken glass and the puddle of spilled lemonade on the floor, she might have cut herself or slipped.

But she was kneeling against the bed, leaning over Matt, trying to hold him. His body was jerking and flailing, snapping like a fish on a line, his head tossing uncontrollably, his arms sweeping in every direction. As Brent watched, one fist slammed across his bedside table, shattering the lamp against the wall. A sound, halfway between a grunt and a scream, was coming from deep in his throat.

Carol was clutching him desperately, her face white. "Call an ambulance," she screamed, as their son rolled off the bed and pulled them both to the floor.

"Has he ever had a seizure before?" the older medic asked.

Carol shook her head. "No."

Brent tried to look around the clean-cut medic's back, to see what he was doing.

"Is there a family history of epilepsy or other seizure disorders?"

"Not that I know of," she said.

Carol stepped toward Brent and he wrapped his arms around her shoulders.

The younger medic wrote on his clipboard. "Might be the heat. Was he exerting himself today? Any sports?"

Brent shook his head. "No, he's been in here all morning."

The medic looked up at him as if to ask what sort of thirteen-year-old boy spends the Bicentennial inside with his parents rather than out with his friends. Brent had been asking himself similar questions since school ended a week ago.

"He was reading." Brent felt compelled to explain, even if he didn't understand it himself. He gestured at the book splayed open in the fragments of the shattered lamp.

"His pupils are non-reactive," the older medic said. "But they are moving."

"Tracking?" asked the other.

He passed an extended finger slowly in front of Matt's eyes. "No. No tracking."

The medic made a note.

"Is that . . .?" Carol struggled again to find the words. "Is that strange?"

"No reaction to noxious stimulate," the medic said, as if he hadn't heard her.

"What does that mean?" Carol asked.

"Weird," the younger medic said, jotting a note.

"What does that *mean*?" Carol asked again, stepping toward the bed.

The medic looked up at her, his expression fixed and stern at first. Then, taking in the fear on her face, he seemed to relax.

"We don't know, Mrs. . . ."

"Corvin."

"Mrs. Corvin. It's not clear what's going on, what's happened to your son." He glanced over at the younger medic, who then slipped out of the room. "He'll grab the stretcher. We're going to take Matthew to University Hospital to run some tests and get him hydrated."

"Oh God," she said, under her breath.

He shook his head. "Your son's vital signs are pretty close to normal. He's running a little hot, but everybody is these days."

After the younger medic returned from the ambulance, they lifted Matt effortlessly onto the stretcher, securing him with straps across his chest and legs. His head lolled slightly to one side, his eyes still darting back and forth.

"University Hospital," the first medic reminded them. "One of you should ride with us."

Matthew was white against the green sheets, his eyes wide, staring unblinkingly toward the ceiling.

PART ONE

✿ ✿

VICTORIA – MAY 2010

I

DAVID'S EYES GLEAMED as I set the package on the coffee table in front of him. I had wrapped it in the comics pages from last Sunday's paper, the way my mother used to wrap all my birthday presents.

"I wonder what this could be," he said, bouncing the package in his hand, teasing me.

"Only one way to find out."

Jacqui was clearing the far end of the table, stacking the cake plates, crushing the torn wrapping paper into a Thrifty Foods bag.

"It feels like a book," he said, running his fingers around the edges of the package.

"From your father?" Jacqui asked. "How odd."

David giggled as he tore at the paper. He looked up at me when he saw the leather cover and a corner of a faded, silver-embossed seal, and I smiled. He pulled the rest of the paper off with a flourish, no longer able to bear the excitement.

Then his face fell.

"Oh," he said, turning the book over in his hands. "*To the Four Directions*," he read, furrowing his brow. "By Lazarus Took."

I forced myself to keep smiling. Jacqui shook her head and plucked the comics in which I'd wrapped the book to tuck them away.

"He's a good writer," I said, leaning toward him. "I haven't read this one, but I used to read his books when I was your age."

He looked down at the book, then back at me.

"You'll like it," I said, hopefully. "There's a quest, and—"

"Is it as good as *Lord of the Rings*?" He ran his fingers over the silver seal on the cover.

"It's—it's different."

"Oh."

I probably should have expected this reaction. I probably should have bought him a copy of *The Lord of the Rings*, like he wanted.

"What do you say to your dad?" Jacqui prompted.

"Thanks, Dad," he said weakly, coming over for an obligatory hug.

"You're welcome," I whispered into his hair.

"And this one's from me," Jaqui said, placing the last box on the table.

Separate gifts for David. Something else I'd never expected.

Under the bright paper was the box from David's latest pair of sneakers. She had taped the edges of the lid down, and David grinned as he tore at them. There was nothing forced about his reaction as he worked the box open.

"A new glove," he practically shouted. "Thanks, Mom!" He almost knocked her over with his hug.

"You're welcome," she said breathlessly, ruffling his hair. "I got some oil as well. It'll need to be broken in."

He looked at the glove, studying every stitch and seam. "Rob Sterling says that if you put a ball in it and put it under your mattress it helps."

"Sounds like that would make it pretty hard to sleep," I said, as lightly as I could.

They both ignored me.

"You can do that," Jacqui said. "We'll look up some other ideas on the computer."

"Cool," David said, before spontaneously throwing his arms around her again. "I love you, Mom."

"I love you too, Davy," she said, looking at me over his shoulder.

"Can we go out and have a catch?" he asked her, bouncing on the couch.

"Sure we can," Jacqui said without hesitation. "Just a quick one, though. You don't want to be late for your game." He was already wearing his jersey.

David bounced to his feet and started toward the front door. He stopped partway and looked back at me.

"Do you want to come too, Dad?"

Both of them waited for my response.

"Not right now," I said, feeling a little raw from his disappointment. "I'm gonna finish cleaning up in here. Maybe later, though."

He didn't look surprised, or particularly disappointed. Clearly he'd expected that answer.

Minutes later, listening to the sound of leather on leather through the front windows, I crumpled the last of the wrapping paper into the plastic bag and took it and the stack of plates into the kitchen. When I came back, I picked up the book, riffled through the pages.

Seeing it through Davy's eyes, it really didn't look like much: just a novel, no movie or videogame connection, nothing he could talk about at school. And it was used, at that: someone had written their name on the inside of the front cover.

Not much of a present for an eleventh birthday.

I turned the book over in my hands.

It was a thick hardcover, bound in brown leather, with a ding in the upper right corner, where it looked like someone had dropped it. The round symbol on the front cover was faded silver, with a band of strange lettering, almost Arabic-looking, circling a star in its middle. Within the star was another circle, which looked like it had been red at one time, but the colour had faded, leaving just a rusty mark against the brown leather.

The symbol also appeared, in miniature, on the spine of the book, separating the title from the author's name.

To the Four Directions.

Lazarus Took.

I had found the book at Prospero's on my way for my weekly lunch with Dale the week before. I had had to look twice at the spine when I first saw it: I had never seen a Lazarus Took hardcover before. The four books I had read had all been paperbacks: this was something new. Well, not new—the copyright page read: Alexander Press, 1951.

Turning to the first chapter, I couldn't help myself: with the first sentence it was like I was eleven years old again, reading in the apple tree or the hayloft at my grandparents' place in Henderson.

TO THE FOUR DIRECTIONS

"I'll get a beating if I am late to the stables," Tamas complained. But that didn't stop him from following Matthias through the winding alley in the dark.

"You worry too much, Tamas," Matthias said. "You have time for a little food. The stable-master will be asleep for hours yet. Besides," he said, hopping over the short wall into the back garden of The Mermaid. "I would be more worried about my mother." Matthias flashed his best friend a sly grin.

"Oh, I am," Tamas muttered, heaving himself over the wall. He almost fell on a stack of discarded bottles.

"Shush. We don't want to wake—"

The water hit Matthias in the face as the back door swung open, soaking him from head to foot.

"What—?" he sputtered.

"Oh, I am sorry," Mareigh, said, smiling sweetly. "I thought you must be a thief. No respectable person would be stealing through the yard at this hour of the night." She passed the bucket to Arian.

Matthias tried not to stare at the serving girl.

"And you, Tamas, what are you looking at?" Mareigh demanded, glaring past her sopping son, hands on her hips. "Does your mother know where you are?"

"She knows I am with Matthias."

"Sad thing for a mother to give up on her son like that." She stepped back from the door. "Well, come on," she said. "You're better off inside. Someone has come looking for you."

Matthias glanced at Arian, but she was already busying herself at the stove. He sat down at his usual spot at the table, Tamas across from him.

"So, would either of you know why I had Zekariah and Jarrett and their friends pounding at the door an hour after closing?"

Matthias hid his hands, with their scraped knuckles, on his lap.

"He said he was looking for you, son of mine," she said. "And he seemed to have fewer teeth than when he was gracing us with his custom earlier."

He tried not to look at Tamas, not wanting to give anything away, but his mother noticed something in his expression. "What did you do?" she asked, sounding defeated.

"Nothing," he said. As Arian leaned past him to set cups on the table he became almost dizzy from her closeness, the sweet smell of her.

His mother brought her hand down on the table with a hard smack. "This is not funny," she said. "If there are people looking for you in the middle of the night, I should at least know why." She turned to his friend. "Tamas?"

Matthias almost groaned.

"There was a fight," Tamas said quickly.

"And I suppose they had it coming."

Tamas risked a nervous glance at Matthias, and Mareigh caught the look.

"Matthias," she said, her voice dropping sternly.

"He did have it coming," Matthias said weakly.

Arian had stopped her work, holding a cloth in one hand as she listened, ready to spring into movement should his mother happen to look her way.

"These are *customers*," she said, not waiting for him to explain. "They put the bread on our table, and a little coin in our pockets."

He looked at Arian again. His mother always claimed poverty, but one as poor as she claimed to be didn't have a servant like Arian to jump at her every command, to keep the bar and the taps in the tavern shining. And she was the only woman to own one of the taverns on the island, close to the castle, safe behind the walls.

She sighed heavily. "You know what you need to do."

"I won't," he said.

"You will," his mother stressed, in the voice that had settled hundreds of tavern fights. "You're fifteen years old—when are you going to learn there are consequences to your actions? You will give them a few hours to sleep off the worst of it and then you will apologize."

"I will not," he said, pushing back from the table. "They had no right—"

"Matthias, they are our livelihood."

"And that gets them as much ale as they can buy. It doesn't give them the right—"

Again his mother turned to Tamas. "What did they do?"

Tamas sank on the bench. "You know how they get when they are in their cups. Joking and bragging." He glanced at Arian, who was making a good show of wiping the counter. "They started in on Arian. Saying she would make a good wife. Someone to come home to. And then Jarrett said that there was no reason to marry her, when you could just pay her by the hour."

As Tamas spoke, Matthias watched Arian, the long, slow stretches of her arm with the cloth, the way the raven hair that escaped from her kerchief fell over one eye.

He and Tamas had been drinking at a table close by, had heard every word the fat drunkard had said about Arian, every piggish laugh that his friend had given in response. Arian had kept her head down, her eyes averted, but he had seen the scarlet on her cheeks.

He had almost come to his feet when Jarrett's clumsy paw circled her waist and tried to pull her close. But Arian moved lightly away, made off to the kitchen, to safety.

Both men laughed, and Jarrett said, "It's more fun when you have to chase them a little."

That decided it for Matthias. He slapped Tamas's arm as the two drunks left. Tamas did not even try to argue—he had seen that look in Matthias's eyes before, and he followed his friend out the door.

They trailed behind Zekariah and Jarrett for a while, putting some distance between them and the tavern. They each picked up a good-size chunk of wood from in front of the butcher's shop, and when the two men staggered into the noxious alley behind, Matthias simply nodded at Tamas.

The drunks were leaning into the alley wall, looks of hard concentration on their faces as they pissed, trying to keep their balance.

"So," Matthias said, and both men started. "You think it's funny to mock a bar girl, do you?"

With a glance between them, Zekariah and Jarrett straightened up, fumbled with their belts, and pulled themselves to their full height. "And what are you, then? Her prince come to her rescue?"

Jarrett laughed. "Looks more like the bastard cur of that tavern wench, come for a beating."

His laugh faded when he saw the wood in the boys' hands.

The fight was quick and dirty, and left the two men in sodden heaps in the muck of the alley.

"Is that true?" his mother's question jarred Matthias out of his reverie, but she wasn't talking to him. She had turned to confront Arian.

The girl paused a moment, not able to meet the older woman's gaze. Finally, she nodded.

"You should have told me," she said, in a voice as close to understanding as Matthias could ever recall hearing. "I would have taken a round or two out of them myself. You need never tolerate that, do you understand?"

Arian kept her eyes on the ground, looking more uncomfortable with the sympathy than she would have been with Mareigh's temper.

Tamas sighed and deflated a little, obviously relieved.

Matthias, though, knew that it was not yet over.

"And as for you," his mother said, rounding on him. "What business is it of yours if some customers have a little fun at the expense of the help?"

"She was—"

"That is her business. And mine. It has nothing to do with you."

She took a long look at his face, and he willed himself to be stony, to give nothing away. But she had seen something. And she did not like what she saw.

"Unless—"

A furious pounding at the front door seemed to shake the whole tavern.

"Open in the name of the King."

"Matthias," Mareigh whispered hoarsely, turning toward the front room.

"Mother, I didn't . . ."

She shook her head. "I've told you your temper was going to be the end of you." She looked at the serving girl, who shrank under her gaze, and back at Matthias. "You've brought this down on all of us."

He could barely breathe.

Mareigh tied on a fresh apron. "I'll get the door, and pretend that I don't know exactly why they're here. You two"—she looked at Matthias and Tamas—"take the back door. Don't go home," she said sternly to Tamas. "They'll be looking for you as well. Find a place, maybe on the shore, to wait this out."

Matthias was stunned; the idea of running from the King's Men had not occurred to him, and now to have his mother suggest it . . .

"Go," she snapped, pushing her way through the swinging door into the tavern.

He didn't move. What was she doing? She had worked so hard to build this place, and now she was suggesting that he run. It could ruin her. If anyone even suspected that she had helped in his escape, the Royal Fiat that allowed her to run the tavern on the island, inside the walls, would disappear like a night of drink. How could he have been so stupid?

But then he looked upon Arian, and he realized that he'd really had no choice. He would do it all again, and damn the consequences.

Her eyes were wide and dark, shining against her ivory skin. She was looking at him as if she was about to cry.

Tamas tugged at his sleeve. "Matthias, come on," he whispered frantically.

He could hear his mother shouting, "All right, all right, give a poor woman a chance . . ."

Matthias wanted to go to Arian, to say something to comfort her, but there was no time.

"All right," he said. "Let's go."

They ran out the back door and retraced their steps, again not bothering with the gate. It seemed like hours since they had tumbled over the stone wall. This time they pushed themselves over it—

—and into a small group of King's Men, facing them in an orderly row.

Waiting for them.

The captain of the King's Men stepped forward. "I command you halt, in the name of the King."

The soldiers lowered their halberks toward the boys, backing them against the wall with the gleaming metal blades, then herded them into the tavern kitchen.

Mareigh was already sitting down, her hands on the table in front of her. Arian was sitting beside her; she bit her lip as Matthias walked through the door.

More of the King's Men stood surrounding the table, their halberks at their sides.

When Mareigh saw her son, her face fell.

They had caught him anyway.

"Matthias," the captain said, grasping the boy's sleeve. "Take a chair."

Matthias shook off the captain's grip, then stumbled as the captain pushed him onto the bench across from his mother. How did the captain know his name?

The captain turned to Tamas. "You, boy." Tamas wilted under his gaze. "Aren't you supposed to be at the stables?"

Tamas looked blank at the question, then nodded.

"Then I suggest you hie yourself over there and not give the master further cause for a whipping."

Tamas barely hesitated. Matthias watched his friend race out the back door—it was only right. Following the men from the tavern, the beating in the alley—it had all been Matthias's fight. It was better that Tamas avoid the consequences.

And given the number of King's Men gathered in the kitchen, the consequences would be dire indeed. He tried not to think of the stories he had heard of the dungeons, buried deep within the castle. The stories of men who went in and never came out.

The captain stepped to the head of the table, and with both hands lifted the bronze helmet from his head. His hair was long, damp with sweat. He had bright blue eyes and a short, well-trimmed beard.

He set the helmet carefully on the table, and nodded toward Matthias's mother.

"Good morning, Mistress Mareigh," he said.

"And to you, Captain Bream." Matthias's mother met the captain's gaze and held it.

Matthias looked between them: his mother knew this soldier?

Matthias had seen him in the street on occasion, but he wasn't one of the soldiers who frequented The Mermaid's Rest.

Arian shuddered next to him, close enough to touch.

"I trust you are well," the captain said.

Mareigh looked pointedly at the men ringing the kitchen. "I've had better mornings."

Matthias flinched at his mother's tone. He expected the captain to lash out at her, with either words or, more likely, his hands.

Instead, he looked at the guards. "Gentlemen," he said.

At the single word, the men broke rank and filed out through the swinging door.

"They'll wait in the tavern," he said. "Out of sight. I am aware that the sudden appearance of the King's Men can be bad for business."

Mareigh nodded. "I appreciate that."

"We're here about your son," he said, turning to look at Matthias.

Matthias pushed back from the table, starting to rise to his feet. "I'm sorry," he said quickly. "I didn't mean to, but I couldn't . . ." He glanced at Arian, then back at his mother. "My mother, she told me to wait here while she answered the door, but I was scared so I ran."

The captain listened to him, his face set in a dark scowl that broke, surprisingly, into a smile. "What are you talking about, boy?"

The question stopped him. "About what happened this morning."

The captain took a satchel from one of the men. He tossed the bag as if it weighed nothing, but it landed on the table in front of Matthias with a heavy smack.

"About Zekariah and Jarrett."

"That is none of my concern. There are clothes in there. Boots. You'll need to clean up."

Matthias glanced at his mother; she seemed as puzzled as he.

"Clean up," the captain repeated. "The Queen has summoned you."

☙ ❧

The sound of the door slamming brought me back to myself. Davy's footsteps were already fading into the house, up the stairs toward his room. Jacqui was standing in the doorway, her keys in her hand, her purse under her arm.

"You're not coming to his game?"

It wasn't really a question, and I didn't answer. I just closed the book slowly.

She shook her head. "You should have bought him *The Lord of the Rings*."

She walked away before I could say anything.

⟞ ⟝

Mareigh swept aside the heavy curtain and stepped into Matthias's sleeping room without warning. He hurriedly finished pulling the new shirt over his head.

"I'm worried for you," she whispered, so as not to be overheard by the guard at the foot of the narrow staircase.

Matthias was scared too, more than he would let his mother see. His insides had turned to water when the captain delivered his summons, and the feeling was only getting worse.

"You know the captain?" he asked.

"Captain Bream," she said. "He served with your father."

"But . . ."

She squeezed his arm so tightly it hurt. "Stop," she said firmly. "We don't have much time."

He pulled his arm away from her and took a step back. His legs pressed against his low bed.

She moved closer to him. "You have to be careful," she whispered. "The Queen . . ." She shook her head as if she had decided something. "She gets what she wants."

Of course she gets what she wants, she's the Queen. He didn't dare say so; his mother's face was white and taut.

"I'll be all right," he whispered, though he feared the words were a lie.

He hugged his mother close, holding her tight until Captain Bream called for him from the tavern below.

"Be careful," she said, as he started down the stairs.

The captain looked at him appraisingly as he descended. "That will have to do, I suppose."

Matthias had hoped to see Arian one last time, but the captain led him directly into the street, where the King's Men formed a tight circle around him. There was nowhere for him to turn, no way for him to run, and he fell into step with them as they led him away, up the sharp rise of the island, toward the castle.

≈ ≈

"Are your teeth brushed?" I asked, up to my elbows in soapy water. "Nolan fed?"

"Yup." He was already in his pyjamas, and his face was red and shiny from a recent encounter with a washcloth.

"Okay. I'll be up in a sec."

I finished the dishes and opened a bottle of red wine, leaving it on the counter to breathe as I went upstairs to read David his story.

Jacqui and I passed on the stairs: she was coming down after kissing David good-night. I tried smiling at her, but her face displayed the same stony rigour she had maintained since dinner.

I tried to put it out of my mind before I got to David's room.

Davy's bedtime was my favourite part of the day, and we had stumbled into it by accident. When Jacqui had gone back to work at the ER after her maternity leave, we had talked about the importance of consistency and routine. Knowing how crazy her schedule was going to be—shifts all over the map, on-call so often—we had decided that it would be best if bedtime were my domain.

It worked for me, too. I was at home, busy with the new book, and finding routine was essential for both my writing and my sanity.

At first it had been easy. Babies don't need much of a bedtime routine. As Davy got older it became more involved: fights about toothbrushing, constant negotiations for extra time, arguments about TV shows.

That was before we discovered reading together.

Standing in front of the bookshelves beside his door, my back to him, I asked, "So, what shall we read tonight?"

"Daaaad," he said, drawing out his exasperation. Playing along.

"All right . . ." I slid the hardcover of *The Hobbit* off the shelf and carried it over to the chair beside the head of his bed.

He was already nestled under the covers. Nolan the hamster was running merrily in his wheel.

The bookmark was leather, rough-cut and almost rectangular, with faded, painted letters, some of them backwards, that read, "To the best Dad in the world." He had made it for me for Father's Day when he was six, and we used it in all of the books we read together.

"We're getting pretty near the end of this," I said. "We'll have to figure out what to read next." I didn't want to be the one to suggest the book that I had given him, still sitting on the coffee table in the living room.

"*The Lord of the Rings*?" he asked. Again.

We had watched part of *The Fellowship of the Ring* on DVD, the parts before it got too violent and gory, and he had been wanting to read the book ever since.

"We'll see," I said measuredly. "Those are some pretty meaty books, so we might want to wait for a bit."

He pouted deliberately.

"There are plenty of good books out there." Not hinting. Not really.

David had always been a reluctant reader, only doing his Language Arts homework under duress. We learned why when he was eight and his teacher sent him for some testing: dyslexia. Reading was a struggle for him, and since then we had done everything we could to make it easier.

But our nightly ritual wasn't about work, or learning, it was all about pleasure.

"Dad," he said tentatively, before I could start. "None of my friends get a bedtime story every night."

"No?"

"Darren Kenneally says stories are for babies."

"Do you think he's right?"

He shook his head.

"Good. Because I know for a fact that he's wrong."

"Because you write stories. For grown-ups."

I smiled. "Right. And you know what? Darren Kenneally doesn't know what he's missing."

His face brightened.

After that he was quiet for so long that I was about to start reading when he said, "Dad?"

"Yeah?"

"When am I going to be too old for you to read to me?"

The thought brought a thickness to my chest. "Someday. That's up to you." Hoping silently that day would be a long time coming.

He watched me carefully for the first few minutes I was reading. Every time I looked up our eyes would meet, and he would grin a little and press himself deeper into the pillow. After a while he turned onto his back, folded his arms over his chest and closed his eyes. His breathing slowed.

He never fell asleep when I was reading, but he always closed his eyes. Once when I asked him why, he explained, "When I close my eyes I can see what you're reading. It's like a movie inside my head."

Although it took more than an hour, we finished *The Hobbit* that night; there wasn't really a good place to stop in the last few chapters.

I was slipping the book back into the space on the shelf by the door when he said, "*Lord of the Rings* next?"

I turned back to him, setting the bookmark on the edge of the shelf. "Maybe," I said, trying not to sound hurt. "We'll have to see."

He snuggled more deeply under the covers. "Okay."

"Time for sleep now, though."

"Yeah."

"Sweet dreams," I said as I stepped into the hallway. "Happy birthday."

I left the door open a foot or so, the way he liked it.

⚮

The soldiers marched Matthias quickly toward the castle, their boots echoing off the cobbles and the stone walls. Few people were out so soon after sunrise, but those who were gave the men wide berth, stepping into gutters or doorways to let them pass.

He gasped when they rounded the corner and the castle came into view.

The castle gates were closed.

For as long as he could remember, the gates had stood open, guarded, but swung wide onto the broad castle boulevard, the gardens within, and the towers that always seemed to shine against the blue sky. People would come and go freely. But this morning the entrance was blocked with towering wooden doors braced with iron.

Matthias stumbled slightly when Captain Bream stopped at a narrow iron door cut into a shallow recess in the castle wall, a short distance from the gates. The captain tapped three times on the door, and an eye-slit opened. The eyes behind the door surveyed them carefully, and after a moment a tumbler chunked into place and the door opened.

Matthias peered into the narrow opening, expecting to see the castle grounds on the other side of the wall. Instead, there was a dim tunnel, lit with torches, sloping into the depths of the castle. Armed guards stood inside.

"Come on," the captain said, directing him through the door.

Matthias's heart jumped into his throat as he stared ahead, his mind filled with his worst imaginings of the castle dungeons.

The captain dismissed his men, and they swung the heavy iron door shut as they left. The captain took a torch from one of the guards and started down the hallway.

Matthias followed silently, the torchlight wavering on the walls. The tunnel angled downward for a while, the walls growing damper, the air thick. Men stood guard at the openings of other tunnels, and they straightened as the captain passed.

Then the tunnel began to climb. In time, the air became fresher, cooler. The walls and the floor dried. Matthias had lost track of how long they had been walking when they came to a sudden stop at a dark archway, covered by what seemed to be a heavy curtain.

The captain pushed his torch into a bracket on the wall, then led Matthias through a barely noticeable seam in the middle of the curtain.

No, not a curtain, Matthias realized as he passed through it: a tapestry.

He found himself in a wide corridor, flanked on one side by a row of tapestries down the length of the stone wall through which he had just passed, and on the other by a series of high windows. A breeze blew cool from outside.

Matthias stopped in the middle of the corridor. The captain turned to him. His face was hard, and his mouth opened to speak, but he stopped himself.

Matthias was overwhelmed, and confused. To go from the backroom of the tavern to the heights of the castle . . .

He looked first at the wall.

The tapestries were all about the kingdom. He was standing in front of a weaving of his home: the island at the mouth of the Col River with the walled lower city rising toward the castle, and on the shore, Colcott Town. The next tapestry over was a battle scene, soldiers fighting, and falling, the Sunstone crest bright on their standards. One soldier was rising from his mount, driving his sword deep into the chest of a Berok warrior, the blade piercing the bearskins the savages wore instead of armour.

He took several steps toward the windows and looked down, first, on the castle and its gardens, then, beyond the castle wall, on the narrow streets of the lower city winding down to the protective wall at the shoreline. From this direction there was nothing but the sea beyond the outer wall; if the corridor had been on the other side of the castle, he knew, he would have been able to see Colcott Town on the shore.

"It is difficult to tell how far you've walked in the tunnels," the captain said. He looked toward the windows. "Or how high you've climbed. Only the royal chambers and the battlements are above us now."

The royal chambers? Matthias glanced down the hallway at the huge double doors, the pair of guards standing in front of them. His heart thrummed in his chest.

"The Queen's receiving rooms. Come."

The guards pushed the doors open as they approached.

Inside, the heady smell of spices and flowers and perfumes filled the bright, sunlit air. Without warning, the captain fell to one knee, bowing his head so it almost rested on his other knee.

"My Lady," he said.

Not having any idea what else to do, Matthias copied the soldier. He didn't dare look up. His stomach lurched, and he trembled with fear.

"Rise." The voice, rich and melodious, had come from the far end of the room.

Matthias waited until Captain Bream started to his feet before he stood up. He kept his eyes fixed to the floor, knowing better than to look on the Queen unbidden.

"Come," said the voice, and Matthias followed Captain Bream forward.

He glanced about surreptitiously, curious about his surroundings. The room was large, but seemed cozy, with tapestries on the walls, low couchettes in the corner, carpets over much of the floor.

"Matthias."

He couldn't help but look up.

The Queen was the most beautiful woman Matthias had ever seen, with long dark hair and pale skin that seemed to shine in the light. She reclined on a low divan on a raised stone platform, a small bowl of dried fruit and a goblet close to hand.

"Y-yes, Your Majesty," Matthias choked.

"Has Captain Bream told you why we bid you come?"

He shook his head, conscious of every motion. "No, Your Majesty."

He tried to look away as she stood up. Her blue-grey gown trailed behind her as she stepped down carefully from the platform.

"You're here because we need you, Matthias," she said, close enough that he could smell the sweetness of her breath.

He almost jumped when she reached out and took his hand, holding it warmly between her own.

"The kingdom needs you."

🙝 🙟

When I got down to the kitchen, I poured Jacqui and me each a glass of wine. As I carried the glasses and the bottle into the living room, I pictured myself passing the glass to Jacqui, reminding her of what we had been doing eleven years ago right now, the night that David was born. I imagined a moment of shared history, of tenderness.

She had been flicking through channels, but she turned the TV off as I set her glass on the end table next to her.

She didn't say anything.

"Davy's to bed," I said as I sat down. Anything to break the silence.

She picked up her glass.

"We finished *The Hobbit*."

I wished she had left the television on, for the noise, the distraction. I lifted my glass toward her.

"Eleven years," I said.

She smiled a small, sad smile, and sipped her wine.

"What's wrong?" I asked. Odds were the answer was going to involve me somehow, but I couldn't bear the silence, the feeling of things hanging in the air.

She shook her head. "It's the same old stuff," she said dismissively. "Is it really worth getting into it, all over again?"

I could feel myself deflating. "Okay."

"I mean, seriously, Chris. You couldn't even be bothered to come to his ballgame? On his birthday?"

"I—"

"And that book. It's like you don't even know him. You spend more time with him than any other dad I know spends with his kids, and it's like it doesn't even register."

"That's not—"

"Do you even know who Rob Sterling is?"

She was so quick with the question, I knew that she had been waiting to use it. And I couldn't answer.

"I didn't think so." She shook her head and looked away. "He's his coach, Chris. Coach Sterling. David talks about him every day. Do you even listen?"

I leaned forward on the couch. "Of course I listen."

"Really? Then why didn't you get him what he wanted for his birthday? Instead, you get him that . . ." She nodded toward the book on the coffee table. David had taken all of his other gifts upstairs to his room.

"He's going to like it," I said, aware even as I was speaking the words that they weren't going to make any difference. "When I was a kid—"

"Exactly," she said, so loudly I almost flinched. "That's exactly it, Chris. When *you* were a kid. This isn't about you. This is about David. It's *his* birthday. And you couldn't even be bothered—"

"Right," I said, leaning forward to set my wineglass on the coffee table and pick up the book. "You're right." I stood up. "It's probably not worth getting into it all again. I'm gonna go."

"Chris," she said to my back as I turned out of the room, but I didn't respond.

I walked through the house and out the back door. I navigated the narrow path in the spill of light from the kitchen window and unlocked the door in the back of the garage.

He sat up slowly, listening to the faint sound of his parents' voices as they rose up the stairs, drifted through the partly open door.

After a few moments, the voices grew louder, not really shouting but definitely upset. It was impossible to ignore them, to tune them out. He couldn't make out actual words, just a texture of voices raised in anger.

Biting his lip, he stood up and walked across the room, careful to be quiet. He closed his door fully, and darted back to bed in the dark, pulling the covers up to his chin and burying his head in the pillow.

He could barely hear the voices, now.

I'm not gonna cry, he told himself. *I'm not gonna cry.*

The narrow staircase was dim with the light from my desk lamp, which I left on from four in the morning until I went to bed. In the shadows of the small kitchen, I filled a glass with vodka from the bottle in my freezer. I set the glass on top of the morning's pages and sat down at my desk.

Why did it always have to go so bad so fast?

I pulled my cigarettes out of my pocket and set my lighter on the desk next to this morning's work. The engraving caught the light. After tapping a cigarette out, I put it to my lips, savouring the feel of it there, its light presence.

For a long time, I had allowed myself a single cigarette each day, just before I turned in. It was a holdover from my days as a smoker, and was supposed to be a reward, a way of recognizing a good day's work, a capstone to a productive time. Now, I was smoking compulsively again, my hands shaking as I flicked the lighter, as I held the flame to the paper waiting for that subtle crackle.

As I drew in the first smooth lungful of smoke, I ran my thumb across the lettering on the lighter.

COASTAL DRIFT

CHRISTOPHER J. KNOX

SPRING 2000

The Zippo had been a gift from my Canadian editor. He had lit my cigar with it at the launch party for my first book, then handed it to me with a broad grin and an arm draped drunkenly across my shoulders.

"To the first of many," he had toasted me.

"Right," I muttered to the memory, throwing the lighter onto the desk and taking a healthy swallow of the icy vodka. It chilled all the way down, and when the burn hit my stomach I shivered.

That had been a perfect night: my life was on track, unfolding as I had always dreamed it would. My novel was just out, and already on the best-seller lists. Jacqui and I had just bought the house, and every time I met her eye across the crowded bar, she smiled. The future was wide open.

And this was where it all led: me sitting in what once had been my office over the garage, trying to ignore the bed in the tiny adjoining room. There had been no more books, no more launch parties. And, over the last couple of years, precious few of those smiles from across the room.

I sat quietly for a moment, watching the shadows of the smoke play along the desk in the pool of golden light. As I opened David's book to where I had left off—since I had started reading it, I'd been sneaking in a few pages whenever time allowed, and when it didn't—I deliberately kept my back turned to the bookcase next to the desk, the top shelf with the different editions of *Coastal Drift*, the second shelf stuffed with bulging notebooks, stacks of loose-leaf, battered files. Ten years in the life, waiting for a match.

⫷⫸

It felt like the floor had tilted beneath his feet. Matthias couldn't think, could barely breathe, with the Queen so close to him, holding his hand, staring into his eyes.

"Let us sit," she said, turning him toward a cluster of divans and chairs against the wall.

"That's better," she said, a smile of comfort softening her face as she settled on a divan. "Sit."

"Yes, Your Majesty," Matthias said as he sat, not sure of how to speak.

"Comfort is a fine, fine thing," she said, almost to herself. "Save for the price that must be paid."

Her smile disappeared as she looked at Matthias again. "Five days ago, the watchtowers fell. Three of them. All under cover of a single night. The Berok have taken them."

Matthias stole a glance at Captain Bream; the man's face was hard and still.

"Our most feared enemy is at the borders of the kingdom, less than two days' ride from the city. From this castle—" She broke off as handmaidens entered the room with wine.

Matthias's mind reeled: the Berok?

Matthias and Bream waited while the maidens tasted from each cup before serving them, and then until the Queen had taken a sip before they drank. The wine was cool and strong.

"The King has brought you here today," the Queen said, "because we think you can help."

Matthias bit back a protest. He knew only tavern fighting, and all he knew of the Berok were the stories his mother had told him when he was a boy. The country to the north was the stuff of myths and children's stories, of blood-thirsty warriors and epic betrayals. Surely there was nothing he could do. He drowned the words he was tempted to say with another swallow of wine, knowing better than to argue with the Queen.

"I know you believe there is nothing you have to offer," she said, seeming to read his thoughts and expression. "But others think differently. Loren," she called, barely raising her voice.

From a doorway at the far end of the room a man appeared, a long, grey beard falling to the middle of his chest. Within the folds of his tattered robes, Matthias could see he carried a large, leather-bound book.

"Loren is an historian and a scholar. One of the King's most trusted advisers," the Queen said, not even glancing at the man as he took his place beside her. "He has been working in the libraries, both in the castle here and at the monastery," the Queen said. "He has found some startling information."

The monastery: the old man was one of the Brotherhood.

"I am a translator," Loren said in a thin voice, "of the ancient texts. When I learned of the attacks on the watchtowers, I was reminded of a manuscript that I translated, some years ago. Not a book. Private papers, from the reign of King Harkness."

"And why did it remind you of that?" the Queen prompted.

"Because of when the attacks happened," he explained. "On a night when the moon was swallowed by the dark."

Matthias remembered the night, almost a week before, when he had stood outside the tavern next to Arian as the moon seemed to disappear momentarily into the night sky. He sat forward to listen more closely to the translator.

"There is a prophecy," the old man said. "In those scrolls. A prophecy which I am only now beginning to understand. It is mostly fragments, scattered within another text." He opened the book in his hand, balancing it carefully as he turned the pages. "It begins:

> *The fall of man shall come,*
> *As a fall comes to all things.*
> *The mighty walls of Colcott shall crack*
> *And bleed*
> *On the night the moon dies in the sky."*

The old man looked up from the book and fixed his eyes on Matthias. "There is more. Much more. And it concerns the boy."

"Me?" Matthias asked, before he could stop himself.

"You," the translator said.

"But—"

The old man shook his head, and Matthias closed his mouth. Loren continued speaking, but Matthias barely heard him over the rushing in his ears. It *couldn't* be him. He was . . . nobody.

"Hidden as it was, the prophecy has long puzzled scholars. But the confluence of events, the attack on the watchtowers on the night of the disappearing moon . . ." His voice trailed off. "I believe I know what it means."

Matthias shifted, uncomfortable in his chair.

"The prophecy describes a treasure, a relic so powerful that it was hidden away before the time of King Harkness. A relic that will save this kingdom. The Sunstone."

"A sunstone?" Matthias asked. It was the symbol of the kingdom, on every flag, every gate, and sewn onto the shoulder of Bream's tunic.

"Not *a* sunstone," the scholar corrected. "*The* Sunstone. The first Sunstone, carried into battle by Stephen the Bold, before he was the First King."

There was a long moment of silence before the captain said, "That's just a myth. A children's story."

"It's much more than that," the old man said. "Do you know why the Sunstone is the symbol of our kingdom? Not because it was Stephen's sigil, but because of what it could do. What it *did*, in our darkest hour."

"What could it do?" Matthias heard himself asking.

"It is believed the stone held great power. How else to explain the victory at Corindor Field, when the brave five hundred broke the army of the Berok, more than ten thousand strong, turning them back and forging this kingdom in blood and iron?"

Matthias recognized the last few words from a poem that every child was taught, the chronicle of the founding of the kingdom.

"Tactics," the captain said. "Bravery. Loyalty. As battles have always been fought and won."

"You would believe that, of course," the old man said. "But the truth is much stranger. The truth is that Stephen rode into battle with the Sunstone, the first Sunstone, on his breast, and a magus at his side."

"Are you talking about magic?" Matthias asked.

"Indeed I am. A magic so powerful it can render an army unbreakable. A magic so powerful that King Stephen, even in the flush of victory, could see its dangers. After Corindor Field, he ordered the Sunstone hidden where no one, not even he, could find it. He entrusted his dearest friend Gafilair, the first of the Brotherhood to be paired with the king, the first high mage, to hide the stone. To wrap it in mysteries and magics such that no man could ever find it.

"The magus did as the new king instructed, hiding the stone away where it would remain for more than a thousand years, until the kingdom once again was in such grave danger that the stone's powers would be its only salvation."

"If it is hidden so well—" Captain Bream began.

"There is one who can find it," the scholar said. "*That* is the reason for the prophecy. That the Brothers of Gafilair, his heirs and followers, might follow the signs, might find the right person at the right time to recover the stone and return it to the King. The clues to finding the stone are in here," he said, gesturing to the book. "As is the information we needed to find the one who could retrieve it."

"Me?" Matthias asked incredulously.

The captain nodded.

"Captain Bream has selected a troop of his finest men," the Queen said. "His most loyal and true. You will ride out with them to find the Sunstone, and bring it back that it might protect the kingdom once more. Loren will ride with you to decipher the signs left by the first high magus."

"But it can't be me," Matthias blurted.

The magus spoke slowly: "There are signs, portents, in this book. We have studied them. Studied you. The signs of your birth. Your parentage. There is enough for us to be sure."

"Matthias," the Queen said. "You'll ride out at dawn in three days' time. You'll be well cared-for, well protected. And when you return with the Sunstone, you will receive a hero's welcome. Do you understand?"

He nodded slowly. "Yes, Your Majesty."

He had no choice.

"Come," she said. "The importance of this journey cannot be overstated."

The Queen led the three men around the stone platform at the end of the room, to a double door hidden behind a tapestry. The captain opened the door, and stepped back to allow the Queen to enter. Matthias followed.

In the centre of the room stood a huge bed. The man lying on it was tiny, and clearly sick, his skin yellow and waxy, his hair missing in patches. He lay facing the door, considering his guests with pale, milky eyes.

Loren took several steps toward the bed before falling to his knee. "Your Majesty," he said, almost in a whisper.

Matthias looked at the Queen.

"This," she said, "is why we need the Sunstone so badly."

The crumpled figure on the bed raised a shaky hand. "Loren," he said weakly. "Loren, my friend."

The mage rose to his feet and stepped to the bedside. The King took his hand.

"Have you found the boy?"

Matthias could feel his heart in his throat.

"I have, Your Majesty. He's here."

The King's eyes searched the room, and prompted by a gentle push from the Queen, Matthias stepped to the old man's side.

"This is him?" the King asked.

"It is, Your Majesty."

A weak smile came to the King's face as he took Matthias's hand. The King's grip was sticky and cool, and Matthias tried to breathe mostly through his mouth; the air near the bed was sweet and acrid with the smells of sickness.

"Yes, so it is," the King said, as if finally able to see him. "It is all yours to do now," he said to Matthias. He winced and strained with each word. "The future of the kingdom is in your hands."

Dumbstruck, Matthias nodded. The King's grip tightened, then fell away. His eyes sank shut. For a moment, Matthias's hand hung in the air where the King had held it. But then a rough, wet breath brought a sense of relief. The King was only sleeping.

"The great secret at the heart of the kingdom," the Queen said slowly.

Matthias turned back to face the Queen and the Captain of the Guard, both still standing in the doorway.

"No one knows of the King's illness. Your mission, therefore, must remain a secret, known to as few people as possible. You cannot go home. Not now. Not before you leave. Do you understand?"

"I do, Your Majesty."

II

I WOKE UP WITH THE ALARM at four—there wasn't really an option. I keep the clock-radio on an old wooden chair partway across the room, so I have to stumble out of bed when it goes off, fumbling with the plastic box in my desperation to silence it.

Standing there, half draped in covers, I faced the usual choice: the bed looked so enticing, so warm, so soft.

I stumbled toward the door and turned on the light. If there ever came a day when it all fell apart, finally and irrevocably, I would know it by the fact that I wouldn't be up in the pre-dawn hours, sitting at my desk, willing the words to come.

After starting a pot of coffee, the next order of business was to throw the empty vodka bottle into the overflowing recycle box. As the coffee perked, I pulled on some clothes, then stood behind my chair, looking at the framed article hung over the desk. "Where are the books?" the headline read. It was a bitchy piece about the long-overdue second novels from a wave of new West Coast writers, all of whose first books had met with the sort of critical praise one dreams of. And then, nothing. No follow-ups, no new books, despite huge advances and early publicity. I had enjoyed writing the article, a year and a half after *Coastal Drift* was published.

A year after the article appeared, the framed copy had arrived in the mail. An inscription in the corner read: *How does it feel, asshole?* It was signed by one of the writers I had mentioned in the article, and the package it came in had also included clippings of the rapturous reviews her second novel had just received.

The paper my article was printed on was now yellowed and dark, and every one of the writers I had written about had since published a second book, or third, and in one case his fourth, while I had produced nothing.

Fresh coffee in hand, I sat down at the desk and turned on the lamp. I ignored the laptop, not even daring to open it. My routine demanded that the writing come first, that everything else—e-mail, websites, online writers' forums—wait until the day's words were down. Avoiding temptation was the only way I knew that I would actually get the work done.

There was no temptation greater than the book sitting on the table beside my reading chair. I could just read one chapter, right? While I tried to wake up a little. One chapter wouldn't hurt, would it?

I didn't give in, and opened my latest notebook to the first blank page. Pen in hand, I stared down at the white expanse, trying to figure out what was wrong.

Right. The music. My secret weapon.

Once I had the Miles Davis CD playing, everything started to move. I wrote, head down, for almost two full rotations of the disk, filling almost four pages. It was good stuff. But then, I always think that.

It took me another hour, sipping at my second coffee of the day, to type in the day's writing, making a few changes as I went. When I printed out the pages, I wrote the date in the bottom margin and set the sheets face down on the top of the eight-inch stack on the bookcase.

Normally, I would have gone straight into checking e-mails and the usual online haunts. Instead, I carried my coffee cup over to the reading chair and sat down with David's book. I had a few minutes before it would be time to get David up and off to school. And besides, it's not like I was just reading: now this was research. I had a column to write, and the beginnings of an idea.

≈ ≈

At the top of a stone staircase, Captain Bream led Matthias through a heavy wooden door. The air was bracingly cold as Matthias stepped onto a walkway at the top of the highest tower overlooking the city. The Queen had told the soldier to escort Matthias to sleeping quarters, but he had led the boy behind another tapestry, through another secret door.

"I know you do not believe this, but you're very important," the captain said, breaking the silence that had overtaken them. "As important as this castle. As those battlements."

"But I don't understand . . ."

"I don't either," the captain said. "Not completely. But the Queen does. And the magus. I do understand this, though."

He directed Matthias's gaze beyond the battlements. Matthias was facing inland, and he could see Colcott Town stretching along the shoreline, facing the castle from across the bay. With the tide in, the causeway was swallowed under the churning tides, the single road between the castle and Colcott Town impassable, as it was for half of every day. A swarm of small boats and flat-bottomed skiffs ferried passengers and supplies to the island.

"Do you see those mountains?" He pointed at the distant, dark swell that seemed to rise out of the smoky green forests deep inland.

Matthias nodded.

The captain moved his fingers as if to trace the mountaintops. "They mark the edge of the kingdom, two days' ride from here. There is a watchtower on each of the seven passes through the mountains, a ring of soldiers watching the King's borders every moment of every day. Less than a week ago, three of those towers fell. Those soldiers died defending this land against an army that came under the cover of night, that stole through the gates and slew every man. They took no prisoners." He took a heavy breath. "Do you know what this all means?"

Matthias had heard the emotion thick in the man's voice. "No," he said quietly.

"It means the Berok have no interest in diplomacy, no intention of treaty. They will not be satisfied until they level the kingdom to the waterline, taking every man, woman and child with it. They will not be satisfied until the crown falls in the dirt, until it can be crushed beneath their heels."

Matthias nodded slowly, thinking about the savage Berok warriors just over the rise, picturing the village below in flames, the screams of his mother, of Arian—

"These are desperate times, Matthias."

I got David to school about five minutes later than normal, but still well before the opening bell. Not a crisis. On the walk home I started mentally composing my column, trying to find the perfect opening line. Once I had that, everything else would fall easily into place.

I usually spent Monday mornings, after the real writing was done, working on my column for the *Vancouver Sun*. It would be nice if my fiction paid the bills, but that was still a fair ways off, especially with how late the new book was. I had been writing *Off the Shelf* for almost five years. It gave me the best of both worlds: a regular pay cheque, and the freedom to spout off on whatever I wished.

I brought up my e-mail and poured myself another cup of coffee, set David's book on the desk next to the laptop.

I winced as the new message headers started to pop up. I had been waiting for an e-mail from Roger, my agent, for a couple of weeks, and here it was. He would, no doubt, just be confirming dinner for when I was in New York in a couple of weeks, but the subtext would be plain: *Where's the new book, Chris?*

Ignoring the looming shadows of the inevitable, I opened a Google window and typed "Lazarus Took" into the search block.

Google came up with 947 hits.

Several of the entries on the first page were rare books dealers—I ignored them for the moment and clicked on the link to Wikipedia.

The entry on Lazarus Took was a stub, little more than a paragraph.

Lazarus Emile Took was an English writer, briefly popular in the mid-1940s. His first novel, *Shining Swords and Steel*, was published by Bartley-Knox in 1945. A purveyor of clichéd, derivative, post–Second World War British fantasy, Took benefitted from the new popularity of the paperback format for his readership, and is rightly overshadowed by his contemporaries including C.S. Lewis and J.R.R. Tolkien.

Not really useful, and it looked like the page hadn't been updated in years. It was strange to think that in the age of the Internet, when people could get obsessed about the most meaningless of things—from obscure silent film stars to the toys inside Cracker Jack boxes—no one seemed to have the slightest interest in "derivative, post–Second World War British fantasy."

The next hit made me feel better immediately. The LazarusTook.com page was entitled "Servants Bold, Treasures Untold" and described itself as "The Ultimate Resource for Readers of Lazarus Took." I clicked on its Books page, and scrolled down, looking for mention of *To the Four Directions*. Nothing. The final book listed was *Long Journey Home*, published in 1949.

I went to the Biography page. It showed a painting of a dour-looking, slim man, middle-aged and greying, leaning against a short stone wall with an ocean in the background, one hand resting on the crystal head of a straight cane.

I lingered over the picture for a moment: I'd never actually known what Took looked like, and the deliberate asceticism came as something of a disappointment. For someone whose books were so full of life, he looked like a prat.

Trust the art, I always say, not the artist.

But then, I would, wouldn't I?

The picture was the most interesting thing on the page. The biography added little to the Wikipedia entry. Took was born in 1895 into a wealthy family. It seems he was a conscientious objector during the Great War, and was involved in one of the many mystical societies that flourished during that time, the Order of the Golden Sunset. The writer took pains to point out that other writers, including Yeats, had been involved in similar organizations. Took married Cora Agatha Tinsley in 1930, and the two settled in Norfolk in the middle of that decade. The biography listed the four novels that Took wrote before his death in 1950, but, again, there was no mention of *To the Four Directions*.

I brought up a new Word window and started to type.

The summer that I was eleven, my life was changed forever. No, more than that—the world was changed forever, and I was pulled along with it.

⌘ ⌘

A soft scratching at the door jarred Matthias from his sleep. For a moment he didn't recognize his surroundings: a large bed, plush down blanket, a crackling fire. Where was he? And then it all came rushing back: the Queen, the quest, the Berok, the captain leading him to the palatial guest quarters.

"Matthias?" a voice called gently, before the door opened a crack. "Might I come in?"

He recognized the voice as that of Loren. "Yes," he said, standing up from the bed, straightening the covers. "Come in."

The gaunt old man slid into the room, barely opening the door. He smiled. "I trust you rested," he said. He crossed the room toward the fire.

"A bit," he said, watching the old man carefully.

The magus settled in the chair closest to the fire, his grey robes settling around him. He began unpacking the bag he had been carrying over his shoulder.

"I thought you might have some questions. I've brought books and maps."

Matthias sat in the other chair by the fire. There was a low table between them, which the magus was piling with books and scrolls. "I tried to follow along with what you were saying this morning, but—"

"That's understandable," Loren said. He seemed to have finished unpacking the bag and was now tamping golden tobacco into his pipe. "Where to start?" he asked himself. "Where to start?"

Loren drew a long splinter of wood from inside the folds of his robe and, after extending it into the fire, lit his pipe, puffing huge clouds of sweet-scented blue smoke as he considered his words.

"Perhaps the Brothers of Thomas," he said slowly. "Well." Another puff on the pipe. "For as long as there have been kings and queens in Colcott, there have been magi. Scholars. Historians. Advisers."

"Sorcerers," Matthias said, thinking of the stories he had heard when he was younger.

Loren smiled. "Our magical powers have been greatly exaggerated."

"Then what about the Sunstone?"

"The Sunstone is something altogether different," he said. "Gafilair, the first high mage of Colcott, wasn't the founder of the Order. In fact, he was little more than an adept when he rode into battle with Stephen the Bold. The Order had been around for hundreds of years, even then. He was the one, though, who forged our relationship with the royal family, with the kingdom. He was the first to ride with a king of Colcott into battle. And he saved him, with the Sunstone."

"But how—"

"No one really knows. The true Sunstone is shrouded in mystery. It is the tradition of our order that adepts go out into the world, beyond the frames of any maps, to explore, to discover themselves and the worlds beyond. When they return—*if* they return—the knowledge they bring is added to the knowledge of the Brotherhood. Only then are they considered for advancement." He puffed on his pipe. "When Gafilair returned, he brought with him not just knowledge, but the Sunstone itself. He never told anyone where it came from, and he spent years investigating the full extent of its powers."

"So what does it do?" Matthias asked, feeling a thrum of excitement.

"It's an object of almost unparalleled power. It lent that power to the army of the King. It shielded them from the perils of the battle. It might"— Loren paused—"it might even have the power of life everlasting."

"What?"

Loren smiled. The air was fragrant with smoke from his pipe. "There are stories. It is said that during the battle of Corindor Field, Stephen took a Berok arrow to the breast, that he fell in the opening moments of the fighting."

Matthias straightened in his chair.

"According to some who claimed to have seen it, the magus leapt from his horse and, without a moment's hesitation, pressed the stone to Stephen's heart. Moments later, Stephen took his mount and led the next charge himself. The stone had healed him, even from the point of death."

"But that's—"

"Impossible?" He puffed at his pipe. "Perhaps. But there are many who believe that story. The King is one of them. He needs the stone to protect the kingdom."

"To heal himself."

The magus's lips curled around the stem of his pipe.

"Why didn't King Stephen keep the stone?"

"Its powers made him cautious. So he ordered Gafilair to conceal the stone, to keep it safe in a place where even he would not be able to retrieve it."

"And only one person—"

The magus nodded. "And that person is you."

"I can't," Matthias said, shaking his head. The words that he had been holding back since the morning came flooding out of him. "I don't know how to fight, I barely know how to ride. I've never even seen a Berok. It can't be me."

"As I said, the descriptions which Gafilair left are very detailed. I compared them against the records kept by the Brotherhood. A child of common birth, born under the sign of the Wolf with the evening star in its ascension . . ." He lifted his hands to show how effortless the whole process had been.

"It's you," he said plainly. "I know you don't believe it, but it's true. I could show you the charts and calculations."

Matthias shook his head. "No," he said, slumping back into the chair. There was no point in arguing, no matter how terrified the idea made him. "So what do I have to do?"

The magus reached into his bag. "First this," he said, laying a knife in a leather sheath on the table between them.

Matthias stared at the knife, then up at the magus.

"It's yours," the magus said. "Wear it in your boot. Keep it with you always."

Matthias thought of the captain, taking care to lock him in the room when he left. He was virtually a prisoner, and now the magus was offering him a weapon.

"You will be well protected as we travel," the magus said slowly. "But there are great dangers ahead, and you must be prepared to protect yourself, should it come to that."

He looked at the knife again.

"Take it," the magus said. "Keep it close. Keep it hidden. No one else needs know."

Dale and I met outside Ferris's, waiting in the short line for a table.

"You know," he started, as we inched forward. "Neither of us has an actual schedule. Is there any reason you insist on having lunch at the same time as everybody else in the city?" We'd had the conversation before. At this point in our lives, we've had every conversation before.

"Routine is important."

He nodded. "Right. But why can't one-thirty or two be the routine? Let the cubicle dwellers get back to their desks?"

I was going to answer, but he stepped into the doorway and exchanged a few quick words with the host.

"Are you hungover?" he asked me over his shoulder.

"What? No."

"Outside is fine," he said to the host.

The host led us to a sunny table in the corner of the back patio.

I sat with my back against the wall, looking out at the outdoor room. The place was full, tables of people in suits and ties, a small sea of blue against the plants on the far wall. There was a lightness, a whirl of conversations punctuated by laughter. Everyone seemed to be smiling, moving with a casual pleasure in the warm sun, jackets over chair-backs. There was still a slight coolness to the air, but it felt, finally, like spring, and the . . .

Dale was smirking at me.

"Sorry," I said. I felt compelled to apologize, but there was nothing I could do to change: there's a part of me that's always writing, always mentally capturing a scene, trying to determine how best to present it, what details are important, what can be glossed over. Even when Jacqui and I were at our worst—fighting, crying—part of me was outside of the moment, watching the words as they moved back and forth, noting the way Jacqui tightened her hands into fists as she spoke.

"You always are," he said.

Every day—multiple times every day—David was reminded of just how much the universe must hate him.

The school assigned lockers by grade, then alphabetically by last name, which meant that he was two metal doors down from Darren Keneally.

Most of the time he tried to avoid making eye contact. He would walk slowly up the hallway, timing his arrival for a moment when it seemed like Darren was focused on something else, then lunge for his locker, spinning the combination lock and swinging the door open as quickly as he could. He would tuck himself behind the light metal door as if it were a shield.

The only problem was, if he was tucked behind the door, he couldn't keep an eye on what Darren was doing. More than once he had swung the locker door closed only to find his nemesis standing right behind it, inches away, a cruel smile on his face, his laughing friends shifting and bobbing around him.

David had delayed his departure from the science lab for as long as he could after the lunch bell rang, giving Darren and his friends time to get to their lockers and head down to the cafeteria. When he assumed he had waited long enough, he crept out into the hallway.

He sighed. It was mostly deserted. No problem.

He was almost smiling by the time he got to his locker and opened it. Stacking his books carefully on the shelf, he grabbed the lunch that his father had packed and his Nintendo and headed down the corridor toward the exit at the end. His best friend Liam had detention, so David was on his own, but the sun was shining. No reason not to eat out in the corner of the athletic field, far from anyone who might bother him.

"So how's the book?"

I shook my head. "It can't possibly be a month already."

Dale smiled. "I put it in my Palm. 'Ask Chris about book.'"

I had suggested, the year before, that perhaps asking me about the book every time we met might be counterproductive. Too much pressure. So he had decided to take me at my word and only ask me once a month.

"So?" he prodded.

"It's going fine. I wrote four pages this morning."

"Any closer to finding the end?"

I puffed out a long breath. "No. Not even close." I opened the menu.

Dale, however, was not to be put off quite so easily. "Can I suggest, again"—he stressed the last word— "that perhaps your . . . domestic situation . . . isn't entirely conducive to your work?"

"It's fine," I said. "I wrote a great column this morning. I think—"

"Your column isn't your writing," he said, undeterred.

"Did you miss the part where I wrote four pages on the novel this morning?" I tried to keep the defensive tone out of my voice; it didn't work.

He nodded slowly. "Okay."

"Seriously, it's fine."

He made a point of waiting until I had started looking at my menu before speaking. "I just wonder . . ." He let the words trail off as he buried his nose in his own menu. It seemed like he was distracted, but I knew better.

"Wonder what?" There was no point in resisting; it had been almost twenty years, and Dale always ended up saying what he wanted to say.

"Have you considered the possibility that it's time for a new start?"

I shook my head. "I can't," I said. "There are too many people waiting for it. And I've already spent the advance."

"That's interesting," he said, still poring over the menu.

"What?" I asked, resigned.

He lowered the menu. "I think it's interesting that neither of those reasons were about the book itself. They were all about obligation and expectations and money. Not about the book. Nothing about how good it was, or how strongly you felt about it. Not a bit of passion."

He shrugged and closed the menu.

I wanted to argue with him, but he had me dead to rights and we both knew it. "Yeah," I sighed.

"I wasn't talking about the book, though," he continued. "I was talking about you and Jacqui. And my guess is that if I asked you if it was time to make a more permanent change with Jacqui, you'd give me exactly the same sort of answer. Expectations. Obligation. Money." He shrugged. "That's all."

He had timed it perfectly: before I could respond our server had arrived at the table, her wide smile at odds with the words in my mind.

By the time David looked up from his Nintendo to see them coming across the field toward him, they were already between him and the school. With the fence at his back there was nowhere for him to run. He blinked slowly and shook his head: nothing he could do now but take it.

He was thankful that he had time to tuck his Nintendo into his hoodie before they got close enough to notice.

"Sitting out here with all your friends?" Darren called as they grew closer. It was him and three others, the usual crew. The three laughed at the joke, one of Darren's favourite lines.

David didn't know if he should respond or not. Sometimes it was better if he said something, sometimes it was better if he kept quiet— there was no way to know for sure.

He kept his eyes low as they approached, watching Darren's shoe-laces flopping on the grass, the cuffs of his pants dragging.

"Hey, loser, I was talking to you."

Clearly not saying anything wasn't the right choice.

"Are you deaf, too?"

As David lifted his eyes to where Darren stood looming over him, the boy kicked at his lunch bag, knocking the plastic container that had held his sandwich several feet away.

"Aw, did your mommy pack your lunch?" His friends laughed.

Trying to control his breath, David stood up. It was a no-win situation: if he stayed sitting he wouldn't be able to get away if Darren decided to kick him too. But standing up put him in range of his fists.

"Did you hear me, loser? I asked if your mommy packed your lunch."

David shook his head, not daring to meet his eye. "No. My dad—"

"Aw, his daddy made his lunch. Isn't that sweet?" Guffaws from the hyenas behind him.

Darren shoved him first, almost knocking him off his feet. "Where's your daddy now?" he asked.

As David righted himself, he came within arms' reach of one of the other boys, who shoved him again.

They kept him spinning, off balance. David did his best to close his eyes, hoping they would get bored soon and stop.

Dale and I had gone to school together our whole lives, but it wasn't until our first year at UVic that we got to know each other. We lived in buildings in the same quad, a bleak expanse of sharp angles and brutal concrete. A perfect place for warehousing hundreds of hormone-addled, hard-partying, emotionally fragile seventeen- and eighteen-year-olds. The next summer we ditched work for almost a month. The plan had been to follow the Grateful Dead around for a few weeks, but plans, as they do, had gone awry. It had gotten a little hairy, but I had come out of it with a blood-brother, and a novel. *Coastal Drift* was all about that summer. About Dale and me. His Dean Moriarty to my Sal Paradise.

He knew me better than anyone.

I chafed with words building up inside me until we had ordered and the waitress walked away.

"It's not like that," I said. "Jacqui and I—"

"I'm not sure this quasi-separation thing is the best idea."

"Well, tell that to Jacqui. It was her idea."

"That's not what I mean. This whole thing with you living in your studio but spending most of the day at the house—it's been, what, six months now? I think you need to retire any fantasies of reconciliation you might have and think about getting a little distance. It's not doing David any good to have you guys fighting all the time. It's not doing you any good, floating in limbo like this. And it's not doing Jacqui any good."

I sagged into the chair, incapable of speech.

I want to say that the words took my breath away, that they hit me like a punch, that they were a sudden piercing insight: none of that would be true.

If I were honest about it I would have to say that the marriage had disintegrated long before I'd moved out of the house. We had spent years growing further and further apart, not really fighting, but not really talking either. We had spent less and less time together, both of us with our attention elsewhere, more roommates than a couple.

There hadn't been any single point where it all fell apart; the marriage had been worn away by apathy, by the slow grind of things not said. Money brought it to a head, a conversation about renewing the mortgage turning into the same fight we always had. I had slept in my office that night.

And I had spent every day since then trying to get back.

"And furthermore," he continued, his tone changing. "It's not doing *me* any good." He smiled, trying to break the tension. "Seriously. I love both of you guys, and this whole thing . . ." He shook his head. "It's not healthy."

"Jacqui and I—" I said, "it's just . . . we're in a rough patch."

He nodded slowly. "Here." Reaching into his pocket, he placed a manila envelope, smaller than a credit card, on the table beside my water glass. An address was written on it, in Dale's careful hand.

"What's this?" I asked, looking at it, deliberately not touching it.

"It's a key," he said. "To one of those live–work places in Dragon Alley. Three floors, big enough for one, space for a pullout for Davy when he spends the night."

I shifted uneasily in my chair.

"I've been trying to find a buyer, but the seller is willing to settle for a rental."

"No." I shook my head. "I can make it work," I said. The idea of moving, of that sort of finality between us, sickened me. It wasn't that bad, was it? We couldn't be at that point already.

The way Dale looked at me, the sadness in his eyes, made me think that I was the only one who thought so.

～ ～

The captain burst into the room without knocking. When he saw Matthias sitting across from the magus, the table between them heavy with books and maps, he stopped.

"My apologies," he said grudgingly.

The magus waved away the comment and rose slowly to his feet. "It is no matter," he said. "I think young Matthias's head is probably full enough for one afternoon." Setting his satchel on his chair, the magus began to pack the books.

Matthias was reeling from all the old man had told him, the blurring together of truth and legend.

"The Queen," the captain said, "has requested our presence for dinner. There are clothes in the wardrobe. It would be best if you washed yourself first."

Matthias could not remember ever having had a true bath. There was a small tub for linens in his mother's kitchen, but he had spent his life doing little more than scrubbing himself with a cool cloth in his room above the tavern, and so now he watched, fascinated, as the tub was filled by a line of servants. Languishing in a tub of steaming water was an alien idea, but once the magus and Captain Bream had departed, he took to it quickly.

Afterward, he dressed in a uniform similar to the one that the captain was wearing when he returned to collect him.

Bream led him down several flights of stairs, from the apartments and sleeping quarters to the main level of the castle. In a wide, marble corridor, the captain stopped and straightened his uniform.

"Shall we?" he said, stepping toward the double doors at the end of the entry hall.

Matthias tried to calm his racing heart as the captain pushed the doors open and he had his first glimpse of the throne room.

The space was huge, with mammoth pillars supporting a high, vaulted ceiling. The Queen was on her throne on a dais at the far end of the room, the King's throne empty next to her. Below, several large tables sagged under the weight of food and wine, and another was set with silver and crystal.

"It is quite a sight, is it not?"

Matthias was overcome, unable to speak. He looked around the room, trying to consign the details to his memory to be able to tell Arian when next he saw her. But there was simply too much to see, too much beauty for him to even begin to absorb.

As they approached, the Queen rose slowly from her throne, the folds of her gown seeming to fall into place in a cataract of silk and jewels. Loren was there as well, standing between the two thrones, a step back, almost lost in the shadows.

"Captain Bream," the Queen said as they stopped in front of the dais. "Matthias."

Matthias knew enough now to take a knee, dropping to the cold stone floor in unison with the soldier.

"Your Majesty," they said, almost in a single voice.

"Gentlemen," she said, stepping down toward them, "please." She gestured for them to rise. "The kitchen has sent us a handsome feast. Let us not watch it grow cold."

As they settled around the smaller table, a servant poured a clear liquid into a small glass before the Queen, and then into those of her guests.

A handmaiden sipped from Matthias's glass, and as she did so his eyes met hers. She smiled and looked down at the table, her face glowing red.

"A spirit," the Queen said, "to honour the fallen."

The spirit burned as it touched the back of his throat. He tried to sip gingerly, but everyone else poured the entire contents of their small glasses into their mouths, closing their eyes as they swallowed. When he followed suit, he almost choked. It was stronger by far than anything he had ever drunk before.

He had only heard whispers about grand meals like this, which always began with the strongest of liquors. The next thing, he thought, would be—

The magus cleared his throat and bowed his head. "We offer our service to you, oh Father and Mother . . ."

The captain bowed his head automatically. As Matthias was lowering his, he glanced to where the Queen was sitting, implacably, at the head of the table. She didn't lower hers.

"A toast," the Queen said after the magus finished the prayer. The handmaidens were now pouring wine into huge crystal goblets. "To the success of this expedition," she continued. "To the three men who will be the salvation of the kingdom. And to the King."

"To the King," Bream and the magus said in unison, before drinking.

Matthias tripped over his words trying to catch up, and drowned his embarrassment in his glass. The wine was slightly cool, hearty and spicy.

Matthias glanced at the empty thrones as he set his glass back down, thinking of the dying man, and the captain's vision of the crown trampled in the dirt.

"Brother Loren has told me of your star signs and the particulars of your birth, Matthias," the Queen said. "But I know little else about the young man I have charged with so dire a mission. I understand that your mother owns a tavern?"

"Yes, Your Majesty," he said, swallowing a little uneasily. "The Mermaid's Rest."

"On the island itself?"

"One of the only taverns within the walls, Your Majesty."

"That's quite an honour for a woman," she said. "And quite a responsibility."

"She works very hard, Your Majesty."

"I would imagine she does. And your father?" Her handmaiden slid a bowl of steaming soup in front of her; the Queen did not seem to notice.

"He . . . my mother doesn't really speak of him, Your Majesty," he said awkwardly.

For all her larger-than-life forthrightness, Mareigh was tight-lipped about Matthias's father. Over the years her son had managed to glean a few details, like crumbs fallen to a hungry dog. She had been a tavern girl, only a little older than Arian; he was a guardsman. They had met before the last war with the Berok. By the time she found that she was with child, he was deep in battle, gone from her life. The money that he sent, after the war, had provided the means for her to buy the tavern where she had worked. Matthias imagined that the Royal Fiat, allowing his mother to move the tavern within the walls, had come as a result of his father's heroics, a favour from the King which he then passed to the woman he had left behind and the son he had never met.

"It must have been difficult for you," Captain Bream said, "growing up without a father." He leaned back to allow a bowl to be placed in front of him.

When Matthias looked at him, Captain Bream turned his eyes away, but not before Matthias saw in them something that looked like understanding.

"My mother is very strong . . ." His voice trailed off.

"That she is," the captain said quietly, still staring down at his plate.

"You know the boy's mother, then, Captain?"

"I do," he said slowly. "Though before last night I had not seen her since I received my rank."

"She must be a very fine woman to elicit such loyalty from her son."

"That she is."

Matthias leaned back to allow the handmaiden to place the bowl in front of him. Her shy smile, the way she kept her eyes lowered, reminded him of Arian. "Thank you," he whispered, and her smile widened.

She seemed to move closer to him as she picked up a spoon, filled it carefully from his bowl, and lifted it gently to her lips.

"The Mermaid is very popular among the men," the captain said. "And Mareigh runs it—"

The captain snapped to his feet at the same moment that Matthias heard the anguished cry from the handmaiden. Her hands were grabbing at her throat, her face livid and red. She clutched at the front of her gown, tugging at it, as her body heaved. She gave a choked, pained whoop, and swayed on her feet, stumbled, then fell to the floor of the throne room. Her body heaved for a moment longer, then fell still. Her wide eyes stared sightlessly at the ceiling as a tendril of blood ran from her nose.

Matthias glanced away from the body, frantically looking around the table. He expected to see the other handmaidens so afflicted, but they were staring back at him, their mouths wide.

"Poison," the Queen hissed, shoving her bowl off the table with the side of her hand.

Loren had come around to study the face of the fallen girl. She looked so young, lying on the floor. "But just for the boy."

Bream pulled himself to his full height. "Your Majesty, the Berok have infiltrated the castle."

≥ ≤

I must have drifted off while reading, because the next thing I was aware of was the sound of David's footsteps on the front steps. His stride was slow and heavy, every footfall thick and deliberate.

"How you doin', sport?" I called out as he opened the front door. Thankfully, the micro-nap had taken the edge off: the one thing about getting up so early every morning was the need for an afternoon sleep.

"Fine," he said quietly, closing the door behind himself.

"You don't sound convinced."

He came around the corner, looking at me, not saying anything.

"How was school?"

"Fine," he repeated as he kicked off his shoes.

He wasn't meeting my eye.

"Do you want a snack?"

He let the straps of his backpack slip off his shoulders, dropping it to the floor. Everything about him seemed slow, dispirited somehow.

"Sure," he said.

I waited for him to say something else, anything else.

"I'm gonna go upstairs," he said, finally.

"Okay. I'll bring you up a sandwich."

He didn't reply, just trudged through the house.

Jacqui glanced down at the paper, then back up to my face, questioningly.

I had been waiting all day for this moment, and I wanted to get it right. Jacqui was covering a half-shift this evening, so after getting David his snack I waited while she changed and bustled around the kitchen, making some toast to tide herself over.

"It's my column," I explained, though it should have been obvious.

"I can tell," she said. "It's been a while."

"I thought you might like this one."

I tried not to watch her as she read; the piece wasn't long, but the time seemed to stretch agonizingly slowly. I ran water in the sink, started taking things out of the fridge, put a pan on the stove—anything to avoid even glancing at her. She hated me watching her read.

Which was too bad. She was beautiful when she was reading.

Jacqui had been my first reader almost since the day we met. She would give my English papers a quick once-over, but when it came to those early short stories, she was tireless. I would hand her fresh pages and she would hand them back to me so covered in red ink they seemed to be bleeding.

I became a better writer, writing for her.

OFF THE SHELF
CHRISTOPHER KNOX

The summer that I was eleven, my life was changed forever. No, more than that—the world was changed forever, and I was pulled along with it.

The summer that I was eleven, my father died. His death was neither quick nor merciful: he died of lung cancer, and spent weeks wasting away in a hospital bed. He had always been a strong man, a builder, and I imagined that I would grow up to be like him: broad-shouldered and confident, always with an easy smile and a kind word. My father was the sort of man that I wanted to be. That I still want to be, truth be told.

The last time I saw him, I barely recognized him. The cancer had laid waste to his body: the man who had towered over me was now tiny and frail. His hair was gone, and his hands shook when he reached out to touch me. He still had the same smile, though—that was how I recognized him, the only way I could be sure that this small man was really my father.

That was three weeks before he died—I didn't see him after that. My mother sent me with my younger brothers to stay with my father's parents on their farm in Henderson, B.C. Even if you've heard of it, you've probably never been there—it's that sort of town.

My brothers took to country life with a passion. Too young to understand what was happening to our father, they treated our displacement as a vacation. They spent their days playing in the fields, or exploring the woods behind the farm, cutting trails and building forts.

I mostly stayed in the house, close to my grandparents, close to the telephone, waiting for it to ring with my mother's frequent updates.

It was a terrible, nightmarish summer, and I'm not sure I would have survived it, save for the discovery I made in the basement one afternoon. I don't even know what I was looking for—probably something my grandmother had sent me to find to keep me out from underfoot—but I discovered a box in a stack in one corner, a box marked with the name Richard Knox. My father's name.

I didn't take it upstairs: I dug into it right there, angling it so the ceiling light would shine into it.

At first, the box seemed like a disorganized mess, a hodgepodge of newspaper clippings, ribbons and trophies, yearbooks and photographs, report cards and a few envelopes that still held letters. It took me a while of digging through to realize that I was actually holding my father's childhood in my hands, sifting through his memories, all the things he had chosen to preserve.

At the bottom of the box, I found a handful of books—paperbacks in fairly poor shape, battered and spine-broken, obviously well read and deeply loved. I ignored the westerns (I still do), but there were four other books, books that promised adventure and daring, with bright pictures of knights and swordsmen, battles and beautiful maidens on their covers.

I put everything else back into the box, but I carried those books with me out into the summer afternoon sunlight. It would probably be an exaggeration to say that those books, four fantasy novels by an author named Lazarus Took, saved my life, but they saved me in a way that only the experience of reading can. I devoured those books, one after another, then I went back and began to reread them, more slowly, with greater attention and devotion.

I spent those weeks reading, lying in the field or perched up in one of the apple trees, up in the room that I was sharing with my brothers or in the privacy of the hayloft.

Like the best books, the novels I found in my father's box were capable of magic—they took me to another world, made me feel more deeply there than I could allow myself to feel in the real world. While I was reading, I ceased to be little Christopher Knox—I became someone else entirely.

And that's what books should do for us. I haven't thought about Lazarus Took in decades, but I still recall how it felt to read those novels, the impact they had on my life, on my heart. Everyone has books like that in their past, forgotten treasures from their childhood. What are yours?

She cleared her throat, and I turned toward her.

"This is good," she said, gesturing with the paper.

"Thanks." I could feel my face warming.

"I didn't . . ." she began, and glanced away. "Why didn't you tell me how important that book was to you?"

I shrugged. I had been thinking about it since the day I found *To the Four Directions* at Prospero's. "I wasn't really able to put it into words," I said lamely.

Jacqui gestured with the paper again. "You seemed to do just fine with this."

"Yeah." That was my curse: I was always better with words on paper than I was with actually talking to people. Especially the people closest to me.

"You should tell David," she said. "Maybe . . ."

I shook my head. "No. I don't want—" I broke off. "I don't think it's something that I want to talk to him about yet. My dad dying . . ."

She nodded, and seemed about to speak, but we both heard a sound outside the kitchen door. Seconds later, David appeared, clutching his sandwich plate.

"I brought my dishes down," he said, with a wide smile. "What's for dinner?"

I hadn't heard him come down the stairs. How long, I wondered, had he been standing outside the room, listening?

"So are you all brushed up?" I asked as I came through Davy's door. He was sitting up in bed, covers draped over his lap, holding his new baseball glove. "Had a pee?" He nodded. "Nolan fed?" I glanced over at the hamster cage.

"Yes, Dad," he said in the much-exasperated tone that was part of the routine.

I stopped at the bookshelf by the door and picked up our leather bookmark. "So, what do you want to start next?"

"What about the one you gave me? I brought it up from downstairs."

When I turned to him, he gestured with the baseball glove toward his bedside table where *To the Four Directions* lay beside the lamp.

I stepped toward the desk, rested my hand on the back of his chair. He wasn't looking at me.

"Are you sure?" I asked, pulling the chair over to the bed. "You didn't seem too keen on it."

He shrugged, pushing a ball into the web of the glove. "I don't know," he said. "It's not *The Lord of the Rings*, but it might be all right."

I resisted the urge to kiss the top of his head. "Well, let's find out," I said, opening the book. "Assume the position, sport."

He didn't lie down the way he usually did. "Dad," he said, extending the glove slightly toward me. "Can you help me with this?"

I looked at the glove, with absolutely no idea what to do with it.

"Can you help me put this under my mattress?"

"Isn't that going to be uncomfortable?"

"It's just for another couple of nights. Coach says—"

"Right."

Together we managed to get the glove set firmly in place. When he lay down he shifted several times, twisting and contorting, the way a cat will settle to the contours of its bed and manage to look completely comfortable once it's done.

"You all right?" I asked, when he seemed settled.

"I think so," he said, shifting a bit more. "It's a bit lumpy . . ."

"Pea under your bed, Princess?" I asked, putting on a fake British accent.

"No, I didn't!"

We both laughed. Quick-witted, my boy.

"Okay." I opened the book again. "*To the Four Directions*, by Lazarus Took."

"Read by Christopher Knox," he said, imitating the introductions used in the audio-books we listened to in the van.

I smiled, at home in at least this little bit of routine.

A few pages into the first chapter, he stopped me.

"You don't have to do that anymore, you know."

"Do what?"

"That thing you do where you call the people in books David for me? You don't need to do that anymore—I'm eleven years old now."

"I didn't." It was an old trick, a way of helping David relate to the story and the characters, but I hadn't done it in a long time. David Baggins just hadn't seemed right.

Had I slipped into the old habit?

I glanced down at the book.

"No, look here." I held up the book to him.

"I'll get a beating if I am late to the stables," Tamas complained. But that didn't stop him from following Dafyd through the winding alley in the dark.

"You worry too much, Tamas," Dafyd said. "You have time for a little food. The stable-master will be asleep for hours yet. . . ."

"And here." Flipping a page.

Tamas risked a nervous glance at Dafyd, and Mareigh caught the look.

"Dafyd," she said, her voice dropping sternly.

"It's spelled differently, with an *f* and a *y*, but it's all David. I wasn't making it up."

"Okay," he said, turning onto his side again. "I believe you."

"Shall I go on?" I asked, with mock obsequiousness.

"By all means."

⊱ ⊰

After the death of the handmaiden, Captain Bream and the chosen twenty of his men took to the road earlier than planned, riding hard in formation around Dafyd and the magus. If the Berok had infiltrated the castle, time was of the essence. They had ridden out of Colcott before dawn, and for the first day, the men took the River Road through the heart of the country. Outside of Colcott Town, the country had given way to smaller villages, clutches of buildings gathered at the edge of the Col River. The road was busy, but the merchants and travellers gave the King's Men wide berth.

The horsemen did not slow, and arrived at the garrison as dark was beginning to fall. The horses were boarded, the men fed, and Dafyd collapsed into the first bed that could be found for him, sleeping dreamlessly.

There had been no idle conversation as they rode, and Dafyd was left alone with his thoughts of the handmaiden who had died in the throne room, who had given her life for his, and of the King who was, even now, dying, hoping for Dafyd to save him. He ached not only from the riding, but for his mother, and Tamas. And Arian. Always Arian.

The next morning, they forded the Col at a town called Donder.

On the south bank of the river, the road was quiet. What few settlements they passed were little more than fishing camps. They rode hours without seeing another face.

The country began to change around them. The great trees and green that Dafyd had known all his life seemed to shrink and turn brown the farther they rode from Colcott Town, and the air was dry, dusty, without the constant moistness of the sea breezes.

Partway through the afternoon, the magus rode up on Dafyd's right.

"I am guessing that this is the farthest you have ever ventured from the island," he said.

After hours of silence, Dafyd was surprised to be spoken to, and it took him a moment to respond. "Yes."

"To see the country, its people . . . it gives us a sense of what is at stake." A touch of sadness had entered the old man's voice.

Dafyd nodded. The thought had weighed heavily upon him for days. "I had no idea that the King was ill," he said.

"It is the best-kept secret in the kingdom," the magus said. "Or it was, until the Berok attacked. Now . . ." He paused. "The two go hand in hand. The King has been sick for some time, and when the Queen had to step in, no one could know. If the Berok ever got a hint that the

King was incapacitated"—he shook his head—"they certainly would have invaded before now."

"But would the kingdom not rally around the Queen as much as around the King?"

"It is not a matter of the kingdom rallying," Loren said solemnly. "Were such a grave illness to become known, it would embolden the Berok, knowing that without an heir, one of their own is next in line for the throne."

Dafyd's face betrayed his confusion.

"Ah. You are too young to recall," Loren said.

"Too young to recall what?" Dafyd asked, his head reeling at the thought of a barbarian on the throne.

"Fifteen years ago, after the Battle of Deren Plain, King Horace and the Berok king met to broker what they both hoped would be a lasting peace between the kingdoms." Loren spoke quietly, and Dafyd had to strain to hear him. "To seal their bond, they arranged a marriage between their children, between the prince, Horace's only son, and Tanis, the eldest daughter of the Berok king. Their union, the royal wedding, was to unite the kingdoms."

Dafyd struggled to understand. "Then why are the Berok—?"

"Because their old king is gone. Died nearly five years ago now, in the Berok fashion. Killed by his eldest son, Queen Tanis's brother, who now sits on the Berok throne. He was one of the strongest critics of his father's diplomacy, and now that he rules, the agreements are worthless. The only bond that remains is the marriage of Tanis and the King. And now that they know of his illness—"

The magus didn't have a chance to finish his sentence. A whistling sound came out of the air and with a startled gasp the guardsman closest to Dafyd fell backward in his saddle.

"Dafyd, get down," he heard the captain cry when he noticed the red shaft of the arrow lodged in the guardsman's chest. "We are under attack!"

☙ ❧

"So how was that?" I asked after we'd read for almost half an hour. I tucked the bookmark into place. "Do you think it's got some potential?"

"Maybe," he said, but his tone of voice and his little smile told the real story. "He's only fifteen—that's not much older than me. Bilbo Baggins was fifty."

"Well, not so long ago someone who was thirteen or fourteen was almost a grown-up. Kids were getting married and starting families when they were that age." I stopped for a moment, trying to wrap my head around the idea. "People lived shorter lives in those days, so they had to start everything younger. That's why when you see someone like a wizard or a mage in books like these, someone with white hair and a long beard, they're important because they've lived so much longer than the people around them. Does that make sense?"

He nodded, but he was fading.

I couldn't shake an odd feeling as I put the book onto the shelf and kissed my son good-night. It stayed with me as I pulled the door part-way shut, making sure the light from the hall didn't spill onto his face.

It was strange I hadn't noticed that the main character of the book was named Dafyd—that sort of detail usually jumps out at me, especially when it was something I could have used as a selling point in winning him over with the book.

Maybe I had been thrown by the *f* and the *y*.

Dafyd froze, unable to look away as the guardsman's horse bolted, the soldier's body tumbling from the saddle and dragging in the dust from one foot tangled in the stirrup.

His own horse reared as the remaining guardsmen turned their mounts toward the rise to their left.

"Dafyd, get down!" the captain shouted again as he spurred his horse.

Dafyd's horse turned to follow, and he felt a sudden streak of wind, a sharp burning against his cheek. He heard the same high, whistling sound follow: an arrow!

He reached up to touch his cheek as the magus launched himself toward Dafyd, knocking him from the saddle and pushing him to the ground.

A moment later the whistling came again, and Dafyd's horse screamed and reared, flailing for a moment against the sky, then crashing to the earth mere inches from where Dafyd had fallen.

"Get close," the magus commanded, pushing Dafyd toward the body of the horse. "Take shelter."

Dafyd did as he was told, tucking himself behind the horse's haunch.

"Keep your head down."

But Dafyd couldn't help but peek over the horse's body.

Leaving a handful of men behind, the guardsmen rode furiously up the rise, the captain at the lead, his sword flashing in the sun, dust rising behind them like smoke.

At first, Dafyd couldn't see what they were riding toward, but as he watched he noticed that parts of the dusty brown hillside seemed to be moving. Men dressed to match the landscape were running toward the charging guardsmen.

Were there three? Four? Dafyd couldn't tell. As the guardsmen rode into them, their swords arced into the sky, then down, and again.

It was over in moments. As one rider broke from the pack and turned back toward them, Dafyd realized he had been holding his breath.

"Are you hurt?" the magus asked from somewhere nearby.

Turning, Dafyd saw the man hunched low behind the horse, his fingers wrapped around the medallion at his neck.

Dafyd shook his head.

The sound of hoof beats grew closer. The captain was at the base of the hill, riding toward them. His face was stern, masked in blood. His dripping sword hung loose in his right hand. When he saw Dafyd looking at him, a grim smile crossed his features.

"That was too close," he said as he reined his horse to a stop beside the body of Dafyd's own.

Dafyd stood up, and the captain flinched. "Your face."

Dafyd brought his fingers up to touch the welt, now sticky and sharp with pain.

"Much too close." The captain turned his attention to the magus, who was rising slowly, carefully, to his feet.

"Was it a scouting party?" Loren asked. "From the watchtowers?"

The captain shook his head, and his face turned even darker. "No. There were too few." He glanced meaningfully at Dafyd, then back toward the hillside, at the bodies in the dust. "These were assassins, sent with only one purpose."

I puttered around downstairs for a while. I straightened the living room, and took the garbage out to the can at the side of the house. I drifted into the kitchen, ran a sinkful of hot water over the dishes and left them to soak as I poured myself two fingers of vodka.

At the foot of the stairs, I flicked off the light, looking upwards toward David's room. I wasn't expecting to see what I saw: he'd been on his best behaviour lately, knowing that we'd confiscate his video game if he was caught playing it after lights-out again.

When I was a kid, I couldn't figure out for the longest time how I was getting caught reading after I was supposed to be asleep. I finally realized that my parents were able to see the light under my bedroom door. Busted.

Oh, David.

I crept up the stairs, avoiding the creaky spots. I hated coming down heavy on him, but he'd had fair warning. If his video game was interfering with his schoolwork or his sleep, we, the almighty we, would have to take it away. He'd already lost it once for three days; next time, a week-long period of cold turkey.

I was halfway up the stairs when the light went out, a click from the lamp echoing down the hallway. I hadn't been as quiet as I had thought.

His bedroom door was closed—I remembered distinctly leaving it open a crack. Clever kid. As if to myself, I said, "I could have sworn I left this open."

Pushing the door wide, I paused before entering the room. In the spill of light from the hall, David looked almost like he was really sleeping, curled on his side, head tucked slightly, no telltale smile on his lips.

I stepped across the room, touched the ball of my hand to his bed-side lamp and pulled it back from the heat.

"That's strange," I said for his benefit. "That lamp's awfully hot."

His composure didn't falter.

I glanced down at the bedside table, looking for his video game, ready to put an end to the performance we were both participating in, but I stopped short.

His video game wasn't there.

It was on his desk, right where he had left it earlier in the evening, its charging light bright.

Next to his lamp, though, was *To the Four Directions*.

I smiled.

"What's this?" I asked. "I could have sworn I put this on the shelf when we were done reading it. I wonder how it got over here. Hmm." I picked up the book. "Maybe I'm losing my mind."

That got a smile out of him, the slightest upturn of the corners of his mouth.

Leaning over, I pulled his covers up and kissed him on the forehead. "Good night, Davy."

He didn't respond.

I tucked the book under my arm.

"Strange things are afoot in this room tonight," I said, leaving the door open a crack. "I'll have to keep a closer eye on things up here."

⁓ ⁓

After the attack, they rode at full gallop to the garrison. Dafyd rode the fallen guardsman's mount, head heavy with the thought that another person had given his life to protect him.

At the gate, Bream waited impatiently while the gatekeeper examined the writ of passage the captain had been given by the Queen. Bream's face was crusted with blood, dark and gritty from the dust of the journey. The gatekeeper finally nodded and shouted for the gate to be opened.

"Made a good show of it," Bream muttered, as he folded the letter back into his saddlebag.

"What do you mean?" Dafyd asked.

"He can't read," Bream said, his voice laced with contempt. "Few of the men can. But none of them want to look stupid, so they'll stare at the paper until they think they've fooled you." He shook his head. "At least he recognized the royal seal at the bottom."

Dafyd could feel his face heating up.

Bream noticed. "My apologies," he said. "Perhaps upon our return, someone can teach you to read." He steadied his horse with a gentle pressure on the reins.

Dafyd nodded, spurring his horse to a canter.

As they passed through the gate, Bream shouted at the first uniformed man he saw. "I need your commander," he barked. When the man hesitated, he shouted, "Now!"

≈ ≈

I was elbow-deep in dishwater when Jacqui got home from work.

She didn't say hello when she entered the kitchen. "So how were things tonight?" she asked, leaning into the fridge to pull out a beer.

"Quiet," I said.

She twisted off the cap and took a long swallow. I watched her throat move, her head tilted back. She was wearing a set of lavender scrubs, her hair messy, her face flushed.

"And how was work?"

"Freak show," she said. "I'm glad it was only a half-shift. By the time I left we were already three hours backed up." She shook her head. "Apparently there's some really good heroin out there right now: we had three ODs before nine o'clock."

"Wow."

"Yeah." She took another swallow of beer. "And how are you?"

I was surprised: she didn't usually ask anymore. "I'm all right."

She nodded. "How did the reading go?"

Her questions were unsettling.

"Fine," I said guardedly.

"Even just for your sake," she said, not meeting my eye, "you probably should have got him *The Lord of the Rings*."

And then it clicked: she was feeling sorry for me.

"I think it'll be all right."

She shrugged. "I'm just saying, he's only eleven. He wanted something that he knew, something that he could talk about at school, you know?"

I let her talk, not arguing, not saying anything.

"I think—" She leaned against the counter, angled away from me. It looked like she had given this a lot of thought, like she had things she wanted to say. "A present like that, it's nice, and it was very thoughtful, but it was more about you than it was about him, wasn't it?"

I didn't rise to the bait.

"Why didn't you just buy him what *he* wanted?"

"He's not ready for it yet."

She looked at me as if she was expecting something more.

"I'm gonna go," I said quietly, draining the sink.

"Chris—"

I stopped at the back door, my hand on the knob. "By the way," I said, as if it had just occurred to me. "I caught him with his light on tonight."

That galvanized her, and she glanced at the top of the fridge. "Where did you put his game?"

"He wasn't playing it." I tried to sound distracted, like it was unimportant. Setting her up.

"Then what—"

I turned the doorknob. "He was reading," I said as I stepped outside. "His new book." I closed the door and headed for the garage.

Time for my cigarette du jour.

⤞ ⤝

"What should have been the easy part of our journey is now behind us," Captain Bream said, dropping his fork onto the tin plate which, only moments before, had been heaped with his breakfast.

Dafyd, Loren and the captain were eating in the garrison captain's private rooms, masses of eggs and meat and crunchy crusted bread. At first Dafyd had boggled at the amount of food, but he wolfed it down without another thought. The welt on his face burned every time he chewed.

"We'll be travelling through territory held by the Berok now," the captain continued. "The watchtowers, once our greatest strength, are now a liability. From them, the Berok can watch the entire valley, and what passes through it."

Dafyd felt a sickening wave of fear settle into his stomach, and regretted eating so much.

The captain cocked his head toward Loren. "Magus, a map?" he said.

The old man moved his plate aside. Bream and Dafyd followed suit as the magus unrolled a battered scroll onto the table.

"We're here," the captain said, pointing.

Dafyd traced the road they had followed from Colcott on the coast along the river, to the unmarked area on the map at which the captain was pointing. The spot was ringed with the jagged shape of mountains, several peaks crested with crowns: the watchtowers.

"Our best course east is through this pass here. It's a good road. Not busy. Miners, mostly, from the iron mines at Comaric." He traced the road toward the mountains. "And this pass, Loren?"

The old man considered for a moment, then nodded. "That sounds like a prudent course."

"I spoke to some of the men last night. There have been no sightings of the Berok, but with the attempt on your life yesterday . . ." His voice grew thoughtful. "We will need to proceed with utmost care."

"To say the least," Loren added, and the captain nodded grimly.

"Our destination is here," he said, pointing at a spot nestled within the mountains. "A small village near the mine heads. We'll stay there tonight, and from there"—he gestured at the map, sweeping his hand over the green expanse at the top of the sheet, only rarely broken by roads and even more rarely by towns—"we're truly on our own."

III

I SET TO WORK the next morning still thinking about Lazarus Took, and *To the Four Directions*. Castle intrigue? A quest? Sure, it was hoary old material, but he had hooked me again, just like he had when I was a kid.

I managed to push the thoughts to the back of my mind while I wrote, but after that I surrendered. I went back to LazarusTook.com and clicked through to the Biography page.

Shining Swords and Steel
The Road to Honour
The World a Stage
Long Journey Home

No mention of *To the Four Directions*. If it weren't for the familiar style, I might have wondered if there was another Lazarus Took. Why wasn't there any mention of the book here, or in any of the bibliographies I had found? I had certainly never heard of Alexander Press, but you would think that the webmaster of the official Lazarus Took website would have.

Well, nothing like going to the source.

I clicked on "Contact Us."

To: info@lazarustook.com
From: Christopher Knox
Subject: Lazarus Took details

Good morning –
I recently stumbled across your website and I wanted to take

this opportunity to thank you for all your hard work. It is very difficult to find any information about Lazarus Took, and I was thrilled to see that he has not been forgotten.

Took was one of my favourite authors when I was a child, and now my son has started reading his books.

As a freelance journalist and writer, I am fascinated by Took's story (as well-told in your scrupulously researched Biography page), and I am considering writing a piece on "forgotten" writers whose work continues to have an impact on those fortunate enough to find it. Would it be possible for me to interview you regarding Took and his work? Or, at the very least, consult with you on background for the story? Any help you can provide will be greatly appreciated.

With best regards,
Christopher Knox

I added the most significant lines as a postscript, hoping they would read as a casual afterthought:

PS: While I've got your attention: I've always wondered, did Lazarus Took only write the four novels that you list? Did he ever work under a pseudonym? Did he leave any unpublished papers at the time of his death?
Thanks, CK

I sent the message and leaned back in my chair.

That would do for the moment; if anyone was likely to know about *To the Four Directions* it would be someone at Took's official website. If they even bothered to reply.

In the meantime, though, it was still early enough to read a bit of the book while David got ready for school. And then maybe have a wander downtown.

That sounded like the start of a good day.

Coming out of the garrison captain's quarters, Dafyd was surprised to find the mustering area full not of soldiers, but of miners. It took him only a moment to see through the disguise, but the deception had worked. The men were in clothes tattered and greyed with age and dirt. They seemed broken down, moving with a slowness that Dafyd recognized from seeing men in the tavern who spent their days pulling nets from the sea, or cutting trees to build houses in Colcott town.

Even the horses seemed drab and dull, and Dafyd watched as one of the men picked up a handful of dirt and rubbed it into the shining coat of his mount.

"We're ready," Captain Bream said from behind Dafyd.

It was a slow day's ride, and a long one. The captain sent the men out in three staggered parties. Dafyd, Loren and the captain rode out with the second. Dafyd was just barely able to see the first men ahead of them whenever the road straightened. The road to the pass was narrow, and the trees on either side pressed in on them. They kept the horses at an ambling pace.

"We're just coming to the pass," the captain told Dafyd after they had been riding for several hours. "Steady now."

Looking up, Dafyd was dizzied by the sight of two sheer rock faces towering above him. Deep shadows swallowed the trail ahead.

He shifted uneasily in his saddle. He knew that up there, somewhere, was a watchtower, manned not by soldiers of the Crown but by Berok warriors. He could feel their savage eyes on the small crew of men, studying them. Would the disguises hold?

His neck prickled with the expectation that, at any moment, he might feel the sudden driving thrust of an arrow piercing his back, the cowardly enemy staying safe and unseen as they slaughtered the King's Men.

He tried to focus on the motion of the horse beneath him. The dull sound of hoofs echoed up the stone walls. How easy it would be for the Berok to come at them from above, or behind. The knife tucked in his boot was faint comfort.

The sky narrowed to the thinnest of lines overhead. The sun had disappeared behind the walls of the pass. Tense to the point of snapping, the men glanced warily around, twisting in their saddles at the slightest noise.

They rode through the half-light for hours. Dafyd wearied after being alert for so long to every noise, every shadow.

When the road widened again, a rush of relief passed through the group of men. It was as if they had all been holding their breath, and had all exhaled at once. The captain's grim visage broke into a small smile.

Once through the pass, they gave the horses their heads. The trees were shorter here than they were along the coast. Hardier stock. The air was noticeably drier, and it burned Dafyd's nose.

Once again, they did not break for a midday meal. The mine heads were a full day's ride from the garrison, and their deliberate pace through the pass had slowed them. Dafyd was ravenous by the time they arrived at the mining camp, just before sunset.

It was a tiny, squalid place, not quite a village. There were several bunkhouses for the miners, a few scattered houses, a general store, and an inn. Huge piles of ore littered the ground at the foot of the mountains, and black smoke belched into the sky from behind a scrim of trees. The air was grey, and tasted of smoke.

The first company of King's Men was waiting in the shade near the inn. Captain Bream handed his reins to one of them as he dismounted. He took off the miner's shirt he had been wearing, revealing his uniform.

Dafyd climbed gingerly from the horse, trying to ignore the gnawing pain in his legs. He followed the captain into the cool dim of the inn's common room. It was larger than his mother's tavern, and every table and glass was already full. But where The Mermaid's Rest would have been filled with the boisterous laughter and good cheer of men at their rest, this place was silent, the drinkers barely looking up. The room stank of spilled ale and old soup.

Captain Bream strode over to the fat man working behind the bar. "I'm looking for the innkeeper."

The man looked at the captain the way one looks at something he's stepped in. "You've found him," he said.

Bream drew the folded letter of passage from within his uniform. "I come bearing a letter of mark from the King. My men and I require lodging for the night, and board for our horses." He unfolded the letter and laid it on the bar face up. Dafyd could see the King's seal.

The innkeeper didn't even look at it. "There's no rooms tonight," he said flatly.

Bream pushed the paper closer to him. "I have a letter of passage—"

"And I have no rooms," the innkeeper said, leaning forward. "Would you have me put all these men out into the cold?" He pushed the letter back across the bar.

Bream's jaw tightened. "By order of the King—"

"The King," the innkeeper snorted. "The same King who refused to quarter soldiers here for the last year, even though we warned of the Berok encroaching? The King who would throw us to the wolves rather than send a company to protect his own iron? And now he wants me to put you up for the night as you pass through, before leaving us to the wolves again?"

Dafyd didn't see the captain move. One moment he was standing, stock-still, hands at his sides, and the next his fist was crashing into the innkeeper's face. There was a popping noise, and blood poured from the man's nose.

Bream caught the front of the man's shirt and pulled him over the bar as if he weighed nothing, calling out "Men!" as the fat innkeeper hit the floor.

Within seconds, several of the men were at the captain's side, bodies tight and coiled as they surveyed the room.

No one else moved.

"Find someplace to stow this."

As two of the men hauled the innkeeper to his feet, the captain leaned in close. "You'll be lucky not to find your neck in a noose come sunrise," he said loudly. "That talk is treason, no matter how far from the castle you might be."

Around the room the miners, who had been watching the confrontation, wearily cast their eyes down to their glasses.

🙢 🙠

First, I saw her feet: her sensible black shoes, her black pants.

I was crouching in Munro's fiction section, browsing the *N*s and *O*s.

At first, I thought she was standing so close because I was blocking a shelf that she wanted to look at. I shifted away.

She stepped into the space I had just vacated.

I pulled a Tim O'Brien novel from the shelf and started to read the description on the back cover.

"Excuse me?"

I looked up. "Yes?"

She was young, maybe in her early twenties, with dark hair and wide eyes. She was smiling uncertainly.

"Are you Christopher Knox?" she asked uncertainly.

I stood up. Should I remember her? Had I met her at one of Jacqui's dinners with people from the hospital, one of those interminable nights where not even name tags would help? Or was she someone from David's school? Had I met her at a parent–teacher night?

Jesus, I'm terrible with people.

"Yes."

She fumbled with her shoulder bag.

"I love your book," she said, pulling out a battered copy of *Coastal Drift*. She was blushing, and she wouldn't meet my eye.

I was speechless.

"I wasn't sure it was you," she said, the words rushing over one another. "I thought you looked like you, but I think it's an old picture."

It was the original hardcover, with the picture of me on the beach. "I wouldn't have recognized me from that picture either," I said.

She smiled and looked down at the floor. "Anyway, I really like it."

"I'm glad to hear that," I said, playing it as cool as I could, trying to make it seem like this was something that happened all the time, a pretty girl telling me that she had loved my book.

"I'm reading it for a summer class at Camosun College. Contemporary Canadian Fiction."

"I didn't know it was being taught." That was good news. "It's nice to know that I'm still considered contemporary." I tried for a wry chuckle.

She didn't get it.

"It's my favourite book in the course. I'm writing a paper on it."

"Well, thank you for that . . ." I said, leaving a space at the end of the sentence for her to fill. I had no idea what to say.

She shook her head. "I'm sorry. I'm Tara," she said, extending her hand.

I took it. "Chris." Her grip was soft and cool. "Did you want me to—" I gestured at the book with my chin.

"Oh, please." She dropped my hand and passed me the book.

"So are you full time at Camosun? I asked, looking for my pen in my bag.

"No, I'm transferring to UVic in September."

"What are you taking?" I balanced the book on the edge of the shelf, and opened it to the title page.

She shifted a little, uneasily. "Creative writing," she said, almost like she was unsure whether she should be admitting it. "And English. Double major."

"Nice," I said, trying to think of something to write in her book. "The department's very good."

"That's what I've heard."

She smiled again as I handed her book back to her.

"Thank you," she said, holding it to her chest.

I shook my head. "No, thank *you*. It's nice to know that somebody's reading it." I couldn't think of anything else to say.

Apparently she couldn't either.

"Listen," I said impulsively. "Do you want to grab a cup of coffee or something? There's a Starbucks—"

Her face fell. "No, I can't. I'm on my way to work." She gestured down at her clothes—the black pants, the sensible shoes, the pressed white shirt.

I nodded understandingly. No, of course not. I don't even know why I said it.

"But listen," she said, taking a pen and notebook out of her bag in a smooth, well-practised motion. The Moleskine was battered, its pages bulging. It looked like one of my own notebooks.

"Why don't I give you my number," she said, scrawling on a page near the back of the notebook. "You can, you know, if you have some time or something you can give me a call, maybe we can, you know, arrange something." Talking almost too fast for me to follow the words.

She tore the sheet out of the notebook and handed it over, suddenly flustered again. "I know how busy you must be, though. You must get lots of people wanting to pick your brain . . ." Offering me excuses, offering rationalizations in her own mind for when I didn't call.

I looked down at the paper: *Tara Scott*, and her phone number, written in green ink. "Thanks," I said, folding the paper and tucking it into my front pocket, the corner of the envelope containing Dale's key digging into the back of my hand.

"I'll give you a call."

Her smile was hopeful, but dubious. She shrugged. "Sure. Whatever. If you get a chance."

⤞ ⤝

Dafyd tried to avoid making eye contact with the innkeeper's wife as she brought them their breakfast and made sure their glasses were kept filled. She looked worn to the point of exhaustion, as if she hadn't slept at all the previous night.

After, she followed a short distance behind Dafyd and the magus as they walked from the grey of the tavern into the bright morning of the inn-yard, staying close to the doorway as they went to their waiting horses. The guardsmen were already mustered and ready to ride.

"Ready?" Captain Bream asked. As his eyes adjusted to the light, Dafyd noticed a length of thick rope draped over Bream's lap. He was working one end of it between his hands.

Dafyd nodded and pulled himself into his saddle. He was getting better: this morning, he barely ached at all.

"The first company has already departed," Bream said.

The captain twisted the rope and curled it around itself. Dafyd didn't envy the captain—he was always on his guard, constantly watching the people around him, surveying their surroundings.

He probably slept with a knife in his hand, Dafyd thought, watching as Bream pulled two lengths of the rope, tightening a knot. His heart dropped in his chest when the captain held up the rope, now tied into a noose, just wide enough to allow the passage of a man's head before it was tightened.

"Are you ready?"

Dafyd had a hard time answering, not sure what the captain was asking. "I am," he said carefully.

"Good. We'll ride out next. Hide yourself in the middle of the pack. Before we do that, though—" The captain draped the noose over his lap as he tugged at his reins and brought his horse around toward the woman by the tavern door.

"The innkeeper," he said, his voice booming. "Is he your husband?"

The woman looked terrified. "He is, sir."

The captain held up the rope, seemed to study his knot. "He has an unwise tongue."

"I've told him, sir. I've told him many a time."

"Tell him again," the captain said. "And tell him that if all he believed about the King were true, his neck would be in a rope this morning."

The woman gasped as the captain tossed the noose gently toward her, the rope landing in the dust at her feet.

"Give him that, so he doesn't forget."

⪢ ⪡

David's footsteps pattered up to the front porch, oddly light, and his key was in the lock and the door open before I had a chance to mark my place in the novel I was reading for next week's column and look up.

He slung his pack off his back and dropped it to the floor, tugging off his jacket and swinging the door shut in the same motion.

"Hey, sport," I said. "What's up?"

He turned toward me sharply, as if surprised to see me sitting there, same place I was every day at this time.

"Hey, Dad."

He kicked off his shoes and picked up his bag.

I set the book on the side table. "You all right?"

He nodded, his eyes flickering between me and the rest of the house. The nod seemed like an afterthought, distracted.

"How was school?" I felt like I was interrogating him with pleasantries.

"It was okay." His body seemed tense, oddly coiled, as if I had interrupted his momentum.

"Just okay?"

He shrugged. Then he stood there like he was waiting for me to dismiss him.

"Do you want a snack? Dinner's going to be a little later tonight . . ."

"Sure."

They say that changes in your children seem to happen overnight—had I missed the moment when he turned into a teenager?

"Do you want to come down for it, or should I bring it up to your room?" A question that couldn't be answered with a monosyllabic grunt.

Another shrug. "I can come down." He hefted his bag back onto his shoulder.

Apparently we were done.

"Okay, give me a couple of minutes."

He nodded, and then he was gone, bent a little under the weight of the pack.

"Homework first," I called after him. "No video games until after your schoolwork is done."

Nothing.

☝ ☝

For two days the King's Men gave their horses a bit of lead, but never let them reach a full gallop. They rode the faint riverside trail from early in the morning until late in the afternoon, when they would start looking for places to make camp. They rode through the heat of the day, the sun baking down, a thick sheen of sweat on their faces catching the dust and darkening their skin. They rode through the rough, brown-grey landscape, through the tall dry grass and over the slow rolling hills.

Dafyd had never been more than a short walk from the seashore; caught up in the streets of the city on the island and Colcott Town he had never imagined that the world could open up like this and be so vast, so empty, so utterly devoid of people. They passed only occasional farmhouses, a few fisherman's shacks along the river. The air seemed filled with spice, a sharp, savoury scent he couldn't quite identify.

Each company of riders made camp separately for the night. Though "making camp"'was an exaggeration: preparations included little more than finding a flat place off the trail, close to the river for fresh water, where the horses could be tethered and the men's bedrolls opened.

"No fires," Captain Bream said as the sun sank low. "A fire can be seen for miles in this country, and the smoke can be smelled even farther."

The slight cool of the evening came as a blessed relief. The dried meat and crusty bread that the men had brought were more than satisfying, the river water cold and almost sweet it was so fresh.

That first night, Dafyd had difficulty getting to sleep. He kept getting lost in the stars. The sky on the plains stretched from flat horizon to flat horizon, seeming almost to swallow him.

They rode again all through the next day, following the curve of the river to the southeast.

As they finished eating that night, the captain leaned back against a log. "By this time tomorrow . . ." he began, looking at Loren.

The magus nodded. "That's what I reckoned as well."

Dafyd looked from one man to the other, not following their meaning. "What?' he asked.

"We should get to the canyon by early afternoon tomorrow," the captain said.

That didn't help Dafyd. "What canyon?"

"The canyon we've been riding for." A hint of impatience crept into the captain's voice. He looked at the magus.

The old man rose and walked to his horse. "I didn't see any need to burden the boy with the specifics." He brought back his saddlebag from the tall grass near where his mount was tethered. "Especially since he was concentrating so hard on keeping to his horse."

The captain smirked.

"We're going to a canyon?" Dafyd asked, trying to shift the conversation back.

"I believe so," the magus said. He sat on another piece of driftwood, three of which formed a rough triangle near the river's edge. "The book presents us with a bit of a puzzle, actually." He began to flip through the pages. "According to the book, the secret of the Sunstone will be found in 'the rainbow chasm at the moment the sun slips and the doorway to the secret world is revealed.'"

"So is that the name of the canyon?" Dafyd asked.

"No, that is what the men have always called it."

"Then . . . how do we know if we're going to the right place?"

"We don't," the captain said drily.

The magus unrolled a map, laying it on the ground close to the hooded lantern. The evening light was almost gone. "We're here," he said, pointing at a nondescript spot along the twisting line of the river. "We'll stay close to the river in the morning, and a half-day's ride"—he slid his finger along the line, toward the mountains in the east—"will bring us to this canyon. Which I think"—he looked at Captain Bream—"is the canyon described in the prophecies."

"Why do you think that?" Dafyd asked.

"Because of this," the magus said, poking his finger at a series of arching lines on the map.

"And because of something I saw in the war," the captain said.

༅ ༅

"I called you twice," I said as I pushed David's door open with my free hand. "Didn't you—?"

He looked up at me as if caught, holding his place in the book with one finger. He was sitting on the bed, his pack on the floor.

"Who—? Pardon?" His eyes were glassy, unfocused. He must have been deep into it.

I gestured toward him with the plate. "I've got your snack, Your Highness," I said. "I hope peanut butter and jelly is okay."

He nodded. "Sure. Yeah. Sure. Thank you."

I handed him the plate, which he set down on the pillow next to him.

"I called you a couple of times, you know."

He shook his head. "Sorry," he said. "I guess I didn't hear."

I looked down at the book in his hand. "No, I guess you didn't. You're not reading too far ahead, are you?"

"I'm trying not to. It's hard to stop," he said, bursting out with a smile.

For a moment it felt like my heart might explode. "I'm glad you like it," I said.

"Dad, I've never read anything like this before. It's like I'm right there."

I wished I could remember the last time a book had had that effect on me. "I'll leave you to it, then. I've got to get started on dinner. Don't read too far ahead," I said. "And make sure you get your homework done. You know what your mom'll say if you start to fall behind."

He was reading the book again before I was out the door, ignoring the sandwich on the plate beside him. I stood and watched him for a moment from the doorway, feeling a combination of pride and wonder. Getting him to read anything had always been such a struggle, and it usually ended with David in tears of frustration. Seeing him so engrossed made it all worthwhile—like I had finally given him something of myself, like we finally had common ground to meet on.

☙ ❧

The next morning they headed east along the edge of the river. As the hours passed, the land to the south, to their right, seemed to rise away from them. By noon, they were riding along the foot of a sharp hill carved out by the rushing Col alongside them.

Dafyd heard the canyon long before he saw it, a sound like faint thunder in the distance, barely noticeable over the rumble of the hoof beats.

By the time they were close to the canyon, the sound drowned out the pounding of the hoofs. When he glanced at the magus, the older man nodded.

"That's the waterfall," he said. "The source of the Col."

A cool mist hung in the air as they slowed their horses near the entrance to the canyon, where the lead group of guardsmen were already setting up camp.

"This is the place I remember," the captain said as he dismounted.

Dafyd climbed easily off his horse, tethering it loosely to a low branch. He couldn't help but stare at the great vertical fissure in the otherwise solid wall of rock, out of which burst the mighty Col.

"The Rainbow Canyon," the magus said. "The waterfall is at the far end. As you'll see."

Dafyd and Loren skirted the river's edge, the water frothing and foaming at their feet, toward the crack in the towering rocks. At the foot of the canyon, to the side of the rushing river, they clambered up a fall of rocks. They both leaned forward to keep their balance.

To Dafyd's surprise, they found a path at the top of the rocks, a trail not quite so wide as the well-travelled road out of Colcott, but just as smooth. The path quickly rose high along the canyon wall, well above the rapids.

He glanced at the magus. "How . . .?"

"This is but one of the wonders you shall see, I think."

The smooth path grew dark as they followed it deeper into the canyon. The thunderous roar echoed around them, though the river was now as far below their feet as the rock walls soared above their heads. A strong wind blew cold from the depths of the canyon.

"So what do we do now?" Dafyd asked, his voice sharp and echoing off the rocks before it was swallowed by the rushing water.

"We wait," the magus said. "The book refers to the moment that the sun slips."

"Sunset?"

The magus nodded, and pointed back at the entrance to the canyon. "Due west," he said.

"So we have to wait here all afternoon?" Dafyd asked, wrapping his arms around himself against the chill in the air. The thought of spending that much time on the narrow ledge, the continuous thunder pressing in on his ears, gave him the shivers.

"We can wait back at the camp," the magus said.

"Good."

"You might want to wait a little longer." The captain stepped out from the shadows between them and the canyon entrance.

"Captain," the magus said, clearly surprised. "I thought you were at the camp."

"I had to see if it was as I remembered," he said, looking out into the canyon. "It should be any time now."

Dafyd knew better than to question him. Instead, he stepped away, picked up a handful of stones and threw them one at a time into the roiling white foam.

They didn't have to wait long.

As the sun crested above the canyon walls, its light warmed Dafyd. It also drew the wet rock walls out of shadow, revealing the full length of the canyon for the first time. From where they were standing, it cut into the hillside almost straight back to the waterfall at the far end.

Dafyd had never seen a waterfall. The white, raging wall of water, with the sun seeming to hang in the sky above it, was perhaps the most beautiful thing he could imagine.

He changed his mind a few moments later.

As the sun rose still farther, the light fell directly onto the falls, and Dafyd saw rays of sunlight taking shape in the mist thrown up by the falling water. The light spread out into thick bands of colour which reflected off the river's surface, filling the canyon with the soft, rich glow of a rainbow.

It was like something out of a dream.

Looking down, Dafyd saw that he himself was stained red by the light. When he looked up, the magus was smiling.

Captain Bream nodded, his face strangely soft. "This is what I remember," he said.

Dafyd felt like laughing; in the warm, rainbow light he almost forgot their mission, was almost able to put his fears out of his mind.

"That's why it is called the Rainbow Canyon," the captain said, half closing his eyes. "I feared I would never see it again."

The magus nodded.

"You've seen this before?" Dafyd asked, his voice almost breaking.

"Once," Bream said slowly. "A long, long time ago." And then he didn't say anything more.

IV

I WAITED UNTIL WE HAD polished off the plate of nachos, until we had each had a couple of beers, before I reached into my pocket, set the small yellow envelope on the table and slid it toward Dale.

"Here," I said.

"What's this?"

He wasn't going to make this easy for me.

"It's the key. To your apartment."

He didn't pick it up. Didn't look away from me.

"I mean, I appreciate the offer, but I'm not going to take it."

"Why not?"

Dale had a way of asking questions and then waiting, not saying anything, forcing me to answer.

"It's not . . . I'm not ready to take that step. It's not like we're estranged. Not really. I see her every day. We talk."

"You fight."

No argument there.

"When was the last time you had sex?"

"Come on."

"All right. Made love."

"I don't think . . ." A not-very-convincing stalling tactic.

"I'll tell you when it was. It was on your anniversary last year."

I had to remember to stop telling Dale everything.

"So?"

"So you're not estranged from a woman who you're not living with, not sleeping with, and who you're unable to have a civil conversation with? What do *you* call it?"

I lifted one hand in a gesture of surrender.

He picked up the envelope from the table and held it close to his face, studying it in the half-light.

"Do you ever think about how you're going to die?"

To say that the question caught me by surprise would be a serious understatement.

"What?"

He leaned forward again, taking me into his confidence. "Your own death. How do you see it?"

I looked around the bar for a moment. "I don't spend a whole lot of time thinking about it," I said, like I was confessing something shameful.

He sat back, nodding sagely. "I didn't think so."

I didn't want to ask: I knew better. He waited. I couldn't resist, and he knew it. "So?"

"I've been doing a lot of thinking about this lately. About how important it is to live with an awareness of your own death. A constant awareness of it."

"You've been reading self-help books again."

"Self-*improvement*," he corrected. His fondness for pop-psych books was a long-running joke between the two of us. "I'm serious, though. That's what whoever-it-was meant when he said that the unexamined life wasn't worth living."

"Plato."

He waved my reply away. "Whoever. The important thing is, if you don't have a keen awareness of your own death, you're not really able to live your life. You'll always be putting things off to the future, operating under the faulty assumption that the future is unlimited."

"What does this—?"

"Chris, there's no future. And there's no past, not one that you can climb back into, like you're trying to do. There's only this, this moment, right now." He raised his hand slowly, and snapped his fingers. "And gone. All you can do is make each moment, each day, the best that it can be."

I looked at him for a long moment.

"So, you're Yoda now?"

He shook his head, and looked at me with such sadness I had to turn away.

"Hello?" Jacqui called as she closed the front door. "Is anybody here?"

"Back here," I called, my face bathed in steam as I dumped the spaghetti into the colander.

I could hear her footsteps through the house.

"Something smells good," she said from the kitchen doorway. Dark purple scrubs tonight, matching the circles under her eyes.

"You've been busy." She looked pointedly at the table, set with three places, the pots and pans on the stove and on the counter.

"We thought we'd have a late dinner, once you got home."

"David hasn't eaten?"

I tried to ignore the tone of reproach. "He had a snack a while ago," I said.

I added a dollop of butter to the noodles, let it start to melt.

"I opened some wine."

"What's the occasion?"

"No occasion," I said as I began to cut the bread into thick slices. "I just thought we might all have dinner together for a change."

When I looked over at her, she was staring at me.

"I thought it might be nice."

She nodded slowly. "Okay. I'll get changed. Should I get Davy on my way? Are we close—?"

"Sure," I said, hoping she'd walk in on him neck-deep in his homework. "We're almost ready to go."

She took one last look at me, at the food, at the kitchen, before she turned away.

"Should I pour you a glass of wine?" I called after her.

"Oh, I think so," she said from the stairs.

David came down a minute later.

"How'd the homework go, sport?"

"Fine," he said, slipping into his place on the far side of the table. "I'm starting to really hate French, though."

I grinned. At least he was talking again. "Why?"

He shrugged as I went to the fridge for milk. "It's hard to remember all the words for things, and all the ways to conjugate the verbs. I don't see why we have to learn it anyway."

"It's good to have a second language," Jacqui said from behind me. She had changed into a T-shirt from a breast cancer fund-raising walk she had done a few weeks before and a pair of yoga pants. Her relaxing-at-home clothes. "And if you ever want to get a job with the government—"

"Which I don't," he said, with such certainty that Jacqui and I both smiled.

"Well, never say never," Jacqui said, sitting down at the table.

"I have a hard enough time with my own language," he said.

I brought the basket of bread to the table. "There is that," I said.

"How's math?" Jacqui asked.

He shrugged. "I don't know why I have to learn that either. I can do it on a calculator faster."

"So the homework didn't go well?" I asked.

"It's all done."

"I think that calls for a toast." Jacqui lifted her wineglass.

Was she really going to get into the spirit of this?

"To getting it done," she said, and looked at me as she sipped.

⚶ ⚶

Dafyd spent most of the afternoon exploring the near reaches of the canyon. The path of the sun overhead was keeping it lit and warm. He didn't venture too deep between the walls. He went a short way into the canyon and sat down on the path, leaning back on his hands as he watched the play of light in the misty air.

The canyon walls weren't smooth, as they had seemed to be in the earlier dark; they were rugged and pitted, worn from the crumbling of time, the passage of the river before it had cut so deeply into the earth. The rainbow colour played across every crevice, every crack.

When the afternoon drew late, the sun remained visible through the open end of the canyon as it sank heavily onto the horizon. Dafyd heard the sound of voices approaching. Bream and the magus led a column of the guardsmen up the narrow path toward him.

"It's beautiful, isn't it," Bream asked, looking into the canyon.

"When did you see it?" Dafyd asked.

"Years ago," he said. "The last time we were at war. Before you were born. This canyon has always been . . .". He seemed to struggle for the right word. "Special. We try to camp nearby when we can.

"It's sacred," the magus offered.

The captain turned away.

"Stephen and Gafilair camped here during the first war," the magus continued, "almost a thousand years ago. I suppose that's why he decided to hide the Sunstone here."

Dafyd stared at the old man. The Sunstone was here?

As the sun crept lower, and Bream spread his men along the length of the chasm, Dafyd grew anxious. So much was depending upon him, and he had no idea what he was doing, what he was supposed to be looking for. The rays of the sun shifted as it set, and the rainbow light gradually faded, replaced with the rich honey glow of evening. The air grew cold again, and Dafyd wrapped his arms around himself as he searched for something, anything, that might answer the questions raised by the magus's book.

At the moment the sun slips and the doorway to the secret world is revealed, Dafyd remembered.

The waterfall roared on. The shadows shifted and crept on the canyon walls.

"I don't see anything," the captain grumbled to the magus.

"Patience," the magus said, his voice less than sure.

"If your book is to be believed . . ."

Dafyd tried to ignore their voices. The sun was mostly sunk into the earth now, only the barest curve of light remaining over the river past the canyon's mouth.

There was nothing here. No secrets. No Sunstone. He thought of the handmaiden, the man who had died on the road; their sacrifices for him had been for nothing.

The last edge of the sun slipped below the horizon. And with the final ray of light, Dafyd saw it.

It happened so suddenly he thought he had imagined seeing anything. But the magus was pointing across the river, and a shout came from a guardsman up the line.

The shadows on the rocks across the canyon had seemed to straighten and solidify, forming, for one passing moment, the perfect, symmetrical, unmistakable outline of a door in the canyon wall.

As quickly as it had come, though, the image disappeared, and the canyon was dark.

≫≪

I left the dishes to soak while Jacqui took a bath. David was in bed, so while dishes and wife were immersed, I read a few pages of the novel I was reviewing for my next column, absorbing next to nothing, letting the words wash over me.

Once we had all gotten past the initial weirdness, dinner had been quite pleasant: a reminder of better times. The three of us together, eating, drinking, talking: anyone looking through the window would have thought we were a normal family.

After David was finished he put his plate and glass on the counter beside the sink and headed back up to his room, Jacqui and I sat for a while longer, working the wine down in our glasses. We hadn't talked about anything important, and avoided any topics that might provoke a fight. We talked about the Emergency Room, about David's fight with the French language, about the book I was reviewing. When I offered her more wine, she waved it away, mentioning how much she would like to take a bath. She offered to do the dishes—"Doing my fair share, with you making dinner"—but I shook my head and poured her more wine to take with her.

The dishes were just about finished when I heard her coming down the stairs. Taking one last swipe across the rim of the last pot, I held off looking at her as long as I could, wanting to delay the pleasure.

"I think I needed that," she said as I hung the dishcloth on the faucet.

"Glad to be of service." I turned to face her.

That first moment was worth the wait. She had on one of my old T-shirts, which clung to her, hanging just to her upper thighs. Her legs were bare, shiny. Her skin was flushed, glowing from her soak, her hair glistening. Her eyes were relaxed, soft.

"I'm probably a little late with this," she said, handing me the empty wineglass.

"There're always more dishes to be done."

"Thank you," she said. "For all this." She gestured around the room. "It's been a rough few days at work."

I took a step toward her, shaking my head as if it were nothing. "No big deal," I said.

"No, it was. I really appreciate it."

I was close enough to feel the heat radiating off her, smell the sweetness of whatever she had put in her bathwater. I gently put my hands on her hips, barely touching her, the softness of the T-shirt over the warmth of her skin. I leaned forward.

She took a step back, shaking her head as if to clear it. "Chris, what are you—?"

"It wouldn't be the worst thing in the world, would it?"

Thankfully, she ignored the question. "Chris. It's a bad idea." She folded her arms across her chest. "Don't you remember our anniversary?"

I'd been thinking about that night since Dale had mentioned it. Dinner and a few drinks, talking the way we used to, then falling together, our bodies fitting like two pieces of a whole.

"I remember," I said.

"It made everything crazy for weeks. We were fighting all the time."

"We fight all the time anyway."

"Things are pretty good right now. I don't want to mess that up by jumping into something that we'll both regret."

"Sleeping with my wife isn't something I'm going to regret."

"It's not the sex, Chris." She took a step forward and touched the back of my forearm, just below the elbow. "I do love you. I really do. And the idea of messing up the sheets with you"—she allowed herself a naughty, knowing smile—"definitely has a certain appeal. It's what comes after . . . It's your thinking that this would somehow make everything else better, too. That you could start moving your things back in."

I shook my head, but she wasn't wrong.

She squeezed my arm. "I don't have the strength for it."

We said good night. I stopped on the back stoop in the light from the window, my chest tight, my eyes burning, not even really sure of what had just happened.

Closing the door lightly behind myself, I lit a cigarette, and tried not to hear Dale's voice in my head, tried not to reach into my pocket to touch the key to his apartment.

David had woken to the sound of voices in the kitchen, right underneath his bedroom. His mother and father. Again. Not fighting this time. "Having a discussion," they would call this.

He waited for a few moments, the covers pulled tight to his chin, his head pressed into the pillow, hoping that it would stop, that the voices would fade again, that the bad feeling would disappear.

When it didn't, he reached out for the lamp on his bedside table and turned it on. He climbed out of bed and walked across to the door, not really taking care to be quiet.

As he closed the door, he took *To the Four Directions* off the shelf.

Lying back down on his stomach, he opened the book and tucked the leather bookmark inside the back cover.

As he started to read, his parents' voices disappeared.

❧ ❧

The sun was still low in the sky when Dafyd opened his eyes the next morning.

He had fallen asleep at the river's edge outside the canyon, listening to the magus and the captain discussing how long it would take to ride back to Donder where they could ford the river, and he awoke to find them already awake and sitting a short distance away.

"We thought it best to let you sleep," Bream said. "It could be a long day."

Dafyd nodded.

"If any daylight remains when you return with the Stone," the captain said, "we will take to the road. The sooner we return to the Queen, the better."

"But you should eat," the magus said, standing up and gesturing for Dafyd to sit, passing him a metal plate with a hank of bread and some dried meat. "He does have time to eat, doesn't he?" the magus asked the captain pointedly.

"Of course." The captain's voice made it clear that he was not in agreement. "Not too much, though," he warned. "You'll want to stay light."

Dafyd wanted to ask what the captain meant, but he contented himself with a mouthful of bread.

When they entered the canyon a short while later, the captain's meaning became clear.

Dafyd was speechless: the guardsmen had been busy. Overnight, they had constructed a primitive rope bridge over the raging river.

"How?" he muttered. The bridge was little more than two thick ropes strung across the canyon, one above the other, woven together with a third rope that looped between them like a loose spiderweb.

"The men did a good job," Captain Bream said proudly.

Dafyd looked at the shadowy wall at the other end of the bridge, where he knew, though there was no sign of it, the mysterious doorway waited. The bridge swayed in the wind, stretched uneasily across the river, no more substantial than the web it resembled.

"Very well, then," he said, fighting a tremor in his voice and taking a deep breath, reminded of something his mother always said. "Sooner begun is sooner done."

⟳ ⟲

I poured myself a glass of vodka from the bottle in the freezer and took my first swallow standing in the kitchen with the freezer door still open. The vodka was a short, sharp shock, exactly what I needed.

Maybe Dale was right. Maybe it was too far gone, too late to change anything between Jacqui and me. Maybe it was a salvage operation now, not a rescue.

I sagged into my desk chair. As I shifted, the keys in my pants pocket pushed into my leg. I emptied the contents of my pockets onto the desk. Keys. Lighter. Two twenty-dollar bills. A handful of change.

A receipt from Munro's Books. The yellow envelope with the key to Dale's apartment.

And a beige, frayed-edged piece of paper with a name and a telephone number written on it in green ink.

I stared at the paper on the desk as I poured myself a glass of vodka.

Tara Scott.

I picked up the note, looked at it carefully. Took a swallow of vodka. Looked at the clock: a little after ten.

I lifted the phone, and looked back down at the paper.

Salvage or rescue?

I set the phone down and dropped the paper on the desk.

NOTHING BREAKS THE WRITING SPELL like the telephone ringing. Only a few people have my number: it could have been my agent, one of my publishers . . .

I answered anyway.

"Mr. Knox?" It was a woman's voice, brusque and impersonal. There was a slight hollowness to the line, a buzz of noise and voices in the background.

"Yes?" I said guardedly. I reached for my coffee cup but it was empty.

"I'm Barbara Kensey. I'm calling from George Jay Elementary."

I straightened in my chair. "Is there something wrong with David?" I imagined him lying in a narrow bed in the nurse's office, his face flushed and sweaty, or sitting with a bucket between his knees.

"Your son is fine, Mr. Knox. He's with me right now. I'm calling because there was an incident this morning."

"An incident?" Suddenly craving a cigarette. Not a good sign.

"Yes, Mr. Knox."

"What happened?"

"I'm afraid that I'm unable to discuss that over the telephone, Mr. Knox. Mr. Davis, the vice-principal, has requested that you or Mrs. Knox come into the office to discuss it in person."

Oh shit.

"Sure," I said calmly, mentally scrambling. "I don't have my wife's schedule right here, but I can call her—"

"Actually, Mr. Knox, this is a matter of some urgency. Mr. Davis has cleared a spot in his schedule at 11:30."

I looked at the clock: 10:58.

"Right now?"

"It's quite a serious matter, Mr. Knox. Your son was involved in an altercation this morning—"

An altercation? "He was in a fight?"

"—with Monsieur Vert, his French teacher," she went on, as if she hadn't heard me. "David isn't welcome to return to class until Mr. Davis has had a chance to discuss this matter with one of his parents. Will you or your wife—?"

"I'll be there," I said slowly, sagging in the chair.

I didn't say anything to David for almost two blocks. I had hoped that maybe the walk would be the best thing for both of us. Give us a chance to cool off. Keep us from saying anything we might regret later.

It didn't seem to work.

"Jesus, David. What the hell were you thinking?"

He was walking a couple of steps behind me, looking down at the concrete. I stopped and turned to see his answer: a soundless shrug.

He hadn't said much of anything since I had arrived at the school.

The secretary had shown me into the vice-principal's office, and I had spent the next fifteen minutes listening to a painfully one-sided chronology of events, from which I could only glean a few unassailable facts: David hadn't been paying attention in French class, and when Monsieur Vert noticed this, he also noticed that David was preoccupied with something under the edge of his desk. Expecting it to be the video game that he had confiscated before, he had approached David quietly from behind and caught him reading.

I had had to contain a smile.

What Monsieur Vert said happened next, though, purged any amusement. He had taken the book, and David—

"You threatened a teacher."

"I didn't threaten him," he said, sounding surly.

"You said you were going to kill him."

"No, I didn't."

I stopped, feeling a twinge of optimism. "That's what Monsieur Vert said."

"Monsieur Vert." He snorted. "He's not even French. His name's Mr. Green. He was the social studies teacher until Mademoiselle Rochelle got pregnant."

"David . . ." He had a good sense for the ridiculous. "He told the vice-principal that you threatened to kill him. If you didn't say that—"

"I said I should strike him down."

I almost laughed; it sounded like something from the book.

"And I didn't say it *to* him. I just . . . said it. To myself. I didn't think he would hear me."

"Well, apparently he did. And now you're suspended for the rest of the week."

We started walking again, David falling into step beside me this time.

"It's only a day and a half."

"You're lucky you weren't expelled."

He shrugged.

"And it goes on your permanent record." Jesus, I had actually used the words *permanent record*. "And you have to apologize to Monsieur . . . to Mr. Green before you can go back to French class."

"Like I want to go back."

"You don't really have a choice," I said.

"It wasn't my fault, you know."

"Come on, David. You were reading in his class. He caught you red-handed."

"He said it was stupid."

We turned onto our street.

"What?"

"He said the book was stupid. He said that if I wasted my time reading things like that, I'd end up being stupid too."

I had to breathe through the anger I felt rising in me. What sort of thing was that to say? Especially with all the problems that David had had with his reading, his insecurity about how smart he was. What sort of teacher . . .

Breathe.

We were almost to the house when he asked, "So what's going to happen now?"

"Well, your mother and I will have to talk about it when she gets home from work," I said. "I think you'll probably be grounded."

His face fell.

"That's the way it is, David. You just got suspended. For threatening a teacher. You can't actually think that there won't be consequences."

A moment of consideration, then he shook his head. We started up the front stairs.

"In the meantime," I said. "You can spend the afternoon working on your irregular French verbs."

He had to look at me to see if I was kidding.

"Hey, Dad," he said as I opened the front door. "Is that—?" Pointing at the package under my arm.

I had forgotten that I was carrying it. "Is this the book, you mean? The cause of all this trouble?"

He waited a beat. "Can I have it back?" Looking at me guilelessly.

"Are you serious?"

He nodded. Of course he was.

I ran through all of the arguments, I tried to weigh all of the conflicting stories, tried to remember how angry I had been when Mr. Green told me of what happened in the classroom.

But then I would picture the weedy little man telling my son that he was stupid, that his book was stupid. Power-tripping.

I held out the package. "French verbs first, right?"

·   ᘓ ᘔ

"Slow and steady," said the captain, as Dafyd shuffled along the lower rope, his hands gripping the upper line.

The only good thing about being scared for his life, Dafyd thought, glancing down at the rushing water far below, was that he didn't have time to worry about what to do once he reached the other side.

He took a deep breath, and another step.

The bottom rope lurched under his weight, pulling away from the top one as far as the cross-woven line would allow, pulling at his arms and throwing off his balance. He swung in the air, and for a moment it felt like the ropes might spin him all the way over, and drop him into the river.

"Spread your arms and legs," the captain called out. "Spread your weight on the lines."

Dafyd shifted his right hand and foot a bit farther out on the ropes. The swaying of the lines immediately slowed.

"You've got it now," the captain said.

Dafyd didn't feel like he had anything; he felt spread out like a hapless insect. Even through the gloves the ropes dug into his hands, while the weight of his body pushed the bottom line painfully into his feet.

"Slow and steady," the captain called.

It was like crawling through the air. As he moved, he stared down at the water, never sure if the roaring white foam was immediately beneath his feet, or a great distance below. Distance and time had lost their meaning. The only thing that meant anything was keeping his grip, the line burning in his hands.

As he neared the middle of the canyon the wind caught at him, buffeting him. For a moment he imagined himself as a kite, lifted into the sky. His concentration faltered and his feet slipped along the rope. As the lines swung and wavered, for a moment he felt weightless, the world spinning out of control. But he did not fall.

He started again, shuffling slowly to his right.

So focused was he on the feel of his hands and feet on the ropes, the slow sideways motion, hand-width by agonizing hand-width, that he was surprised when, on extending his hand for another piece of the rope, his fingers closed instead on cold iron: a bolt, driven into the stone.

He had done it. He had made it across.

But his heart sank.

There was no ledge, no path, no place for him to go.

᷾᷾

"Starting a little early today, aren't you," she said, looking at the empty glass as she came into the living room straight from work. Green scrubs today.

"It's been a day," I said, trying to get the right sense of warning into the words.

"Is it David?" she asked, glancing toward the stairs.

I nodded. "He's up in his room." I gestured to the couch. "We need to talk," I said. "You should probably sit down."

I told her about the meeting in the vice-principal's office, about Mr. Green's story and David's suspension. A couple of times I had to pause to calm her down, to keep her from rushing upstairs to confront David before she knew the whole story.

"David says it happened differently," I explained, as soothingly as I could. "He says that he only muttered it"—she started to speak, but I shook my head—"and that was only *after* Mr. Green told him he was stupid."

I paused, waiting for the same anger that I had felt, her inevitable defence of our son, her outrage at what the teacher had said.

"So David threatened him?"

It wasn't the reaction I had been expecting. "He told David he was stupid, Jacqui. Don't you think—"

"That doesn't give him any right to threaten anyone. I'm surprised that they only suspended him for two days—in a lot of places, you'd have been picking him up at the police station."

"He was upset."

She shook her head and looked away. "And I suppose you brought him home and made him lunch and told him that everything was going to be all right."

I bit my lip, holding back the response on the tip of my tongue. "No, actually," I said slowly, as if it were costing me considerable effort to make myself understood. "I told him that you and I were going to talk about it and figure out the appropriate consequence for what he did."

"And what do you think an appropriate consequence would be?" she asked.

"Well," I said, as if I hadn't been thinking about it all afternoon. "I think he needs to write Mr. Green"—she gave me a quizzical look—"*Monsieur Vert* a long and heartfelt apology."

She nodded.

"And I think he should be grounded. For at least a week, probably two. No TV, no video games, computer for homework only—"

"So where's the book?" she asked.

"What?"

"Where did you put the book? I want to have it with us when we're talking to him."

In the pause that came before I could get an answer out, Jacqui understood.

"Oh for Christ's sake, Chris—you gave him back the book?"

☙ ❧

Clinging with one hand and balancing on one foot on the bolts that secured the lines, Dafyd felt a moment of panic: surely the guardsmen wouldn't have built the bridge with nowhere for him to go. Why would the captain have sent him across?

Craning his neck, Dafyd looked back, his eyes scanning the canyon wall. At first glance, the rocks behind him looked just like the rocks in front of him, pitted and rough, a solid wall stretching from the water to the sky.

As he faced forward again, however, he caught a glimpse of something. He wasn't sure what—an edge? A right angle where there shouldn't have been one? He couldn't be sure.

Carefully he twisted so he was almost pressed against the wall, still clinging to the top bolt with his left hand. As he moved, the wind caught at him again. He crouched, lowering his centre of gravity as much as he could, trying to ignore the sick feeling in his stomach as he started to trace his fingertips along the rock face, the rough surface. Nothing even hinted at a door.

And then his fingers seemed to slip over a sharp edge, the rock wall disappearing into a space so deep he couldn't reach the end of it. Looking at where his hand had disappeared, Dafyd could almost make out the doorway's sharp edge. Whoever had made the door had done a good job of concealing it.

Taking a deep breath, he extended his foot along the wall in the direction of his hand. It was terrifying, watching his foot hovering in the air, feeling it bump along the wall. He tried not to believe his eyes, which told him that there was nothing there, nowhere for his foot to land.

But he knew better. He knew, now, that his eyes couldn't always be trusted.

Stretching his leg, he found another edge, and a flat surface deep enough to hold his foot.

From the fleeting glimpse that he had caught of it at sundown yesterday, he knew that the doorway was more than wide enough for him to stand in. Without giving his fear any more chance to take root, Dafyd planted his foot, gripped the edge of the wall and pulled himself away from the bolts.

For one dizzying moment he hung in the air, and then he was standing, pressed against the back of a shallow nook in the canyon wall. Dafyd fought to keep his balance, fearfully aware that the slightest misstep would send him into the rushing river below.

With barely enough space to turn around, and the wind pulling at his clothes, he struggled to get a good look at the rock wall he was pressed against. He could find no handle, no latch. The stone's surface was smooth, almost slick, different from the canyon walls themselves. If this was a door, there was no way to open it.

Dafyd cried out his frustration. Here he was, all but clinging to the edge of the canyon, having risked his life in crossing the river, and now he was stuck. He pounded on the rock wall with both fists, half screaming, half growling in the back of his throat.

That was a mistake. The pounding on the wall, the momentary loss of control, threw off his balance, and he wavered over the drop to the river. He threw his arms out at his sides to brace himself against the door frame, such as it was.

He took a moment to let his heart slow.

As he calmed himself down, he noticed that the rock under his fingers wasn't as smooth as the back wall of the alcove. The side walls looked smooth, but shadows obscured some roughness where one of his hands had come to rest. Dafyd ran his fingers lightly over the stone surface. There. A ridge, and a dip. Another. Another. Each sharp ridge led into a vaguely rounded recess. He cursed the shadows. If only he could see.

As he moved his hand over the shapes, his fingers slipped into them.

They seemed to fit there, perfectly. He shifted his palm into place and felt a surge in his chest.

It could have been his own handprint, so well did his fingers fit into the stone. Was this how the door was to open? Dafyd pushed excitedly against the handprint, turned his wrist to see if the impression would turn.

Nothing happened.

He muttered a curse to himself. It should have done *something*. Why would someone put a handprint there if it didn't have something to do with the door?

Unless . . .

Turning his head, Dafyd scanned the opposite edge of the door frame. His guess was correct: another handprint was visible, and he could see the skill that had gone into its carving. The amount of detail was astonishing.

He stretched his arms across the doorway, careful to keep his balance, straining toward the far wall. He barely had enough reach left to apply even the slightest pressure.

It was enough.

As he pushed, both handprints gave way, retreating slightly into the stone. Then they stopped with a muffled clatter, and the rear of the alcove began to slide with surprisingly little sound into the canyon wall.

☙ ❧

David was lying on his stomach when we came into his room, the book splayed open on his pillow. He didn't look up, just slid his index finger down the lines of the page as he read.

"David," I said. "We need to talk to you."

It would have been easy to miss the slight nod of his head if I hadn't been watching.

"David," Jacqui said, her voice rising with warning.

There was a beat, a moment, a movement of his fingers along a line of text before he turned to us.

"Oh. Hey, Mom," he said innocently, as if completely unaware of the reason for our coming to his room, together.

"We need to talk."

"Okay." Breezy, casual.

"Sit up," she said.

He carefully turned the book over on the pillow to hold his place before shifting into a sitting position. His movements were slow and deliberate, unconcerned.

The colour was rising in Jacqui's face.

"Would you like to tell me what happened at school today?" she said.

He looked from her to me, then back. "Didn't Dad—?"

"I want to hear it from you."

He thought for a moment. "Well, Mr. Green—"

"Monsieur Vert," she corrected him.

He looked at me again. "Monsieur Vert got mad at me in French class and—"

"Why did he get mad at you? Were you doing something wrong?"

A slow nod, his eyes drifting downwards now.

"Well? What were you doing?"

I shifted on my feet.

"I was reading," he said quietly, a hint of contrition colouring his voice.

"What were you reading?"

He glanced down at the book on the pillow. "That."

"Why were you reading it in French class?"

He looked up, appealing to me. I wanted to do something to comfort him, or maybe I could say something to Jacqui.

When I looked at her, I saw that Jacqui had caught our silent exchange. She pursed her lips and looked back toward the book, nodding slightly.

"Pass me the book, David," I said, as evenly as I could.

"What?"

"Give me the book."

"Why?"

I took a deep breath. "I told you there were going to be consequences," I said, trying to sound reasonable. "You can't threaten people." I held out my hand.

He shook his head, pulled himself back on the bed. "Why? I'll do anything. Anything you ask. I'll do the dishes. I'll mow the lawn. I'll give up the computer."

I glanced at Jacqui, but she wasn't wavering.

"David," I said, still trying to be reasonable. "Don't make it worse. Give me the book."

He moved his hand toward it, and for a moment I thought he was going to pass it to me. Instead he picked it up and held it tightly to his chest. "No," he said. "You can't. It's mine. You *gave* it to me."

"David."

Fed up, Jacqui stepped forward and reached for the book.

David's next movements were a blur—he shifted, curling himself around the book so that he was kneeling on the bed, sheltering it with his body. His arm rose and he shoved Jacqui back as he shouted, "No!"

Jacqui stumbled and I reached out automatically to steady her. She pushed my arm away.

"David," I said in my sternest voice.

"No, no, no," he repeated. He hunched more tightly around the book, pulling himself farther up the bed, farther away from us.

Jacqui didn't hesitate. She grabbed his arm, twisting sideways to avoid a sudden flurry of kicks. "No." His voice was louder, and he squirmed to get away. His ineffective thrashing shook the bed.

Jacqui looked at me, her face tight with the effort of holding his arm. "Chris," she muttered.

I tried grabbing his other arm, but he pulled out of reach. I had to turn myself to avoid his kicks.

"Chris, the book."

She leaned into him, using her weight to slow his thrashing. As he tried to push her off, I could see the spine of the book and I grabbed it away from him. I stumbled back from the bed, lifting the book high as he grasped for it with his free hand.

"Do you have it?" Jacqui asked, still trying to hold him down as he thrashed.

"Yeah," I gasped. "Yeah, I've got it."

She released him and stepped back quickly from the bed.

"No!" he howled, his body shuddering to rest.

Jacqui looked at me. Her hair was wild, her face flushed from the exertion. A red spot was forming under one eye. She reached up, touched it gingerly. "I think he got me."

We both turned to look at David.

He was lying on his stomach, his back heaving with sobs I could barely hear from the depths of the bedding where he had buried his face.

"David," I said, starting forward, but Jacqui laid her hand on my arm.

"Stop," she whispered.

"David," she said, her voice cold and even. "You need to calm down. We're not done talking about this."

She didn't touch him, didn't try to comfort him. Instead, she turned and left the room, beckoning for me to follow her.

As I turned to follow her, David looked up at me. His cheeks were wet with tears, his eyes filled with a look of incomprehensible betrayal.

In the hallway, I handed Jacqui the book. I didn't want to touch it, didn't want to have anything more to do with it.

She took it.

"I hope you're happy," she said.

VI

It was all David could do to wait.

He forced himself to keep his hands in his lap as his father's footsteps faded down the stairs. He desperately wanted to reach under the blanket, but he forced himself to stay still, just a little longer. Like holding his breath, it gradually became almost unbearable.

Far away, the back door closed with the faintest of sounds. Dad was outside now. Probably smoking. It was safe.

Reaching under the covers, he pulled out the book and opened it to his page. He tried to keep one ear open, ready to hide it again. But what was the worst thing that could happen if his dad discovered that he had been taking the book down from the top of the fridge, reading it when he was supposed to be sleeping or banished to his room? It didn't matter. What was important was the book, and what happened next—especially now, with Dafyd so close.

⤜ ⤛

The stone door slid silently into the canyon wall. Dafyd took small steps into the corridor that had opened before him. He could breathe again, relax, turn and face the canyon without fear of falling.

He shivered at the sight of the simple rope bridge swaying in the wind, fading into the mist and distance.

He could barely see the far edge of the canyon. He held his hands high above his head and waved to the tiny figures of Loren, Bream and the guardsmen, indistinct and blending into the canyon wall behind them.

No response. Had he disappeared into whatever shadows hid the doorway from view? No matter the reason, he was truly on his own.

Dafyd turned back into the passageway. The stone door had come to a stop. He was stuck, again, it seemed, this time inside a rectangular stone box.

He had just begun to wonder what else he would need to do when the stone wall began to tilt slowly away. Dafyd flinched reflexively, expecting a loud crash. But there was no crash—it slowly continued to fall.

In the dim light, he made out a niche cut into the passage wall. A torch rested in a metal bracket. A small leather bag hung below it. He touched the torch-head carefully. It was sticky. His fingers came away smelling of pitch.

Fumbling under the bracket, he opened the leather bag, and smiled as a number of tinders spilled into his hand. Dafyd struck one against the cavern wall and touched it to the head of the torch. The pitch caught almost instantly, bursting with a warm golden light.

Dafyd could see now that the gentle descent of the stone wall was controlled by heavy chains on both sides.

"A drawbridge," he muttered to himself.

But over what?

The door settled flat, and Dafyd stepped forward cautiously, stopping at the narrow seam between the stone floor and the drawbridge. Water lapped at the length of the drawbridge: a narrow stream ran beneath it through the cavern.

He set one foot carefully forward. The stone didn't move. He pushed down and it remained firm.

Taking a deep breath, he stepped quickly across.

His torchlight flickered back at him from another smoothly carved edge, another doorway, this one open. Angling the torch forward, he found himself looking down a set of damp stairs that disappeared into the black far below him.

There had been a time when the house, our house, was as comfortable as a familiar jacket, something warm that could be pulled on, nestled into. But it was all different now. I couldn't relax, couldn't get comfortable.

Every sound made me start, pulled me out of the book I was reading.

Finally I put on a Philip Glass album, hoping that the repetitive, slow-building melodies might help.

It didn't work. I ended up sitting there, thinking of David huddled asleep in his bed above me. Nothing I could say could console him now. What had I done? What was I even doing here?

The cordless rang, and I jumped.

"Hello?" My voice was rough, tenuous, after hours of silence.

"It's me," Jacqui said quietly. "I wanted to be sure you got my message."

She had called in the afternoon to say that she wouldn't be home for dinner.

"I did. Is it busy there? Friday night and all . . ."

"It's steady," she said. "It looks like it's starting to ramp up now."

The house shifted and sighed—it almost sounded like someone moving.

"How's David?"

"Quiet," I said. "He didn't want a story again tonight." In fact, he'd barely spoken to me all day, sequestering himself in his room, lying on his bed staring at the ceiling.

"He'll get over it," she said. "It's important—"

"I know," I said. "Consistency. Boundaries."

She didn't speak for the longest time.

"Listen, why don't you head to bed?" she said, sounding genuinely concerned. "You sound exhausted."

"But David—"

"He knows to use the intercom if you're not in the house. And he doesn't usually wake up anyway."

Just thinking about it, I had to restrain a yawn.

"I'm going to be here for a while yet," she said. "I've got to finish up my charting."

"I won't wait up," I said.

"I'll see you in the morning, then."

I waited for her to say something else, anything else.

—

Jacqui cradled the cell phone in her hand.

She was staring out the windshield at the front windows of the house. The blinds seemed to glow with an inner warmth, an illusory comfort. She was parked just far enough down the block that Chris wouldn't see the van if he happened to look outside.

She waited and watched, hoping to see his shadow on the blinds, an image of his body as he stood up and disappeared from view. As he turned off the light and left the house. As he went away.

There was no movement. Nothing.

She sighed and turned the key in the ignition. She couldn't do it. Not again. She'd find a coffee shop, someplace she could wait for an hour or so.

VII

DAVID WAITED EXTRA LONG. It was one thing to sneak down to the kitchen while his father was outside smoking, the house empty except for him. But his dad had left before bedtime, headed out with Uncle Dale, leaving him with his mother. And *she* wasn't going outside.

She wasn't doing much of anything. She had tucked him in a while ago, not even offering to read him a story. Not that he would have let her read to him anyway.

He waited until he could hear the faint, tinny sounds of the television through his open door. Then he waited a little longer, until it had been almost fifteen minutes since he had last heard any sound from the kitchen below.

Then and only then did he creep out of bed, rolling softly on the balls of his feet, slowly stepping across his room and out the door, edging down the stairs. He waited on each stair, his ears tuned to the slightest sound from below, the barest disturbance of the air that might hint that his mother was in motion.

⁂

It was quiet on the stairs within the canyon walls. Dafyd could faintly hear the roaring of the river behind him, but the only other sounds came from him: his ragged breathing, and the slapping of his feet on the stone.

As Dafyd descended, he marvelled at the construction of the passage. It must have taken dozens of stonecutters years to carve all of this out.

But Gafilair had written of the person who would find the Sunstone a thousand years before Dafyd's birth. He thought of the way his hands had fit so perfectly into the stone to open the door, and he knew, then, that no workers had slaved over building this cave. Gafilair had done it all himself.

Dafyd was descending into a world built by magic.

☙ ❧

David stopped at the bottom of the stairs before turning toward the kitchen. There was no sound of his mother moving, no faint footsteps, nothing, just the noise of the TV from the front room.

He moved quickly, silently, keenly aware that this was the most dangerous time, when he faced the highest chance of getting caught. He was in and out of the kitchen, the book liberated from the top of the fridge, before she could notice.

☙ ❧

Dafyd lost all track of time as the stairway drew him deeper into the earth. He felt like he had been walking for days. And then, one more turn of the stairway, one more blind corner, and suddenly the stairs ended.

Dafyd stopped. His torch was still burning, sending up plumes of black smoke, and he held it high to see where the stairway had brought him.

The chamber was small. The smooth, wet floor, and the pointed rocks that hung from the ceiling and dripped all around him glimmered in the torchlight. The rough walls beside him curved up into the rounded ceiling, and in some places mist obscured their features.

The wall at the far end of the cavern, however, was as flat and smooth as the doorway in the canyon had been. Dafyd's torchlight flickered off a bright glint of red in the middle of the wall, a shimmering object the size of coin in what looked to be a silver setting the size of the mouth of a flagon.

Dafyd took two steps forward, holding his torch far ahead of him.

The Sunstone. It had to be.

He could hardly believe his eyes. Having come all this way, done everything that he had done, the Sunstone was now close enough to touch. Almost his.

As he stepped forward, mesmerized by the stone, he didn't notice the wisps of mist drift away from the wall, though there was no breeze.

※ ※

David kicked off the blankets without even realizing it. He suddenly felt too warm, as his eyes flashed across the page. Despite the sheen of sweat gathering on his skin, a chill ran over him as he read of Dafyd in the cave, and the mist coalescing and moving behind him.

※ ※

The closer Dafyd got to the red stone, the more certain he was. It pulsed with its own power and light. The silver in which it was set looked like an amulet, carved with drawings and symbols.

Behind him, the patches of mist grew more distinct and solidified as they drew closer. Shapes like arms extended, and hands, fingers flexed as they reached out for the boy.

Dafyd was about to touch the stone in the wall when he felt the cold, damp hands upon him. He screamed as they clutched at his shoulders, grabbed him by the arms. He squirmed and turned, trying to get free, trying to see who was dragging him away from the Sunstone.

※ ※

David could almost feel the cold grip of the creatures in the mist.

He tensed in his bed, his legs twitching, as his eyes raced across each line. His breathing was ragged. A slow ache pounded in his temples.

The Sunstone was almost his.

※ ※

Dafyd's torch fell to the floor as faces formed in the misty figures now surrounding him. Distended mouths shaped words.

"Stop," they said faintly. "You can't."

The mist wrapped around his chest, threatened to pull him backwards off his feet. He struggled, but he could not break the grip.

"Stop . . ." The faint voices echoed in the cave.

Their arms tightened around him. If he didn't do something soon, Dafyd feared they would drag him to the ground, swallow him.

Summoning all his strength, he pushed himself forward, shaking from side to side to break loose. The apparitions held for a moment longer, then shredded apart, leaving Dafyd free and stumbling forward, falling at the foot of the wall he had been trying to reach. Turning, he saw the mist re-gathering itself into vaguely human shapes, arms reaching out for him once more, mouths crying out, "Stop, stop."

In seconds they would be on him again. He didn't know if the Stone's powers would protect him, but what other hope did he have?

Pulling himself to his knees, Dafyd reached out for the Sunstone.

As his fingers brushed the cold surface, a bolt of red light jumped from the stone to Dafyd's hand. His body buckled and snapped as the charge went through him. As he slumped to the floor he could smell something burning.

Himself.

It was the last thing he smelled.

In the cave of the Sunstone, deep within the earth, Dafyd, son of Mareigh, closed his eyes and died.

⁂

David's body snapped and writhed as if an electrical current were running through him. He fell off his bed, dragging the covers with him, as he twitched and flailed. His lamp fell to the floor and smashed, and there was the smell of burning in the air, a metallic taste in his mouth as he bit through his tongue. He tried to scream, tried to cry out, but no sound came.

"Sorry," I said, standing up. "I should . . ."

Dale waved it away. "More wings for me," he said brightly.

I answered my cell as I was walking through the restaurant toward the front door. "Jacqui?"

"Chris, where are you?"

It was hard to hear her, to get any sense of emotion from her voice. "Downtown," I said, stepping onto the sidewalk. "Why? What's going on?"

"It's David. He's in the hospital."

My stomach heaved. "What happened? What's . . . he's okay?"

"He collapsed," she said, her voice tight. "I'm not sure. They're checking."

"Okay, I'll meet you. I'll be right there."

Every aisle inside the restaurant was thick and clogged. I dodged and shouldered my way back to the table. I wanted to scream.

"I'm sorry," I said when I finally reached the table. I pulled out my wallet. "I have to go."

Dale rose halfway to his feet, throwing his napkin onto the table. "What's going on?"

I shook my head, distracted, counting out enough cash to pay for the meal twice over, dropping the bills on the table.

"It's David. He's in the hospital."

I was already moving before he could react, dialling a cab with my cell phone as I stumbled back out of the restaurant.

Outside, without thinking, I lit a cigarette, drawing on it heavily, frantically, as I waited for the cab.

PART TWO

I

JACQUI PROBABLY WOULD HAVE called it a typical Saturday night crowd: drunks hunched over cardboard basins; small children whiny and flushed with fever; a young man cradling a broken arm, too long and bending at the wrong angle. In one corner a young man rocked in a chair, muttering an unceasing stream of obscenities, his eyes fluttering back in his head: strangely, no one seemed to notice him, all too wrapped up in their own crises to register the presence of another crazy person in their midst.

No sign of David.

I stepped up to a nurse taking the temperature of a boy about David's age. The boy noticed me waiting. He had sick eyes, burning with colour, half hidden under drooping lids. He didn't acknowledge me when I smiled at him.

As the nurse packed up her cart and turned away from the boy, I stepped forward. "Excuse me," I said.

She didn't look up. "Sir, someone will see to you shortly. If you'd take a seat and wait for your name to be called."

"I'm looking—"

"If you have any questions"—she set her stethoscope in her basket decisively—"the reception desk is over—"

"I'm just looking for my son," I said sharply. "My wife told me that he was here."

She seemed to see me for the first time. "Are you Jacqui's husband?"

I nodded.

"David's back here," she said, taking the handle of her cart and leading me through a swinging door and down a narrow corridor.

I followed her into a warren of curtained beds and beeping machinery to a large nursing station. Nurses bustled back and forth, pastel blurs, the officious squeak of soft-soled shoes.

Jacqui was standing at the counter, talking to one of the nurses. I was shocked when she threw her arms around my waist, pulling herself tight against me.

"Oh God, Chris."

"What happened?" I asked. I hugged her reflexively. "Where's David?"

She pulled away. Her face was pale, and her eyes were wide, darting. She looked like she wanted to bolt.

She hesitated a moment, then gestured with her hand. "In 17."

I started forward, but she put her hand on my arm.

"The doctor's with him." Her voice came out small and fragile.

Following the numbers above the curtains, I spotted 17. Two pairs of feet, and tan pants and blue-green scrubs, moved in the space between the curtains and the floor. "Shouldn't you be . . ."

She was bouncing one foot slightly as she leaned against the counter, her lips tight and pale. "They asked me to wait out here. They're doing a lumbar puncture. They think it might be meningitis."

The word chilled me. "What happened?"

She shook her head. "I heard a noise. Upstairs. I came into his room—"

The curtains around the bed slid back with a metallic rattle and the doctor and a nurse I vaguely recognized stepped out. The doctor was writing on a clipboard as we moved toward him.

"How are you holding up, Jacqui?" he asked.

"Hanging in," she said quietly.

"I'm Stephen McKinley," he said. "You must be Christopher."

"Chris," I said, craning my neck around him to see the metal bed. David.

"Is he going to be okay?"

The doctor took a half-step back and I edged around him.

"We've done a preliminary examination," he began as I reached David's bedside. "And a lumbar puncture. David is stable. I do have a few questions, though. Is there any family history of epilepsy?"

Epilepsy? What the hell was going on?

"Not that I know of," Jacqui answered.

"Diabetes?"

I let Jacqui answer the doctor's questions. David's face was white, almost translucent, his lips grey and dull, and crusted with dried blood. His body was entirely still, save for the slow expansion and contraction of his chest. His hands, though, were moving, ever so slightly. Twitching.

"We're going to get him in for a CT scan as soon as we get a slot. We've sent the blood work out. We'll take a look at everything," Dr. McKinley was saying.

"So what is it?" I asked, turning back to face him.

"We're not sure," he said, in a warm tone at odds with the terse matter-of-factness with which he and Jacqui had been communicating moments before. It was a tone intended to placate, to soothe: it set my teeth on edge.

"It's possible it's something as simple as food poisoning," he continued leadingly.

"We both had the same thing for dinner," Jacqui said, ruling that out.

"Or it could be something viral. Seizures are often seen in children fighting a fever."

"What was his temperature?" Jacqui asked.

The doctor hesitated a bare moment, a stutter in the conversation that most people probably wouldn't even have noticed. Jacqui looked down at the floor.

"It's normal," he said. "We're running tests. We want to exclude meningitis, cancer, metabolic disorders. You should know, most cases of epilepsy are idiopathic: there's nothing ominous or obvious that triggers them. And the majority are well controlled. We'll know more in the next few hours."

I glanced pointedly at the bed. "He seems calm now."

The doctor turned toward David. "We've got him sedated. The convulsions had slowed by the time the ambulance picked him up—"

Ambulance?

"—but we needed to draw blood and confirm his vitals. We had to sedate him."

The thought of David in the back of an ambulance . . . I couldn't say anything, watching the tiny spasms in his fingers.

"You can sit with him, if you'd like," the doctor said. "I'll be back as soon as the test results come in. And I'll see about the CT." He touched Jacqui quickly on the upper arm before turning away.

Standing at David's bedside was a slow agony. I wanted desperately to take Jacqui's hand, to rely on her strength. I was stunned when I felt her fingers touch mine, felt our hands interlace easily, naturally.

David's body was covered almost entirely with a nubbly flannel sheet, antiqued with constant use.

"What—?" Staring at the blood on David's lips, I gestured toward my own mouth.

"He bit into his lips. And tongue. When—"

"What *happened*?" I interrupted. "I don't know. You haven't said."

"I'm sorry," she said. She took a deep breath. "David went to bed at about eight-thirty, no argument, no bargaining. I was watching TV a while later and I heard something upstairs. I thought it was David going to the bathroom, but then there was a crash." She shook her head. "When I got upstairs, he was on the floor beside his bed. Convulsing."

She looked down at the bed, her gaze lingering on David's pale face. She crossed her arms and held herself like she had a sudden chill.

In our silence, the tiny space seemed to swell, the narrow opening at the edge of the bed, too tight for the two of us to stand in comfortably, seemed to grow, a gulf opening. I had never felt so small, so helpless, so inconsequential.

I leaned forward against the steel rail of the bed. "How you doin' there, sport?" I asked in a whisper. I reached out and gently cupped my hand over his, which throbbed and jerked. It felt like Nolan, David's hamster: it pushed and seemed to struggle against my hand, trying to get free.

"It's gonna be all right," I said, wincing at the platitude.

His face was a pale cold mask, utterly devoid of expression. His puffy lips were parted slightly. He didn't look like he was sleeping, he looked— I couldn't bring myself to think the word.

Except his eyes were moving. I could see them behind his closed lids, shifting and distending the thin skin like an undersea creature about to break the surface. The motion was unnerving, like watching him drown.

But it wasn't irregular, like the twitching in his hands: his eyes were bouncing regularly from side to side, in unison.

The night seemed to pass like moments in a dream. Sitting in our quiet corner, we could watch the unceasing traffic into the Emergency Room— the slow, shambling, uncertain steps of people looking for signs, unsure of where to go or what to do with themselves; the decisive slamming of gurneys through doors and raised voices of the paramedics, joking with the nurses, holding court in the lobby as they waited for their patients to be handed over, for their stretchers to be returned.

Neither of us said much. Periodically, Jacqui and I, alone or together, would wander into the ward, slip between the curtains to David's bed, hoping for some change, some development.

"They've got him pretty sedated," she said at one point, staring down at him. "They'll see what happens when he starts to come around in the morning."

"I know."

As I moved past her, I touched her softly in the small of the back and then walked away.

Standing outside, just around the corner from the ER entrance I lit a cigarette. I was blowing out the first lungful of smoke when the doors slid open and Jacqui stepped out.

I reflexively tucked the cigarette out of sight, though I knew she had already seen me.

"Busted," I said sheepishly.

"Can I have one?" she asked.

I fumbled with the pack, then cupped my hands around the Zippo to light it for her. I was stunned.

She took a deep drag and held it for a moment, shuddering slightly as she restrained a cough. "Almost twelve years," she said. "When did you start again? With more than the token one or two a day, I mean."

I tried to think. "It's been a pretty rough year."

"Yeah."

We puffed in silence for a long moment, watching the smoke curl up toward the streetlights.

"We don't both need to be here," she said. "Nothing's going to change before morning."

"Do you want to—?"

She shook her head. "I can't." She gestured at the ER.

"Right." Not with her co-workers watching. Not when she felt she could, maybe, do something, anything, if she needed to. "When are you supposed to work next?"

"Monday. Afternoon." She took a drag off her cigarette. "We're going to need to get some sleep."

"Yeah."

I dropped my cigarette and crushed the butt with my heel. I didn't want to leave. I could see what she was saying, but it wasn't just David that I wanted to be there for.

How long had it been since we had shared a cigarette late on a Saturday night? How long had it been since we were on the same side in a fight?

"So you think I should—" I gestured toward a cab waiting a short distance away.

"Is that okay?"

"Sure," I lied. "I understand."

"I'll call you if anything—"

"Yeah." I nodded emphatically. I took a couple of steps toward the cab and then it hit me. "You're thinking this is going to be a long-term thing."

She hesitated, and the sudden weight of our situation crushed in on me. That look on Jacqui's face, that pause: David wasn't going to be better when I returned in the morning.

I let myself in through the front door. I had to see it for myself.

Everywhere I went there were signs of a tragedy: a knocked-over stack of magazines in the living room; the kitchen sink full of cold grey dishwater; a pile of Davy's laundry that I had folded and placed on the stairs for him to take up to his room now scattered and strewn. I imagined the heavy shoes of the paramedics kicking at the clothes, a T-shirt catching in the wheels of the stretcher.

I tried to breathe evenly as I climbed the stairs. David's bedroom was the worst of all.

His blankets had been pulled across the floor. The mattress had slid partly off the bed frame, its corner bright blue where the sheet had pulled away.

I surveyed the chaos slowly, trying to build a story around what I knew and what I was seeing. Davy in the early stages of the seizure, falling out of bed, trying to hang on but dragging the mattress with him. His flailing arms catching the bedside table, knocking it over, smashing the lamp, scattering all of his most prized possessions—baseball, glove, video game, book—onto the floor. I could see my son staggering around the bedroom, crashing into the shelf by the door, knocking books to the floor, smashing the glass of a picture of the three of us at Disneyland. Falling against his desk, spilling the glass of water, pens falling to the carpet, Nolan's plastic cage tumbling onto its side.

I could see him in the middle of the floor, his body heaving and shuddering in the rounded, clear space amidst the chaos, his teeth uncontrollably gnawing into his tongue, his lips.

Unable to bear where my imagination was taking me, I kept noticing small details: the way the spilled water pooled around the edges of his computer keyboard. The faint, blue glow from the video game, which had fallen open. The way the baseball seemed to sit at the lip of the glove, as if about to be caught.

Standing there, surrounded by his life, by those things he loved, I wanted to take David something, something to comfort him, something to tuck into the hospital bed with him. Something familiar that would be there when he woke up.

Until he was about six, David had loved a battered brown teddy bear. He had called the bear Pik, after a Pokemon, and he carried it with him everywhere, usually by the ear. Jacqui and I had thought there would be a fight when it came time to separate the two of them, but David took care of the separation on his own. We had only noticed the absence of the bear after a few days.

I wished I knew where the bear was: it would have been perfect. Something to hold, something soft, something familiar and meaningful.

I stepped into the room and righted Nolan's cage. The hamster was all right, cowering in the corner beside his overturned food bowl. David's old baseball glove lay on the floor; it was dingy and battered and soft. That would have to do.

As I bent to pick it up, though, I spotted *To the Four Directions* beside it on the floor, partially concealed by the sheet. I had noticed it before, but it hadn't really registered: what was the book doing in his room? Jacqui had put it on top of the fridge, homeland of exiled objects.

"That little . . ."

I could picture it; it was something I would have done.

No wonder he didn't put up any resistance to going to bed.

I replaced the book on top of the fridge before going out the back door. No need for Jacqui to know.

It was only lying in my bed, staring at the ceiling, that it occurred to me: the book was in his room. He wouldn't have forgotten to replace it in the kitchen before he went to sleep, risking his mother's wrath. And it was partially under the sheet.

David had been reading when the seizure hit.

II

On my way back to the hospital the next morning, I half expected to find David wide awake, sitting up in bed, playing that damn video game, as if my absence and a few hours in his mother's tender care were enough to bring about a full recovery.

I found him exactly the way I had left him, broken and still.

I tucked his baseball glove into the crook of his arm, and kissed him gently on the forehead. "Good morning, Davy," I whispered, before sitting down in the chair beside the bed.

Jacqui went home then, and I spent the morning at David's side. I didn't see a doctor at all until Jacqui returned several hours later: she was back less than three minutes and here he was.

He was older than the doctor we had seen the night before, balding, but with a bushy beard, almost sloppy in what looked like his street clothes. He glanced at me over the top of his glasses, but didn't acknowledge me as he leaned against the bedrail and started flipping through the chart.

As Jacqui bent to brush David's hair back from his forehead, she looked at the baseball glove. Biting her lower lip, she smiled at me.

"Has he ever had a seizure before?" the doctor asked.

"No—" Jacqui said, but he cut her off.

"Is there a family history of epilepsy?"

"Not that I'm aware of."

The doctor nodded, still looking at the chart. I don't think he had glanced at David at all.

"Does"—he had to glance at the top of the sheet for his name—"David have any allergies? To food, or to any medication he might be taking?"

"Not that we're aware of," Jacqui said, her voice growing cold, impatient. All the same questions.

The doctor nodded again, but he still wasn't looking at David. "And has he suffered any injuries to his head recently?" he asked. "Sports, perhaps? Or a fight in the schoolyard?"

"No."

The doctor pushed his glasses up. "Well, the tests came back negative for meningitis." He looked at Jacqui, not at David. "I think the first thing we need to do is send your son . . ." He couldn't even remember David's name. "For some tests. I'll order an MRI and a CAT scan."

"Dr. McKinley put in a request for a CT last night," Jacqui said.

"Then I'll make sure that happens," he said, momentarily focused. "He'll get priority if he's coming from Emergency. After, we'll get him admitted and we'll see what the tests show us."

"Doctor," I asked, "is it possible we're jumping the gun a bit?" Jacqui looked at me—I couldn't tell if she was agreeing with me or not. "Isn't it possible that once the sedative wears off, he'll just . . ."

The doctor was flipping through the file, and I had run out of words. I couldn't shake the feeling that David was just going to wake up, that all of this would vanish behind us like a bad dream.

"According to this," the doctor said, "your son was treated early last night with a single intravenous dose of lorazepam." Jacqui nodded. "That should have worn off a little while ago."

He pushed his glasses higher on his nose and looked up the bed at David. "Ah yes. It seems our patient is awake."

My knees buckled at the words. I turned to smile at my son, my mouth tightened to say good morning.

But I stopped.

His eyes were open, but David didn't look at me. He didn't look at anything; his eyes were flat and dull, rolled partway back in his head, twitching from side to side.

"David?" I said quietly, trying to get his attention, to break the spell. And then more loudly, "David?"

He didn't respond. A thin trail of saliva trickled from the corner of his mouth.

"David?"

Two and a half hours after taking David from the ER for an MRI and CT—with a promise to return him within the hour—the attendants brought him back. Jacqui and I tucked him under the covers. His body was heavy and slack and I couldn't help but think of all the nights I had rolled and snugged him under his quilt after he had kicked it off.

His eyes were open, his pupils wide and darting from side to side. I leaned in close, trying to get his attention, hoping for a moment when his eyes would widen, when his face would set in a smile of recognition and he would say "Dad!" and throw his arms around my neck, but there was nothing: no recognition, no smile, no words.

Just an occasional blink, and that constant and oddly familiar flicker, back and forth.

"I'll take the first shift," Jacqui said quietly.

I glanced at her. I had been staring at David for a long time.

I didn't want to leave, but I agreed with her, already thinking ahead to the night to come, building elements of routine out of what had been unimaginable just the day before.

I ruffled Davy's hair.

Back at the house, I went into the kitchen to check the answering machine. I was bone-tired, but I knew there was no chance I'd fall asleep. My mind was whirling.

No messages.

I took the copy of *To the Four Directions* off the top of the fridge and let myself out the back door.

In my apartment, I ignored the bottle of vodka beckoning me from the freezer and ran myself a glass of tap water.

I wasn't sure why I had brought David's book up with me. I certainly wasn't in the mood to read, and the book should have been a reminder of David being mad at me, his last words to me either sullen or laced with bile.

Last words—what was I thinking?

Curiously, though, all I could think about was how excited David had been to read it, the warmth I felt when I saw the light under his door when he was supposed to be asleep.

I sat in my reading chair and turned the book over in my hands, started idly flipping through the pages. The book felt loose, worn-in, the result of him—and who knows how many other kids—carrying it around, reading it, loving it.

I found the bookmark, which David likely had tucked randomly near the back of the book as he was reading.

World's Best Dad.

Yeah, right.

Cupping the spine loosely in my hand, I let the pages fall open. It felt right to read the words that David had been reading. I had no way of knowing if this was where he had left off, but it looked like a good part. Something about Dafyd in a subterranean chamber, ghosts coming out of the walls. God, how I had eaten this stuff up.

I was shifting to cross my legs when I happened to catch sight of myself in the mirror across the room, a sudden glimpse of my face looking up from the book. A chill ran through me. I stood up, holding my place in the book with my forefinger, and walked slowly toward the mirror, never looking away from myself.

It couldn't be . . .

I stopped almost against the mirror and gazed at my own eyes, watching the way they moved when I glanced to the right, then to the left.

I opened up the book and started to read a line, but I couldn't read and look at my reflection at the same time. I shook my head—there had to be a way.

I turned the book around so the printed pages faced the mirror, and lifted it in front of my face until the top of the spine was across the bridge of my nose. In the mirror, I looked crazed, only my eyes visible above the book.

I ran my eyes along the reflected lines of text, not trying to decipher the words but trying to catch sight of myself reading, trying to see what my eyes looked like as they traversed the lines of the story.

I couldn't do it—every time I tried to see what they looked like in the mirror, my eyes would stop and I'd be staring into my own pupils. Physicists have a term for it, the way observing something changes the thing being observed.

I pulled the book away from my face in frustration.

But it didn't matter if I couldn't prove it.

I considered the book in my hand with a mounting certainty: David's eyes weren't moving randomly. They were moving metronomically, from side to side, left to right.

He was reading.

III

WITH DAVID ADMITTED, we saw a different specialist the next morning. It was just as well—every time I thought of Dr. Whatever-the-hell-his-name-was, the way he barely looked at David, a cold fury built in me that made me want to hit something.

On the other hand, Dr. Rutherford, a stately, middle-aged man with silvering hair and a plummy South African accent, spent a long time with David. He tested reflexes and flexibility, checked his eyes and his ears, all of the usual measurements that the nurses had been tracking in his chart, and then asked us to step out of the room.

"I'm going to test his reaction to noxious stimuli," he explained. "It's not something that parents usually like to see."

I was still waiting for an explanation when Jacqui took my arm and directed us into the corridor. A few seconds later David let out a sharp exclamation of pain and surprise. It was the first time I had heard my son's voice in days, and I turned around and threw back the curtain.

The doctor was leaning over him with a needle in his hand.

"That's the test, Chris," Jacqui said from behind me. "It measures a patient's level of consciousness by checking their reaction to pain."

I let Jacqui turn me away.

We spent the next half hour with Dr. Rutherford as he pored over the MRI and CT results. Finally, he held up his hands and said, in his warmest voice, "I'm very sorry that I don't have any more concrete information for you."

After the doctor was gone, I cleared my throat. "Can I ask you something?"

Jacqui regarded me suspiciously.

I probably should have mentioned it to the doctor, but I knew it didn't make much sense. Still, the thought had been weighing on me.

"I think David might have been reading when the attack hit."

"What makes you think that?"

I pulled the book out of the pocket of my jacket. "This was on the floor of his room, under the rest of the mess."

It took Jacqui a moment to respond. "We put that on top of the fridge," she said. "Did you—?"

I shook my head. "I think he snuck it off the fridge after you put him to bed."

"It's no wonder he didn't put up a fight."

I nodded. "I think he was reading—reading this—when he had the seizure."

"But reading wouldn't . . ."

"I know. I'm not saying that it caused the seizure, just that the two things happened at the same time."

For few moments I watched the relentless movement of David's hands, the constant flicker of his eyes.

"There's one more thing," I said slowly, not sure if I wanted to share this. She'd think I'd gone crazy.

"What?" she asked, looking at me.

I glanced at David's eyes again.

"Look at this," I said, opening up the book. "Watch my eyes."

I started reading from the top of the page, exaggerating the reading movement somewhat, moving my eyes past both ends of each line, hoping it would be obvious to her.

When I stopped, Jacqui looked puzzled. "What?" she asked.

"Look at my eyes," I stressed, repeating the whole pantomime.

"You're reading," she said. "I don't . . ."

"Now look at David," I said. "Look at *his* eyes."

Jacqui looked down at David, then back at me. "His eyes are moving."

I almost smiled. She saw what I was getting at.

"Chris, that's called nystagmus. It's involuntary." Suddenly a nurse again. "It's a symptom. We see it in patients with neurological problems, head injuries, that sort of thing."

"I think it's more than that," I said. "The movement, it's so regular, so consistent. It's like his eyes are actually focused on something."

Jacqui shook her head. "It's just the way he's manifesting the symptom."

"I think it's more than that," I repeated, trying not to get frustrated. "Look at how his eyes are moving. Doesn't it look like he's reading?"

"Chris."

I stopped.

"I'm going to get a coffee and stop by the ER to check in with Marla," Jacqui said slowly. "Do you want anything?"

I felt a rush of anger at the thought of her leaving, walking out when I was trying to explain, but then I recognized it for what it was: de-escalation. Cooling off.

"Just a coffee'll be fine," I answered, not looking at her. "Thanks."

The curtain rattled as she left.

I turned back to David, smiling down at him, hoping he could at least sense my presence.

"Looks like it's just the two of us again, sport," I said. "So what should we do now?" I held the book up to him before I sat down. "A bit of a story?"

I imagined him smiling the way he always did when it came time for stories at home. Teeth brushed, face washed, jammies on, tucked warmly into bed.

I flipped through the pages. "It's kind of tough," I said, "not know-ing where you left off. I don't want to read you anything that you've already read—" Then louder, as I leaned back in the chair, "Well, how about this?" I settled on a page. "I think this is about where you fin-ished. Looks like a good part, too."

Their arms tightened around him. If he didn't do something soon, Dafyd feared they would drag him to the ground, swallow him.

Summoning all his strength, he pushed himself forward, shak-ing from side to side to break loose. The apparitions held for a moment longer, then shredded apart, leaving Dafyd free and stumbling forward, falling at the foot of the wall.

I looked up from the book. "Does that seem about right to you?"

He didn't answer, save with the twitching of his eyes, and the clenching of his hands. I continued.

Turning, he saw the mist re-gathering itself into vaguely human shapes, arms reaching out for him once more, mouths crying out, "Stop, stop."

In seconds they would be on him again. He didn't know if the Stone's powers would protect him, but what other hope did he have?

Pulling himself to his knees, Dafyd reached out for the Sunstone.

David's body jerked on the bed. His back snapped upward, his hands flying uncontrollably. A gasp escaped his mouth and I stood up, dropping the book to the floor.

☙ ❧

"What the hell?" David muttered, opening his eyes.

It was dark and cold. And it felt like he was lying on the ground. Not in his bed. When he tried to roll over, his whole body protested, and there wasn't even a hint of give to the cold surface beneath him.

☙ ❧

I thought it might be the beginning of another seizure, and I glanced at the curtain, wondering if I should call out for help, wishing that Jacqui was there. She always knew what to do.

I was reaching for the call button, and just as quickly as it had come on, David's body relaxed back onto the bed.

I waited a moment. "Davy?" I whispered, touching his face, his arms, his hair, trying to soothe him. "David?" My mouth was dry, and I could hear the beating of my heart.

It was a long time before I could sit back down. I pulled away slowly, tentatively, reluctant to break the contact between us. "You gave me a scare there."

I thought about calling a nurse, but he seemed back to normal. I'd let Jacqui know when she got back.

I picked the book up off the floor. "Should I continue?"

I would pause in my reading every so often to look at him. Something was different. It took me a couple of glances to determine what it was.

His hands were now absolutely still on the hospital blankets, no clutching, no grasping. And his eyes had stopped flickering: he seemed to be staring directly upwards, focused unwaveringly on a spot somewhere in the middle distance.

Like he was listening.

> 🙢 🙠

The last thing David could remember was dropping the book on his bedroom floor, watching it fall away from his shaking hands in slow motion, trailing streaks of light. The blinding pain in his head. The taste of blood in his mouth, in his throat, choking him.

But he also remembered stumbling, falling, almost burning himself with his torch, turning toward the stone wall, reaching out for the Sunstone, then a burst, almost like an electrical shock, his whole body shuddering, the smell of burning flesh.

But that was the book. That was Dafyd, in the cave in the canyon.

He had been in his room. Mom was downstairs. He could hear the tinny voices on the television. He had been in bed, holding the book, and his hands had started to shake, a headache coming on so fast he thought his brain might explode.

But he had just come down the stone stairway into the chamber of the Sunstone. He had been attacked. The only thing that could save him was the Sunstone.

No, that was the book again.

Why was he remembering scenes from the book as vividly as he was remembering scenes from his own life? Was he sick? Sick in the head?

Where was he?

"Mom?" he croaked out, his mouth dry and tasting of metal. "Dad?"

"Shh . . ." came a voice in the darkness, a cool, comforting hand on his forehead. "It's going to be all right."

The voice sounded like it belonged to a child.

Turning, looking up again, David saw that he was surrounded by the mist creatures who had attacked him.

No, that was Dafyd they had attacked.

Vaguely human in form, glowing faintly in the darkness, reaching out to him with long, misshapen hands.

David screamed.

⤳ ⤶

When Jacqui got back to the room, Chris was sitting in the chair on the far side of the bed, reading aloud.

He glanced up at her, and she shook her head slightly: he shouldn't stop on her account.

She listened to Chris read as she pulled the cups from the tray, not really paying attention to the words, but letting the rise and fall of his voice comfort her. It reminded her of home, of the old days, when she used to stand in the doorway of David's room and listen to his storytime.

When she glanced over at Chris, he gestured with his hand as he read that she should look at David. She looked at their son, then back at Chris, wrinkling her brow. What did he want her to look at?

Chris lifted one hand from the book and pointed at his eyes; Jacqui leaned over, looked more closely at David's face.

His eyes were perfectly still, staring straight ahead.

Chris's voice rose slightly, his words coming a little more urgently. Things were building up in the story. And at the perfect moment, he stopped—Jacqui knew the sound of a cliffhanger when she heard one.

He stood up as he finished reading. "He's not moving his hands, either," he said excitedly.

"No, he's—"

"His eyes and his hands stopped moving when I was reading." Chris was breathless.

"That's a good sign," she said. "He's probably responding to the sound of voices around him. It means—"

"We've been standing here for two days, talking, and it's never made any difference before."

"That's what I mean," Jacqui said. "Maybe he's coming out of it. That he's developing more awareness of . . ."

She stopped.

David's eyes were moving. And the fingers on his right hand had started to twitch. She looked at Chris. He had noticed it too.

Within a few seconds, the twitch had spread to his left hand. Then both hands jumped slightly off the bed, bending and grasping.

⟳ ⟳

David screamed and pulled himself across the stone floor, trying to get away from the long, grasping fingers of the mist creatures. They followed him, floating effortlessly through the dark room as he scraped and banged his hands and elbows on the rocks.

"It's all right," one of the creatures said, the shape of a face emerging out of the mist: a nose, the curve of a mouth, dark shadows where the eyes should have been. "We don't want to hurt you."

It was the same childlike voice that had spoken to him before.

David wasn't falling for it. That was one of Darren Keneally's favourite tricks, to pretend to be all friendly, and then just when David started to trust him, bam! And Darren would walk away laughing not only at what he had done, but at how stupid David had been for trusting him in the first place.

David kept pulling himself away, trying to put as much distance as he could between himself and the mist creatures. But they kept coming, shifting like mercury as they floated through the air toward him.

"Stop it," he cried out.

A moment later he backed hard into the wall of the cave, banging his head. He was trapped in the dark, pinned against the wall.

⟳ ⟳

I was running a little late: Jacqui had sent me home mid-afternoon, ordering me to take a nap. I had said I'd be back by eight, but it was almost nine by the time I got the van parked and took the elevator up to the ward.

I pushed through the curtain and stopped. A nurse was leaning over David, gently withdrawing a needle from his left arm. He was restrained with wide leather straps at his arms and feet, blood on his face and on the sheet under him.

It wasn't the sight of the blood that stopped me, or of the straps.

It was the sight of Jacqui pushed back into the corner. Her face was white as paper, but streaked with tears. Her eyes were wide, and when they met mine, she started crying again.

I crossed the room and held her as she rose to her feet. She shuddered in my arms. I willed my heart rate to slow. I had never seen Jacqui like this, completely helpless, completely out of control. She was usually so level, so calm—it made me dread asking her what had happened.

"I went out to talk to Judy. I talked to her, maybe a couple of minutes, and when I got back to the room . . ." She lowered her head, trying not to lose her composure again.

"He was having another seizure?"

She shook her head. "No. Not right then. I came back to the room and he— Just as I came through the curtain, he screamed."

"He screamed?"

"I've never heard anything like it, Chris. It sounded—it sounded like he was in pain. And scared. Terrified." Tears left silver streaks as they ran down her cheeks. "And then, he was out of control." She shook her head. "His arms and legs . . . He tore out his IV."

She threw her head back and sniffed, trying to shake it off. "I rang for the nurse, but they were already coming. They'd heard him."

"Jesus."

"It took three people to restrain him so the nurse could give him a sedative."

"If he's sedated . . ." Looking at the broad leather straps.

"They've ordered him restrained, at least until they can run some more tests. They're worried that he's going to injure himself."

The blood on David's arm, where the IV had pulled free, was drying on him like rust.

"What can we do?"

Jacqui shook her head.

It wasn't until hours later, flipping through the pages of David's book, holding a solitary vigil while Jacqui tried to get some sleep at home, that the thought struck me: the seizure had come shortly after eight in the evening.

Storytime.

The twisted, misty fingers hung in the air in front of David's face.

"It's just a dream," he whispered, trying to convince himself. "It's just a dream, it's just a dream."

He pressed himself against the wall as hard as he could, turning his face away when he could go no farther. He flinched as he felt the cold tendrils touch his cheek.

"It's not a dream," the voice said, and David choked back a sob.

But the fingers weren't reaching for his throat to choke him, or his eyes to gouge. They were stroking his cheeks, as if trying to comfort him.

"Shh," the voice said, as its fingers continued to brush against David's face. "It's all right."

"But, but . . ." David couldn't even form full thoughts, let alone full sentences.

"We're not going to hurt you," the voice said, with such sincerity that David almost believed it. Except . . .

"You tried to kill me," he said, his voice bouncing off the rock wall, surprisingly deep.

"No," the creature said simply.

"When I was trying to get the Sunstone. When I—" David stopped himself.

That wasn't me.

So why could he remember it so clearly?

"No," the voice said again.

David half turned his head in time to see the face emerge from the mist again.

"You tried to keep *me* from the Sunstone."

Him. To keep Dafyd from the Sunstone.

The face was moving, as if the creature were lowering its head. "We tried to stop you from touching the Sunstone." The misty lips moved to form the words. "We tried to save you."

IV

DALE PARKED HIS VAN at the curb and stepped down, carefully balancing the cardboard tray of coffee. It was too early to be visiting anyone normal, but Chris made such a fuss about getting up at four every morning to write. He'd be awake.

Or he would be, soon enough.

He knocked heavily on the back door of the garage and waited in the silence, surveying the barbecue, the picnic table, the Adirondack chairs, the lawn in need of a mowing, then knocked again, a little more forcefully. The smell of the coffee made his stomach growl. He was about to knock again when he heard Chris on the stairs.

He put on a smile when Chris opened the door, but the expression quickly receded. "Hey," he said cautiously.

Chris didn't say anything, and held on to the doorknob with one hand.

"I brought coffee." Dale gestured with the tray. "It looks like you could use some."

Chris was pale and haggard, his shirt hanging loose, his hair messy and dirty. Dark circles around his eyes against the white of his face made him look like he was wearing a mask. He stepped to one side to let Dale enter.

The apartment looked as rough as Chris did. Clothes were strewn across the floor, books and papers on every available surface, the air thick with the smell of cigarette smoke.

He passed Chris a cup. "I thought you might be at the hospital."

"I came home a couple of hours ago. Nothing I could do there." His voice was ragged.

"So," he said, looking pointedly around the room before letting his gaze settle on Chris. "I guess I don't have to ask how you're doing."

"Surviving," Chris said as he sat down in the desk chair and gestured for Dale to take the Stickley-style reading chair.

"Barely," Dale said as he sat down. "You look like hell, actually."

"Thanks." Chris tipped his cup toward Dale in a mock toast.

"Have you slept? At all?"

"A little bit," Chris said, with a guarded tone that Dale knew meant he was lying.

"Right," he said. "How's David?"

Chris didn't say anything for a moment. "He had another seizure. Last night, at about eight."

"Was it a bad one?"

Chris nodded.

"Is he okay?"

Chris exhaled a sharp, sad laugh. "That's the question, isn't it. I've been going through my books—" He gestured at the table beside Dale, at the stack of home medical encyclopedias. *The Merck Manual* was on top of the pile. Since when did Chris have a *Merck Manual*? "And trying to find something online, but I can't figure it out."

"You don't need to figure it out, Chris," Dale said, rattled by the pure desperation in his friend's voice. "That's what the doctors are there for. They'll figure it out."

Chris sighed heavily.

"What?"

"I don't . . ." He leaned back in his chair. "I'm not sure they will."

"You're just tired," he said. "You need to take care of yourself, and of Jacqui, and let the doctors take care of David."

Chris shook his head, fiercely and decisively, a look of frustration flashing across his face. "I don't think they're looking in the right place."

"What do you mean?"

He reached past the laptop and picked up a book from the desk. "Ever since I gave him this for his birthday, David's changed."

Dale took a sip from his coffee, avoiding looking at Chris.

"I don't know what happened. I liked it when he started reading, all on his own. You know how hard that is for him. But then he, I don't know, he seemed to get obsessed with the book."

"And you think it had something to do with the seizure?"

Chris ran his fingers through his dirty hair. "I know how stupid that sounds. I've been doing all this research . . . Reading doesn't cause seizures. The brain doesn't work like that."

Dale was about to speak, but Chris cut him off. "But I can't help it," he said, arguing against words that Dale hadn't had a chance to speak. "I saw how the book was affecting him. I mean, come on, threatening a teacher? And now, when I read to him, he calms right down. He stops fidgeting, his eyes stop moving."

"His eyes?"

Chris leaned forward excitedly. "His eyes. Even though he's . . . unconscious . . . his eyes are moving. Back and forth, back and forth. It looks like he's still reading."

He slumped back into the chair.

"It's not the book," Dale said, quietly and carefully. "You need to get some sleep. You're not going to do anybody any good if you're too tired to even think straight."

"I know," he said, nodding slowly.

"Listen," Dale said, standing up. "I'm gonna hang around here for a bit. Why don't you crash for a while?"

Chris looked at him for a long moment.

"Seriously."

He smiled a grateful smile as he rose unsteadily to his feet and went to his room.

Dale started to straighten up the apartment. He didn't try to be quiet—it was probably better for Chris to have a reminder that he wasn't alone. He avoided Chris's desk, knowing better than to interfere with the organization of his work. He put mugs and glasses into the sink to soak, emptied the ashtrays and dumped the take-out containers that littered the counter. He threw the loose clothes into the laundry hamper and put out the overflowing garbage.

Finished tidying, Dale leaned into the bedroom doorway. Chris was lying flat on his back, arms thrown out, his breathing rough and deep and regular. Dale looked at him for a few moments, then washed the dishes and let himself out of the apartment, closing the door quietly behind himself, the locks clicking sharply into place.

⋙ ⋘

"We tried to save you."

As the mist creature spoke, other faint voices echoed its words. David could make out other shadowy figures forming in the flickering light from the torch on the floor across the room. He relaxed slightly against the cavern wall.

"Save me?"

The creature had taken on a small, shimmering humanlike form. He seemed to be standing in the air next to David. "We tried."

David could almost read sadness on his grey, indistinct features.

"You saw what the Sunstone did, when you touched it," the voice said. "We tried to stop you."

David remembered the shock, how it had made his heart jump in his chest.

"I thought you were trying to kill me," he said, still suspicious. "I thought you were one of the tests, the traps set by Gafilair." The words came so naturally to him now.

"No, not a test. We've seen what the Sunstone can do . . ." The voice trailed off.

"We touched it, too," said another voice, which sounded as boyish as the first, if not younger.

"We all touched it," said the first figure. "That's why we tried to save you."

And failed, thought David.

"The Queen sent all of you as well?"

The shapes looked to one another again. "Yes and no," the first voice said.

"What does that mean?" David asked, starting to lose patience.

"I'm the only son of Mareigh, who runs The Mermaid's Rest tavern within the walls of the lower city," the first voice said. "Captain Bream came for me one morning. I thought I was in trouble for attacking two of my mother's customers the night before . . ."

As the first voice continued speaking, another voice began. "I'm the only son of Mareigh . . ."

"But instead I was introduced to the Queen, and her adviser, a magus by the name of Loren . . ."

Another voice started to speak. "I am the only son of . . ."

"I was told that I was the only one who could save the kingdom," said the first voice. "That I had been written of in a prophecy . . ."

David struggled with the words, trying to figure out some sort of explanation, anything that might help him make sense of this.

"We were attacked on the road by Berok assassins . . ."

David felt himself growing cold.

"And the morning that we left the inn, the captain called the inn-keeper's wife to him, and said—"

"Tell your husband he lives by mercy of the King," David muttered at the same time the mist creature spoke the words.

The room fell silent as the voices stopped.

"Yes," the first voice said quietly.

"But that's my story," David said weakly.

"That's *the* story," the grey figure said. "That's the story that brought all of us here. It ends with a flash, and death. It ends with the Sunstone."

David had to take a deep breath to hold down the bile he felt rising in his throat. He looked between the grey, misty figures. "But . . . who are you?" he asked.

"We're all that remains," the first voice said, heavy and slow, "of those who have come before you. Each of us the one and only hero who could save the kingdom."

⁓ ⁓

I waited in bed for several minutes after I heard Dale lock the door and walk down the stairs. It was stupid, lying there, faking sleep in case someone checked on me—now I knew how David felt. But this way Dale got to feel like he was looking after me, and I could avoid his skeptical looks about David and his reading.

In the distance, there was the sound of a van door closing, of an engine starting. I crept from bed and skulked over to the window to peer out. Dale's van was gone.

Back at the desk, I tossed the medical books onto the reading chair; the medical stuff was a dead end anyway. Dale had said something near the end of the conversation: "It's not the book." He'd been debating a point I hadn't made, firing a connection that I hadn't even considered.

What if something about *To the Four Directions* itself had caused David's attacks?

I flipped slowly through the pages, trying to find the place where the book had fallen open in the hospital room, the place in the story where David had been overcome.

> *He didn't know if the Stone's powers would protect him, but what other hope did he have?*
> *Pulling himself to his knees, Dafyd reached out for the Sunstone.*

David had been reading a suspenseful section of a novel that he'd been obsessed with for days, and at the moment that the hero of the story is overcome by unknown forces, rendered unconscious and senseless, David had a seizure that left him unconscious, senseless.

It was a bit of a stretch, but was it possible that he could identify so deeply with a character in a book that he might physically respond to the injuries that the character suffered? Could his unconsciousness be his way of responding to the trauma suffered by Dafyd in the book?

The first time I could really recall being that immersed in a book was reading those first Lazarus Took books at my grandmother's place. Those few weeks when I was eleven, I wasn't really in Henderson at all—I was taking to the road with the travelling players in *The World a Stage*, hiding in the woods from the King's Men in *The Road to Honour*, trying to find my sword and my destiny in *Shining Swords and Steel*.

I remembered vividly the way it had felt when I had to stop to have dinner or to go to bed: the real world seemed a strange and disappointing place, and a pale substitute for the life I was living in the stories.

I'm sure that I had had similar experiences before then—Lazarus Took probably came to mind because of David's book—but I couldn't think of any other books that had taken me quite that deep.

It made sense to start with Lazarus Took.

I had just gone to LazarusTook.com when I heard a soft knock at the door at the bottom of the stairs, then the gentle rattling of keys.

Jacqui.

≫ ≪

"You're ghosts," David said in a whisper. "Spirits."

The grey figure who had been speaking the most nodded his head. "I guess we are."

"Then who . . . who are you?"

The spirit looked at him. "The name the book gave me was Matthias. My real name is Matt. Matthew. Matthew Corvin."

Matthew Corvin.

David knew the name, but it took him a moment to place it. "Seattle," he said excitedly, as the pieces fell into place.

The shade nodded.

"You read the book before me. You wrote your name in it!"

"We all read it before you," the spirit said. "That's what brought us here, the same as it brought you."

"Brought us here?" He thought of reading the book, the way the letters didn't move and flip on the page like they usually did when he read. And after a while the words had seemed to disappear altogether: everything had seemed so real, it was like he wasn't reading at all.

A coldness crept into David's belly. "Does that mean . . .?"

He looked at the spirits around him, the grey faces that hinted at what they had looked like as children.

"Does that mean . . .?" He couldn't bring himself to say the word, could barely speak at all. "Does that mean I'm a ghost?"

"No," Matthew said, his voice uncertain for the first time. "No, you're something different."

≫ ≪

"You're up," Jacqui said, surprised. She stepped into the apartment and closed the door. "I thought you'd be asleep."

"Too much to do," he said warily. How long had it been since she'd been in his apartment? Months, probably.

"Did you at least try to get some sleep?"

He straightened up in his desk chair slightly, unsure why her mere presence was making him so tense. "I lay down for a bit."

Her eyes drifted to the desk, to the books and papers on the chair. The medical references. Her eyes went to the laptop screen, but Chris reached out and closed it, trying to make the gesture look casual.

"I called the hospital," she said, and he turned to her. "David's resting. The sedatives have worn off and he seems calmer."

"For the moment," he muttered.

She flinched.

"But what happens when the next seizure hits? And the one after that? How much damage does each of these seizures do to him?"

She gestured helplessly with her hands. "I don't know." "That's just it—nobody has the first idea what's wrong with him. He's supposed to be getting better but he's not, and nobody knows what's going on."

His eyes darted toward the desk, a glance so quick that Jacqui thought she might have imagined it, especially when he fell back deep into his chair, shaking his head.

"I'm sorry," he said, rubbing his eyes. "I'm sorry. I shouldn't be taking this out on you. I'm just . . ."

"I know," she said, almost in a whisper.

Neither of them spoke again for several moments.

"Anyway," she said finally, carefully. "I came over to leave you a note. I'm going back to the hospital."

He stood up. "I'll come with you," he said. "Do you mind waiting a couple of minutes? I should probably change my clothes."

She tried to smile. "You might want to wash your face and comb your hair while you're at it."

"What would I do without you?"

She stood up. "I'll wait for you in the van. Take your time." Taking the keys from the counter, she started down the stairs.

Once she was gone, Chris went to the Biography page at LazarusTook.com and pressed Print. He cleaned himself up as three pages dropped into the hopper.

He folded them into the book and then, before leaving, grabbed a new Moleskine notebook, still in the plastic, out of his top desk drawer.

≈ ≈

"Something different?" David repeated.

"Look at yourself," Matthew Corvin's spirit said.

Lowering the torch a little, David looked down at himself, drawing a short breath at what he saw.

Leather boots. Brown pants. The guardsman's training uniform that Dafyd had been wearing—David understood what it was immediately, though it was different from how he had envisioned it. The fabric was heavier, rougher cut, the boots battered and workmanlike.

"It's not what usually happens," the spirit said, the words seeming to emanate from the mist without any movement now.

"What usually happens?" David asked.

"Usually the hero gets to the bottom of the stairs and sees the Sunstone. He hesitates for a moment, then goes toward it. And as he reaches out for it . . ."

David flinched, remembering the sudden, heart-stopping jolt. "You died," he said, trying to think it through.

"You died too."

For a moment, David couldn't move, couldn't breathe. "What?"

"The blast blew you partway across the room," Matt said. "You weren't breathing. You didn't have a heartbeat. You died."

David looked down at himself again. He didn't look dead.

"After touching the Sunstone, our bodies vanished. We're all that was left," Matt said. "Your body didn't disappear. And then you woke up. Back from the dead."

David flexed the fingers on his left hand. But not really *his* hand. This hand, it was bigger than his own, stronger, rougher. This body had spent its childhood working in a tavern, not sitting at a school desk.

"So why me?" He asked. "What's different for me?"

David was "resting quietly" according to the nurse on duty. His eyes were open and moving, his hands twitching and pushing against the leather restraint.

I leaned over the bed, over his face. "We're back, sport," I whispered, kissing him on the forehead.

David had no reaction, not even the slightest hesitation in the movement of his eyes. He was in his own world.

I straightened up and looked at Jacqui, shaking my head.

She smiled a tight, sad smile. "I'll go check in at the nurses' station."

The waiting was terrible. I could almost hear the drip of the liquid in the IV as each drop pulsed down the clear plastic tube and into my son's bloodstream. People passed in the hallway in flashing blurs of colour and sound, loud voices echoing off the cold walls and floors. Beds slid past, bodies shrouded, faces pale and yellow in the harsh institutional light. My own breathing was too loud, every motion in the chair echoing in the still air. I tried to read David's book, but the words swam off the page.

The only thing I could focus on was David's face: the smoothness of his cheeks, the pale length of his eyelashes, the slackness of his mouth.

When Jacqui returned, I stood up.

"I was thinking of getting something in the cafeteria," I said.

"And having a cigarette." She smiled.

"And having a cigarette."

I took David's book with me, double-checking with my thumb for the pages I'd tucked inside.

"I'm not sure what's different for you," Matthew said. "We didn't save you, David. You still touched the Sunstone. You still died."

"Then why . . . How is it I'm still alive?"

"Something is keeping you alive," Matt said. "Something is keeping your story going."

Something about the way Matt said "story" made David think of his father, the way he would keep reading even after David closed his eyes.

David felt his knees weaken at the thought of his father, and he wished desperately for someplace to sit down, other than the cold wet floor.

He understood.

"You were reading the book yourself, right?"

"Right," Matt said slowly. "What—?"

"I'm not stupid, okay?" David said, more forcefully than he felt. "But I've got a problem reading. So every night . . ." He slowed down. "My dad reads to me. Like a . . . a bedtime story."

He braced himself for Matt's reaction.

Instead, Matt said, "That's cool."

David had no idea how to react.

"What if . . . What if my dad's still reading to me? That would keep the story going, right? When you . . . when you touched the Sunstone, here, you stopped reading there, in the real world. But if my dad is still reading the story to me . . ."

⁂

I sat down as far from the cafeteria doors as I could manage. This early, the room was almost empty. It was mostly doctors and nurses, talking loudly and laughing. Others, "civilians," as Jacqui called them, sat quietly alone or in twos, staring into their food or talking in hushed tones. Their faces were tight and pale, a palpable anguish just below the surface. They looked broken, beaten.

Like me.

I finished a bowl of oatmeal and unfolded the pages that I had tucked into the back of *To the Four Directions*.

Reading the biography carefully, making notes, I suspected that there wasn't much point. Just the life of a writer that nobody remembered. What in this essay, this list of dates and acquaintances, moves and publishers, could possibly help David? What difference did it make when Lazarus Took was born, where he lived, when he died? It was all just trivia.

Or was it?

I flipped back through my notes. There, barely legible in my own handwriting: *Died suddenly, Seaside, Oregon, Sept 14, 1950.*

I flipped to the copyright page of *To the Four Directions*.
"Alexander Press, 1951."

It was probably nothing: books got published after their authors'
death all the time. Hell, V.C. Andrews and Robert Ludlum have made
second careers out of it. The publication had probably been scheduled
already when Took died, and the publisher fulfilled the contract. It
was probably nothing.

But I couldn't shake the feeling that I'd caught someone in a lie.

⫷ ⫸

David thought of the book, the pride on his father's face as he had
handed him the birthday gift, the sound of his father's voice as he read,
the feel of the book in his hands as he read the words for himself.

"The book's not finished," he said.

"What do you mean?" Matt asked him.

"*To the Four Directions*. This part, in this chamber, with the Sunstone.
That's only, I don't know, not even halfway through. There has to be a
mistake."

Matt's features condensed enough to look quizzically at David.

"You don't kill off the main character halfway through."

The look remained on Matt's face.

"My dad, he's a writer," David tried to explain. "We talk about this
stuff sometimes. A writer wouldn't just kill off the main character halfway through the book. Nobody would read any further. He'd end up
having to start again and again with a new . . ." Looking around at the
shades, gathered in a loose knot around him, David saw that his point
seemed to make sense.

"So we shouldn't have died here," Matt said slowly.

"Exactly," David said.

"That means—"

"The story *doesn't* end here. It goes on. It has to."

David turned toward the Sunstone, the ruby glimmering like a spot
of wet blood on the wall.

⫷ ⫸

"You look like you're feeling a little better," Jacqui said when I came back that evening. She was sitting in the chair by the bed, reading a copy of *Maclean's* she had probably purloined from the nurse's station. "Did you sleep?"

"A bit," I lied, setting the book on the bed at David's feet. "How's he doing?"

Jacqui's smile disappeared.

"More of the same," I said.

"Yeah." She flipped the magazine onto the table. "The nurses came by to take his vitals and change his IV pack." She pointed at the bulging new bag of clear fluid. "It's shift change coming up."

I was getting to be almost as familiar with the hospital's routines and schedules as she was. "I thought maybe I would read him a bit of his story."

She almost smiled as she stood up and edged past the bed.

This was taking a toll on her. Jacqui's face was hollow and etched with deep lines of worry. She hadn't been eating, and she looked like she'd lost weight.

"Half an hour?" she said.

"Sure, that'll be fine."

I watched her as she walked away, then sat down.

My watch read 7:50. Just about our usual storytime. A little less than twenty-four hours since his last seizure. I studied him carefully. Was he flexing harder, longer, now than he had been earlier in the day? It was impossible to be sure.

"Hey there, sport," I said as I looked for the page where we had left off. I hadn't marked it: superstitiously, perhaps, I couldn't bring myself to move the bookmark from where he had left it in the back of the book.

"It's about that time," I continued. "Are you ready for bed? Are you ready for your story?" Observing the rituals, imagining his answers.

I found my place and started to read.

Within seconds I wanted to look up, to check on what effect, if any, the reading was having on him, but I forced myself to keep going, to give him several minutes of pure, uninterrupted listening.

When I finally did look, David was perfectly still, his eyes unmoving, his face loose, his arms limp at his sides. I felt both relieved and vindicated. As I watched, his eyelids sank shut.

"You like that, don't you?" I asked him. "It does something to you. This book." I held it up, as if he would be able to see it.

I closed the book and set it on the bed in front of me, then reached for the magazine Jacqui had abandoned on the table. I flipped it open, turned toward the back to the review section.

"I'm sorry about this," I said quietly. "But I have to check."

I started to read the review out loud. I wasn't paying attention to the words at all, and after less than a minute of reading, David's eyes were flickering, his fists clenching. Slowly, at first, but the motion grew more intense as I watched, his forearms flexing and pushing against the restraints, the muscles in his neck drawing and contracting, his lips pulsing and wavering. His back started to arch, his head jerking from one side to the other.

I threw the magazine back on the table and fumbled for our place in the book. I was out of breath as I read the first few lines, but I slowed and paced myself, calmed my voice.

Within a few lines, David began to settle again. His body seemed to sigh as it sank back into the bed.

By the time Jacqui got back, everything was disturbingly normal: just the two of us enjoying the nightly ritual. She stood silently at the end of the bed as I finished reading.

When I closed the book, she whispered, "How did it go?" as if afraid of waking him.

I gestured vaguely at the bed. I didn't want to lie to her outright, but I knew that there was no way I could tell her about the book again without it turning into a fight.

"He seems pretty relaxed now," I said.

≽ ≼

David lowered his torch to look at the Sunstone, but he kept a safe distance, wary of it still. His hands shook.

"It doesn't make any sense for me to be trapped here. For any of us to be trapped here," he said as he leaned in closer to the wall. There were carvings, faint, above the silver circle that held the stone. "There's something there," he muttered.

"But the Sunstone . . ." Matt said.

David took a half-step forward, trying to make out the markings.

"David." Matt sounded frustrated. "What are you going to do?"

He wasn't sure how to explain it. At best, it was only a guess. "We all got here by reading the same book, right?"

"Right."

"We've got to get back into the story. I think that's the only way to get out. To go through the book, all the way to the end."

"For you," Matt said sadly.

"What?"

"You said 'we,' but we can't. We've tried to get out, to escape, but we can't set foot on the stairs. It's like there's a wall holding us in. If you're right . . ." He seemed to sigh, and David looked past him at the other shades, hanging limply in the still air. "Only you can get to the end."

"I'm sorry," David said quietly.

Matt's shade turned to look at the others, then back to David. "Maybe if you make it through . . ."

"If the Queen gets the Sunstone," David added.

"If you can make it to the end, maybe . . . maybe it will be a happy ending for all of us."

David could feel his eyes burning with tears. His voice cracked when he said, "I hope so."

⁂

Pulling into the driveway, Jacqui turned off the engine and sat in the silence. She stared up at the faint glow in the window above the garage. It was well past midnight: was he hard at work, head bent over one of his notebooks, pen in hand? Or had he fallen asleep in his reading chair again, his book falling to his lap, the way it always used to, back when . . .

Her hands were shaking as she punched the numbers on her cell phone. It took him a couple of rings to answer, and with each passing second she fought the desire to hang up.

"Is something wrong?" he asked, without saying hello.

She imagined the worry on his face.

"No, no. Everything's fine. David . . . there were no problems."

"That's good."

Then they both waited in silence. Jacqui imagined that she could see his faint shadow on the curtains, but it was probably a trick of the light.

"I came home," she said faintly.

"I heard the van."

"There was nothing . . . He's stable, and . . ." She wasn't sure if she could actually hear him moving over the line, but a moment later the curtains parted and he was leaning toward the window, cupping one hand against the glass.

"Did I wake you?" she asked. "I wasn't sure if I should—"

"I was just getting ready for bed."

"That's good." She looked from his window to the front door of the house, then back to his window. It was hard to see his face with the light behind him, but she imagined their eyes meeting. "Do you— Would you like to sleep in the house? Tonight. With me?"

He was silent for so long she wondered if they had been cut off. She almost hoped they had.

"Just to sleep," she said, rushing in to fill the space between them. "I just—"

"Sure," he said, with a quiet intimacy and understanding that stirred a deep part of her.

Her hands were shaking harder as she opened the van door.

≥≈ ≈≤

David bent low, as close as he dared to the Sunstone. In the wavering torchlight, the symbols carved into the wall were difficult to see.

"I can't quite read it."

"Let me try," Matt said, as he drifted past David. "Hold the torch closer."

Instinctively, David reached out to keep him back. "Matt, don't." His hand slid through the grey mist, no more substantial than cold morning fog.

"I think I'll be all right," Matt said. "It can't kill me again, right?"

David extended the torch until it was almost touching the wall. "What does it say?" he asked excitedly.

"Hang on a sec," Matt said. "It's pretty faint."

David leaned in closer, despite himself.

"Okay, it's like a little poem:

> WITH MY TOUCH I FORSAKE ALL CLAIM,
> AND TO YOU I FREELY GIVE.
> FOR YOUR GLORY I GIVE MY HEART.
> FOR YOUR STRENGTH I GIVE MY STRENGTH.
> FOR YOUR LIFE, I GIVE MY LIFE."

David waited for him to continue.

Instead Matt straightened up and slid back. "That's it," he said. "That's all there is."

"But what does it mean?" David asked.

"You've got me."

"It sounds like an oath. The sort of thing the captain might say."

Matt nodded thoughtfully. "It does. But it doesn't really help you, does it?"

"No," David said, disappointed. He rubbed his hands together, trying to psych himself up. There was no point in delaying.

JACQUI FELL ASLEEP WITH ME holding her, lying on my back as she nested into me, her head resting on my shoulder, my arm loose over her, the smell of her hair, her skin, enfolding and enveloping me. I lay there as she drifted into sleep, and as she unconsciously rolled away, back to huddling on her side of the bed, the way she preferred to sleep.

I spent most of the night awake, listening to her slow, steady breathing.

When the numbers on the clock radio changed silently to 4:00, I slipped out of bed. Jacqui didn't move or even sigh as I stood up and took my clothes out to the hallway to dress.

The next few minutes all unfolded like a memory, or a dream. The silent walk through the darkened house. Lifting the doorknob on the back door a little as I closed it to dull the sound of the lock clicking shut. Smoking a cigarette on the back walk, looking into the dark mystery of the yard and at the second floors of the neighbouring houses, all that was visible over the cedar fence. The ritual of letting myself into the office, turning on the lights, making a pot of coffee.

It was the way my life had been, once.

When I turned on the desk-lamp, any illusion of normalcy vanished at the sight of the stacks of medical texts, the black notebook I was using to keep track of information, writing to make sense of my thoughts.

I flipped idly through the notebook, hoping for some lightning flash of inspiration to strike, some arc of connection, of synchronicity, to pull it all together.

It didn't happen.

I logged on to the laptop and went back to LazarusTook.com. The biographical essay had been thorough enough that I was disappointed to find that the rest of the site was fairly pedestrian: a few covers, an excerpt from each book.

No luck with the author; what about the publisher?

Searching "Alexander Press" brought no hits. Adding Took's name, then Belden, Oregon, didn't help any. A search for "Took Publishers" didn't work.

I tried Sprite Press, the house that had published the four paperbacks I had read at my grandmother's house.

Sprite Press—Founded in 1949 by Trevor Williams following the success of Penguin's expansion of the paperback market, Sprite focused primarily on science fiction and fantasy reprints. Although never as successful as Ballantine or DelRey, the house's peak years came in the 1960s with the widespread interest in its specialty genres. At the height of its success, following the publication of JM Chadwick's *The Grail Travellers*, Williams sold his company to Davis & Keelor, where he continued to operate it as a specialty imprint until 1983. Williams died in 1986.

Williams's name was a link, but his Biography page made no mention of Took, unless one considered the inclusiveness of the phrase "republication of mid-level British genre writers."

I scratched a few notes into the black notebook.

The mention of Davis & Keelor was probably a dead end. With the publication of the four novels coming decades before the sale of Sprite, the books were probably long out of print, rights reverting to Took's estate. Still, it was something to pursue.

I checked my watch—not even nine-thirty in New York. No point in calling.

I brought up the D&K website and hit the link for General Information. The Contact Us button opened a new email window.

Good morning,

As a freelance journalist in Victoria, Canada, I have recently
begun writing a feature piece about "forgotten" writers from the
1940s and 1950s. I was wondering if you could provide me
with any information with which to contact the estate of
Lazarus Took, a writer who was published by Sprite Press in
the 1960s. I realize that this was prior to Sprite's purchase by
D&K, but I'm hoping

I leaned back in my chair. What was I doing?

The publisher wasn't going to be able to tell me anything, and even
if they could connect me with Took's estate, what could I possibly ask?
I was grasping at straws.

It was just a book, that's all.

What the hell was I thinking?

I finished the note with a few half-truths about hoping to get in
touch with some of the authors I was writing about, and hit Send. A
wave of exhaustion washed over me, and I closed my eyes just for a
moment, the book resting in my lap.

"David! Remember what happened last time," Matt said, alarmed. "You
can't touch the Sunstone."

As if David would ever be able to forget that.

That wasn't you, he thought to himself. That was Dafyd. None of
this is real.

But it was. David knew that this was as real as the life he had left
behind.

"Of course I remember," he said. "But I have to try. It's the only way
to get out of here, to make the story keep going. Can you think of any
other way?" He tried to sound confident and strong, tried not to let on
just how much the thought of touching that stone again terrified him.

Even though he couldn't see Matt's eyes, David could feel him looking at him for a long moment, before the mist slid, slowly, out of his
path.

The Sunstone shimmered in the silver plate. He held his breath, his gaze never wavering as he steeled himself and reached out.

≫ ≪

One of the nurses shook her finger at me good-naturedly as I hurried away from David's room, pulling my ringing phone out of my jacket pocket.

"Chris? It's John."

The voice was gruff, familiar, though I rarely heard it. My editor at the *Vancouver Sun* usually e-mailed.

"John," I said. "How are you?"

We exchanged pleasantries. I didn't volunteer anything. Jacqui and I had decided to keep the news of David's "condition"—as she called it—close, at least until we had more information to give.

"Any problems with your e-mail?" There was a bemused tone to his voice.

"Not that I know of."

"Then is there any chance I might get your column sometime soon?"

At first I didn't really understand what he was asking. Had I committed to an extra column? Was there a special—?

And then it hit me. "Oh shit," I muttered. "It's late."

"Only if you believe in press deadlines and that sort of thing," he drawled, teasing me.

"Sorry, John," I said. "I completely lost track of time."

"Must be nice to be a freelancer."

"No, it's . . . it's been a bad couple of days. David's in the hospital."

"Jesus, Chris, why didn't you say something?" All trace of amusement had vanished. "What happened?"

As I explained about David's seizures and collapse, I was sharply aware of myself crafting the story, constructing the narrative. We had told only a few people what had happened—Dale, David's school. Jacqui's parents and sister, my mother and brothers, all lived too far away to be here right away, but we'd been on the phone with them regularly since early Sunday morning. I became aware, as I was talking to John, that I was structuring what would become the official version of what had happened.

"Jesus," he repeated. "Last thing you should be worrying about is a newspaper column."

"No—"

"We'll run something off the wire," he insisted. "Run a cutline saying that you're away for a few weeks."

For years, I had filed a column every week. Even when we were on vacation. It was practically a ritual. Reluctant as I was to let my obligation slide, it was like having a weight lifted from me.

"Thanks, John. I appreciate it."

"All right," he said, gruff again. "Listen, give your wife a kiss for me. Tell her I'm thinking about her. If I can do anything, you just let me know."

"I will."

～ ～

David braced himself and took a deep breath. He had no choice. He couldn't face Bream and Loren without the stone. And he couldn't ask for their help: this was his quest, right down to the handprints on the wall.

Dafyd's quest.

He let his fingers brush against the stone.

There was no spark, no shock, just the cool, smooth surface of the gem, and the sound of his breath escaping from him.

He turned to Matt. "Nothing happened."

The mist figure smiled.

David turned back to the wall. The blood-red stone was set into the silver plate, the centre point of a complex geometrical design. It was firmly embedded: David tried to pull it free, but it didn't move. He shook his head. No tools, no way to get the stone loose. Then he took a closer look at the silver disk.

"It looks like there are some grooves here," he said, and Matthew drifted back toward him. "Do you see?"

He pointed at two half-moon indentations carved into the stone wall at the edge of the silver disk, where the *1* and the *7* would have been on a clock face.

"I wonder . . ." Stretching his hand, he could just manage to slip the tips of his thumb and forefinger into the two grooves.

"It's very thick," he said. "I'm just gonna . . ." He gripped the edge of the disk, holding it tight, and pulled.

To his surprise, it slid forward about an inch, then stopped with a sharp click.

"Dammit!" He shook his fingers for a moment, sore from the effort, then tried again, but the disk didn't budge.

"It's stuck."

"Try turning it," Matt suggested.

The disk extended far enough from the wall now that David could get a better grip. "Lefty loosy," he muttered as he started to twist.

The disk turned easily in the wall.

"It's working," he said excitedly. He kept his grip tight, expecting the silver plate to pop free at any moment, but it just kept turning, protruding farther and farther from the wall with every revolution.

"How thick is this thing?" he muttered.

Without warning, the disk froze into place again with another click. Gripping with two hands now, he pulled.

The disk slid from the wall easily and smoothly. What he had thought was a silver plate, a setting for the Sunstone, was actually the top of a silver cylinder, a shiny tube about the size of a large soup can.

David leaned his torch against the wall and held his hand under the tube. He didn't want it falling to the floor. It was a wise decision.

The tube burst free of the wall, heavier than David had been expecting, propelled out of the hole by the force of the jet of water behind it. The white froth drove the cylinder painfully against his chest, and knocked David backwards halfway across the chamber.

༖ ༒

I told Jacqui it had been John on the phone.

"Deadline," she said, resigned.

I didn't tell her that he had let me off the hook for the column. Instead, I took a cab home.

Sitting down at the computer, I saw John's two messages, along with a note from my agent's assistant, confirming dinner with Roger when I was in New York the following week. I made another mental note to cancel the trip.

There were two messages remaining, one from rights@daviskeelor.com, one from webmaster@lazarustook.com. I clicked on the one from the publisher first. Thankfully, I wasn't expecting much.

"Thank you for your message. Your e-mail is very important to us . . ."

I closed the window without reading the rest.

I clicked on the second message, expecting nothing more than an auto-reply from the Took site as well. I was shocked when a lengthy note opened on my screen:

Mr. Knox –

I cannot express how pleased I am that you found LazarusTook.com, and that you were impressed with the website. As I am sure you will understand, it really is a labour of love, and it does thrill me to hear from readers like yourself. Especially readers who still remember the works of Lazarus Took who, as you rightly note, has been largely forgotten by modern readers. I'm not sure why that is: one would think that in this age of Harry Potter, and with renewed interest in J.R.R. Tolkien and C.S. Lewis, there might be more attention paid to a writer like Lazarus Took.

By way of responding to your questions, I have something of a confession to make: I do not come by my interest in Lazarus Took by chance. Lazarus was my grandfather. Although I never knew him myself, I grew up with him as a significant presence in my life: his stories, both his books and the stories of his life, were like mother's milk to me, and my work on the website is just a small way of keeping his memory alive. I hope you'll forgive me for not mentioning on the site that this was a "family project"—I wanted it to have as much credibility as possible.

I turned to a fresh page in my notebook and took the pen out of my pocket.

> To reply to a few of your questions: yes, I would be delighted to be interviewed for your article. I'll answer your questions to the best of my knowledge and, failing that, I do have some of my grandfather's papers to draw upon. E-mail is fine, or by telephone. My contact information is below.
>
> Lastly—as far as I know, the four published novels are the bulk of my grandfather's work. There are unpublished stories in the papers, and notes for other planned novels, but no books beyond the four which you remember so fondly. He did write some ritual guides when he was involved with the Brotherhood of the Stone, although he is not credited as their author. I don't believe he ever wrote or published under a pseudonym.
>
> I look forward to speaking with you further.
>
> With all best wishes,
>
> C. Agatha Took (but my friends call me Cat!)

I sat back in my chair and stared at the screen. I had expected at best a terse and unhelpful response from the webmaster, who I had imagined to be a middle-aged male book collector somewhere in Scandinavia, a devotee of children's literature from the ancestral home of children's literature. But here I was, in correspondence with Took's granddaughter, who was not only being helpful, but had the keys to the archives.

From the sound of her note, though, it didn't seem like she knew anything about *To the Four Directions*. How was it possible that a relative devoted to his memory and his work had never heard of it?

I scratched a few notes into my notebook, then leaned forward to the keyboard.

Hello Cat, I typed, I hope you don't mind me calling you that.

Jacqui's telephone rang partway through the afternoon; she glanced at the display before she pressed the button to connect.

"Chris," she said.

"God, it freaks me out when you do that."

She grinned; she couldn't help it.

"You can't use your cell in David's room," he said. "Where are you?"

"In line at Tim Hortons. Should I get you something?"

"Not quite yet," he said, his words measured.

"It's not going well?"

"Not really," he said, his voice faint, almost overwhelmed by a sudden noise on his end of the line.

"What was that?" she asked.

"Some idiot in a tricked-out car."

"Aren't you at home?"

"I'm out front having a cigarette, checking the sidewalk for inspiration."

"Why don't you just tell John that you can't do it this week? I'm sure he'd understand."

"Nah, I'm all right. It shouldn't be too long. I've got a few ideas. I'm just waiting for it to gel."

"It's just—there's a physiotherapist coming and it would be—"

"A physiotherapist?"

"They're worried about his muscles atrophying, and they want to show us some exercises to do with him. When do you think you'll be back?" she asked again, taking another step forward in line.

"I'll get this done and I'll be there as soon as I can. All right?"

She wanted to tell him that he could bring his laptop in, that he could work in the room, close by. Instead, she said, "Whatever works for you."

There was a long pause. "I'll see you later, then," he said.

"Yeah." She folded the phone shut and slid it back into her pocket as she stepped to the counter.

I pressed the button to disconnect the call, and stepped through the front door of Prospero's Books. The bell over the door jangled as I walked in.

"You're late, Chris. I thought maybe something was wrong with the universe." Brian's smile was unforced; he seemed genuinely happy to see me.

My expression must have given me away, though.

"Something *is* wrong with the universe, though, isn't it?" He stood up behind his desk, his heavy body lurching over the stacks of books.

He didn't say a word as I gave him the same story I had given John earlier. I was already getting better at telling it.

Brian was shaking his head when I finished. "And it was just his birthday too, right? He's eleven now?"

He had given me the opening that I needed. "Yeah, eleven. It was his birthday last week." I reached into my shoulder bag. "That's actually what I wanted to talk to you about." I laid the book on the desk between us. "Do you remember this?"

He picked it up, looked at the spine, turned it over in his hand. "You bought this for your son a couple of weeks ago. 'Something other than *The Lord of the Rings*.' I remember that, sure." He set the book back down on the desk. "Why? Is there something wrong with it?"

I shook my head. "No, there's nothing wrong with it. I'm just trying to figure out what it is. Do you happen to recall where you got it from?"

He looked at me as if he might start laughing. "Jesus, Chris, you know this place." He gestured at the crowded bookshelves and the stacks teetering on his desk. "Do you really expect me to remember where one book came from?"

"Actually, I do," I said, one book aficionado to another.

"Chis, I'd like to help, but . . ." He stopped himself. "What do you mean you're trying to figure out what it is?"

I had no idea how much I could tell him. "I'm not really sure," I confessed. "David fell in love with the book when he started reading it. I tried to find some history on it and I couldn't. It doesn't appear on any of the online databases; there's a website for the author and there's no mention of it there. I can't seem to track it down anywhere."

He looked at me for a long moment without speaking. "And you're looking into this to take your mind off your son in the hospital?"

I didn't say anything. Probably better to have him think me overcome by grief, obsessing over something other than David.

"Anything you can remember, Brian, anything at all. It would be a big help to me."

He examined the book, flipping to the inside of the front cover.

"I do remember this," he said. He held up the book to me, open to the front endpapers. "This name right here?"

I'd looked at the inscription dozens of times: *Matthew Corvin, Seattle, 1976.* "What about it?"

"I remember thinking to myself that it was going to be a crying shame to have that writing in the book if it turned out to be worth anything." He hefted the book in his hand. "It was in pretty good shape, except for that. But then I punched it into some of the collectors' databases and there wasn't any listing for it, so I figured it wasn't worth anything anyway." He shrugged, looked at the book ruefully, as if staring at a missed opportunity. "You're telling me that this is too rare to even have a profile on the collectors' market?"

"I don't know," I said honestly. "I can't find any mention of it. Do you remember where you got it?" I tucked the book back into my bag.

"Portland," he said, sitting back down. "There's a dealer down there I do business with sometimes. More of a collector, really. He'll give me a call every few months when it comes time to cull his collection a bit, make space for new acquisitions. I've gotten a nice couple of Hemingway firsts from him over the years."

"You bought it from him?"

"Bought it? Nah. He always throws in a couple of extras. Nothing really valuable, you can be sure of that. A little something to help me break even on the shipping and the customs fees. It's a nice arrangement."

"Can you put me in touch with him?" I asked, trying to keep the excitement out of my voice.

Brian shook his head. "He's a really private guy."

His refusal took the wind out of me. "Brian, I wouldn't ask if—"

He held up a hand to stop me. "But," he said firmly, lowering his hand before continuing. "I could send him an e-mail if you'd like. If you have any particular questions."

The relief hit me so hard it almost brought tears to my eyes.

"I have to warn you, he's not the most dedicated correspondent."

"That's okay," I said. "At least I know there's someone out there who might know something."

Uncapping a pen, he asked, "So what do you want to know?"

"Everything," I said, without hesitation. "Anything he can tell me. What it is, where it came from, how he got it."

Brian jotted down a few notes in handwriting worse than my own.

"Thanks, Brian," I said. "I really appreciate it."

"Don't expect any miracles," he said, re-capping his pen.

⇜ ⇝

"What is that?" David choked, spitting out a mouthful of water as he struggled to his feet.

The water shooting from the hole in the wall had buffeted him toward the far wall of the chamber with the force of a fire hose, but he had managed to retain his grip on the cylinder.

"It's the river," Matt answered, shouting to be heard.

"The river?" David crammed the cylinder inside his shirt, tucking it under his left arm.

"This chamber is under the river," Matt said, as the shade drifted across the room toward David.

Already there were several inches of water on the floor. David's boots were soaked, his feet chilled, his clothes sticking cold to him.

"That wall," David said, pointing toward the hole left by the cylinder. "It's like a dam. It's holding back the water."

"It was," Matt said, looking at the lump under David's shirt. "I guess you were right. About the story going on."

David didn't take any pleasure or comfort in the words. As he watched, cracks started to appear, trailing out from the hole in the wall like the cracks in a windshield. "That wall's not going to hold," he shouted. "We've got to go!"

He turned for the stairway, expecting Matt to follow, but he didn't.

"Come on," David said, the water spilling over the tops of his boots now, water starting to seep through the cracks in the wall. "We've gotta go!"

"I can't," Matt said. "Remember?"

A sound almost like ripping fabric shook the chamber as a huge crack opened from the hole in the centre of the wall to the upper corner, spewing torrents of water into the room.

"It's your story now. You have to finish it."

➳ ➳

There was another e-mail waiting for me from Cat when I got home from Prospero's. Another lengthy reply.

Chris,

I'm fine with you calling me Cat, so long as I can call you Chris. ;)

You've probably got a deadline to meet so I wanted to get back to you quickly. Besides, I don't get many opportunities to talk about Lazarus these days. I like to seize these chances when they come along. I trust you don't mind.

You've certainly asked some interesting questions: I'll do my best to answer them from what I recall hearing my mother and grandmother say, and if you need more details I'll venture into the archives.

The reason for Lazarus's move to the United States has never been entirely clear to me. Coming as it did so soon after the war, I suspect it had something to do with that. Lazarus and Cora were great believers in personal liberty, and I think the experience of Europe in wartime, and the restrictions they suffered at that time even in England, soured them on the land of their birth. I don't think it's any accident that they ended up in Oregon—we've always had a strong live-and-let-live attitude here.

I stopped reading and picked up my pen, writing the work *Oregon* into my notebook, circling it several times.

In the spirit of full disclosure, I must admit that there were always whispers in the family about something that had happened in England, an accident of some sort that created a certain amount of notoriety which apparently plagued them for a long time. This may also have contributed to their decision to leave England, but I don't really have any concrete information—it wasn't something that was much talked about.

As to the question of magic—that's a long story, and I'm not really clear on a lot of the details. I do know that both Lazarus and Cora, in their younger years, were members of a group called the Order of the Golden Sunset, a group run by a man named William Thorne, with some vague lineage to Aleister Crowley and the Order of the Golden Dawn. They left this group in the 1930s, I believe, along with several other members of the group, forming a new group called the Brotherhood of the Stone. Again, this is not something that was spoken of much when I was growing up.

I wrote the name of the Order down in my notebook, then scrawled: *Stone = Sunstone???*

The sense that I got, however, was that Lazarus wished he could have the same renown in magical circles as Thorne, but he lacked the selfish sadism which contributed so much to Thorne's legend. I don't think Lazarus was a wizard or anything like that—as I mentioned, he wrote volumes of lore and ritual for the Order, but my impression is that he was more of an observer. A "pagan-type earth-devotee" as you put it in your e-mail. Suffice it to say, I never heard of any blood sacrifices or satanic orgies, but we did observe the solstices and equinoxes when I was growing up.

I'm sorry for going on so long—as I mentioned, I don't get a lot of opportunity to talk about Lazarus.

Yes, I represent the literary estate. My mother let his books go out of print before I was born, and they've stayed that way ever since. Frankly, it's a matter of laziness and nervousness on my part—I simply don't have any idea how the publishing industry works or how one would go about getting the books published again. Do you have any advice or connections that you can share?

As for Lazarus's papers, there are still pages and outlines and books from his time here in Oregon, but he sold his earlier papers to the Hunter Barlow Library in New York prior to coming to the United States. In fact, I suspect the sale helped finance the move. If you're ever down this way, I'd be delighted to show you what I have, though.

I suppose I should sign off here—I'm starting to feel like one of those little old ladies who prattles on and on about things you probably have no interest in. I'm sorry about that. Please feel free to get in touch with me if you have any more questions.

With best wishes,

Cat

Oh, and no, I've never heard of Alexander Press. Is that a publisher that might be appropriate for Lazarus's books?

I leaned back in the chair, rubbing my eyes. It took a while to sort out what I was feeling, to try to separate my inherent interest in a good story from my need for answers. This correspondence with Cat was interesting, but she clearly didn't know anything about her grandfather's fifth book. And there were much more important matters at hand.

Matters of life and death.

The ringing of the cell phone woke me up. I was startled to find myself in my reading chair, *To the Four Directions* open on my lap.

"Chris? Where the hell are you?" Jacqui's voice was ragged, and I could hear the thickness of tears in her throat.

"What's wrong?" I asked, adrenaline surging, burning off the vestiges of unexpected sleep.

"David's had another seizure. Where the hell have you been?"

I glanced at the clock on the kitchen wall and my heart plummeted. 8:51 p.m.

"There has to be a way," David cried.

"Maybe," Matt said as the raging river filled the small chamber.

"What?" David said. There could be only seconds before the wall collapsed.

"This might not work—"

"Matt," David warned, as another ripping sound echoed through the chamber, a crack suddenly running to the opposite corner of the wall.

The spirit drifted close to him, the mist coalescing into a face, looking back at him.

"Do you trust me?" Matt asked.

David nodded.

"Then breathe out. Push all the air out of your lungs."

The stone screamed as the wall cracked again. The solid rock seemed to bulge under the river's pressure.

David tried to focus on his breathing, on pushing all the air out of his lungs. He flexed his diaphragm until it hurt, until he felt completely empty.

"Now breathe in," Matt urged him. "Breathe deep."

The air rushed into his empty lungs, sweet and cool.

The mist in front of him dissipated, as if blown asunder by the force of the water.

"Now run!" Matt screamed, as the wall exploded.

I darted out of the elevator, my bag swinging on my shoulder as I raced toward David's room, and I didn't even see Jacqui as I rounded a corner.

"Chris," she called from behind me.

When I turned around she was standing motionless, her arms folded across her chest. Her face was pale, except for the red, moist patches around her eyes.

"Where were you?" she choked as she stepped toward me. She pushed against my chest, slapping it with the flat of her hands. "Where were you? Where . . .?" She kept repeating herself, kept slapping at me. Fresh tears rolled unchecked down her cheeks.

I did nothing to stop her.

When the anger gave way to anguish, she fell into my arms, small and defenceless, her back heaving.

"I'm sorry," I said. "I lost track of the time." I couldn't tell her what I had actually been doing: I had to add another lie.

"I can't do this alone," she whispered.

"Is he okay?"

She shook her head. "He's bad. He's really bad."

My eyes slipped closed as I tried to fight the sense of vertigo that came over me, the feeling of the world opening up under my feet like it might swallow me whole.

"It was the worst one yet. I had to come out here while they . . ."

"Should we go back in?"

She hesitated for a moment, then nodded.

Two nurses and a doctor were leaning over him, their backs to the door. Jacqui and I waited. When they straightened up and turned toward us, I had to look away. I could never have prepared myself for the sight of my son.

David was the same white-grey as the hospital sheet. His lower lip was thick, bloody and swollen, and stitched in a wide U almost its complete width. It looked like a second smile, a black, rough line under his lips.

"He bit through his lip," Jacqui said. "And his tongue. There was blood . . . there was blood everywhere."

I brought my arm up around her shoulders, eased her closer to me.

His hands were twitching and flexing. There was a new leather strap across his chest, holding him fast to the bed.

"He dislocated his shoulder as well," Jacqui choked. "It took four orderlies to hold him down so Jane could give him an injection."

The doctor looked familiar, and he stepped toward us. "Mr. Knox, I'm Dr. McKinley. I treated David when he was admitted the other night." The doctor from the ER. "I'm guessing that Jacqui has brought you up to speed."

"A bit," I said.

He nodded. "I've got a call out to Dr. Rutherford. He should be in in a bit. I'm—" He paused, as if trying to decide how to proceed, and whether he should. "I'm very concerned about the increasing severity of the seizures that your son is suffering. We've got him on Dilantin—that's a powerful anti-epileptic." He shook his head. "With the dosage he's on now, we should be seeing a reduction in the attacks."

He glanced at his watch, and at his colleagues who were standing between him and the door. "I've got to get back down to the ER, but if anything happens—" He looked at me, then at Jacqui. "Have me paged."

The moment the doctor and nurses were out the door, Jacqui dipped a tissue in the plastic cup of water and brought it to David's lips.

"Hey, Davy," she said, her voice a singsong whisper. "Let's get you cleaned up a little bit, okay? I'll be gentle."

She touched the tissue to his lips, lifting the blood away in the subtlest of increments. How many times had I watched her scrub something away from David's mouth with a tissue, dampened with the tip of her tongue? But never with such attention, such tender care.

"It's not coming off," she said, in a voice I had never heard from her before, a sound of barely suppressed anguish. "It's not coming off."

"It looks okay."

"It's not coming off," she said, her voice breaking. "I can't do it," she wept. "I can't get it off. I can't do it. I can't do anything."

꙾ ꙾

The wall exploded. Water smashed through the chamber. The remaining shades, drifting near the edges of the room, dissolved with the force. The torch winked out, plunging the chamber into absolute darkness.

David stubbed his toe on the edge of a step, stumbling a little, catching himself with the hand not holding the cylinder. A wind out of the chamber urged him up the stairs as the roar of the water grew behind him.

He held his free hand out as he ran, wishing he still had the torch. It was so dark, and he didn't dare slow down. His hand and shoulder bounced and scraped off the stone walls as the stairway twisted upward.

He could hear the water coming closer, the full force of the river swallowing the Sunstone's chamber, then forcing itself up the narrow stairway, the pressure building and building, like soda foaming up into a bottle's neck. He could picture the water bursting out of the cave and washing his battered body all the way back to the castle.

His chest burned and heaved; his legs screamed in agony.

"Come on, David," Matt's voice urged, very close to him. "The water's getting closer."

"I know," he gasped, through gritted teeth.

The staircase, which had seemed endless when he was climbing down, seemed even longer now. And then a hint of light appeared far above his head. He redoubled his efforts, knowing that the end was in sight.

The water was so close now that he could smell it, a cold metallic odour that would have made him choke if he had been able to take a deep breath.

"Almost there," Matt said. "Almost there."

With every step the light grew larger, brighter, a sliver of warmth seeming to expand as he watched it, until it resolved itself into a doorway, a tall rectangle of daylight.

David threw himself through it.

The light was almost blinding, but David couldn't stop. Tucking the cylinder into his shirt, he ran across the entry chamber, the thunder of the river seeming to surround him now. The water exploded through the door at the top of the stairs, a silver-grey jet that shot into the room.

The wall of water chased David across the stone bridge, down the short corridor, and, without even a momentary pause, right off the edge of the canyon wall, into the cool air above the river.

≋ ≋

"I'm sorry," he whispered into David's hair, worrying that someone might overhear. Chris had sent Jacqui, tearful still and barely coherent, home in a cab to get some rest. "I'm sorry. I meant to get back, I really did."

He was aware of how pathetic it all sounded.

"Can I make it up to you a little?" He reached for his bag and pulled out the book. "Can I read you a little bit now? I know it's late, but I thought you might like to hear some anyway."

He started from where they had left off the day before. As he read he kept glancing up, comforted by the way David's hands stopped moving as he read, the way his body relaxed.

He read longer than he should have, long past the point where the words stopped making sense, long past the point where his mouth stopped moving, where the words stopped coming from him.

The next time the nurse checked on David, she found Chris asleep in the chair beside the bed, an old book fallen open on his lap.

The nurse smiled to herself and thought of small mercies as she checked David's pulse and temperature, taking care not to wake his father. When she left, she dimmed the light and closed the curtain as quietly as she could.

꙲ ꙮ

As David's feet stepped into the air high over the river, he thought of two things.

The first was those old cartoons that his dad had made him watch with the coyote and the roadrunner, when the coyote runs off a cliff and hangs, motionless, in the air for a moment, until the full reality of his situation hits him, and only then, with wide eyes and scrambling feet, does he fall with a puff of dust.

And he remembered his swimming instructor from last summer, that day his class had first gone off the high-diving board.

"Right now we're just jumping," he had said. "No fancy diving. And no belly flops." Everyone had laughed. "Keep your body straight, and your feet together. You can wrap your arms around your chest if you want, it doesn't really matter."

David did as he had been told.

"Take a deep breath, and remember, stay relaxed. Don't tense up. That's how people hurt themselves."

David inhaled as deeply as he could and willed his legs to soften, his knees to unlock. He didn't let himself think about how high up he was, or the possibility of rocks in the river under him—there was nothing he could do now but close his eyes.

He entered the water with a cold, sharp shock. He had to fight to hold his breath, and flailed instinctively, struggling against the current to get up to the surface.

His breath exploded from him the moment he reached the air. He took a deep breath, struggled to open his eyes.

He didn't have time to take another breath before the water from the cave crashed down on him, pushing him deep below the surface of the river, spinning him out of control.

VI

I GOT BACK TO MY apartment at about four-thirty the next morning. It was cold and quiet, the way I had liked it when I used to come in every morning to write.

I sat at my desk.

If Took's granddaughter had no idea about *To the Four Directions*, I'd exhausted every possibility, hadn't I?

I flipped through the notes that I had been taking, and it occurred to me: every possibility save one. The e-mail from the rights department at Davis & Keelor had been useless, and I knew that I probably wouldn't hear from them for weeks, if at all. I'd need to get their attention in a different way.

I quickly scanned the bookshelves behind my reading chair. There it was: *The Last Family*. I had reviewed it the year before: I had been expecting another trashy true-crime book, but I had been surprised. The book was a surprisingly well-written history of the Marcelli crime family from Sicily to New York, and an account of the life and misdeeds of the author, Anthony Marcelli. His decision to become a federal informant, and the brutal, damning testimony that had brought down his family, followed a crisis of faith right out of classical tragedy. I had praised it in my review, and I hadn't been alone in my assessment. The book had spent several weeks on the *New York Times* best-seller list.

I flipped directly to the Acknowledgements.

I skipped past the usual stuff—though one had to admire a mafia traitor who nonetheless thanks his family—scanning almost to the end before the sentence that I was looking for jumped out at me.

"And finally, my editor, Tony Markus, without whom this book would not exist."

Tony Markus—I'd forgotten his name. He'd gotten a lot of coverage in the trades when the book was camped at the top of the charts—the young editor who, for his first book, had gone after a mafia soldier, a confessed killer, and convinced him to write the story of his life and crimes. That sort of thing gets you noticed in the publishing world, and Markus had been hailed as a wunderkind, heir apparent to a generation of editors on their way into retirement.

"But what have you done lately?" I muttered as I searched his name online.

The answer, as near as I could tell after going through the first six pages of mostly obscure results, was *nothing*. In the year since *The Last Family* had been published, Markus had not been credited with publishing or acquiring anything remotely of interest.

I clicked on the Contact button under his bio on the D&K page and took a moment to mentally compose my opening line.

I titled the message "Possible Future Project."

Mr. Markus,

My name is Christopher Knox—I'm a writer and freelance journalist based in Victoria, BC, Canada. I'm approaching you because I was an admirer of *The Last Family*. You may have seen my review in the *Vancouver Sun*.

Back in the mid-60s, Sprite Press (which was later acquired by D&K) brought out four books of young adult fantasy by a British writer named Lazarus Took. You may not be familiar with the name, but at that time the novels attracted quite a following. The books are now, sadly, out of print.

Given the popularity of young adult fantasy these days—from Harry Potter to the incredibly successful re-brandings of Tolkien and Lewis, as well as the legion of new writers following in their footsteps—it seems to me that the time is ripe for a relaunch of Lazarus Took, a previously forgotten writer who could be introduced to a new generation of readers.

What separates this from a simple reissue campaign, however, is the fact that there is a previously unknown fifth novel by Lazarus Took, entitled *To the Four Directions*. It seems that this book was published in a very limited edition in the early 1950s and completely forgotten—it was not published by Sprite Press with the four other titles, and doesn't appear in any of the online databases or bibliographies.

In fact, I believe that the Took estate—which I have been in contact with— is unaware of its existence. While C.A. Took, the executor, has expressed some interest in seeing the four previously published novels back in print (and would, I think, be delighted if Davis & Keelor were interested, given the relationship with the Sprite imprint), I have taken this preliminary step of approaching you independently and directly regarding the fifth book.

I think that the combination of factors is fairly compelling for this project: young adult fantasy is in vogue at the moment; Took's previously published novels have a proven track record, and would be well received by a contemporary audience; and given the reception and media typically accorded to "discovered" books, I think that this has tremendous potential.

My first step would be to find out if D&K has any contractual claim to a fifth Lazarus Took novel. While the rights to the previous four books have long since reverted to the estate, there might be something in the original contracts regarding *To the Four Directions*.

Mr. Markus, could you please let me know at your earliest convenience whether this project might be of interest? If it isn't, I'll need to inform the estate of the existence of *To the Four Directions* and allow them to put it out to wider consideration.

With all best wishes,

Christopher Knox

I included my telephone number and address and reread the message.

The e-mail left me with a slightly dirty feeling. I hadn't lied—there really was a fifth book, and Cat had asked for my help in getting her grandfather's books back into print. I never claimed to be working for the estate, or empowered to make deals on their behalf.

All I was guilty of, really, was using the craven interests of a young editor, probably hungry for his next success and vulnerable to a little flattery, to get access to information that might somehow help David.

And it might work out to everyone's benefit, no matter what I got out of it. Fantasy was huge in publishing circles these days, and *To the Four Directions* could be a huge success, just as I had described. Hell, it had gotten David reading. Wasn't that the surest testament to its appeal?

Tony Markus pushed himself away from his desk and spun to face his printer. "Come on," he muttered, tapping at the arm of his chair. The wait was excruciating, but not surprising: the printer was probably a cast-off from two floors up. Certainly the rest of his office was made up of crap that nobody upstairs wanted.

At least he had the luxury of a private office, even if rumours and lingering smells suggested it had once been a janitor's closet. Four walls and a door beat a cubicle every time, and Markus knew that he was the envy of most of his colleagues. If the fast track took him through a janitor's closet for a couple of years, that was the price to be paid.

"Come on," he urged the printer again. When it finally roared into action, he yanked the paper free of the rollers before the machine had even finished.

He took his time on the stairs. He needed a chance to think this through, to make sure that his story was in place. Plus, he didn't want to arrive at Sharon's office winded and sweaty.

In his own mind, Tony Markus was a solid, imposing presence: not fat, solid. Impressive. The way his uncles were: broad-shouldered and hard, good-looking without even needing to try.

The reality was somewhat different.

Despite the slow pace, he was still out of breath by the time he got to the executive floor.

"Is she in?" he asked Traci, Sharon's assistant, stopping at her desk with feigned confidence, as if his meeting with Sharon Cahill, publisher of Davis & Keelor, was an everyday occurrence.

Traci glanced down at Sharon's calendar and Tony's eyes drifted to the neckline of her blouse. "She's got a ten-thirty," she said, glancing up and catching him looking. She sat up straighter.

"I just need a couple of minutes," Tony said, gesturing with the printed e-mail as if it were the most important thing in the world.

"Just a sec."

He watched her fingers as she dialled the phone: they were small and fine, pale, with delicate pink polish.

"Sharon, I've got Tony Markus out here. He says he needs a couple of minutes." She listened a moment, then hung up. "Go on in."

"Thanks, Traci," he said, smiling broadly, but she had already gone back to whatever she had been doing before.

He found Sharon leaning over her desk, studying two cover designs side by side. She didn't look up.

"What do you need, Tony?"

"I've got something I'd like to pursue," he said, the words coming out in sharp, stuttering blocks.

She raised her eyes over her glasses and looked at him.

He took a deep breath, trying to calm himself. "Are you familiar with the name Lazarus Took?"

She shook her head, pursed her lips.

"He was a fantasy writer, back in the fifties. Young adult stuff. Pretty good. I read a few of them when I was a kid." He held the e-mail from the journalist in his left hand: it was a prop. The last thing he wanted was to let his boss know that this had dropped into his lap.

The expression on Sharon's face was one of rapidly dwindling interest.

"It occurred to me," he said, hurrying, "that with fantasy being so popular right now we might want to take a look at Lazarus Took, maybe relaunch him—"

"What does that have to do with me?" she asked, firmly but not unkindly. "Take it to Maria over at Magic Wand or whatever they're calling themselves these days." The Young Adult division had changed its name several times in the last decade, attempting to capitalize on precisely the trend that Markus was talking about. "God knows she's overdue for a hit. Or just bring it to the next editorial meeting. We're always up for a reissue campaign." She smiled a conspiratorial smile at him. "Especially at a reasonable cost."

She was studying the covers on her desk again by the time he managed to say, "The thing is, it wouldn't be just a reissue program."

She looked up at him again. He wished he weren't sweating quite so much.

"Imagine what it would be like," he said, finally able to start the presentation he had worked out, "if someone were to publish a new Narnia book. Or a new Tolkien."

"Are you saying that there's a new novel from this . . . what's his name?"

"Lazarus Took. And that's exactly what I'm saying."

"But who cares?" she asked. "Nobody's heard of him."

"Exactly," he said, making virtue out of weakness. "We can use that very fact to our advantage. Rediscovering a lost author, beloved, a big reissue campaign leading to the debut publication of his long-lost, final novel. A nice pretty edition, suitable for kids *and* adults. Pub right before Christmas . . ." He snapped his fingers, already picturing the sales in his mind.

As he finished his spiel, she was smiling and nodding. "It would be nice," she said, mostly to herself. "Lock up the film rights. What's the name of the book?"

It took him a moment to remember. "*To the Four Directions*."

"Hmm. That should probably change . . . although if we're looking at the historical rediscovery angle . . . What's the book like?"

"I . . ."

She noticed his hesitation. "You do have the book?"

"I will have," he said. "Probably in the next couple of days. It's been a bit of a chore . . . "

She looked at him over her glasses, and it felt like she was looking right through him.

"All right," she said. "Keep me posted. I'll mention it to Peter when it comes in. If it's any good."

Peter Oates was the executive vice-president, the hands that held the purse. If he was interested, Peter would get behind a project in a very public way. If he wasn't interested, or didn't think it had financial merit, Tony might just as well disappear back into his janitor's closet.

"Thank you," he said, backing toward the door. "I'll keep you in the loop."

Sharon's attention was already back on the art on her desk, but Tony could feel the weight of her interest. That sort of weight could crush a man.

I had assumed, at the peak of my optimism, that I might hear back from Tony Markus within a day or two. I wasn't expecting it to be him when my cell phone rang a few hours after I sent the e-mail.

"Mr. Knox, it's Tony Markus calling from Davis & Keelor. You sent me an e-mail earlier today." The voice was nasally, with a New York accent.

I had to smile: never underestimate the curiosity of an editor. Especially a hungry one.

"I didn't want to let this lie. First off, tell me, how did you come by a copy of a book that no one seems to know exists, not even the author's estate?"

"I bought it," I said, trying to push a sense of amusement into my voice. "At a used bookstore. For my son's birthday."

"Amazing," he said, with a distracted tone that made me think that he was taking notes. "So it has been published, then?"

"Sort of," I said, reaching for the book. "The copy I've got is a hard-cover, from Alexander Press."

"Never heard of them."

"Me neither," I said. "And there's nothing online. I asked—" I almost said Cat. "I asked someone from the estate about the publisher, and she had no recollection of them either."

"I see." Probably scribbling away.

"I wanted to talk to you before I said anything to the estate."

"Looking for a finder's fee?" The words were pointed, but said with just enough humour that I could have taken them as a joke, had I been so inclined.

I didn't say anything. Best to let him think that we had covetousness in common.

"Well, I appreciate you getting in touch with me," he said, filling the dead air. "Oh, and I have to say, I really appreciated your review of *The Last Family*. I meant to send you a note at the time."

"It was my pleasure," I said, laying it on thick. "It really was quite an impressive book." Gratuitous ego-stroking goes both ways.

"And your son—"

For a moment, all I could wonder was how he could possibly know about David in the hospital.

"—what did he think of the book?"

"He loved it," I said without hesitation. "David—that's my son—he's never been much of a reader, but he devoured *To the Four Directions*. He even got in trouble at school when they caught him reading in class." I threw in that last comment to really whet Markus's appetite.

He chuckled and I could hear the faint clatter of his keyboard.

"Well, I should probably see the book," he said thoughtfully, as if that weren't the main reason for his call.

"I'm not really comfortable sending the only copy of it across the continent." I had rehearsed the line in my head, expecting this to come up.

"No, of course not." He dismissed the request I hadn't given him a chance to make. "I don't suppose you're going to be in New York anytime soon?" he asked.

"I was supposed to be, but—" I didn't want to give too much away. "I've had to cancel my trip."

"Ah, well. That's too bad." A leading silence.

"I'm sure we'll think of something. Say," I began, as if the question had just occurred to me, "did you have a chance to look into the rights situation?"

"Oh, it's a mess," he said. "Apparently the older books by Lazarus Took were published by a company D&K bought out in the 70s." Just like I had written in my e-mail. "All of their papers are warehoused off-site. If they even exist anymore. I'm sending an intern over to sift through the boxes."

As I listened, I realized that my real question about the book had already been answered. How many different ways did I need to hear that *To the Four Directions* didn't exist, save for the one copy? I wasn't going to learn any more from D&K.

So what was this book? Had it really caused David's first seizure on Saturday night? I was pretty sure it had. Why, then, did the same book ward off seizures now? I knew how ridiculous the questions sounded, but there had to be answers.

"Well, please let me know what they find out," I said, trying to bring the conversation to a comfortable close.

"Oh, I certainly will," he said. "Listen, Mr. Knox, what would you think about photocopying the book and overnighting it to me? Of course, I'd reimburse any expense." He made the suggestion quickly, as if he was aware of my attention waning. I started to feel a little sick again about leading him on.

"We should probably wait until we hear about the rights situation, shouldn't we?"

"Oh, of course. I just thought that we might save some time if I could see the book now, rather than waiting for the rights department. It's a pretty big job that they've got, sorting through all that stuff." His voice never lost its cool tone, but the words were increasingly desperate.

"That's a good point," I said. "Still, it wouldn't be fair to go further down this road without knowing where we are, legally speaking, would it?"

"Certainly." Clipped and cold. "Of course, Mr. Knox. I'll get back in touch with you once I hear from our rights department, then."

Hanging up the phone a few moments later, I almost felt bad for Tony Markus. To have something dangled in front of him like that, an opportunity he probably desperately needed, only to have it jerked away.

I felt worse, though, knowing that David's condition was becoming more serious by the day, and there was still nothing I could do.

I looked down at the book lying next to my laptop. The answers were all there, between those covers. But how to get them out?

David choked and coughed as his eyes opened to bright sunlight. He managed to turn slightly to his side before he threw up, coughing up river water from his stomach and lungs. Bright patches danced in his eyes as his body heaved, struggling to purge as much water as it could.

For a long time, David knew nothing but the agony of waking, and the dull cold that suffused his belly. He wondered if he had died, if this was what it felt like to be dead: hanging suspended in a space of warm light, but unable to shake the cold that had worked its way into his bones.

After a while the world started to come into focus around him. He wasn't suspended: he was lying on rough ground, rocks digging into his back. He couldn't get warm because he was half submerged in icy water, no longer able to feel his legs and feet.

It all came back to him in a rush: the fall into the river, the struggle not to drown. He must have blacked out and drifted along on the currents who knows how far.

As he struggled to sit up, his arms buckled beneath his weight. His teeth were chattering, his hands shaking. But he had no choice. He had to get out of the water, figure out some way to warm up before hypothermia set in.

Turning onto his stomach, David half crawled, half dragged himself up the rocky bank until he was out of the water. In the distance, a green strip looked like it might be the edge of a grassy plain. Someplace soft, warmed by the sun. He pulled himself forward. A few feet, and he collapsed again.

As he fell back onto the rocks, he heard a dull, metallic thunk, and something dug into his ribs. Something large, cylindrical, inside his shirt.

The Sunstone!

It took all his energy to smile before his eyes sank shut once again.

The doctor laid the file carefully on the bed.

"We need to broaden our parameters," Dr. Rutherford began. "The continued seizures, and the increase in their severity, are at odds with both the medication and the results of the tests we ran on David on Sunday. Now, those results are five days old—I've got your son going in for a CT scan and an MRI this morning—but going over the existing tests, there's nothing to indicate David should be experiencing continued seizure activity."

All of which was to say that he had no idea what was going on, either.

"It's possible that this is an allergic reaction. Do either of you wear perfume or cologne?"

We both shook our heads.

The doctor picked up the chart and made a note. "Do either of you smoke? Vestigial tobacco smoke—"

"I do," I said. "Are you saying that he could be having these seizures because I have an occasional cigarette?"

"Not typically." The way his voice trailed off left no doubt where he was leading: this wasn't a typical situation.

"It's something else to check," he finished, making another note. "We're trying to eliminate as many possibilities as we can."

"Would mould be a possibility? Or dust? The sort of thing that might have come off an old book?"

Jacqui shot me a look but I ignored her.

The doctor made another note. "It's certainly something to consider," he said. "Mould in particular could be a factor, either as an acute allergen or as a source of infection."

I nodded slowly.

"But there's no evidence of infection, is there?" Jacqui asked.

The doctor shook his head. "David's running a slight fever, but no more than we would expect given his symptoms. We'll do some broad spectrum blood work and see what comes up."

Jacqui nodded, her lips set in a hard line.

"I have to caution you, though," the doctor said, closing the file. "I don't think it's environmental. If it were, the symptoms wouldn't be increasing in severity with his removal from the initial environment. If it were cigarette smoke or perfume, we would have expected to see some warning signs with earlier exposure, and the allergen would have to have

been present, in concentrated form, at the time of the initial attack."
He glanced between us. "You would have had to have been there."

After the doctor left, Jacqui stared down at David in silence. I waited
for a long moment, then said, against my better judgment, "I think it's
the book." I tried to keep my tone neutral, my voice matter-of-fact.

She turned to me, her expression caught somewhere between shocked
and oddly hurt. "Chris, you heard what the doctor said. There's no way
it can be the book. And even if it were mould or dust there's no sign of
infection. Chris, it's just a book."

"That's the thing," I said, my voice rising before I had a chance to
rein it in. I told her, in the most general of terms, about the research I
had been doing, the web searches and the e-mails. "The thing is, as near
as I can tell, the book"—I hefted the weight of it in my bag—"doesn't
exist. No one's heard of it. The publishing house doesn't exist. Aside
from this copy, there's no trace of it."

I looked at her, waiting to see the effect of my words, my research.
"So?"

I felt myself crumbling. "What do you mean, so? I just . . ."

She shook her head. "Chris, all you've got is a rare book. Unless it
was printed with toxic ink or something, there's no way it could have
caused this." She gestured at David.

"But he calms down when I read it to him. And the seizures have
come on nights that I *didn't* read to him." As if that were conclusive
evidence.

She put her hand on my arm, obviously believing that I needed sympathy. "He likes the sound of your voice, Chris. It probably soothes him."

"The other night, I tried reading to him from that magazine." I
pointed to the table beside the bed. "And it didn't do anything. It's not
just reading. It's not just the sound of my voice. It's the book."

The pity in her eyes stopped me.

"I know how helpless this makes you feel," she said in a consoling
tone. "Hell, I spend my days surrounded by this kind of thing and I'm
still feeling completely overwhelmed. But all we can do is hope that something comes up in the blood work or on one of the scans. All we can do
is wait, okay?" Talking to me like I was a child. "One step at a time."

I nodded as if her words had convinced me, all the time feeling myself standing between David in the bed and the book in my bag, unsure if I was part of the solution, or part of the problem.

☙ ❧

Voices. Voices around him in the dark, low murmurs that seemed to blend with the burbling of the river.

"David?"

Like the sounds of his parents having friends visit, distant and unclear as he tried to sleep. He could almost make out what they were saying, if he tried, but it was easier to just—

"David?"

—let the voices wash over him. There was something warm and comforting in hearing them, in knowing that he was surrounded by people, that he wasn't alone.

"David?"

He could feel himself moving toward them as if rising toward the water's surface, the sound of the voices gaining a shape, a physical presence, a location. Up.

"David?

Except that one voice, clear and loud, a child's voice repeating his name. But not above him. Not around him.

Inside him, somehow.

Matt? he said, without speaking.

David! He could feel the other boy's joy, his relief. *I thought you were gone!*

Aren't I? Seeing nothing but the black, knowing nothing else in the world but the sound of voices.

He thought he heard Matt laugh. *They've found you*, he said. *You're going to wake up.*

☙ ❧

We were in the cafeteria when my cell phone rang. They had taken David down to the Medical Imaging Lab about half an hour ago.

Jacqui looked at me over the rim of her coffee cup and gave me a bemused smile. I answered the phone as I negotiated my way toward an exit.

"Chris Knox," I said, dodging past an employee shifting a huge cart of dirty dishes.

"Chris, it's John."

I stepped out into the small side-yard, crowded with smokers. "John?" I couldn't guess why he would be calling.

"Yeah," he said gruffly. "Twice in the same week." His voice softened a little, with concern. "How's David doing?"

"He's the same," I said. "The doctors are having a hard time figuring out what's going on."

"Diane wanted to send flowers," he said. I'd only met his wife on a couple of occasions. "I told her a bottle of Scotch might be more appropriate." He chuckled. "She vetoed that pretty quick."

"That's too bad," I said. "A bottle of Scotch would be just what the doctor ordered."

"Well, check your mailbox," he said. "Just because she vetoed me sending it doesn't mean your friends at the paper can't send you a little something."

"Thanks, John. I'm touched."

"Anything I can do to make it a little easier," he said. "And that's why I'm calling. A bit of good news. Your piece from Saturday? It's been getting a huge response. Tons of e-mails."

"Really?"

"Yeah, really," he said. "It's different from your usual curmudgeonly approach. I like that stuff; I think everyone likes it. But this is a nice change. And people noticed."

I racked my brain, trying to remember what exactly I had written.

"I especially like the way you wrapped it up."

"How was that?" I asked. "I'm not at my computer, so I don't have the piece in front of me."

"Just a sec." There was a rattling sound as he reached for something on his desk. "The paragraph that starts 'Like the best books . . .'"

When I didn't say anything, he started to read "Like the best books, the novels I found in my father's box were capable of magic.'" It was strange hearing my own words in someone else's voice, knowing that they were mine but not remembering them. "They took me to another world, made me feel more deeply than I could allow myself to feel in the real world. While I was reading, I ceased to be little Christopher Knox. I became someone else entirely.' That's good . . ."

I wasn't listening to him anymore, overwhelmed by the thoughts rushing through my head. Of course. The answer had been right in front of me all along.

"Chris?"

Lazarus Took's interest in magic, his skills as a writer: what if he had figured out a way to build on the inherent power of storytelling, to add to it in such a way that a book, a single book, could literally carry the reader away?

"Yeah, I'm here, John." It was all I could do not to hang up on him.

"I thought I'd lost you there."

"Just a blip, I guess." I was curling and uncurling my toes I was so desperate to get off the phone.

Jacqui looked up when I joined her at the table. Something must have seemed off with my expression. "Is everything okay?"

"Yeah, everything's fine. That was John at the paper—apparently my column got lost in the e-mail, so he wants me to resend it."

I couldn't very well tell her the truth.

She smiled wryly. "Technology."

"I was in a rush to get back to the hospital," I explained. "I just hope I didn't delete it." Might as well play it out for all it's worth. "Do you have the keys?"

She passed me the keys for the van, still half smiling.

"I'll be quick," I said.

She waved the comment away. "The tests will take a while."

Apparently last night's sleep had done her good. I kissed her on the top of the head as I left, surprising both of us, and practically ran for the parking lot.

🙢 🙠

"Wake up!" A commanding voice, impossible to resist.

David flinched as he opened his eyes to bright sunlight. Dark shapes loomed over him.

"He's awake." This voice gentler, calmer.

"Loren?" he whispered.

One of the shapes nodded.

"At least he hasn't lost all his faculties," said the other.

As David blinked into wakefulness, the shapes became clear—Captain Bream and Loren looking down at him. The old man looked concerned, his face pale and drawn, while the captain looked as stern as ever.

They were both pretty much as David had pictured them.

"I'm cold," David stuttered, his jaw shaking, his body trembling uncontrollably.

"The men are building a fire," Bream said, looking behind himself to check on their progress.

"But the Berok . . ."

"Let us worry about them," the captain said.

"Where . . . where am I?" His tongue felt too thick for his mouth, lazy and uncooperative.

"A good ride downriver from the canyon," the magus said. David struggled to focus on his face. "You had been in the cave for a long time when we heard a roar, and then we saw you running and jumping into the river. We didn't think there was any way you would survive, you were under the water for so long, but then you came up. We rode after you. Thankfully, the river takes a bend here and you washed up, or you would have floated all the way back to Colcott Town." The old man was frowning, obviously concerned. "What happened in the cave?"

David nodded, then suddenly remembered, bringing his hands to his chest, feeling for the outline of the cylinder. He couldn't find it.

"Not to worry, Dafyd," the magus said. "We've got the Stone. You've done well. Now let's get you to the fire, see if we can't melt some of that ice out of your bones."

John's phone call kept rattling in my head as I drove home. I had exhausted, as far as I could, my inquiries into the book and its publishing history. But there was more to it than that, wasn't there?

What about other readers?

And what about magic?

Sitting down at my desk, I punched "Matthew Corvin" into the Google entry field and pressed Search. Google spat back more than half a million results for the name. When I added the word "Seattle," the first entry brought a chill to my forearms: The Matthew Corvin Foundation.

I clicked on the link. The home page had several photos: a gala dinner, a crowd of children in front of a bus, a doctor in a laboratory, an operating room.

My hand was shaking as I clicked through to the Mission Statement.

"The Matthew Corvin Foundation is a charitable trust devoted to those suffering from brain injuries and related disorders. With a two-fold approach, the Foundation provides support for ongoing research into the causes and treatment of mental disorders, and for those suffering with those and related conditions."

I clicked through to the History page.

"The Matthew Corvin Foundation was established in 1985 as a means to provide funding for both research into brain injuries and support for those living with such injuries. The Foundation was established by Carol and Brett Corvin, and was named for their son Matthew, who suffered a debilitating brain injury at age 13."

"Son of a bitch," I muttered, as an electrical jolt ran through me.

I scrolled down the page: there was a photo of Matthew Corvin with his parents. He looked about twelve years old, and was smiling directly into the camera. It felt like he was staring right at me, daring me.

It couldn't be. There had to be dozens of Matthew Corvins . . .

But what if it wasn't a coincidence?

Only one way to find out.

I clicked on the Contact Us button and took a deep breath. I had to be careful. I just needed information. I was just a reporter, looking for a story.

It took a long time to write the short note.

When I was done, I drove downtown to the parkade next to city hall. It was less than a block from there to the red, dragon-adorned gates that marked the entrance to Chinatown. I skirted the Chinese day-school and bounced anxiously on the balls of my feet as I waited for the light.

Hurrying along the narrow sidewalk, I dodged the slow-moving crowds, avoiding the bins of vegetables and cheap toys for sale that spilled almost to the edge of the street. I nearly missed the entrance to Fan Tan Alley—I usually did. It was easy to miss.

"The narrowest street in Canada" looked like little more than a doorway; in fact, it was a narrow corridor between two buildings, joining Pandora and Fisgard, lined with small shops on both sides, although it wasn't even wide enough for two people to walk along it side by side.

Though people did try.

I ended up stuck behind a pair of ambling tourists, Americans by the sound of their accents, as they cooed over "the old world charm" of the alley. I waited behind them for what seemed like hours before saying "Excuse me" in as clipped a tone as I could manage and pushing past them, narrowly avoiding the man's dripping ice cream cone.

I stopped in front of a glass door backed with a red silk curtain, which bore a sign in ornate, faux-Renaissance lettering: ALCHEMY: A PLACE OF MAGICKAL LIVING. A smaller sign, on a piece of tan paper taped to the inside of the glass, read CONSULTATIONS WITH MME SARAH. DAILY. PLEASE INQUIRE.

I'd exhausted all of the Took resources online: Alchemy seemed like a reasonable next step.

A small chime tinkled as I opened the door. The air was heavy with incense, musky and sweet. The small shop was crammed: bins and jars of incense, statuettes, crystal balls, a display of tarot cards. I was the only customer in the store.

Back when we still spent family afternoons exploring the nooks and crannies downtown, the three of us had ended up here several times. David loved the dragon statues, and Jacqui always found a way to fill the time at the jewellery display at the counter. I, naturally, spent my time with the books.

I went straight to the bookshelf on the side wall. There were none of the cheesy paperback occult tomes that one might expect for the tourist trade, no exposés, no horror stories: the books, like the shop, were a resource for the practising Wiccan—the unofficial faith of the city—and those with a serious interest in magic.

I started at the upper left corner. I wasn't sure what I was looking for, but if it was anywhere, it would be here.

"Can I help you?"

Startled, I turned toward the soft voice.

"I'm sorry," said a tall, striking woman with thick, curly red hair that fell past her shoulders, beads and crystals woven into small braids throughout. "I didn't mean to sneak up on you." She smiled enigmatically. "Is there something I can help you find?" Too angular to be called pretty, she was probably in her forties, but her green eyes looked younger.

"Answers," I said, smiling back.

"I hear that a lot. Is there anything in particular?"

"Yes," I said haltingly. "But I'm not quite sure what the question is."

She nodded sagely, a gesture that didn't seem at all affected. "I hear that a lot, too. Do you think it's something that might benefit from a consultation with Madame Sarah?"

It hadn't occurred to me before she mentioned it. "Maybe," I said. "Is she here?"

"Right in front of you," she said, her eyes sparkling.

"You're—"

"Madame Sarah," she said, extending her hand.

"Sorry." I took her hand and shook it. "I guess I was expecting—"

"You were expecting a gypsy, maybe?" she said, putting on an accent. "Lots of scarves, kerchief, long fingernails?"

I looked at her, dressed in a plain, cream-coloured peasant blouse, faded blue jeans, with bare feet. "Something like that."

"Or," she said, reading my reluctance correctly, "I could start off by helping you find a book or two." She smiled again as she let me off the hook. "What are you looking for?"

"History, actually. Twentieth-century stuff. Occult orders in the U.K. in the first half of the century. Do you have anything that gets into that?"

"Well, our magical history books are down here. There's not much on the twentieth century, though. Hermetic Egypt we've got loads on." She smiled. "The twentieth century, less so. And I'm getting the sense that you're looking for a bit more than Aleister Crowley and 'do what thou wilt' . . . " I nodded. "I don't think I've got any books here that are going to help you with that," she said. "But you could talk to my mother."

"Your mother?"

Sarah nodded. "It's her shop. She trained me, like her mother trained her." More than retail skills, I assumed. "She's the one you should talk to if you're interested in magical history."

Any little bit of information, anything at all.

"Could I?" I asked. "I mean, if it's not too much of an imposition."

"Hang on, I'll check." She stepped to the cash desk and opened the small door behind it. "Mum, are you busy?" she called, traces of an English accent surfacing. "Got a man out here who'd like to talk to you."

I couldn't hear any response from the backroom, but Sarah nodded and waved me over. "We were just having tea," she said, as she led me through.

～ ～

David half walked, half stumbled the few steps to the fire, supported by the magus. Although the old man looked fragile, his body was sinewy and strong.

Captain Bream drew a heavy blanket from one of the packs. "You should get out of those clothes."

David nodded. Every few moments another wave of shivering racked his body, started his teeth rattling inside his mouth.

He tugged at the collar of his shirt, pulling the cold fabric away from his skin, struggling to get it over his head, and it came off with a wet suck. His fingers were too stiff and thick to easily manage the hook on his pants, but eventually they came free and he pushed out of them like a snake shedding an old skin. He wasn't wearing anything under them, and he tried not to look down at the strange body he was inside, the muscles, the hair.

The hair?

This is worse than gym class, Matt muttered inside his head, but David was too cold to care.

He wrapped himself in the blanket. It was rough, and smelled of horse and smoke, but it was warm, and he crumpled to the hard ground at the edge of the fire, as close as he could get to the flames without getting burned.

"We're heating some wine for you," the magus said, concern heavy in his face. "To build back your strength."

I guess they've never heard of hot chocolate, David thought. He was shocked to hear Matt laugh.

You can hear what I think? David asked silently, lowering his eyes to the flames.

Apparently, Matt said.

The fire leapt and crackled, the colours dancing hypnotically.

What happened back there? In the cave? David asked.

You took me inside of you.

All of you?

There wasn't much left.

Like your soul? David didn't know much about church, but he had a certain sense of how a soul worked: like a personality, or a spirit.

I don't know, Matt confessed. *Whatever was left after the Sunstone . . .*

What . . .? David began, then stopped, not sure of how he should ask.

But Matt had already understood the question forming in his mind. *The others in the cave? I can only guess. The water . . . They might still be there, but you taking the Stone might have released them. Maybe they're floating around somewhere . . .*

David felt a cold sadness, even as his muscles and bones warmed with the fire.

"How are you doing?" the magus asked.

David looked up. "Getting warmer," he said slowly.

"Here," the magus said. He extended his hand, holding a cup. "Be careful. It's hot."

David took the cup gingerly, the scent of the wine and spices in the steam strange and unpleasant. "Thank you," he said, holding it carefully to his chest, trying not to inhale. The smell made him want to throw up.

"Drink up," the magus urged. David caught the sympathy and warning in his voice. "You're going to need your strength."

David heard the crunching of stones under boots on his other side.

"How are you faring?" Captain Bream asked.

"Better," he managed. He took a careful sip of the wine, trying not to gag.

"Good." The captain nodded.

He surprised David by hunkering down next to him. "Then maybe you can tell us what happened after you crossed the bridge. And about this—" He set the silver cylinder down in front of them.

≈ ≈

I don't know what I might have expected the backroom of a magic shop to look like, but it certainly wasn't the bright, modern kitchen that Sarah led me into. And Sarah's mother certainly didn't conform to any idea I might have had of an older witch: she looked like a fairy-tale grandmother, down to the chubby, rosy cheeks and the floral dress, more likely to offer you a cookie than to bake pies out of children.

"Mom," Sarah said. "This is . . ."

I stepped forward and extended my hand. "Chris. Chris Knox."

"And this is my mother, Nora."

She didn't so much shake my hand as clasp it warmly between hers, smiling broadly. "Lovely to meet you, Chris. Please—" Releasing my hand, she gestured at the empty chairs. "Have a seat. Sarah and I were about to have tea. Can I get you a cup?"

I nodded, but Sarah was already on her way to the kettle.

Sitting herself back down in her chair, Nora pushed a plate toward me. "You'll have a cookie?"

I couldn't help but smile.

I was surprised when Sarah sat with us.

"We'll hear the bell if anyone comes in," she explained.

"Ah."

"Mum, Chris is looking for some information about magical orders in England, especially in the '30s and '40s. Aleister Crowley and them."

"Not Crowley," I hurried to clarify. "But people who had been affiliated with Crowley—"

"Fellow travellers," Sarah said.

"—who then went off to form orders of their own."

"It sounds like you have someone particular in mind," Nora said, before biting into a cookie.

I nodded. "A man named Lazarus Took. A writer."

She shook her head. "I can't say I'm familiar with the name."

"He and his wife"— I fumbled, pulling the notebook out of my pocket—"were apparently members of a group"—it took me a moment to find the reference—"called"—flip, flip, flip—"the Order of the Golden Sunset."

"Oh," she said, curling her lip in distaste. "That bunch."

"You know them?" I asked, leaning eagerly across the table.

"I know of them, that's for sure. We *all* knew *of* them. William Thorne. Lots of bad energy there. You know about the scandal?"

I shook my head.

She reached for another cookie. "Well, I suppose you could look it up, but the short version is that around 1920 or so, police raided Thorne's house, found a very young woman being held prisoner, along with her daughter. Thorne was arrested, but the woman refused to testify against him, and went back to him as soon as he was released from prison. The papers all said that he had her under his spell." She shrugged.

I had been making notes as she was speaking, and when she stopped, I flipped back a few pages. "Well, Took was apparently a member of the Golden Sunset."

She thought for a moment. "The name isn't familiar, but I'm not an expert. What's your interest?" She looked at me suspiciously.

God, how to answer *that* question.

"I'm doing some research on Lazarus Took, and I think he started an order of his own after he left the Golden Sunset. The Brotherhood of the Stone?"

Glancing between the mother and the daughter, I could see that my answer was not to their liking.

"You know the Brotherhood of the Stone?"

Nora nodded gravely, but didn't speak.

Time for fuller disclosure. "I think that Took, and maybe that order, are the source of some problems I'm currently facing."

"Well, that wouldn't surprise me," Nora said briskly, taking another bite of cookie. "That bunch was nothing but trouble. Set the course of true magic back twenty-five or thirty years, they did."

"How?" Sarah asked.

"Well, they had that estate . . ."

"Raven's Moor?" I said, checking the notebook.

"Right, Raven's Moor. Apparently it was a family home, but when the new master got his hands on it . . ." She shook her head. "The stories that came out of that place. Rituals, orgies, drugs . . . A lot of the stories that circulate today about Crowley I suspect actually referred to that bunch. One mystical order is the same as another to most people. Especially after what happened."

She took a sip of her tea.

"After *what* happened?" I prompted.

She waited a moment, as if she didn't really want to talk about it. "Well, no one knows what *really* happened, that's the thing. The police and newspapers just referred to it as 'the mysterious happenings at Raven's Moor.' People disappeared, ran, went underground. Not just . . ." She struggled with the words. "Not just that crew, but everyone of a magical bent. That's what my mother did, went underground. Kitchen witch to kitchen witch in three generations. One brief, shining moment of semi-respectability brought crumbling down because of those people."

In my notebook I wrote, *went underground => America?*

"Do you have any idea what happened to the Brotherhood after that?" I asked, already knowing the answer.

"They disappeared," she said.

"Some of them probably turned up in other groups, but no one ever saw the master again. At least"—she paused— "not anyone who admitted to being the master."

"So was this a particular type of witchcraft, or—"

"No," Nora said sternly. "Not witchcraft. Witches had nothing to do with this. You're doing what the newspapers did, lumping together things they didn't understand."

"Wicca is an earth religion," Sarah explained. "Its rituals are built around the seasons—observance of and communion with the natural world. The first tenet, the guiding principle, is to do no harm. It's a sympathetic magic, do you see? Guided by harmony and accord. The magics that the Raven's Moor group believed in, the rituals they performed, were something much different. Completely concerned with power, and with the individual possessing it and increasing it by drawing more from his followers. They sought to conquer death, to control time, to bend the world to their will."

"And sometimes they succeeded," Nora said, her tone one of finality. She was clearly not interested in discussing it any further.

We sipped at our tea in silence for a few moments.

"I'm curious, Mr. Knox," Nora said at length. "You mentioned that you thought this order, the Brotherhood, might be at the root of some problems you are facing."

I took a deep breath, not sure of how much to give away.

"Why do you believe that?" she asked, setting her cup on its saucer.

"I recently . . . An object has come into my possession," I explained slowly, trying to keep it vague. "An object that I'm sure once belonged to Lazarus Took."

"And strange things have been happening since you've had it," Sarah continued on my behalf.

I nodded.

"You have the object with you," Nora stated. "In your bag." She cocked her head toward my shoulder bag.

"Yes."

"May we see it?" Nora asked.

A momentary uncertainty rose at the thought of revealing the book, but I started to take it from my bag. Nora stopped me. She took the plate of cookies to the counter and opened a drawer. When she came back she pushed the cream and sugar containers to the edge of the table and spread out a square of green silk.

"There," she said, centring the fabric. "You can put it there."

"It's a book," I said, setting David's book on the cloth.

"So it is," Nora said, staring at it.

Almost a full minute passed as she leaned close to the table and studied the book. She didn't pick it up, didn't even touch it.

"It always amazes me," she said thoughtfully. "Just how much passes most people unaware. It's like they're living in a black and white world, completely unaware of the colours all around them."

"What—"

"You can feel it, can't you, Sarah?"

Sarah had gone pale.

"Feel what?" I asked.

"Sarah?"

"Cold," Sarah said. "Powerful, but cold."

Nora looked at me. "This is indeed an object of great power, and it bears the touch of a very dark magician."

Her words should have brought me a sense of relief: I wasn't going insane. It really was the book.

But magic?

"What does it do?" I asked, my voice dropping to nearly a whisper.

"Why don't you tell us?" said Nora. "What has it done to you?"

I didn't even hesitate. I told them everything—not the vague story I had told John, but the whole story, from giving David the book to his suspension to his collapse.

When I finished, Nora laid her hands on the table and said, in a flat voice, "Well, that's that then. It needs to be destroyed."

I shook my head. "No, we can't."

I explained about the soothing effect that the book had on David. She looked at it again, thoughtfully.

"Well," she sighed as she stood up. "The first thing we can do is get a better sense of what this book actually is." She walked over to the sink and turned on the water. "Sarah, be a love and pass me the Plexi cake pan, would you? In the drawer under the stove."

A few moments later, Sarah carefully placed a clear Plexiglas baking pan partly filled with water on top of the book, taking care not to spill a drop.

"What's that?" I asked, craning to see.

"A baking pan half full of water," Nora said, sitting back down. "What does it look like?"

She fumbled at her neck and lifted away a necklace, heavy with a large clear crystal. "We seek not to change, but to see." She slid the stone off the silver chain and held it up to me. "Quartz," she said. "For clarity."

Clutching the stone in her fist, she brought it to her mouth, whispering words that I couldn't quite hear. When she was finished she nodded decisively and, reaching out, let the stone tumble softly into the pan of water, near the edge closest to her.

"What is this supposed—?"

"Shh," Sarah said, gazing intently at the pan.

The water, which had been clear a heartbeat before, now shimmered with a slight iridescence, a faint glow along the surface. Through the water, I could see the cover of the book, wavering a little with distortion from the pan and the water, the golden lettering of the title and the author's name, the faint shadow of the stamped shape in the middle of the cover.

As I watched, though, something happened. The gold of the letters faded, the colour becoming a dull grey-brown, almost disappearing into the leather. The symbol, however, began to glow a tanzanite that shone brightly through the water. I could see symbols within the points of the star, and odd characters between the points. The circle around the star symbol was not, as I had thought, a simple line: it too was made up of tiny, unfamiliar letters or symbols.

I started to speak, but Sarah hushed me again.

Another series of letters began to glow, the purple gradually intensifying in a wide band that followed the edges of the cover, a broad line of characters that formed a frame around the cover and the star image.

I picked up my pen and started to copy some of the figures, panicking when I realized the colour was starting to fade.

"Dammit," I muttered, racing to get something, anything, down in the notebook.

"Don't worry," Nora said. "That which has been seen cannot be unseen."

She was right. Although the purple colour lost its intensity, the symbols remained plainly visible, in the same faded gold colour as the title and Took's name.

I sat back in the chair, trying to catch my breath.

"Sarah," Nora said. "If you would be so kind."

Sarah started at her mother's voice, and looked away from the book.

"Could you please?" she gestured at the pan.

As Sarah picked up the pan of water and carried it over to the sink, Nora and I gazed intently at the book, at the new letters and symbols that had appeared on the cover.

"Do you have any idea what it is?" I asked.

"A spell, I'm guessing," Sarah said as she sat back down. She was holding a dishtowel, rubbing it between her fingers, and after a moment passed the crystal to her mother.

"A spell," I said, turning the thought over in my head.

"Or spells," Nora added, as if that would make it easier. "It's not the sort of magic we do." She glanced at her daughter. "Our rituals and spells are very open, and reciprocal, based on agreement and trust. This, this is . . ."

"It's a trap," Sarah said flatly.

Nora nodded.

"I still don't understand."

"Look," Sarah said, turning the cloth so the book was facing us. Neither of them had touched the book directly. "This sigil"—she pointed at the star—"is a fairly common magical symbol. It's got hundreds of variations, hundreds of uses, hundreds of contexts. Based on the symbols within this particular star, though, I'm guessing that it's setting the parameters for the spell. Look, here, that's the symbol for male, governed by"—she shifted her finger—"this symbol, which stands for youth. These two symbols together refer to a young boy. Do you see?"

I nodded, trying to keep up.

"My best guess . . ." She looked at her mother, who nodded her agreement. ". . . is that this is a proscription. The spell will only work on someone who matches all of these criteria."

"You said you'd been reading the book?" Nora asked.

I nodded.

"No sign of seizure?"

"Not so far."

"Exactly," Sarah said. "Without the proscription of this sigil, the spell would work on anyone."

"Or no one, more likely," Nora said. "It's very difficult to create a universal spell. Especially one that has to work on its own."

"So what are these letters?" I asked, pointing at the frame of characters that had appeared under the pan of water.

"I'm not sure," Sarah said. "It's not a language I've ever seen before. It bears a superficial resemblance to Celtic runes, but there are too many characters. Probably it's an invented language."

"So you can't tell what it does?"

"Oh, I think I know what it does, in general terms. I think it's an invocation, perhaps. Or an invitation. It's hidden on the cover, like texturing. It might be a super-conscious thing, or perhaps it registers by touch."

"Only those who are susceptible to it. Young boys . . ." I said.

"Yes, that's right. And then with this in place, the rest of the spell is probably scattered through the book, hidden in plain sight. Is there a dedication?"

They both flinched as I reached out and opened the book. "I've spent the last two weeks reading this book, carrying it around with me. If it was going to affect me, I think it would have already— Here's the dedication," I said, and they both leaned forward to read it. "'For Cora, the greatest gift.' Cora was Took's wife."

"And here," I said, flipping forward, "is what I think David was reading when he had the first seizure." I glanced at Nora. "Even to me, that looks like a spell."

Sarah nodded as she read. "That looks like the final step," she said. "By the time David got to here, he would already have been mostly enthralled. This would have done it."

"Done what? What does the spell do? Did someone go to all this work just to give seizures to some kid?"

"Without being able to decipher the language . . ." Sarah began.

"How can we do that?" I asked. "How can we decipher the language?"

"We can't," she said. "Not without a lexicon. A code key. This Lazarus Took probably invented a new system of runes for precisely this purpose: to keep people from figuring out how the spell works. To keep people from figuring out ways to counter it."

"So that's it?" I asked. I wanted to pound my fists on the table, to throw something at the wall, to burst into tears.

"I'm sorry, Chris," she said, using my name for the first time. "Without a lexicon . . ."

"Sarah, love," Nora said, still staring at the printed text. "Can you bring me a fresh pan of water, please? And make sure the bottom is completely dry."

We both looked at her, equally puzzled.

"There is more here," she said, "than meets the eye."

Sarah repeated the process with the pan of water, this time setting it carefully atop the open pages of the book. Nora dropped her crystal into the pan and I watched in silence, waiting. Time slid by as the three of us sat, staring at the words on the page.

"I'm not seeing anything," I said carefully.

"It's not just you," Sarah said. "Mom?"

"Watch." With what seemed like exaggerated care, Nora flicked the side of the pan.

As the water moved with the impact of her finger, I sucked in my breath: the lines of text, refracted through the water, seemed to waver, and as the black lines shifted, flashes of brilliant purple appeared where they had been hidden by the text. Purple letters, words, sentences.

"It looks . .,." Nora said, still staring into the water as it gradually stilled, as the purple lines settled back under the black print. ". . . like there's more than one text here. There's more than one book to your book."

She tapped the pan with the back of her knuckles. Harder, this time, the water sloshing. Again the moving black lines revealed the purple letters underneath, but this time, with the greater motion of the water, the purple lines also wavered, revealing more purple lines. And more. And a fourth layer. And more.

"By the Goddess," Sarah whispered.

"How many are there?" I asked.

Nora shrugged and looked at me, her face pale, her eyes dark. "There's no way to tell."

In the silence that followed I thought back to my conversation with John, the words I had written, the clues my subconscious had left for me. I hadn't wanted to say anything before I had heard them out, to be sure they wouldn't dismiss me as a madman.

Still, it was difficult to finally put my question into words. "If the book *is* a trap, do you think it's possible that my son's consciousness, his soul or his essence or whatever you want to call it, has been trapped in this book? That he's somehow in *there*?" I gestured at the splayed pages. "While his body is in the hospital?" I almost cringed, but there was no other way to express my suspicion. My own words: *While I was reading, I ceased to be little Christopher Knox. I became someone else entirely.* It was the only idea that made sense.

Once I got past the fact that it was insane.

Nora didn't even hesitate. "Yes. I think that's exactly what's happening."

I was so relieved, I almost wept. If I was crazy, at least I wasn't alone.

"From what I know of the Brotherhood," she continued, "it sounds like exactly the sort of thing they would do."

Sarah looked stunned. She didn't seem entirely convinced, but clearly had too much respect for her mother's wisdom to disagree. "And what's more," Nora said, reaching toward the pan and rapping it with her knuckles again, so hard that the water almost spilled over the pan's edges. The black and purple lines swayed wildly. "I think one of these purple lines is your son's story, the life that he's living within the book."

"David," I whispered.

"If his consciousness, and his soul, are trapped within the book, then his free will is trapped in there as well. There would be no way for the author to control his actions. He's within the world of the book, but able to react autonomously. Independently. Within its strictures, of course."

"The ultimate character with a mind of its own," I muttered.

"And his storyline would have to be present within the book as well as the author's storyline. Hidden by it, but present nonetheless."

It all made perfect sense, except for one detail.

"If David's storyline is one of those purple lines, what are all the other ones?"

My heart sank: in asking the question, I had intuited the answer.

"Other children," Sarah whispered.

≈ ≈

David sipped from the cup of hot wine, trying not to gag, to buy himself time. If his only hope of getting out of this world was to get to the end of the book, it was important that he pretend to be the Dafyd that these people had known. That meant he couldn't tell Bream and Loren anything about Matt, or the shades in the cave. He couldn't say anything about the story they were all trapped in: not if he wanted to get safely out of it.

So he limited himself to a chronology of what he had done to get the Sunstone, and to escape from the cave once the water had started pouring in. He broke up the story every so often with sips from his cup. How could his mom and dad drink this stuff?

"And you managed to hold on to that"—Captain Bream pointed at the cylinder—"even as you struggled under the waves?"

David nodded slowly. He didn't like the way the captain was looking at him. Had he always been this distrusting and Dafyd had just never noticed it?

To his surprise, the captain reached over and patted David heavily on the shoulder. "Nicely done, Dafyd," he said. "I'll be sure the Queen learns of your bravery."

He bent forward and picked up the silver cylinder, looking at it for a moment before handing it to David. "It seems only right that you should be the one to carry it home."

David took the cylinder. He touched the stone tentatively, brushing his fingertips across the smooth surface, still half expecting it to shock him.

The Stone and the disk looked much different than they had in the chamber. The Stone seemed small and dull by the light of the sun, flat and unremarkable.

"This doesn't—" David began, before he could stop himself. Once the words were out of his mouth, all he could do was hope that no one had noticed them.

"What?" Bream asked, looking more closely at the Stone.

David was vaguely aware of the magus rising and walking away.

"I was expecting it to look more important, I guess," David said, touching it with his fingertip.

The Stone sat at the centre of what looked like a sunburst or star, radiating out in four long points at the top and bottom and sides of the circle, with smaller points between them. Around the rim of the disk was a narrow band of writing that David couldn't read.

The magus returned holding his book. He sat and thumbed through the pages as David lingered over the strange inscription. The letters seemed distorted somehow. Familiar, but strange.

"It's mirror writing," he exclaimed, causing the magus to close his book with a surprised snap.

The captain leaned in close to look.

David pointed at the faint writing. "It's written backwards," he said. "You need a mirror to read it."

Both the magus and the captain slowly lifted their eyes from the Stone to look at David.

Be careful, David, Matt warned. *In this world—*

"I've heard stories," he muttered weakly. The captain held his gaze a moment longer, then looked away.

The magus took both the cylinder and David's cup of wine. Leaning toward the fire, he held the cylinder face down above the wine, adjusting its position to reflect the firelight into the mouth of the cup.

Once he got the angles right, he peered intently into the glass.

David leaned forward, catching a glimpse of the reflected silver disk, which seemed to float on the dark surface of the liquid.

"This," the magus said heavily, "is not the Sunstone."

☙ ❧

Something in the air seemed to change whenever Sharon Cahill came down the two floors to the editorial bullpen. A hush would fall, starting with the junior editor closest to the elevator, a palpable stillness of people not just working, but staring deeply at their monitors in an attempt to look like they were *really* working. She wasn't an imposing presence physically. She always had a warm smile if someone happened to meet her eye, and she'd stop occasionally, inquiring casually after a project, or someone's family. But as she made her way through the warren of desks, the usual hum of conversation disappeared, and a wave of silence rolled over the room in advance of her like ripples spreading out from a thrown stone.

In his office at the far end, Queen's *Greatest Hits* playing low from his iPod speakers, Tony Markus was completely unaware of his publisher's stately approach.

"Dammit," he muttered. He had spent most of the day trying to amass as much information as possible on Lazarus Took. What he had assumed would be a simple search had turned out to be anything but. Aside from the usual antiquarian value sites (which all seemed to agree that Took's books were worthless) and a low-budget home page, he hadn't come up with much of anything. Certainly no mention of a previously unpublished book (which he hadn't expected to find) or any reference to the dead author's estate (which he certainly had).

He tried another term in the search field, and came up with no results yet again. "Dammit," he repeated.

"Stymied?" Sharon asked from the doorway.

He spun to face her so fast he almost tipped his chair. "Sharon," he said, trying to effect a tone of fond surprise.

She was leaning against the door frame with a casual ease that was entirely at odds with her aura. Tony wondered how long she had been standing there.

"Is that to do with the kids' book?" she asked, glancing at his monitor.

He nodded. "I'm trying to collate as much information as I can before I present it to the board."

"And how are things looking for the fifth book?" she asked.

It had been only four or five hours since he had brought her the idea in the first place—he had clearly piqued her interest.

"I've got lines in the water," he said, as vaguely as he could. "I've got an intern from Rights trying to dig up any existing contracts we might have had with Lazarus Took. And"—he gestured toward the computer—"I'm trying to get in contact with someone from the estate."

"And not having much luck with it," she observed, bemusement on her face.

"I am having a bit of trouble on that front," he admitted. "There's not a lot of information out there about it."

She nodded slowly. "And I suppose you've already tried the telephone book? I know it sounds old-fashioned . . ."

He raised one eyebrow: as if he would overlook something that simple.

She started out of his office.

"Oh," she said, turning back, treating it like an afterthought. "I spoke to Peter a little while ago, and he's definitely on board," she said. "Depending on the book, of course."

"Of course," he agreed.

No additional pressure there.

After Sharon had gone, he brought up the national phone directory website and searched "Took" in Oregon.

Less than a second later he had eight results.

"Son of a bitch."

"Is there any way to break the spell?" I asked, looking at the book, now closed in the centre of the green cloth in the middle of the table.

"I don't think so," Nora said apologetically. "Without being able to translate the symbols, it's impossible to develop a counter-spell—it would be like trying to make an antibody with no idea of what we were trying to cure. Do you see?"

I nodded, suddenly weary. Heartsick.

"And even with a lexicon, and a translation, I'm not sure if I would be able to create the spell." I must have looked surprised or confused. "This is powerful magic, Mr. Knox. I'm not sure that I have it in me to counter it."

"But you might be able to?"

"If I had the lexicon, I might be able to do something. Maybe." She looked down at the book. "But this is dark stuff. And beautiful, in its own way. Lazarus Took spent a lot of time creating this, a lot of effort, a lot of magic." Her tone was almost admiring.

"What if we destroyed it?" I asked, returning to her earlier, instinctive reaction. "Wouldn't that release all of the trapped . . . energies?"

Nora shrugged. "It might. Or it might destroy them, along with the world they're living in."

All of the hopes that I had allowed to build in my mind, however guardedly, crashed back to earth.

"Thank you anyway," Tony Markus said, forcing a smile into his voice. "I'm sorry for taking up your time."

He hung up the phone and scratched the fourth number off his list. He deeply resented this cold-calling, this spade-work. Surely there had to be a better way.

Grumbling, he went to the fifth name on his list. *C.A. Took. Seaside, Oregon.*

He punched in the numbers and waited. It took two rings for the telephone to be picked up with an uncertain "Hello?"

"Good afternoon," he said. "I'm sorry to be calling like this. My name is Tony Markus. I'm an editor at Davis & Keelor in New York City, and I'm trying to track down someone who might be able to help me—"

"You're calling about my grandfather," she said. "Lazarus Took."

"Yes. Yes, I am." He settled back into his chair, ticking a large checkmark beside her name. "I was hoping to get in touch with someone from the estate."

"You just did," she said.

"This is—" He consulted the list. "C.A. Took?"

"You can call me Cat."

"Well, Cat, I'm calling because, first off, I'm a huge admirer of your grandfather's work. I read all of his books as a boy. I'm not sure if I'd be as much of a booklover as I am now if it weren't for his stories." Tony Markus took great pride in his ability to sling BS. "And I think it's just terrible that these books have been out of print for so long. It must be, what, more than thirty years?"

"Almost forty," she said.

"That's three generations of children who have missed out on these books? I think that's terrible. Cat, I'd like to talk to you about the possibility of bringing your grandfather's books back into print. Is that something you would be interested in?"

"That would be lovely," she said. "I'd just about given up hope of ever seeing them published again."

Sometimes it was too easy. "Well, I've got a few questions. First off, just to be clear: are you the person I should be discussing this with? Is there a board I should be presenting this to, or . . ."

"Oh, no, it's just me."

"So you've got signing authority as far as publication contracts and the like are concerned?"

"Yes."

"And the estate still holds the rights to those books?"

"Yes, it does."

He'd double-check that.

"And tell me, Cat: did your grandfather write anything else? We're definitely looking at reissuing the four novels, but if there were some other work, another novel perhaps, that would really round out the relaunch."

"You know, you're the second person this week to ask me that."

"Hmm," he grunted, silently cursing the Canadian writer. No sense of finesse—the idiot could have given the whole thing away.

"And before that, no one had asked about Lazarus for a very long time."

"So is there another book? Or some papers I could look at? I'm planning on being out in Oregon in the next couple of weeks; I could come by."

The idea of going out to Oregon had occurred to him on the fly, but it made sense. He hoped to have a copy of the book by that time. He'd carry the provisional agreement with him. And even if he didn't have the book yet, sitting down with her face-to-face would probably serve to lock him into a deal before the Canadian could take the deal to someone else.

"No, unfortunately Lazarus wrote only the four books. You'd be more than welcome to go through his papers here, though, if you're thinking of coming out this way."

"Oh, I wouldn't miss it, Cat."

☙ ❧

Captain Bream snapped to his feet as if he were facing a Berok attack. "What?" he spat.

"This is not the Sunstone," the magus repeated.

"Then what is it?" the captain asked, snapping out each word clearly and distinctly.

"It's a compass rose," the magus said, still studying the disk intently. "For a map. The writing is . . ." He hesitated. "It looks like instructions to a traveller. To *the* traveller." He glanced at David. "To you."

"And what does it say?"

The magus squinted into the wine, trying to read. "*To the Four Directions ride,*" he said. "*With stone and silver key to guide.*"

In the silence that followed, the only sound was the popping and crackling of the fire.

"And just what," the captain said, his voice seething, "in the name of the Queen does *that* mean?"

Neither David nor the magus had an answer ready for the captain.

"It's a compass rose," the magus said, as if thinking it through as he was speaking. "So it works with a map."

"Which map?" the captain asked, clearly having lost all patience. "There are dozens of maps."

"Dafyd," the magus said, turning to him. "Was there anything else in the chamber?"

David's heart stopped. Had he missed something?

"I—I don't think so," he stammered, not entirely sure.

"Dammit, think!" the captain barked.

"What about the wall?" the magus continued. "Where the stone was set?"

"It was just a wall."

There was nothing else there, Matt said. *Just the stone. And that poem. I would have seen anything else.*

"So no map?" the magus said.

"That was all," David said, gesturing at the cylinder.

"So this is what it comes to," the captain said in disgust. "We're left with a compass rose to a map that's lost to the river now."

David rose to his feet. "It wasn't there," he said, in his own defence. "If there was a map, I would have brought it out."

The captain stared at him for a long moment, his face setting in anger.

David, Matt said, *don't push him.*

David pulled his eyes away from the captain and sat back down, his face burning.

"So what do we do now?" the captain asked the magus, ignoring David altogether.

The magus was about to reply when David asked, "Did you look inside?"

⁂

I came to a sudden stop in the doorway of David's hospital room—he was sitting up in the bed, the blankets draped over his lap.

"What—?"

As Jacqui turned to me I took a closer look at David. His eyes were still moving rapidly from side to side, his mouth still slack, his hands still twitching.

"The rehab doctor came by," Jacqui said. "Dr. Jonas. He wanted to go over coping strategies."

"Coping strategies." The words had the grim finality of a life sentence: David wasn't going to get any better. Our future would consist of coping.

"The physiotherapist was very impressed with David's responsiveness. She had him up yesterday and taking a few steps with a walker, even. And Dr. Jonas says that if they get the seizures under control, he'll be able to come home." She sounded genuinely excited by the prospect, as if it marked a great victory.

She turned back toward David. "We're just about to have lunch, aren't we, Davy? We're going to practise eating." A covered tray sat on the bedside table.

The notion of my son having to practise eating filled me with a sick feeling that began in my lower belly and crept upwards.

"Did the tests show anything?" Still grasping at faint hopes.

"Dr. Rutherford hasn't been back yet."

"Shouldn't we wait until we hear what he has to say before we . . ." The words died on my lips.

She frowned at me. "It's just coping skills. We might not need them. And if David is this responsive . . ." She gave me a long look. "I know it's not perfect, Chris, but it wouldn't hurt to learn how to deal with this."

I nodded. Nobody knew better than me that need to be doing something, anything. "Okay," I said.

"Let's see what we've got here," she said, cooing a little as she lifted the lid off the tray. "Oh, this looks good. We've got some cream of wheat, and some pudding, and a nice ripe banana. That sounds like a great lunch. And they sent extra napkins."

I looked away as Jacqui unfolded a napkin and tucked one edge into the neckline of David's gown to make a bib.

Hands in my pockets, I watched her feed our eleven-year-old son the same way she had when he was a baby, the same tiny mouthfuls, the same soft food. I clenched my fists until my fingers ached, feeling more helpless by degrees.

How could he do this? How could Lazarus Took take my son as he had, stealing not only his future but the last eight or nine years of his life, all that living, all that growing, reducing him to a second infancy, an infancy that he might never grow out of? What kind of sick joke was this? What power came with crippling a child?

David picked the cylinder up from the ground, shaking it slightly in his hand. Something shifted inside. "Something's in here," he said, although it seemed obvious.

To you, maybe, Matt said. *But they've never seen a soup can.*

The magus leaned closer to the canister. "But how do we—?"

"Easily," the captain said, reaching for the cylinder and for the hilt of his sword in almost the same motion.

"Wait," David said, pulling the canister close to himself. "I think there's a better way."

Anger flashed in the captain's eyes.

He didn't like that, Matt said.

No, he didn't.

"We don't want to risk damaging whatever's inside," David said quickly, to soothe the captain.

The captain adjusted his sword-belt.

"I think," David said, as he curled his fingers around the lettered edges of the disk, which looked like the top of the container. "That if I do this . . ." The stone pressed cold into the palm of his hand as he twisted. "It should . . ." It took a moment of pressure, but a seal broke with a faint popping noise as the lid started to turn.

"There," he said, giving the lid several full turns. Gafilair or whoever had designed the cylinder clearly hadn't wanted to risk damage or rot to whatever was inside.

He had almost finished unscrewing the lid when Captain Bream plucked the container from his hands. David felt himself shrinking, like when Darren Kenneally started in on him.

Captain Bream removed the lid and upended the canister, allowing the contents to fall into his waiting hand: a heavy sack, and a scroll. Dropping the cylinder to the ground, he fumbled eagerly with the knot closing the sack, but as he opened it, his face fell.

"Sand," he said, shaking his head. "Red sand." He passed the bag to David.

Reaching in, David rubbed a pinch of the red sand between his thumb and forefinger. It was cold to the touch.

"And for you," Bream said as he passed the scroll to the magus. As he handed the container back to David, he almost dropped the compass rose.

David was about to say something—

Don't. This is not a place where they tolerate a boy talking back. Especially to a man with a sword.

David bit his lip and re-tied the bag of sand.

Setting his book on his lap to form a small table, the magus broke the twine wrapped around the scroll and carefully unrolled it. He glanced at the canister in David's hands.

"That is quite a remarkable box," he said appreciatively. "The vellum is more than a thousand years old, but perfectly preserved." He held one corner of the scroll between his thumb and forefinger, bending it slightly. It did not crease or tear. "Perfectly."

"Is it the map?" the captain asked.

"It is *a* map," the magus said. "I can only assume . . ." His voice stopped. "Ah, yes. I suspect this is the map we are looking for." He showed David and the captain the round hole that had been cut into the upper right corner of the vellum.

David passed the silver disk to the magus. Setting the map down on the book, Loren carefully placed the compass rose into the hole in the map. It fit perfectly.

Pulling the blanket tight around himself, David craned his neck to see the map more clearly.

"The rose," the magus said, "seems to be centred over the canyon. You can see the entry here." He pointed. "We're about here." He moved his finger to a spot partway downriver.

The river ran from the compass rose along the top edge of the page. It took David a moment to get his bearings. He touched the river near the edge of the vellum.

"So this, where we are, that's north."

The magus nodded.

"Does it tell us where to go?" the captain pressed.

"There's something written here," the magus said slowly, looking intently at the area of the scroll below the silver disk.

Leaning in, David could see the faint writing. It didn't look much like any of the printing in books that he had ever seen, with lots of tails and whorls, but he was able to follow along silently as the magus read the words out loud:

> By the day's first light
> Your journey shall be plain
> To forests of silver
> Through mountains of rain
> To the Four Directions
> The one shall ride
> The chosen your champion
> The Stone your guide.

The captain grunted his disapproval.

"Instructions, I think," the magus said. "It seems clear that something will happen with the Stone at dawn, something to show us the way."

David looked up from the writing to Loren's face. He waited for the magus to continue, but the old man didn't read aloud the final four lines:

> The chosen shall rise to the challenge alone
> Sacrifice all in search of the Stone
> And through triumph over death and betrayal
> Shall return to claim his rightful throne.

David was about to ask about the final four lines, when Matt cried out, *David, don't!*

He snapped his mouth shut.

He's hiding something, said Matt.

But he's not covering up the words.

Because he doesn't know you can read.

After a long meeting with the chief of Nursing, Jacqui's supervisor granted her a one-month leave of absence, with an option to renew if David's condition required it.

I had stayed at the hospital during the meeting because I wanted to be there when Dr. Rutherford returned with the test results. They revealed nothing out of the ordinary: I didn't know if that was good news or bad.

I had also stayed at the hospital for David. I couldn't bear the idea of him being alone.

To be completely honest, though, I stayed also because I had nowhere else to go. My quest was done—I had discovered the root of David's suffering, but there was nothing I could do to alleviate it.

Later, I helped Jacqui bathe him, lifting him slightly from the bed so she could take off his gown, holding one arm up, then the other, as she wiped at him, quickly and efficiently, with a warm, wet cloth. We dressed him in a clean gown, and she used a fresh cloth to wash his face. She lingered over his mouth, his stitches, the inside corners of his eyes, the gentle seam where his nose met his cheeks.

"I'll go downstairs for a bit," she said, after we had lowered him back down to the bed.

The words had come out of nowhere. "What? Why?"

"Isn't it storytime?" she asked. "I thought I'd give you guys a little time alone."

Of everything that Lazarus Took had done, the need to keep reading David the story that had crippled him was probably the cruellest. As I read, I could feel the bile in my throat, and the words turned to dust in my mouth. But I forced myself to read them, wondering what other stories were lurking just underneath. I savoured the moment that David's hands and eyes stilled, but any solace that I had once taken was tainted by the knowledge of Took's absolute control over my son's life, even from beyond the grave.

When I finally went home, I poured several fingers of vodka into a glass and tossed it back without feeling it, then poured two fingers more. I carried the glass over to the desk, shoving some of the books and papers aside to clear a place to set it. I slumped into the chair and stared at the mess. All that work, all those answers, and it didn't make any difference.

Reaching out without straightening, I woke up my computer.

Another message from Roger's assistant, reminding me of dinner in New York. A short note from Tony Markus, asking if there was any way I could send him even a photocopy of *To the Four Directions*.

They were both going to be disappointed.

The last e-mail was from Cat Took, titled, simply, "Thank you!"

Chris,

I just wanted to mail you to say thank you—I received a telephone call this afternoon from Tony Markus at Davis & Keelor, expressing his interest in republishing my grandfather's books. I suspect that there's no coincidence in his interest following so closely on our correspondence.

So thank you, again, for doing whatever you did to pique Mr. Markus's curiosity, and for your continued interest in, and now support of, my grandfather's work.

Yours,

Cat

I smiled bitterly to myself: Tony Markus had taken the ball and run with it.

Picking up my glass, I absently scrolled through Cat's message. Below her thank you was the entirety of our correspondence. I glanced at it idly—it all felt like so long ago, back in the days when every message seemed like it might hold a clue.

Yesterday. The day before.

I stopped scrolling down, but I wasn't sure why. I reread what was on the screen twice, trying to figure out what had twigged my subconscious. Then I saw it.

Reaching into my pocket for my notebook, I fumbled it open for the page where I had written down Sarah and Nora's phone number. My fingers shook as I dialled.

"Hello?"

"Sarah? It's Chris. Chris Knox. I'm sorry for calling so late."

"It's not that late," she said. "We're just playing a couple of hands of gin before Mom goes to bed. What is it? Did something happen to your son?"

"No, no. Listen, I need to . . . I need to see you both."

"Why? What is it?"

I looked at the computer screen, at a paragraph from one of Cat's earlier e-mails.

"I think I know where I can find the lexicon," I said.

PART THREE

New York

THE NIGHT PASSED SLOWLY. They let the fire go out before the darkness set in, and the air was cold. He hadn't felt warm since he had come out of the river, even with his clothes dry again. Still, it was a small price to pay for being alive.

Sort of.

He held his hand up against the moon, marvelling at the size of it.

David. Dafyd.

Where did Dafyd end and David begin?

Triumph over death

The words from the scroll tumbled through his head, like pieces to a puzzle that needed solving. He was utterly exhausted, his body aching and battered, but every time he closed his eyes he saw the lines of verse on the map, the brown ink faint against the cream-coloured vellum.

The chosen shall rise to the challenge alone

The words Loren hadn't read aloud.

What did you mean, when you said that Loren didn't know I could read? David thought.

Remember, they don't know that you're . . . you, Matt said. *All they see is Dafyd, the tavern woman's son. Most people, in books like this, they don't go to school. Unless they're noble, or part of a religious group.*

Like the soldier at the garrison gate, David remembered. *Captain Bream said he couldn't read.*

Captain Bream probably can't read either, Matt said. *Or any of the soldiers. Why do you think they brought Loren along?*

David thought back to all the conversations he had had with Bream and Loren, and with the Queen herself. All that talk about deciphering the ancient scrolls . . .

How do you know all this? he asked Matt.

I love books like this one, he said. *Don't you?*

I'm not sure, David confessed. *I don't read that much.*

Oh shit, man, Matt muttered. *Are you ever in over your head.*

David nodded, his mind flashing back to the last lines on the map.

So what do you think Loren is hiding? David asked.

Something about you, Matt answered, echoing David's deepest suspicions. *I mean, you are the chosen one, right?*

That's what he says.

He was the one who chose you—chose Dafyd—for this. There has to be some reason why.

He said it was written in the ancient scrolls.

David thought about the oversized book that the magus carried with him, and what secrets it might be hiding.

⇁ ⇀

It only took unpacking my laptop bag to recreate a facsimile of my desk in the hotel room, complete with computer, notebooks, a couple of novels, a folder with hotel information and notes for the trip. The only thing missing was an ashtray: the whole of the Grand Hyatt had gone non-smoking since the last time I stayed there.

I had planned on cancelling my trip to New York, but Cat's reference to her grandfather's papers being sold to the Hunter Barlow Library had changed my mind.

"Are you sure it's there?" Sarah had asked when I told her of my plan. She, Nora and I were again sitting around the kitchen table.

"Not one hundred percent, no," I confessed. "But his granddaughter told me that that's where most of his papers ended up. I just need to know what I'm looking for. I have no idea what a lexicon might look like."

"It could look like anything," Nora said.

"That's not really helpful."

"It's a code. A key, for translation. If he was using it for rituals, for the Order as a whole, it might be a pamphlet or a small book, explaining each symbol, why it was chosen, giving a bit of arcane history . . ."

"Pamphlet," I said, jotting notes. "How will I know I've got the right one? What if there are a whole bunch of different codes?"

Nora leaned forward. "I don't think you'll have to worry about that. The symbols used on the book are very powerful. They weren't chosen lightly, and my guess is that they've built up a lot of power from their use by this order. I think that once this system was developed, they stuck with it. We're not talking about dabblers, here."

As I was leaving, less than an hour later, Nora embraced me in the doorway.

"Here," she said as she stepped back. She fumbled at the back of her neck, her hands coming away with the crystal dangling from its length of chain. "I think you should have this." I lowered my head, and she fastened the chain around my neck. "It probably won't help you at all. There's no spell on it"—she smiled—"but crystal does help one focus and see things clearly, so . . ."

"Thank you," I had said, holding the crystal in my hand.

In the days before my flight, I had tried to find out as much as I could about the Hunter Barlow Library, the private collection that had bought Lazarus Took's papers in 1949. There wasn't much information online: the library's own website seemed wilfully unhelpful, while other sites referred to the library's impressive collection of occult materials, "which runs as a counterpoint to the mainstream of the twentieth century."

Even with packing and preparations, I'd spent as much time as possible at the hospital. David was becoming more responsive: he could eat and chew, and was able to walk, haltingly and with a walker, a few steps at a time. But his level of catatonia meant he was incapable of initiating even the most basic of actions. Jacqui could lead him into the bathroom and sit him on the toilet, but left to his own devices he would wet himself and not even notice. His will, his awareness, his initiative, were all gone.

And now I knew exactly where they were.

Under the light from the hotel desk lamp, the symbols on the cover of *To the Four Directions* still glowed faintly.

"I know you don't want to talk," I had said to Jacqui last night, before we left the hospital.

She took a deep breath and stiffened. Preparing herself.

"But I'm wondering if you could do me a favour while I'm gone. For David."

Reaching into my bag, I pulled out a thick sheaf of papers: a photocopy of *To the Four Directions*. "Could you read to him while I'm gone?"

She looked at me disbelievingly.

"Please. It's important."

Pursing her lips, she took the papers.

"Thank you," I said. "I've marked the place where we left off. It's important that he be read to as close to eight o'clock as possible."

She rolled her eyes as she turned away.

"I know you don't believe it. It's probably just a coincidence, but he hasn't had any seizures since I've been reading to him at the usual time, and I'm hoping, even if you do it just to humour me—"

"I said I'd do it, didn't I?" she snapped.

Her response silenced me for a moment. "You didn't, actually."

She'd lowered her eyes. "Well, I will."

Now I glanced at my watch and did the time-zone math in my head. Just before dinnertime at home—a good time to call.

Jacqui answered on the third ring.

"Hey," I said.

"Hey."

"I made it in okay."

Nothing.

"I left you a note with my hotel information, my flight numbers and stuff."

"I got it."

"Good," I said. "How's David?"

"He's home."

"What?" Thinking I must have misheard her.

"He's home. I checked him out today. I've got a bed set up for him in the family room for the time being."

"What? When did this . . .?"

"The doctor said we could try it, with his progress in the rehab and the fact that he hasn't had any seizures in a week. We were about to have some dinner."

"Why didn't you wait till I was home?" I asked, almost too stunned to ask.

"Why?" she scoffed. "If I'm doing all of this on my own, what difference does it make what time zone you're in?"

"Jacqui—"

"I've gotta go," she said. "I'm making dinner."

I sat at the end of the bed for several minutes, the cell phone dead in one hand, the other clutching the solid warmth of the crystal through my shirt.

※ ※

David lay flat on his back, unable to sleep, staring up at the starry sky.

It's beautiful.

It is, Matt agreed, his voice touched with wonder. It took David a moment to realize that this was probably the first starry night Matt had seen in who knows how long.

Do you think they're the same stars here, he asked, *as at home?* The thought of home, his mother and his father, his hamster Nolan, cut him with sadness. He couldn't imagine how much harder it must be for Matt, and he immediately regretted asking the question.

Maybe, Matt said, not giving any indication of sadness. *It's a lot like home in a lot of ways.*

David tried to still his mind as he watched the flickering of the stars. A question was coming together, and he tried not to think it, tried to keep it from Matt's attention. But struggling to avoid the question only seemed to bring it into focus, like that old trick of trying not to think about an elephant.

What do you think happened to us, he thought, *back there? In the real world, I mean. To our bodies?*

The question had been gnawing at the edge of his mind since he had awoken in the cave and realized that his old body, which couldn't

really run, couldn't play baseball, with its too-small hands and too-short
height had been replaced by these tough, rough hands, this rangy height,
this body too skinny to get comfortable on the hard ground.

I think I died, Matt said simply. *I remember*—His voice grew tight.
This was obviously something that he had tried not to think about. *I
remember reading. In my bedroom. It was the Fourth of July. My friends
were setting off fireworks in the alley behind the Bartell Drugs. But I didn't
go. All I wanted to do was read.*

David remembered that feeling.

*I got to that section in the cave, and when Matthias reached for the
stone, it felt like I got a . . . a shock A bad one. The last thing I remember
is dropping the book, and the taste of blood in my mouth. And then . . . I
was here.*

David couldn't breathe.

But that doesn't mean you died, David thought, arguing against the
worst of his own fears.

*You saw me. I don't know of any other way for a spirit to come out of
a body,* he said. *Do you?*

"Magic," David whispered.

It's all magic, Matt said, his words bitter and pointed. *And I think
we both know who's to blame.*

David thought of Loren, and the huge book he carried. The book
the magus thought only he could read.

Exactly, Matt said.

David pictured his room, his body lying lifeless on the carpet. It
didn't feel like he had died. He could still remember everything about
his old life, a connection to his old self like he might be able to pull
himself back to his body at any time.

If only he knew how.

Maybe that's the way ghosts always feel, Matt said. *Maybe that's why
they keep trying to go back.*

THE TELEPHONE JARRED ME from a fractured sleep of strange, unpleasant dreams. Hotel-sleep: one of the reasons I didn't like to venture too far from home.

"Hello," I groaned into the phone, expecting it to be Jacqui.

"Mr. Knox?"

I sat up in bed at the sound of the strange voice. A man's voice. And then it occurred to me that Jacqui would have called my cell.

"Yes?"

"It's Tony Markus calling. From Davis & Keelor. I'm glad I caught you."

Sleep-addled, it took me a moment to recognize the name. "Right. Tony Markus."

"How was your flight?"

It was too surreal to continue having this conversation in the curtain-blotted dark. "Fine," I said as I reached for the lamp on the bedside table.

"Good. I'm glad to hear it. And I'm glad to hear that you changed your mind and decided to come to New York."

"How did you get this number?" I was starting to put things together. I had managed to avoid Tony Markus's e-mails and calls for the past week—there was no way he should have known that I was in New York.

"Oh," he said. "I spoke to your wife. She was kind enough to tell me where you were staying."

Still more questions, but I didn't have time to ask them. And then I noticed the time on the clock-radio: noon.

"I wonder if you'd let me buy you lunch?" he asked without pause.

"Or breakfast, perhaps, from the sound of things." He chuckled. "I'm hoping we could talk about—"

"Lazarus Took," I finished for him, trying to think of ways to avoid lunch.

"Well, yes, that, of course," he said. "But actually, I'd like to talk to you about your own work."

That brought me up short. "My work?"

"I didn't put it together when we first spoke. Different contexts and such, I suppose. But I read *Coastal Drift* when I was in college. I loved it. I just loved it."

Absolutely speechless.

"I was hoping we'd have a chance to sit down and talk about it, and about what you're working on now."

"Sure," I said. "Do you have someplace in mind?"

"Well, that depends on your plans for the rest of the afternoon."

I told him that I was hoping to spend a few hours at the Metropolitan Museum and he quickly suggested a restaurant just off Lexington, a few blocks from there.

"It's a small place, pretty low-key, but the food is fabulous."

He gave me thorough directions, but a subway ride later, still sleep-addled, I almost walked past it: there was a single window and a small, unassuming door with DONOFRIO's on a brass plate and the hours below. I saw no indication at all that it was a restaurant.

I checked my watch. Fifty-five minutes from bed to brunch—not too shabby. Juggling my coffee cup between my hands, I managed to light a cigarette without spilling a drop.

The first cigarette of the day, with a hot coffee on a sunny New York spring afternoon—it really didn't get any better than that. I could almost forget what was happening at home. Almost.

"I can't believe my eyes," said an overweight man who had lumbered up beside me, his voice thick with a Brooklyn accent.

I glanced over at him, assuming he was talking on a cell phone, surprised to see him looking directly at me.

"I thought you West Coast types were all about healthy living and yoga and that sort of thing." He extended his hand. "Tony Markus," he said.

Cocking the cigarette in the corner of my mouth, I shook his hand. "Chris Knox," I said. "How did you know it was me?"

He smiled broadly and took the book out from under his arm. It was the hardcover of *Coastal Drift*, the one with my picture on the fly-leaf. The same one Tara Scott had been carrying.

I already preferred that meeting to this one.

"I'm a little older than that now," I muttered. "It's a wonder you recognized me at all."

"I wasn't expecting to see you out here smoking, either," he said.

I took one last drag and flicked my butt into the street. "I'm a writer," I said, blowing out the smoke as Tony held the restaurant door open for me. "Someone's got to conform to the stereotypes." I wasn't sure who I had stolen the line from.

He grinned. "I guess that means martinis with lunch."

⤞ ⤝

Dawn arrived eventually, the black sky fading to the purple hue of a bruise. The camp came quietly to life with the sound of men stowing their bedrolls, packing their horses. They did not speak.

David rose slowly, his body aching. Shivering in the cool air, he went in search of the magus.

A short distance from the camp, close to the river's edge, the old man was leaning over a flat rock, looking intently down at something by the faint glow of a lamp. He looked up at the sound of approaching footsteps.

"Ah, Dafyd. I trust you slept well, after yesterday's hardships."

His voice was so friendly David wondered if his suspicions, his and Matt's fears, were misplaced. But then he saw the massive book tucked under the old man's arm.

"Not really," he said. He took several steps forward.

"That's unfortunate," Loren said. "There are more hard days to come, I think."

David gestured with his hand toward the rock. "Is that the map?"

"Yes, yes," the old man said. He beckoned for David to come closer. David reluctantly joined him.

The magus had laid the map out on the surface of the rock, with stones on each corner to keep it flat.

"I've lined it up so the compass faces north," he explained, gesturing at the silver disk with the red stone. "And the river on the map is aligned with the actual river. It's just a guess, really, but if something is to happen at dawn it seems to me that it might be best if everything is lined up and ready."

"I'm sure you're right," came a deep voice out of the shadows. David hadn't heard the captain approach.

The captain doesn't like him either, Matt said.

"How will this work?" the captain asked. He didn't acknowledge David's presence.

"We'll know soon," the magus said, looking up at the sky, quickly brightening.

They didn't wait long. Only minutes later, the first light of the sun broke across the crest of the distant hills, a faint sliver of gold against the darkness.

The light struck the top of the red stone, and it burst with colour. A thin ray of red light shot from one of the stone's facets across the map.

David took a half-step back.

Partway down the map the beam touched the vellum in a tiny red dot.

After a moment, smoke began to curl from the spot.

"It's capturing the sunlight," the magus said. "And using it to show us the way!"

David had learned about light and refraction at school: how had Gafilair done it? Had he found a stone with a fault in it that would make the light refract in just the right way, to direct the light to a particular point on a map . . . Or was it more magic?

As quickly as it had started, the beam faded and disappeared. The sun had risen higher, the intensity of those first moments replaced with the steady glow of another morning.

"That's where we're headed next," the magus said, gesturing at the small burn mark, still smoking, on the vellum map.

That was cool, Matt said.

The captain, however, was not convinced.

"How can we be sure?" he asked, looking closely at the map. The hole was far to the south of them, and looked to be nestled in the bend of a smaller river.

"It's as Brother Gafilair planned," the magus said. "He left us the tools, and the instructions for their use."

"But how do you know you read the instructions correctly, Loren?" the captain demanded.

"I lined up the map—"

"But if you were even a degree off, or had your stone at slightly the wrong angle, would not the marking be off as well?"

David flinched at the captain's raised voice.

"I . . . yes . . ." The magus kept glancing between the captain and the map.

"So we should just take it on faith that your calculations were correct and lead my best men hundreds of miles to the south?"

What an asshole, Matt muttered.

The captain glared at the magus, daring him to argue.

When he didn't speak, the captain turned on his heel and called out to his men as he walked away. "Break camp," he said loudly. "We've got a long day's ride."

～ ～

Tony Markus took a care with his actions that straddled the border between fastidious and prissy. He had spent several seconds hanging his coat, making sure the shoulder seams lined up with the back of the chair. Setting his copy of *Coastal Drift* on the table between us, he had lined it up carefully with the table's edge, rubbing a spot on the cover lightly with his thumb to remove a smudge.

When the waitress arrived with our drinks, he carefully arranged his napkin on his lap before picking up his glass. He took a small sip of his mojito and smacked his lips in satisfaction.

"I'm thrilled that you were able to take the time to have lunch with me today," he began.

I smiled and took a deep swallow from my martini. It left a comforting trail of warmth all the way down.

"I really should have recognized your name when I got that first e-mail," he said. "Especially since you were writing from Victoria." He took another tiny sip from his drink. At that rate, it was going to take him most of the afternoon to finish it. "But then, you don't really expect one of your favourite authors to just e-mail you out of the blue."

I didn't know how to respond; it had been a long time since I'd had smoke blown quite so exuberantly up my ass.

"Do you mind if I ask you some questions about it?"

"No, not at all," I said. Another healthy swallow from my martini, which was disappearing all too fast.

He paused briefly while the waiter took our lunch order.

At first, I was comfortable answering the expected questions: my inspiration, whether the book was based on my life, my writing process. It had been a long time, but I slipped easily into the practised patter, the book tour boilerplate. But there was no way he had retained that much from reading the book years before. He had clearly only read the book in the last few days.

It was a set-up. Nicely engineered, I had to give him that. I hoped that he had made someone a little money on eBay, purchasing the book.

I waved the waitress over and ordered another martini, smiling at Tony as I drained off my first one and handed her the glass. No reason not to make the most of it.

A few minutes later I was thoroughly enjoying my steak, crisp and spiced on the outside, pink and cool in the middle. He had ordered a salad, and I managed not to break into laughter when he began to cut each leaf of lettuce into smaller pieces with his knife before placing it carefully between his lips.

"So about Lazarus Took," he began when his salad was done, folding his napkin and placing it on the edge of his plate.

I nodded, allowing one of my last bites of steak to melt on my tongue.

"I've had an intern digging through boxes of old contracts in New Jersey for the last week." He smiled, as if this were the most hilarious thing he could imagine. "And I've been in touch with the estate, just to see if there was any interest there."

I was surprised that he would admit to the end-run. "So much for keeping it between us," I said, setting my knife and fork side by side on the plate.

"The strange thing is, the woman at the estate didn't seem to know about any unpublished writings."

I nodded. "That's what I told you."

"Of course," he said. "You did. It does make it difficult, though, to be talking about publishing a book that a deceased author's representative doesn't even know exists."

"Don't get ahead of yourself," I said, finishing another martini, enjoying the way the world blurred on the edges of my vision.

He ignored my comment and cut right to the chase. "Do you have it? The book, I mean. Can I see it? I need to be able to look at it before I even think of bringing the idea up with my publisher. It's not like she would agree to publish a book that neither of us has ever seen, right?"

I reached for my bag, but immediately second-guessed myself.

He caught the interrupted movement. "You've got it *here*?" he said excitedly, starting to move his plate to clear a spot in front of himself.

In for a penny, I thought, as I reached into the bag and passed him the book. Tony's eyes lit up like a child's at Christmas.

"Oh, that's lovely," he said. He handled the book carefully, weighing it in his hands, turning it over front to back. "That's gorgeous. I mean, we'd want to put a jacket on it, make it more enticing to young readers, but we could print the boards like this, class it up for the adult crossover market." He held it up to show me as if he were a spokesmodel, as if he were practising the pitch to his publisher.

I tried to rein him in. "Like I said, nothing's set in stone right now."

"Oh, I know, I know," Tony said, starting to flip through the pages. "If we do go ahead with this, though, we'll really need to jump on it. It's not like we've got to wait for a manuscript, right?"

"I'll have to talk to the estate," I said.

"Of course," he said, still buried in the book. "We'll have to talk to the estate, make sure they're on board."

A slow wave of anger was rising in me, but it was my fault. This was the monster I had created.

"Have you read it?" he asked, carefully turning the pages.

I nodded. "Most of it."

"How is it?"

And with that question, my stomach lurched. I'd been so caught up in the business, in the lunch, that I had somehow managed to overlook, for a moment, the true nature of what I had handed him. It looked like a book, but it was a bomb. And I had no idea when the fuse would start burning.

"It's good," I said haltingly. "Of its time. I mean, it's worlds away from what kids are reading now. It's a bit dated." My heart was pounding in my chest, and I cursed the third martini as I tried to ease him away from his interest. "To be honest, I'm not sure what someone coming from Harry Potter would make of it."

"Mm-hmm," he said, and I noticed with horror that he had flipped to the first page, that he had started to read. "I see what you mean," he said slowly, running one finger along each line as he came to it.

I started to feel optimistic. He would read a bit more, then decide to pass. Why take on a forgotten mid-level hack? If Lazarus Took was forgotten, there was probably a good reason for it, right?

"I don't think the prose is a problem, though," he said slowly, still not looking up.

"What?" How could an editor not be concerned about the writing?

"I'm not worried about it," he said as he closed the book and set it on the spot he had cleared. "The thing is, when they're done with Harry Potter, there's a whole generation of kids turning to the Narnia books and *The Lord of the Rings*. And there's *nobody* more stilted than Tolkien, is there?"

He looked at me for agreement and I managed a weak smile.

"So how should we proceed?" he asked, his tone tightening, strengthening. For a moment I understood how he could have dragged a memoir out of a convicted mafia killer.

As I thought about my response, he drummed his fingers slowly on the corner of the book.

"Well, there's the matter of the rights—"

He waved the comment away with a flick of his wrist. "Not an issue," he said. "Rights must have reverted to the estate years ago. Hell, everyone who signed that contract is dead now. Long dead. But I don't think we'll need them anyway. I've started to develop a pretty good relationship with Cat Took."

He was calling her Cat. Jesus, I couldn't believe that I had inflicted this man on that poor, unsuspecting woman.

Still, it had seemed to make sense at the time. Anything to help David.

"Well, I guess it's time for me to talk to Cat, to tell her about the book." I gestured at it. "She's probably aware that something's up."

"In that case," he said, shifting, "why don't we concentrate our efforts, consolidate, so she's talking to only one of us. Cut down on the confusion."

I nodded. "That sounds like a good idea."

"Good," he said, laying both hands on the book and starting to move it toward himself. "I'll hang on to this—"

"No."

"What?" He seemed genuinely shocked.

"That's mine," I said, gesturing toward the book. "I'm not handing it over to anyone."

"But if I'm going to be negotiating with the estate . . ."

"You're not," I said, my tone still strong. "I have to talk to Cat, let her know what I've found, and the estate can decide how they want to proceed."

"Can decide on your finder's fee, you mean." The cool strength that he had demonstrated a few minutes before was dissolving into frustrated petulance.

"What I decide to do with my property is entirely my business," I said. "Now . . ." I extended my hand for the book, hoping I could maintain the facade of confidence long enough.

"Can we at least"—he rushed the words, a little desperate, still holding the book—"talk about the timing? Can you keep me in the loop as to how your discussions go with the estate?"

What I said next didn't matter. Once I got the book and myself away from Tony Markus, it would be easy to ignore him. The miracle of the digital age: with e-mail and call display, it was now possible to erase someone from your life entirely.

"Sure," I said, putting on a congenial smile. "I'm not trying to screw you over or anything. I just need to look out for my interests, right?" If he wanted to think me mercenary, I could play along.

He nodded, and his relief was obvious on his face.

"I'll try to get in touch with Cat over the next few days, tell her about the book, see what we can come up with."

"So just a couple of days?" He grasped at what little hope I was leaving him.

"Sure."

"So I should hear something from you by Monday or so?"

I shrugged. "Probably." What the hell. I had no intention of calling Cat while I was in New York, or, potentially, ever again, depending on what Sarah and Nora could do with the book. Once they were done with it, I never wanted to hear the name Lazarus Took again.

"Monday, then," he confirmed.

"Okay."

He nodded, comfortable again.

I reached out for the book and he picked it up off the table and extended it toward me, pulling it back at the last moment, smiling like it was a joke we shared. I don't think the smile with which I reciprocated was all that convincing.

⋙ ⋘

David had a moment of crisis as they broke camp. One of the men tacked his horse and packed his saddlebags, leaving David to stand next to the mount, with no idea what to do.

I've never ridden a horse, he whispered in his mind.

What? Matt responded, sounding shocked.

Well, have you?

The other boy was silent for a moment, and David reached out, tentatively touching the saddle.

Matt, he called out, increasingly desperate. *What should I—?*

Just do it.

But I can't.

Dafyd can, so you can. Just . . . don't think about it.

David wondered for a moment, as he put his foot into the stirrup, if Matt was as confident as he sounded. But then he was in the saddle, his other foot finding the other stirrup, the reins comfortable in his hands.

See, Matt said.

David thought he could hear relief in his voice, though.

They rode out of the dry, rolling hills and into rougher terrain of valleys and sharp rises, the forests growing thicker on either side of the narrow roadway. The forests were different here from those around Colcott Town, the trees taller, the air lacking the sweet coolness of the sea air he was so familiar with. The trees seemed to swallow up the sound of their passing and a stillness settled over them, despite their speed. Captain Bream drove them hard.

When they finally stopped to make camp, David all but fell off his mount, stumbling onto the soft ground just off the road and falling onto his back. His vision swam with flashes of light.

"David?" the magus asked, looming over him.

"Just trying to catch my breath."

The old man half smiled. "That was a hard ride."

David glanced over at Captain Bream, who was methodically unpacking his saddlebags. "It doesn't seem to have affected him too much."

The magus shook his head. "No, it wouldn't, would it? He didn't nearly drown yesterday." He held out his hand, and David allowed himself to be helped to his feet.

The river was just a short distance through the forest, and David knelt beside it and drank from the clear, cold water before filling several skins to bring with him.

When he arrived back at camp, one of the soldiers from the first company was talking to Captain Bream, their voices hushed, their faces grim.

The magus stepped toward them. "There's news?" he asked, ignoring the angry look Bream shot him.

The young guardsman was out of breath. He had obviously just ridden in. "There is, sir. We've found a Berok encampment just ahead. We almost rode right into them."

I waited until I had walked over to the Metropolitan Museum of Art before I dialled my cell. I wanted to put as much distance between myself and Tony Markus as possible, and I wanted to be out in the sun, in the warmth, anything to vanquish the chill I was feeling.

"Hello?"

"Sarah?" It was hard to tell over the shaky connection.

"Yes?" Obviously the difficulty went both ways.

"It's Chris. Chris Knox."

"Do you have it? Already?"

"No, no. The library isn't open until Monday. I do have a question, though."

"All right." Her voice suddenly guarded.

"I just had lunch with someone," I began, then decided to skip the preamble. "What would happen if someone published *To the Four Directions*?"

She was silent for a long moment. Then she said, "Oh, Chris."

"That bad."

"I think so," she said. "Mom's here, though—let me ask her." She put her hand over the receiver, and for almost a minute I listened to a muffled thud and hiss, and then she was back on the line. "Actually, Mom says it probably wouldn't be a problem—"

"Oh, thank—"

"—so long as they didn't use the cover. That's where the first stages of the spell are set, so . . ."

The cold, sick feeling that I had been trying to walk off came back in a rush, and I almost doubled over. "And if they did use the cover? Would the spell still work, even though it's being mass-produced?"

"I don't see why not," she said. "All the recipes in *The Joy of Cooking* work, right? Why are you asking, Chris?"

My silence seemed to say enough.

"Someone isn't publishing it, are they? Chris? How did that—?"

"It's a long story," I said weakly.

"They can't," she said, with certainty. "It's too dangerous. You can't let them."

"I won't," I said, my confidence undermined by the memory of the smile on Tony Markus's face as he described the millions of Harry Potter readers, all eager for a new author to read.

. . . a whole generation of children . . .

⌁

"Berok?" the captain snarled, stepping closer to the guardsman. "We should be out of their territory by now."

"It looks like a patrol group," the young guard said.

"Are they tracking?" the captain asked. "Are they searching for us?"

The guard shook his head. "I don't think so, sir. They were making an awful lot of noise for a scouting party, sir, as they were making camp. That's how we noticed them."

The captain nodded thoughtfully. "They don't know we're here," he said.

The thought chilled David's blood: the attack on the road, the way the arrows had seemed to come from nowhere. He could almost feel eyes upon him, even now.

"Where are they camped?"

"Close to the river, sir, a few miles ahead, where the floodplain starts to narrow into a gorge. They're on the flats, pretty open, but they've got the river on one side and a rock wall on the other."

"So there's no way around them."

"We could go up, sir. Ride back until we can take the higher ground, come around them on the rise. They'd never know we were there."

"That's almost a full day's ride back," the captain said, considering it.

David became aware of the magus shifting uneasily next to him.

The captain paced slightly, his jaw set, his eyes looking out at the darkening middle distance of the forest.

"Ride out," he said, his voice firm. "Bring the third company forward. We'll muster here."

⌁

Tony Markus waited by the phone until 11 that night, giving the Canadian a fair chance to call. He was almost happy when the phone didn't ring. He had no reason to expect Chris Knox to get back in touch with him before he left New York and some opportunities needed to be seized before they disappeared altogether.

At 11:01 he picked up the phone. He had called the number so often he was able to dial it from memory. Martine answered after the second ring.

"Allo?" Her voice was still heavily accented, despite her having left the Ukraine more than five years ago.

"Martine, it's Tony Markus calling."

"Little Tony." Her voice was warm and expansive, almost nurturing. It was that strange combination—earthy compassion and understanding wrapped in a six-foot-two, bleached blonde, voluptuous vixen—that had kept the customers at the strip club where she had first worked when she arrived in New York desirably off balance, and had earned her a dedicated clientele when she was working as a call girl.

Anthony Marcelli had fallen in love with Martine the first time he laid eyes on her. "Like a bolt from the blue," he had told Tony. "I saw her and—boom—that was it."

In his book, Marcelli's journey from mob enforcer to government witness was all about making one right choice after a lifetime of bad, the sort of story that sells a lot of books. The truth was a little more complicated: his wife, Angela, had ordered him to choose between her and his "Russian whore." He had chosen Martine, had taken her into witness protection with him, and there they had been living, happily ever after.

"Everything is okay, yes?" Martine continued.

"Everything is good. And you? How are you?"

"I think I'm getting fat," she said. "Tony says no, but he likes his women a little fat, so he can't be trusted."

"I think you probably look as good as you ever did," Tony said, the words feeling thick and ungainly as they fell off his tongue.

"You men and your lies." He could tell that she was smiling.

"Is Big Tony around?"

"Where else would he be?" she asked. "All day he's around. Never leaves house. Never goes out. People always coming to him and he sitting around the house all day. You think I'm getting fat, you should see him."

"Can I speak to him, please?"

"Ya. I get him." She dropped the phone on the counter with a sharp rattle and click.

"Little Tony." His voice boomed on the line a few moments later. "I thought I told you never to call me here."

They both laughed at the traditional greeting.

"How's it going, Uncle Tony?"

"It's fuckin' Utah," he said, not even pausing for a breath. "It's a hundred and fifty degrees, I'm surrounded by Mormons and deserts, how the hell do you think I'm doing?" His uncle hung up the phone without another word.

Tony Markus paced around his cramped apartment, waiting for his cell phone to ring. It wouldn't happen right away—Tony would need to get to his office, pick one of the cell phones out of his desk drawer, double-check that it was fresh, punch in the number from the call display of his legit line, and then call.

It was convoluted, but it wouldn't do for it to be discovered that a star government witness, a man who had claimed redemption and illumination in the pages of a bestselling book, was still doing business via anonymous cell phones with the boys back east from his Utah rancher, bought and sponsored by the U.S. government.

The cell phone—which Tony had bought with cash at the scuzzy bodega two subway stops away that afternoon—rang. The sound startled him and he pressed the Answer button.

"I'm starting to feel like Marlon Brando," Big Tony said, without preamble.

"Martine said you were getting fat," Tony said, in what he hoped was a sufficiently jocular manner.

Big Tony choked out a laugh. "I meant the way people are always asking for favours. So why the call? You want to write another book and put my name on it?"

"No, nothing like that."

"Too bad."

"I need something, Uncle Tony." He could picture the novel in his hands, remembered the weight of it, the texture of the cover. He remembered how reluctant that journalist had been to even let him hold it.

Tony Markus—born Anthony Marcelli, named after his father's grandfather, just as his uncle Tony had been—had far too much riding on this to let some hick journalist, some fucking Canadian, get in his way.

"I need a book."

≽ ≼

David wanted to say something to the captain after the young guardsman rode away, but Loren's hand on his shoulder stopped him.

When he turned, the old man cocked his head toward the river. They walked along the shoreline a ways before the old man spoke.

"It seems strange to me," the magus said. "The way rivers seem at the heart of such paradoxes. This river, here, feeds into the river that spills into the sea by the castle. In many ways, it is the same river, but it's both here and there. It is permanent, but always changing."

David just watched him.

"Forgive me," he said. "These are the sorts of things an old man ponders." The magus picked up a stick. "You were dangerously close to treason back there."

"What?" David asked. "I didn't say—"

"No," the magus said. He threw the stick into the water. "It was what you were *going* to say. You were about to ask why we wouldn't just ride around, yes?" The look on David's face must have been all the confirmation he needed. "Why we didn't just take the extra two days and avoid the Berok encampment altogether, correct?"

David nodded slowly.

"If you were a soldier, those sorts of questions, to a captain in the field, would have had you beaten for insubordination."

He's not wrong, Matt said.

David started to speak, but the magus held up a hand. "But you're not a soldier. Which would have made those questions, in a time of war, akin to treason."

That stopped David. He thought of the innkeeper, and how close he had come to hanging.

"The truth is," the magus said, "I agree with you. I think we would be wise to avoid a potentially costly fight with the Berok. But this is Captain Bream's decision. It's his command. An extra two days' ride is not insignificant, especially when time is as important as it is right now."

David nodded. That made sense.

"And then there are the men themselves."

"What do you mean?"

The magus sighed. "It has not been long since the watchtowers fell. These men lost good friends that night. They've been waiting for an opportunity to bring the fight back to the Berok. I suspect that that was one of the main reasons so many of them agreed so quickly to join this mission. And after the attack on the road, what the captain is planning will, if nothing else, be good for morale."

David felt sick at the words.

The magus looked at him gravely. "We're at war, Dafyd. It is expected that men do terrible things."

⤝ ⤞

I spilled myself out of the cab in front of the hotel, allowing my fluid momentum to carry me through the crowds on 42nd Street, across the lobby, and into the right set of elevators. Somehow I managed to remember what floor to punch in, and it took only three or four tries with the key card to get into my room.

I kicked my shoes off and fell on the bed, pulling my cell phone out of my pocket to dial Jacqui's number.

"I was beginning to think you weren't going to call," she said, without a hello.

"I'm a man of my word," I said carefully, rolling onto my back and staring at the ceiling, trying to make the multiple smoke detectors merge into the single one I knew was actually there.

"Right now you sound like a man of many drinks."

"I confess I've had a few."

"And how was Roger?"

"Yeah," I said cautiously.

"What is it?" she asked. "Did something . . .?"

"It seems—" I was diligent about forming each word in my mouth. "I need to find new representation."

"Oh, Chris."

"He was good enough to buy me dinner, though, before he cut me loose."

"I'm sorry."

"It's all right," I said, having trouble forming full sentences. "I've been rethinking the book. Where it's going."

"What?"

"How's David?" I asked, desperate to change the subject.

The meeting with Roger and his assistant had been brutal, in a polite, cordial, bloodless way. When he told me that he was no longer interested in being my agent, I couldn't even pretend to be surprised. No new books, not a whole lot of point. He had managed not to be quite so blunt.

"The same," she said, her tone turning dark.

"No more seizures?"

"I've been reading to him, if that's what you're asking. I told you I would."

"I was just checking to see how he was."

She sighed. "Sorry. I have to say, though, I can see why he got so into that book. It's got fights and quests and mysteries . . ."

"Everything a boy might like," I said, thinking of a gingerbread house in a dark forest.

"And how are you?" I asked.

"Better than you, from the sound of things."

"Which probably goes without saying."

"I'm all right," she said. "This is hard. Harder than I thought it would be. Being with him all the time, having to do every little thing."

"I'll be home in a few days," I said, not sure if she would want to hear it.

"I'm glad," she said, surprising me.

"Me too," I said, and then nothing. A long silence.

"So, publicists Monday?"

"Yeah," I lied, grateful that she had changed the subject. "Fall books, review copies, interview requests. The usual."

"And tomorrow?"

I didn't want to tell her that I had nothing on my schedule, that I was just going to kill the day, when she was so busy. "I'm sure I'll figure something out."

"I'm sure you will too. You should get some sleep. You're going to be a wreck."

"Yeah," I said, a sudden exhaustion falling over me like a warm quilt. "I'm headed for bed, but I wanted to call."

"Well, consider your duty done," she said, warmly.

"Okay. I will."

"And sleep well."

I drifted off there, lying on the covers fully dressed, all the lights in the room on, one hand loosely gripping Nora's crystal through my shirt.

III

GETTING UP THE NEXT MORNING was, apparently, a bad idea. I should have stayed in bed and tried to sleep off the hangover.

My telephone rang as I was standing in the coffee line in the hotel lobby, voices and laughter and shouting echoing off the mirrors and marble, and I answered it without checking the number.

"Chris! It's Tony Markus calling! How's your day going?"

His false good cheer made my head pound, and the three ibuprofen I had taken before coming down didn't even take the edge off.

"Hello, Tony," I said, trying not to convey my utter lack of enthusiasm, vowing to myself yet again that I would start checking callers' numbers, the way Jacqui suggested.

"So did you make it to the Met yesterday afternoon? And what did you end up doing last night?"

"Not a whole lot," I said, thinking that keeping up a constant stream of minimal responses might derail his litany of pleasantries—we both knew why he was calling. "Dinner with my agent."

"You're staying at the Grand Hyatt, right? Right on 42nd Street? How is it?"

"It's fine," I said, taking another step forward in the line. "Listen, Tony, I'm sorry but I haven't had a chance to get in touch with the estate yet."

"Oh, no," he said, as if surprised that I would even think that he might be calling to check up on me. "I just wanted to make sure you were having a good time while you were here."

Like the goddamn Chamber of Commerce.

"Oh, I am."

"And how long are you staying?"

"Couple of more days." Back to the pleasantries.

"Well, we should stay in touch while you're in town," he said. "Maybe plan on having dinner Tuesday night?"

"I'll have to check my schedule." Wondering if he was ever going to take the hint.

"Sure, sure. That sounds fine. I'll talk to you in the next few days."

"That sounds good."

I hung up wishing, in my very marrow, that I had never thought to contact Tony Markus.

Tony Markus hung up his phone and tapped it softly as he watched Chris Knox step up to the coffee counter. He loathed the man. Just look at him, Mister High-and-Mighty, Mister I'll-have-to-check-my-schedule. Knox had no intention of calling back, no more than he had any intention of handing over the book. Hell, he probably had it in that shoulder bag right now. He had probably brought it with him because he couldn't stand to be parted from it.

Or . . .

As the thought came to him, he cursed himself for not seeing it sooner. Of course! *That's* what he was doing in New York. All that journalist talk about meeting with publicists, setting up interviews, chasing books to review, all that was crap, a smokescreen to obscure his real reason for being here: he was trying to sell the rights to publish the book! He was probably in constant contact with the estate. All that crap about coming to D&K first—he just wanted to make sure that there wasn't a legitimate claim on the book before he started talking it all around town.

Goddamn him!

He quickly dialled the New Jersey number his uncle had instructed him to use last night.

"Venture Construction," someone answered.

Pretty good service for a Sunday morning, he thought.

"I'm calling regarding the Templeman estimate."

"If you don't mind, sir, we'll call you right back."

The line disconnected immediately. Tony hung up and waited. He could picture it in his head: somewhere, someone was picking up another prepaid cell phone, another untraceable line. Technology had made this sort of thing so much easier.

His cell phone rang.

"Tony Marcelli?"

It was strange hearing the name he had surrendered so long ago again.

"Yes."

"Our mutual friend told me you'd be calling. He said you might have need of our services."

"Yes." He looked across the room at Chris Knox, now sitting at one of the small tables near the coffee bar.

"We're going to need some information."

"Of course," Tony Markus said. Shifting the phone away from his ear, he snapped several quick photos of Chris Knox.

The bartender smiled as I settled onto a stool at the far end of the bar and ordered a drink.

"To your health," she said, setting my vodka and tonic on a napkin and sliding it across to me.

I took my notebook and pen out of my pocket. Flipping the book open, I checked my notes on the Hunter Barlow Library. The place opened at 10 tomorrow morning, so I'd want to be out of the hotel by 9:15 or so. I wanted to maximize every moment: I'd planned on using all day Monday and Tuesday if necessary, but given that I had no idea what I was looking for, or how large a collection of Took's papers the library had, I needed to make the most of my time.

Which meant I didn't want to waste a moment with technical difficulties. Pushing my notebook and drink to one side, I took the cell phone I had just bought out of its bag and tore open the box.

I spent almost an hour at the bar fiddling with it, checking the wireless, making sure that the essential e-mail contacts were programmed in, familiarizing myself with all the camera controls.

When I thought I had it figured out, I turned toward the room and took a photo.

"Excuse me," the bartender said from behind me. "You can't take pictures in here."

I was startled by her voice: I'd been focused on the camera.

"Sorry," I said, turning back around on the stool and checking the photo. "I'm just trying to figure this out." The photo was blurry, probably because of the low light. "These things are easy enough for an eleven-year-old to use," I muttered. "Some of us it takes a little longer."

"Yeah, my sister's daughter has one of these," she said. "She's eight."

"Thanks," I said dryly, as I slid the phone back into my pocket.

I flipped open my notebook again and leafed through the pages. I'd looked at my notes so often I almost had them memorized—there was no new information there, nothing to surprise me.

"Let me guess," came a voice from beside me. I turned in time to see a woman easing down two stools away. "You're a reporter." She pointed at the bar. "Your notebook—it looks like what a reporter would use. Like in an old movie." Her speech was slow, deliberate, ever-so-slightly slurred. The drink that she proceeded to order clearly wasn't her first.

"Ah. Right. No, not a reporter. Not really."

"So how is someone 'not really' a reporter? Isn't that a binary, true-or-false thing?"

"Well, I do write for a newspaper. But it's a column. I'm not really a journalist."

"What are you really?"

"I'm a writer," I said, hating the way it sounded.

"Isn't that the same thing?"

"Not really. I write books, mostly."

I braced myself for the next question, the inevitable *Have you written anything that I might have read?*

Instead, she asked, "So what newspaper do you write for?"

"The *Vancouver Sun*, mostly," I said. "In B.C.—"

"I know where Vancouver is," she said, almost petulantly.

I smiled. "Sorry."

"Us ignorant Americans," she said, nodding. "You talk about Vancouver, you might as well be talking about Vladivostok. That's where you're from, then, Vancouver?"

I shook my head. "Victoria."

"Nice city." She nodded appreciatively. "My husband and I spent a weekend there a couple of years ago. He ran in the marathon."

"Really? Where are you from?"

"Seattle."

"Ah, well, that's the thing. Seattle's practically Canada anyway."

"That's what they say. I'm Marci."

"Chris."

"So what brings you to the Apple, Chris?" She shifted on her stool to face me fully.

"Meetings," I said, before giving her a brief description of my usual June trips to New York: agent, editor, publicists. "What about you?"

She looked a little sheepish. "I'm the enemy," she said. "I work for a software company. They needed me here for some meetings."

"I feel like such a Luddite, with my notebook and fountain pen."

"Don't," she said. "I don't understand most of it myself. I'm more of a coordinator. I make sure the guys who write the programs get along with the guys that sell them."

"Wow."

She shook her head. "It's a lot of this," she said, tapping her glass. "A lot of hotel bars, airports, dinners with developers and clients, me not having any idea what anyone is talking about."

"The glamorous life."

"Something like that. Which reminds me . . ." She checked her watch and downed her drink. "I've got a dinner meeting. Wish me luck."

"Luck," I said.

"And you too," she said, laying a ten-dollar bill on the bar. "With your meetings."

I smiled, and watched her as she walked out.

The bartender swept away Marci's glass and cash and wiped her spot at the bar.

"You're calling early," Jacqui said when she answered her phone, pleased in an unexpected way.

"I could call back later." Chris's voice was slow and thick.

"I can probably squeeze you in now."

"I'm glad," he said. His voice had that end-of-the-night feel to it, that comfortably drunk, completely relaxed tone.

"Are you out, or . . .?"

"No, I'm back at the hotel."

"But you don't usually turn into a pumpkin for a few hours yet." She pulled her knees in to her chest and nestled deeper into the couch. "Did you go out for dinner?"

"I just grabbed something in the hotel lounge. They actually do a pretty good Cobb salad."

"For the amount that they probably charge for it. Not getting together with any of your friends?"

"No. I didn't really feel like it."

She tipped over the line from interested to concerned. Typically, when Chris was in New York, his phone calls became increasingly rare as the days went on. She might get a disjointed, shouted call from some bar, music blaring in the background, Chris slurring and stumbling over his words.

"Are you all right?"

"I'm okay. I just didn't feel like . . ."

He sounded so sad, and she wanted to ask him about Roger, about what he had started to say about his book, but she held back: now wasn't the time.

"It just didn't feel . . ." His voice trailed off. "Besides, this way I'll be well rested for my meetings tomorrow."

"Right."

"How's David?" he asked, almost talking over her. For a moment, Jacqui thought he might be trying to change the subject.

She glanced up at their son, still and silent in the bed next to where she was sitting. She had basically moved into the family room with David, sleeping on the couch, eating at the coffee table, keeping him close. He had been alone for longer in the hospital, but she couldn't help the feeling that she had to stay close, to keep him safe.

"He's the same," she said, almost sighing. "Better now, a bit. We just read his story."

"So it's still working."

"It still seems to soothe him, yeah."

"That's good."

"I didn't read to him too much. Just until he started to calm, then I stopped."

"Why?"

"We're more than halfway through, Chris. Have you thought about what's going to happen once the book is done?"

≫ ≪

David saw the first Berok at the edge of the path, lying on his back as if he had been tipped over. He had been dreading this moment with a sick feeling in his stomach since they had broken camp an hour before.

"Sentry," Captain Bream said, barely looking at the man as they passed.

The arrow had taken the man in the throat; later, it seemed, someone had run a sword across his midsection, spilling blood and guts into the grass.

Oh my God, David. This is . . . Matt said, his voice choked.

I know.

The man was smaller than David had been expecting; from the stories and from his glimpses during the attack, he had assumed any Berok warrior to be a giant of a man, wearing the traditional bearskin, the bear's head crafted into a combination of helmet and mask. This man was wearing a bearskin, but only as a vest over a plain uniform much like the one David wore. The warrior was small, almost frail-looking. He would have been no taller than David. Not Dafyd—David.

And his face . . .

David, Matt said, and David could almost feel him withdrawing.

David wanted to turn away himself, but he forced himself to look.

The Berok sentry was just a boy, no older than Dafyd would have been. His hand, still clutching the shaft of the arrow, was small, the skin of his face smooth and hairless, his eyes blue and clear as they stared sightlessly into the sky.

"Dafyd," the magus said from behind him, and David spurred his horse to catch up with the captain.

Did you see—?

Shut up. David was trying not to cry, trying to rid his mind of the image of the dead boy.

Then they came upon the camp. The captain brought his horse to a stop and dismounted, joining the small group of soldiers waiting there for him.

David climbed off his horse and stepped forward uneasily. The smell of flesh was already rising in the air, redolent with the metallic smell of blood.

At the centre of the encampment was the ashy ruin of a fire, grey and cold. Arranged around it, their feet close for the warmth it would have provided, lay a half-dozen bedrolls, each of them soaked and caked with blood, torn and ragged from untold slashes and stabs of swords. Each bedroll held a body. A few were pierced with arrows, but most had their throats slit, the wounds like dark, bloody smiles under their chins.

David couldn't look away, and the images burned into his eyes. No sign of struggle, no hint of a battle, just corpses on the ground.

The captain and his men were surveying the scene from the edge of the clearing, nodding appreciatively. One of them even smiled.

Don't, Matt warned. *Don't say anything.*

David staggered back to where the magus waited with the horses. He stumbled up to the old man, almost falling at his feet.

"They killed them all," he gasped, barely able to breathe. "They killed them in their sleep."

IV

TRUE TO FORM, I OVERBUDGETED my time the next morning, arriving at the Hunter Barlow Library almost half an hour early. I walked around the neighbourhood, trying to make my coffee last as long as possible.

The Hunter Barlow was housed in a large, nineteenth-century mansion, part of a strip of similar houses that stretched for several blocks. The tarnished brass plaque on the gatepost read, simply, HUNTER BARLOW. Someone could still have lived there.

Not that any of the houses along that ornate row were residences anymore. They were a lingering reminder of a golden age, a time when wealthy industrialists and proto-nouveau-riche separated themselves from the hustle and grime of the city by moving farther and farther uptown, distancing themselves with carriages and private parks, a world of wealth and privilege leagues away from the crowds and the banality of actually working for their money.

I found a bench outside a gated park and sat down. Taking out my notebook I flipped to the last written page, the note I had scrawled after talking to Jacqui the night before:

"What happens when the book ends?"

I had just assumed that we could keep reading to David forever. But Jacqui was right, and more than she knew: if David's life was now inextricably linked to the book, his story wrapped up within its story, what would happen when that story ended? I had read enough of the book to know that it was headed for a happy ending, but that was the story that Lazarus Took had written. If Nora was right, David's story could end very differently.

Not a moment to waste.

The library door was still locked; I double-checked my watch, ensuring that it was after ten, then rang the buzzer.

"Can I help you?" came the voice from the intercom, almost too quickly. Glancing up, I saw there was a video camera in the corner of the doorway.

I leaned toward the intercom. "My name is Christopher Knox. I have an appointment to—"

The lock clicked, and I pushed the door open.

A young man stood up from behind an antique reception desk and extended his hand. "Mr. Knox, I'm Ernest," he said.

He was tall and slim, and everything about him, from his haircut to his sleek suit, subtly suggested money. It was a cool, seemingly effortless air of elegance that he didn't so much project as inhabit. My chinos and shirt left me feeling like a slob.

"I understand that you're here to view the Lazarus Took archive," he said. "Might I ask why?" His voice was precise and seemingly unaccented—he could have been from anywhere.

Fortunately, I had already come up with a story. "I'm a writer myself, and I'm considering a book about Lazarus Took. I've got a feeling that there's a story there just waiting to be told."

He nodded, and seemed to be considering my words. "Oh, I would agree with that, sir. There's quite a story in Lazarus Took." He paused. "And it must be getting increasingly difficult to find writers who haven't already been written about."

I wasn't sure how to respond.

"If you would be so kind as to fill out the blank spaces on this form." He passed me a clipboard from the desk. "I've taken the liberty of filling in most of it from the information in your e-mail."

"What is this?"

"A waiver, sir. Limitations of liability and such. It's mostly for insurance purposes."

I wondered what the "mostly" left out.

I started to fill in the blanks. "So I wasn't able to find much information about the library," I said, trying to make the questioning sound conversational.

"No, you wouldn't have, sir. We try to maintain as low a profile as we possibly can, owing to the nature of our collection."

"I'm not sure I understand."

"Sir, we pride ourselves in being a serious collection, a resource for scholars and committed students." He looked at me with an expression that clearly grouped me with the latter. "And because of the nature of the collection, we have to keep a low profile, in order to allow access to those with legitimate avenues of inquiry, like yours."

"I'm sorry, 'the nature of the collection'?"

"Yes, sir. The Hunter Barlow collection is one of the largest private collections of material pertaining to the occult and the arcane in the world. But then, you already knew that, didn't you?"

I capped the pen and passed him the clipboard. "Actually, I didn't know that," I lied, hoping that he might give me more information than I had been able to find. "I found you from information that Lazarus Took had sold the library his papers."

"Ah, well. Then I can see the source of the confusion. The Hunter Barlow Library is devoted to material having to do with the occult. The library was founded in 1915 by James Hunter and Robert Barlow, initially as a repository for their personal materials and memorabilia. You see, both men had been involved with mystical orders in England, where they grew up. In fact, Mr. Hunter apparently credited magical forces for his success in the shipping industry. Mr. Barlow was more of a collector, and the collection itself is largely his work, and his legacy. While Mr. Hunter chose to focus on his enterprises, Mr. Barlow explored more widely. Over the last century, the collection has grown immeasurably, funded by the estates of Mr. Hunter and Mr. Barlow."

"I see." The idea of all that material, all that information, gave me renewed hope.

"I'm sure you can understand, then, the need for our discretion. If word were to get out about the nature of our collection—" He shuddered. "I can only imagine what sort of people it might attract."

"Of course."

"Oh, and I should mention—one of those papers you signed was a non-disclosure agreement."

Of course it was.

"Certainly if there are materials you'd like to use in your work, permissions can be readily granted, but any discussion of the library itself is strictly prohibited."

"That's fine."

He nodded, and smiled, as if pleased by my compliance. I didn't care about any of the legal mumbo-jumbo—I just wanted to get at the papers.

"Normally I take first-time visitors on a walk through the upstairs gallery, which houses some of the highlights of our collection. There are"—he thought for a moment—"Aleister Crowley's handwritten notes for the *Book of the Law*. A letter from W.B. Yeats to Lady Gregory regarding the faerie tribes of Ireland. A copy of the so-called *Demonic Bible*. A letter from Vladimir Rasputin to Czar Nicholas, telling him of a dream he had in which the entire royal family was killed. A *grimoire*, allegedly bound in the skin of a witch executed at Salem."

He was watching my face as he listed off their "treasures."

"Actually—"

"But I digress. Let me show you directly to the Lazarus Took material."

"It's just that I'm somewhat short of time." Wanting, for some reason, not to seem rude.

"Of course, sir. If you'll just follow me."

He stepped out of the foyer.

"I will have to insist that you leave your coat and bag in this vestibule." He gestured toward the well-appointed check room. "And you are, of course, subject to search prior to leaving."

I hung my coat on one of the hooks. "Is it all right if I take a couple of books in with me? For reference?" I took my notebook out of my jacket pocket, and pulled the copy of *To the Four Directions* out of my bag.

Ernest's eyes followed the book; I could tell he wanted to ask about it, but decorum and training held his tongue.

"Of course, sir. They will, however, also be subject to search prior to your departure."

I nodded.

"Oh, and—" He pointed at my shirt pocket. "I'm afraid that will have to stay out here as well." I pulled the fountain pen out of my pocket and looked at it inquiringly. "Pencils are provided if you need to take notes," he said. "We can't risk any damage to the documents."

He led me through an anteroom and into a study. A stately desk, heavy and masculine, backed onto a bay window with a view of the park. In front of the desk was a stainless steel table and a light table, each fitted with a floor-standing magnifying glass, a chair on wheels between them. A dozen archive boxes had been neatly stacked next to the steel table. I couldn't decide whether that seemed like a lot of material to sort through, or not nearly enough to give me hope of finding what I sought.

"This was Mr. Hunter's private office," Ernest said. "As you can see, we've brought up the materials you requested from the archive proper."

I nodded. He seemed born to say the word *proper*.

"There are pencils and paper there—" He gestured at the steel desk. "And I would ask that you wear these while you're perusing the documents." Reaching down to a table beside the door, he passed me a pair of soft cotton gloves, almost blindingly white, and waited while I slipped them on.

"Very good, sir," he said.

"I feel like a mime."

He showed not the slightest trace of amusement.

"The door will be locked from the outside," he said, half turning to leave. "But you can use this intercom to contact me if you need anything at all. There's an override in case of emergency—simply press 555 and the door will release and an alarm will sound."

I nodded. "That's fine." I hadn't noticed it when I first came in: the office door wasn't wood, but brushed steel.

The sound of Ernest turning the lock behind himself was sharp and loud in the small room.

~~ ~~

"We did what we had to do," the captain said, startling David.

David spun around to face him.

"You killed them in their sleep!" David cried out. The magus flinched and Matt gasped at the words. "You called them cowards when they killed the men at the watchtowers in their beds, but you—"

The captain slapped him across the face with the broad of his hand. David dropped to his knees, his ears ringing.

"Do not speak," the captain commanded, towering over him, "of things you know nothing about."

The captain stared at him for a long moment, then looked away.

"I couldn't risk this mission by waiting to follow the rules of war." The captain spoke, quietly now, still not looking at the boy on the ground. "Returning with the Sunstone is our mission. Nothing can stand in the way of that." He turned away.

David could hear the hushed voices of the men, the gentle rumble of the river, the scraping of corpses being dragged across the clearing.

"Captain Bream," the magus said carefully. "What will you do with the bodies?"

The captain turned to Loren as David stood up slowly, unsteady on his feet. "We'll drag the bodies off the trail. Conceal them in the clearing under branches and brush." He shrugged. "Someone will miss them, sooner rather than later. We'll have to be on our guard: I had thought we were well clear of the Berok."

The magus nodded.

Without another word to David, the captain started back for the clearing.

✦

I had no idea where to begin, facing the sum total of a man's life and work in a dozen identical cardboard boxes. If I hadn't been so conscious of time, I would have started with the earliest box, labelled 1918–20, and used it as a way of getting to know Took thoroughly. But I didn't have that kind of time: I had, at the outside, two days here.

I pulled the lid off the top box and smelled pipe-smoke and incense, old paper and the faint hint of leather.

At first it looked like the contents had been hastily thrown into the box, but that wasn't the case: there was simply too much odd-sized material—notebooks, a small leather bag, a set of medallions and, though I couldn't get over just how hackneyed it seemed, a crystal ball—to file it neatly.

Setting the contents out as neatly as I could on the steel table, I went through the loose papers first. Everything seemed to create more questions than it answered.

Two tickets for transatlantic passage on the SS *Franklin* in the fall of 1949—Lazarus Took and his wife coming to America. Fleeing England, but why?

A letter from James Hunter agreeing to purchase Took's papers for $100,000. I gave a low whistle—such an amount for an author's papers would be remarkable even today. In 1949 it would have been a fortune.

And why did James Hunter address the letter to "Lazarus," and sign it "Yours, J"? Were they friends?

I only glanced at the letters from Took to his acolytes in London, Dublin, Basel and San Francisco. Every letter read the same way: after an ostentatious opening, reminding them of their privilege in serving the Brotherhood of the Stone, he adopted a wheedling tone. Hitting them up for money "to finance my travels in search of truth and enlightenment," clearly Took had reached a low point in the late 1940s. He was outright grovelling for money from the members of his cult.

I skimmed through everything from letters from a lawyer (referring only to "a matter which needs clearing up") to a magical grocery list, detailing what ritual supplies the Order was short of. Then I stopped at a crumpled letter. The letterhead bore a sketch of a rambling building, clearly an institution of some sort, with the words "Barnwick–Hay" below it. It was a report on a patient in a private hospital: Reginald Pilbream.

The letter was addressed not to Took, but to his wife Cora. I scanned it quickly: "condition remains unchanged," "prognosis is unfavourable," "resting comfortably." The letter ended by thanking Cora for her continued support of "this unfortunate soul," and reminding her that the annual payment for care and lodging was due before the first of the new year.

I had no idea what it might mean, but I took notes anyway. Lazarus Took didn't strike me as likely to support an indigent patient in a private hospital, especially at a time when his finances were crumbling around him.

I leaned back and took off one of the gloves to rub my eyes. It was already after eleven, and I had only made it through the household accumulation of less than one year. I needed to speed up.

I started through the notebooks next. A small, battered, black leather book contained almost fifty pages of what looked like a novel. The writing on the early pages was dense and intense, gradually thinning before disappearing altogether, leaving most of the notebook blank. I knew exactly what that was like. Every writer has notebooks like this; Took had five in this box alone. 1949 had been a rough year for him.

The sixth notebook was slightly larger than the others. I felt a rush when I opened it: a journal.

I don't know what I was expecting from the journal of a noted magus and cult leader, but it certainly wasn't anything as banal as what I found inside.

"Jan 1, 1949—I begin the new year with faint hopes, and deepening concern for Cora . . .

Jan 10, 1949—The post brought news from the hospital, and Cora took one of her turns . . .

April 17, 1949—As preparations continue, Cora grows increasingly grim. Perhaps America will have some small, good effect upon her . . .

May 12, 1949—Cora's visage is growing strained and worrying. I know not what to do when she takes these moods."

Page after page of a man worrying about his wife; I dropped the journal on the desk.

I only glanced at the paraphernalia on the table. There might have been a clue in one of the several small medallions I'd removed from the box, but I would have had no way of knowing. I couldn't undo the knot at the top of the leather bag, but whatever was inside felt like a small bone—I was just as grateful not to have to handle it directly.

"Shit," I said, looking at the mass of stuff on the table. With a sigh, I stood up and repacked the box.

In need of a break, I buzzed Ernest to let me out for a cigarette.

When I came back, renewed and refreshed, I opened the second box and my heart sank: more papers, more abandoned notebooks, more 1949 banality. But at the bottom of the box was a large leather notebook. I pulled it out carefully and opened it on the table.

It was a scrapbook.

Someone, I assumed Cora Took, had meticulously clipped and pasted every newspaper mention even peripherally concerned with Lazarus Took and the orders he had belonged to, starting in the fall of 1925 with a small announcement of a meeting "for those who seek truth and power in these dark times," giving a date and a London address.

For a man who had left so little trace, he had made no secret of his existence, at least in the early years. There were regular announcements of meetings and appearances by "Master Lazarus," who would speak, depending on the night, on "Light and Truth" or "Power Over the Self" or "Finding Your Way." An article from 1927 went on at some length regarding "the Master's" charisma and insight—another convert, it seemed. I couldn't help but think of Dale, and all those self-help, personal-growth, power-through-your-thoughts types out there, monopolizing talk shows and selling out lecture halls and weekend retreats.

In the early 1930s, though, the listings and announcements seemed to taper off.

In February 1935, there was mention in a legal round-up column that Lazarus Took, "orator and specialist in personal magic," had been arrested for public intoxication. Later that same year, a small announcement appeared that all correspondence for Lazarus Took, Cora Took and the Brotherhood should be sent to Raven's Moor, their new headquarters, with an address below.

An article with a definite small-town feel to it marked Took's return to Raven's Moor. "The manor on the hill, dark for so many years, returned to life last week with the arrival of Lazarus Took and his wife, freshly returned from London in the wake of a successful European tour." I flipped back, looking for any mention of a European tour that

I might have missed. Hyperbole, perhaps? It would have fit with Took's over-the-top style, and grandiose posturing.

The next page of the scrapbook was a lengthy piece from the same city newspaper as the earlier articles.

APRIL 15, 1935
INSIDE THE DEVIL'S LAIR

This is not a story that I ever imagined myself writing. Nor is it a story for all to read. Some of the subjects I find myself forced to explore, and many of the events I have witnessed, are simply unfit for most company. I am compelled to repeat them, however, to alert readers to the evil that is growing in our midst.

Lazarus Took has developed something of a reputation as an orator and a counsellor. His regular Thursday evening meetings, which, until his recent decampment, took place in his large Mayfair flat, were well-attended and popular. Many people returned, week after week, to hear Took expound on the world at large and, most significantly, on personal mastery through force of will, focused though a system he referred to as "majick." This is no ordinary stage-magic, however, but a system of rituals and beliefs designed wholly to facilitate greater knowledge and control over one's self. These rituals involved a variety of prayers, control of the breath, meditation and devoted study of ancient texts.

I must admit that I fell, for a time, under the spell of Lazarus Took. Little did I know how apt that term "spell" was to be.

Following one of the Thursday meetings, I was invited by Took and his wife, the blushing, quiet Cora, to attend a weekend of intensive study and ritual at the same apartment. Naturally, I agreed.

The following Saturday morning found me back in Mayfair, knocking on the door of the apartment. It was opened by a man whom I had previously seen in the back of Took's meetings, stand-ing near the door. This time, however, he was dressed in a black robe, with a large silver star hanging upside down from a chain around his neck.

In fact, this was the standard uniform of all those attending this weekend meeting, and a similar robe was provided for me.

I skipped ahead, through a tedious description of the other guests and an endless account of dinner—clearly the writer was being paid by the word.

The room in which we typically took our meetings had been completely transformed. There were no chairs, no dais, and candles flickered on every available surface. The carpet had been rolled, and on the floor was painted a large circle, within which was the same inverted star as dangled from every necklace.

"A pentagram," I muttered. Did this amateur occultist honestly not know what a pentagram was?

I followed the group's example, taking my place in a circle around the symbol painted on the floor. Once we were in position, everyone, as if on a prearranged signal, raised their hoods, obscuring their expressions and identities for the whole of the ritual.

A door at the back of the room opened, and two people entered, both of them dressed in matching red robes, their hoods already concealing their faces. I assumed that this was the master and his lady, Lazarus and Cora Took. The foremost of the pair carried a large black book. The second carried a large knife, which was set on the floor next to the golden bowl at one point of the star.

As they entered the circle, a chant began in a language with which I was unfamiliar. As a result, I cannot reproduce it here for you. Nor would I: such words are best left in the darkness where they belong.

As the chanting continued, one of the men in the circle, I believe it was the same man who had greeted me at the door, whom Cora Took had referred to as Pilbream

That shocked me out of my reverie, and I reached for my notebook. I had been lulled by the Edwardian clichés of the hooded circle, the same clichés that had become a staple of B-movies, but the mention of Pilbream at the ritual, almost fifteen years before the notice from the hospital . . .

I made a quick note.

picked up the knife, while one of the red-robed figures picked up the bowl. As they started to move around the inside of the circle, the members of the chanting group extended their left hands.

I watched in horror as Pilbream took each hand and, without a moment's hesitation, slashed the palm with the ritual blade. Not a one gave voice to his suffering, and the red-robed figure caught the falling blood in the golden bowl.

The chanting grew louder as they worked their way around the circle, growing ever closer to me. When it came my turn, I extended my hand and, without a sound, watched as he cut into the flesh of my palm. The pain was excruciating, but I didn't cry out for fear I would be removed, and I watched with a rising feeling of sickness as my blood spilled into the bowl, mixing with that of the others in the circle.

Once the bloodletting was finished, the red-robed figure set the bowl at the centre of the star. Then both of the figures in red stood side by side as Pilbream cut their hands. They let them dangle over the bowl, their blood dripping into the crimson murk.

"Blood," Pilbream called out.

"Power," the group responded in one voice.

"Blood."

"Purification."

"Blood."

"Sacrifice."

At that word, another acolyte led a young, black goat into the middle of the circle. The kid was bleating plaintively as it looked around. Its cries were cut short as Pilbream pulled back its head, exposing its warm throat, and slashed across it with the ritual blade.

The kid screamed in an almost human voice as its life gushed into the golden bowl. The acolyte held the goat aloft as it bled, its legs twitching and kicking, ensuring that not a drop was wasted, then laid the corpse of the pathetic animal outside the circle.

The acolyte then lifted the bowl high, making it the focus of the group's attention.

"Blood," Pilbream called out again.

"Power." The cry of the group came even louder this time.

"Blood."

"Purification."

"Blood."

"Sacrifice."

This time, however, Pilbream spoke the word again as he drew a silver chalice from within the folds of his robe.

"Blood," he called out.

"Communion."

As the word still hung in the air, he dipped the chalice into the bowl of blood and, raising it to his lips, drank heavily of the sickening draught.

"So in the beginning and so too at the end," he said, his lips glistening red.

The group repeated the words.

"The blood is one. The sacrifice pure. Feel his power."

And with that, he and the acolyte began a second round of the circle. They stopped at each person, who knelt as Pilbream filled the chalice and held their mouths wide as he offered them this unholy communion.

I confess, I could stay no longer. As gorge rose in my throat, I broke from the circle and ran from the flat, disposing of my borrowed robes on some nameless Mayfair street. I was utterly sickened by what I had seen, by what I had been a part of, and no amount of prayer seemed to cure me of the fear that, someday, I shall feel Pilbream's hands at my head, and his blade at my throat.

I set the scrapbook on the desk, still open to the article.

What was I to make of that? On the one hand, it was so loaded with clichés part of me doubted that the author had ever actually been part of such a ritual. It would have been easy to crib the details from other sources and sell it as an exclusive.

But there was the matter of Pilbream. I already knew that Took had paid for the man's medical care, and now here he was, fifteen years earlier, not only an intimate of the Tooks but, seemingly, a member of their inner circle. For that reason alone I was inclined to give the piece more credence than I would have otherwise.

Either way, there was nothing in the account that seemed to help me. Time to push on.

The next page contained a rebuttal of the article in the form of a letter from Lazarus Took. In it, he denied ever holding such a ritual, and "certainly I have never had one of my guests run incoherently into the Mayfair night." He described his ritual practice as "drawing on the best aspects of many of the world's faiths, elements which can be used to the betterment of the human soul."

I didn't know which was less credible: the newspaper exposé, or Took's denial.

Apparently the account of the ritual had been greeted with considerable interest. The next several pages contained clippings of articles with titles like "Lazarus Took: Visionary or Villain?" and "Go Home, Took," an account of the townspeople rallying against the new residents of Raven's Moor with "the new information we have gleaned from shocking accounts of what truly happens behind Lazarus Took's closed doors."

And then silence.

The next several pages were dotted with small announcements, mostly for the publication of Took's first novel. I found no mention of the Order over the course of the Second World War.

Nothing.

Until the fall of 1946.

≈ ≈

The next two days passed in a blur of trees, and hoof beats muted by the surrounding forests. Every so often the captain would call them to a stop, wheeling his horse around to the magus to study the map, while everyone else waited, still in the saddle, knowing that the captain's "Hai!" could come at any moment, and the ride would resume immediately.

David ached everywhere. He could barely breathe with the constant rocking of the horse. He was having a hard time focusing, and his head had begun to hurt.

My ass hurts, was all that he confessed to, though.

You're doing fine, Matt said. *It can't be that much longer.*

David hoped that Matt was right—he wasn't sure how much longer he would be able to take it. The riding was wearing him down, but even worse was the cold. He'd assumed at first that it was just the lingering chill of the river and the time he had spent in the cave. But the cold had settled deep into his bones, and nothing seemed to shake it.

You just need to get some sleep.

Matt was probably right. David had lost track of how long it had been since he last slept. The night before he went into the cave? A little maybe. But not much since then. And nothing since the attack on the Berok. No matter how exhausted he had been, he couldn't bring himself to close his eyes in his bedroll at night. Not with the captain right there. Not having seen what the man was capable of.

He's there to protect you, Matt tried to reassure him.

David couldn't put his misgivings into words, couldn't express the sick sense of dread that now came over him when the captain was around.

But then, he didn't really need to.

It's not him you have to worry about, Matt said, and David caught sight of the magus riding ahead of him, his cloak buffeted by the wind of his passing. *It's him and his book.*

Yes, the captain, despite his severity, had never been anything but honest with him.

The magus had been keeping secrets.

❧ ❧

The first mention of Took and his followers in 1946 came in a small article titled "Police to Investigate":

Constable John Barth announced this morning that Norfolk police would undertake a thorough investigation into last weekend's incident at the manor belonging to Lazarus Took which left a member of the household staff grievously injured. While Lazarus Took, who has some renown as a public speaker and was the subject of considerable negative press after moving into Raven's Moor, continues to claim that "it was a tragic accident," members of the community remain unconvinced.

"There are strange things going on at that house," says Mrs. Edwina Trifle. "Dark things."

While Constable Barth would not comment on persistent rumours that the house is the headquarters for a group of satanic worshippers, he did say that "we are definitely interested in getting to the truth of the matter."

Lazarus Took, his wife and staff returned to the manor, a long-time family home

The article was cut off at that point.

Picking up a freshly sharpened pencil, I wrote in my notebook: *Accident – 1946 – Pilbream?*

The next article seemed to bear out my suspicions.

DARK FORCES AT PLAY

A local man who seems to have fallen under the thrall of a noted "dark magician" may be paying the cost of dabbling with forbidden forces.

Reginald Pilbream, who is part of the household staff of Took manor, was admitted to the care of local physician Dr. Philip Carnaby early last Sunday morning following an incident at the manor which left him in a death-like state.

"There is no movement on the part of the patient, and there seems to be no conscious thought," says Dr. Carnaby of Mr. Pilbream's current state. "His eyes are open, but he seems to have some limited awareness of the world around him. An empty shell where there once was a man."

The doctor could have been describing David.

Mr. Pilbream's employer, Lazarus Took, has suggested that "a horrible accident" caused Mr. Pilbream's current condition, but Dr. Carnaby disagrees.

"If an accident caused this condition, there would be some sign of injury," says the doctor. "And there isn't. There are no wounds, abrasions or broken bones. This isn't a concussion or a head injury; this is something else."

There has been much speculation in the last several days, but little is known about the circumstances leading to Mr. Pilbream's condition. A few facts, however, are known. Among them: this past weekend, Took manor (which is referred to as Raven's Moor in various letters and advertisements) hosted one of its well-known gatherings, with more than a dozen guests arriving by car late Friday afternoon. These gatherings have been a concern in the local community since Mr. Took moved here in 1935. Neighbours report hearing strange sounds and raised voices at all hours of the night, and one neighbour, Mrs. Edwina Trifle, reports to have seen strange behaviour in the manor's garden during one of those weekend gatherings. "They came out of the back of the house, all of them in robes, and they made a circle in the middle of the lawn. They was all singing and holding hands and looking up at the moon. It was full that night, that's why I was able to see them so clearly. Not that I wanted to, when they took off them robes, all of them stark naked in the garden like that."

Reports of the strange happenings at Raven's Moor seem to confirm earlier accounts of similar activities occurring in Mr. Took's London home prior to his moving in to the manor, including satanic ritual, animal sacrifice and cannibalism. Mr. Took maintains, however, that he is simply a spiritual teacher, drawing elements of his teachings from the "great spiritual traditions from around the world."

Mr. Pilbream was himself an active participant in Mr. Took's rituals while they lived in London. It is also known that among the guests at last weekend's gathering was rumoured to be self-confessed Satanist Mr. Alton Petty, who reportedly departed the scene prior to Mr. Pilbream being taken for medical attention. Mr. Took, following an initial statement, has refused to comment further on the incident and is apparently not cooperating with the police investigation. The shades at Took manor have been drawn since Sunday morning, and neither Lazarus Took nor his wife, Cora, have been seen in the village since then.

I shook my head as I finished the article, marvelling at the tone of the piece, which boldly ignored the line between reportage and outright libel. A newspaper would never be able to get away with that today.

I wrote Alton Petty's name in my notebook—if I had enough time at the Hunter Barlow, I would look him up, but I suspected it would be a dead end. One of too many.

The next article from the following week was a brief mention that Pilbream had been removed from Dr. Carnaby's care and placed in a private hospital, costs to be paid by the Took family.

"Something terrible happened to that man," Dr. Carnaby said, after the private ambulance removed Mr. Pilbream. "The people of this community have a right to know about the evil that lurks among them."

I had a sense that things were all starting to come together, but time was running out. It was already mid-afternoon; the library closed at five.

The next article detailed a police raid on Raven's Moor. It was dated two weeks after the last one, almost three weeks after the incident.

One of the officers on the scene had told the reporter, "That's a terrible place, that house. It's dark and cold and it smells of something terrible." When asked what evidence was removed, the officer listed "Knives and swords, crystal balls and bowls that look like they've got dried blood in them. Robes and hoods. Skulls. Animal skulls, and one that looks like it might be human. And books. More books than I've ever seen in my life."

The next pages of the scrapbook contained more rumours and speculation peppered with the occasional bit of actual news: Lazarus and Cora being questioned by the police. Took petitioning for the return of his books. A letter from Took to the newspaper accusing them of "slanted and libellous reportage" and claiming that they were "profiteering from a tragedy."

The coverage trickled in for almost eighteen months, until early January 1948, when police announced that they were closing their investigation owing to a lack of evidence.

Between the lines, however, a different story started to emerge. The officer giving the statement "took over the case from Constable John Barth, who is currently on extended leave." Similarly, "Dr. Carnaby, the first doctor to examine Mr. Pilbream, died suddenly last November."

It didn't take much imagination, or paranoia, to suspect that a man like Took might silence his accusers.

The article finished with a call to arms: "While this case may not be active, it is important to remember that the suspect, Lazarus Took, has not been cleared of suspicion. He is best treated with caution and care. This community should not forget, and should not forgive."

"Jesus," I muttered. Why not just start taking names for a lynch mob right there?

And sure enough, the last four pages of the scrapbook chronicled an ongoing campaign of harassment directed at the Tooks and at Raven's Moor: letters to the editor urging ordinary citizens to stand up when the law couldn't. Broken windows and fires on the property. An egg thrown at Cora Took when she dared show her face in the village. And, finally, a triumphant notice:

SATANISTS TO LEAVE
A hum of approval and satisfaction could be heard around the village this week when it was learned that Lazarus Took and his wife, long suspected in the injury of Reginald Pilbream, have decided to leave their manor home and settle in America. We believe we speak for the village as a whole when we say

that this is the best thing that could happen for our community, and hope that perhaps the Americans are as inhospitable to their sort of destructive living as possible.

That was the last article in the scrapbook, but I already knew what happened next: the trip to America, the sale of the papers to this very library, the settling in Oregon, Took dying in 1950.

And the book.

I set the scrapbook on the desk and picked up *To the Four Directions*. Almost a full day in the library, and I still had ten boxes to go.

There was a gentle knocking at the door, the lock clicked open, and Ernest appeared, peering into the room without actually entering.

"Mr. Knox," he said obsequiously. "I'm very sorry for disturbing."

"That's all right," I said. "You're not really interrupting anything."

"Sir, if you'll forgive me, I noticed that you didn't leave for lunch, and I was wondering if you might be interested in a cup of tea. It is about that time."

☙ ❧

At the end of the fourth day's ride, close to sundown, it was the magus who called "Hai," pulling his horse up short. David steadied his own mount, and they waited: Captain Bream was well ahead and had to turn his horse before cantering back to them.

"What?" he barked.

"I think we're close," the magus said, reaching for the map.

Wheeling his horse away, the captain trotted a short distance along the path, whistling loudly for his men. That morning, after consulting the map, the captain had decided to keep the men together, feeling they were finally out of Berok-held territory.

"He's not the nicest guy sometimes, is he?" said David.

The magus turned quickly to face him, his face shocked and drawn. *Jesus, David!*

David sagged in his saddle.

But after a moment, the magus's expression melted into a smile. "No, he really isn't."

"You do have a most careless mouth, Dafyd," he said, his tone warm but cautionary. "You should be careful that your tongue doesn't get you into trouble."

David allowed himself a small smile. "I've heard that before," he said.

⇗ ⇖

"Have a seat, Mr. Knox," Ernest said, gesturing to one of the chairs as he stepped toward the stove. A kettle was starting to whistle. The library's kitchen was almost as homey as Sarah and Nora's.

When he put a plate of cookies on the table in front of me, I had to suppress a grin. "Thank you for this."

"You're most welcome, sir. I thought that perhaps you could use a little refreshment. You've been locked away for quite some time."

My stomach groaned. "I guess I lost track of the time."

"That happens, sir. Can I make you a sandwich?"

I shook my head in spite of my sudden hunger. "No, that's all right. This will be more than enough."

He let the tea steep briefly, then poured two cups. I waited for him to take a cookie off the plate before I took one myself.

"Are you finding everything you're looking for?" he asked.

I shook my head. "It's a bit overwhelming," I said.

"There is a great deal of material to go through."

"I think I'm going to have to come back tomorrow."

"That's fine, sir. You can leave the room as it is, if that would help you get a faster start in the morning."

"Thanks." I finished my cookie, and found myself desperately wishing for another.

"So tell me," I said. "How did you end up working at the library?"

"It's the family business," he said. "My grandfather was Robert Barlow."

"Ah." I took another cookie from the platter, acutely conscious of his eyes on me. "Funny—you're the second grandchild I've met since I started this project." He looked puzzled. "I've been corresponding with Lazarus Took's granddaughter as well."

"I didn't realize he had a granddaughter." He thought for a moment. "But then, that's hardly the sort of information one would find in a collection of papers we purchased more than fifty years ago."

I nodded. "Ernest, if you don't mind my asking, do you share your grandfather's interest in all of this"—I waved my hand loosely in the air—"magic?"

He smiled. "That's why I'm here."

I looked down at the table, reluctant to make eye contact as I asked, "So, are you a believer?"

"I suppose that depends on what you mean."

I started to clarify, but he continued.

"Do I believe in all the chanting and the ritual and the trying to contact the Old Gods, that sort of thing? No, not really. But do I believe in magic itself? Yes." He sipped gingerly from his tea. "There are so many things that can't be explained rationally, so many mysteries that are impervious to scientific examination. Even in the heart of the sciences themselves one invariably reaches a point where rational analysis ceases to work and faith takes over."

"That sounds more like religion than magic."

"Why do you think there's a difference between the two? Magic is just another faith, another way of living with the mysteries in the world, rather than trying to explain them away."

I nodded slowly, trying to accommodate the faith that he was describing with what I knew of Lazarus Took's actions.

"What about spells and rituals and things like that?"

"Aleister Crowley and such, you mean?"

I nodded again.

"I think that words and rituals can have a powerful effect on the human soul, an effect that science can't explain. But then, you must know that, Mr. Knox, being a writer? You must have written something that made people laugh or made them cry. Or made them fall in love with you."

I thought of Jacqui.

"Well, that's what's at the heart of magic—the power of words over the human soul."

—

Sitting on the subway on my way back to the hotel, wedged against the window, I wished that I had brought something with me to read, something to isolate myself from the crowding and the noise.

In desperation, I pulled *To the Four Directions* out of my bag.

I could see why Jacqui thought I was crazy: it was so innocuous. So banal. Just a book.

By now I had read it from cover to cover. The story was pitched perfectly for an eleven-year-old, complete with the hero completing his quest, returning to the Queen triumphant, saving the life of the King and vanquishing the threatening hordes. The closing scene, with the newly healed King riding out at the head of his army, had given me goose bumps such that I was willing to ignore how clichéd it was. A perfect happy ending—a little too pat for my liking now, as an adult, but the sort of thing that David would have loved.

Too bad David wasn't living the events of the book I was reading. If Nora was right, his story would be different. Trapped between the endpapers, his life was, literally, in my hands.

How would his story end?

And what would happen to him when the cover closed on the printed text?

Trying to distract myself from the noise, and the smell of the man next to me who seemed to have fallen asleep, I started flipping through the book absent-mindedly, the way I had done so often in the past weeks.

The book opened to the early scene where everything started to come together, just before the Queen revealed the King's failing health.

"Me?" Dafyd asked incredulously.
The captain nodded.
"Captain Bream has selected a troop of his finest men," the Queen said.

I sat up so quickly in my seat that I almost woke the slumbering man, who grumbled and shifted.

"Son of a bitch," I muttered.

Pilbream.

Took had named one of the characters in the book, the faithful
guard, after his own faithful servant. It was obvious once I saw it, but
that's not how my mind usually works. In my mind, books and the real
world occupied separate places—

And I stopped.

A thought was growing in me, a thought that, once I recognized it,
I knew to be a fact.

"Excuse me," I said, holding tightly to the book and my bag as I
lunged to my feet. "Excuse me." I pushed my way through the crowd,
desperate to get to the doors before they slid shut.

I was already dialling the phone by the time I got to the busy street
above.

Nora answered on the second ring.

"Nora, it's Chris." My voice was shaking. "Can you hear me?"

"Chris, it's very loud where you are."

I ducked into an empty doorway and turned my back to the street.
"Is that better?"

There was a clattering noise, and the sound of another line being
picked up.

"That's Sarah," Nora explained. "On the extension."

"Did you find it?" Sarah asked. "The lexicon?"

"No. But, Nora, do you remember telling me that there was a scandal concerning the Brotherhood, that it seemed to dissolve after that?"

"Yes. In the late '40s, I believe."

"I think I've figured it out. The Tooks had a servant, a man named
Pilbream. Worked for them for years. He was part of their inner circle.
Apparently he was injured at Raven's Moor during a ritual weekend.
People basically ran Took and his wife out of town."

"Of course they would," Sarah said. "Narrow-minded—"

"I think they were right," I said, cutting her off. "I think he was
injured in a ritual. I don't think it was an accident, though."

There was silence on the other end of the line. "Nora, the spell that's
in the book, the spell that pulled David in—would that work if it were
spoken, rather than being read?" I was tapping the fingers of my free
hand anxiously on my pant leg.

"Of course," she said cautiously. "If anything, it would probably be more effective. Especially if the spell were cast in a ritual setting."

"And a spell, even from a powerful magician, still has to be tested, right?"

"There's a certain amount of trial and error involved. Though with a magician as powerful as Took, probably not that much. His spell would likely work the first time."

My stomach sank. "There's a character in the book, a Captain of the Guard, who's sent along with Dafyd"—I stumbled slightly over the name—"on the quest. To protect him. To guard him. The guard's name is Bream." I waited a moment for the information to sink in. "I don't think that's a coincidence."

"No," Nora said. "There aren't many coincidences. Not in the magical world. Especially not where names are concerned."

"I think that back in 1946 Lazarus Took used one of his ritual gatherings to test out this spell that he was working on. I think that Pilbream was the first victim of the spell."

"Chris—"

"The articles that came out after the accident, they all described Pilbream as being injured mentally somehow. He doesn't move. His eyes are open, but he doesn't seem to see. It sounds just like David."

"Chris," Nora repeated.

"That makes sense, right? That Took tested the spell on Pilbream, and trapped him in the book, just like David. Doesn't that make sense?"

"It sounds—" Sarah began, but her mother cut her off.

"Chris, this Bream in the book—he's in a position of authority? Guiding the child, the children, on the quest? Overseeing them?"

"Right."

"Chris, what you're describing could very easily happen."

It seemed my day hadn't been a complete waste after all.

"But, Chris," Nora continued. "What if it wasn't an accident?"

Her words brought me up short.

"What if Took put Pilbream into the book deliberately? What if Pilbream volunteered?"

After camp was set, David wandered into the surrounding woods by himself.

"Don't get lost," the captain had said, without looking up from where he was starting a small fire. It sounded almost affectionate, until he added, "I don't want to have to send the men out for you once darkness falls."

"I won't," David muttered, but he was pretty sure that the captain wasn't listening.

Away from the camp, David allowed himself to be lulled by the solitude, by the rich, loamy smell of the earth, the gentle creaking of the treetops in the breeze high above him.

There were bushes everywhere, but the trees kept the groundcover broken up, with lots of natural paths for walking. David loved the feeling of being alone, of walking among the huge trees, touching them, letting his fingers run over their bark. Some of the trees were so old their trunks were as wide around as a room in his house.

"Did you ever see that picture?" he asked out loud, stooping to pick up a twig.

Which one? Matt asked.

"It's got an old tree, and it's so big that they've cut a drive-thru out of the bottom, and there's a car driving right through this tree. An old car, too. A big one."

I have that on a postcard, Matt said. *From when we drove down to Disneyland a couple of years ago. We stopped in the Redwood Forest.*

"That's what it was called."

Yeah, we stopped there. We drove through that tree. Or another one like it. This place is a lot like that.

"This could even be the Redwood Forest," David said. "Or Lazarus Took's version of it." He slapped the twig against a bush as they went deeper into the forest, unaware of the eyes watching him.

So what do you think we're looking for? Matt asked.

David hadn't mentioned looking for anything, but he had come into the forest with that thought in the back of his mind.

He tossed the twig into the brush.

I don't know, he answered. He was getting used to having no privacy. *With the cave you had to be in the right place at the right time to see the door.*

And the same with the map. Right place, right time.

As David bent to pick up a larger stick, the scent of his hand drifted heavy and rich under a bush spotted with red berries.

But there's nothing else on the map, David said, plucking a berry and sniffing it, then flicking it away. He had no idea what might be poisonous here.

He looked around, nothing but trees and low bushes as far as he could see, a drowsy pall falling over the forest.

No notes or clues.

And no idea if we're even looking in the right place. David thought of what the captain had said about the magus's calculations. One degree off and they would be searching miles from where they should be.

We should get back, Matt said, at almost the same moment that David noticed the thickening of the shadows.

"Yeah," he muttered, and as he turned he whacked his stick into the berry bush.

The undergrowth exploded with a mighty roar, a blur of brown fur and claws, of teeth and muscle suddenly towering above him, mouth open, teeth bared and dripping.

David stumbled backwards and fell onto his back as the bear loomed over him. It roared again, its paws waving, claws glinting in the half-light. The bear reeked of feral wildness, a rank, musky odour that David feared would be the last thing he ever smelled.

⇝ ⇜

I walked the dozen or so blocks back to my hotel in a daze. The sidewalks were packed with the afternoon rush, but I seemed to drift between people, allowing the force of the crowd to buoy me along, my thoughts still racing from my telephone call with Nora.

"What if Pilbream volunteered?"

I hadn't been able to say anything for several seconds after she'd spoken the words.

"You said that in real life he was one of their most devoted servants. Involved in their rituals."

"Yes." My mouth suddenly dry and sticky.

"What if Took placed him, deliberately, into the world of the book? Someone to look after his interests in the world that the spell had created? A way of making sure that the children trapped there, no matter the amount of free will they might have, couldn't interfere with the effects of the spell?"

I shook my head. Everything she was saying made sense. Too much sense. "That's a horrible thing to do to your most devoted servant."

"Maybe there's something more concrete in it for him, some tangible benefit. It's impossible to tell without knowing the full effect, the full aim of the spell itself."

The thought of Pilbream catatonic in a private hospital haunted me as I drifted back to the hotel. How long had he lived, in that mindless, soulless state?

Back in my room I flopped into the easy chair, closing my eyes.

Until my telephone conversation with Nora and Sarah, a small part of me had still believed that David's enchantment must have been a mistake—after all, what sort of person would you have to be to cripple an innocent child?

But now I could see clearly the depths of Took's depravity. Did he just hate children that much?

"Concentrate on the lexicon, Chris," Nora had said.

One day to do it.

One day to save my son.

⁂

David tried to scramble away from the bear, but with his every move back the bear would take a tottering, uneasy step on its hind legs and tower above him again. David watched the animal's chest—when it dropped to all fours, he would be trapped by those paws. The last thing he would feel would be the weight of the bear crushing him, or the crunch as those fangs ripped into his skull.

The bear roared again, shifted its weight, and David braced himself.

But the roar turned into a surprised and pained squeal. The bear twisted its neck, trying to see what was happening behind it, but it didn't seem to be able to turn, to move. It bellowed again in frustration, shaking its head vigorously from side to side.

David saw his chance and scurried away, down the path.

Some distance away, he stopped and glanced back. He couldn't believe what he saw.

The bear was being lifted above the earth, its hind feet kicking fruitlessly. It flailed back and forth, trying to determine what was happening.

As the bear rose, David could see the magus standing emerging from the bush behind it, one hand holding the medallion around his neck, the other arm extended toward the bear, fingers curled as if clutching it by the scruff of the neck.

He's picking it up, Matt said in a hushed, awed voice, *like it's a kitten.*

David could almost see the energy flowing across the clearing, from the magus's outstretched hand to the bear's thrashing body. The magus flicked his wrist, and just like that the bear flew through the forest, crashing into a tree with another shriek of pain.

David waited, breathless, for the bear to attack again, but it lay there crumpled for almost a minute. When it finally stood up, it lumbered away into the woods.

Loren walked over to where David was still shaking on the ground.

Oh shit, Matt muttered, and David agreed. They were in the deep woods, far from the camp, alone with the magus. He wanted to run, but he could only cower.

"Are you hurt?" the old man asked, touching him lightly on the shoulder.

David shook his head, unable to speak.

"You should stay closer to the camp. There are dangers in these parts."

There were only a couple of empty stools at the hotel bar when I sat down. The redheaded bartender smiled.

"The usual?" she asked.

"I find it disturbing that I've been in the city less than seventy-two hours and I've already got a usual," I said.

"That's never a good sign," someone a couple of stools over said. Marci, a highball glass in front of her.

"Hey," I said.

"Are you afraid I'm going to bite?" she asked, looking pointedly at the empty stool between us.

I slid over. "So how was your day?"

"Productive. Had a meeting this morning, then lunch with some Japanese investors. A very *long* lunch." She stretched out the adjective. "They do like their Scotch, those Japanese investors. And their steaks."

"There are probably worse ways to spend an afternoon."

"I like my Kobe beef as much as the next girl," she said. "What about you? How were your meetings?"

"All right," I said. "Actually, I spent most of the day at a private library. I'm trying to find out more about the author of this book I've got. It's my son's . . ."

"How old's your son?" she asked with a smile.

"He's eleven." It felt strange to mention David to her, and for a moment I couldn't see his face in my mind.

"Eleven's a good age."

"Yeah, it is. Do you have kids?"

She shook her head. "No, not yet. Too much work, too much travel, not enough time at home."

"Yeah, I can see that." Sipping my drink.

"Why didn't you just go online?" I must have seemed confused. "For your research, about this book."

"I did," I said. "I tried. There wasn't a whole lot there. And then I heard about this library in New York that had bought all the author's papers." I shrugged. "I thought I'd check them out."

"Did you find what you were looking for?" Her every sentence seemed flirtatious—genuinely interested, but playful. Teasing.

"I'm not sure," I said. "There's a lot of stuff there to go through."
I took another sip of my drink. "I'm going back tomorrow."

"Oh, two days in a library—that sounds like a thrill."

"Well, we can't all spend the afternoon lunching with Japanese bankers."

"Touché."

～ ～

The magus laid a hand—*the* hand—comfortingly on David's shoulder. It was searingly hot. David jumped away from the touch.

"What did you do?" he asked, his voice breaking.

The magus withdrew his hand. "I did what I am here to do. I protected you."

"But . . ." David closed his eyes. It was all too much, the bear, the magus. "That was magic."

"I do have some skills in that regard."

David couldn't take his eyes off the old man. He could hear the terrified bear in the distance, stumbling away through the undergrowth.

The magus sighed. "It is something that the brethren are trained in. Ways of magnifying our natural strengths. Focusing our minds. When we go on our journey, before being accepted fully into the Order, we are alone with our wits and our . . . strengths, to keep ourselves safe."

David thought of the kung fu movies he had watched on TV on Saturday afternoons, of the ability of those monks and peasants to break boards and bricks with their hands.

"That's more than training," David said.

The necklace, Matt said. David had noticed it too, a glint within the folds of the old man's robes.

"You did something with your necklace. You were holding it in your hand."

The magus smiled a half-smile. "You're very observant," he said. "You might have been accepted readily into the Brotherhood."

The magus reached into his robes and withdrew the silver amulet. It looked similar to the Sunstone, except the stone was not red but blue, a deep, rich blue that seemed to absorb even the scant light around it.

The silver mount for the stone was also different: rather than the sun image that Dafyd had seen his whole life, the magus's stone was mounted on a quarter-moon, with bright sparks of stars behind it.

"How does it work?" David asked, still studying the necklace.

"We can discuss it as we walk," the magus said. "The darkness is coming on quickly, and it would be wise to be back at the camp before Captain Bream notices we're both missing."

When I rang the buzzer at the library the next morning, the door unlocked without even a sound through the intercom. Ernest was sitting behind his desk in a different suit, but one just as sleek and stylish as what he'd worn the day before.

I, on the other hand, felt like I had been hit by a bus, and probably looked the same.

In spite of our early start, Marci and I had closed out the Hyatt bar. After a couple of hours, we had moved from our bar stools to a table and ordered some food. And wine. And more wine.

In retrospect, the second bottle of wine had probably been a mistake. Let alone the third.

"Good morning, sir," Ernest said, stepping out from behind the desk. "And how are you this morning?"

I shook my head gingerly. "The less said about that the better."

He nodded and started down the corridor. "I've kept the room locked since you left yesterday, so it's as you left it."

"Thank you," I said, setting my coffee cup on a small table in the vestibule as I took off my jacket and hung it up with my bag. I picked up the coffee cup again and saw Ernest looking at it.

"Oh, right." I swallowed the cool dregs as quickly as I could, then looked for a garbage can.

"I can take that for you, sir," he said.

"Thanks." Not the most auspicious of starts.

"My pleasure, sir." It sounded like he almost meant it.

"Chris."

"Of course. Chris."

I nodded as he opened the study door.

"If you don't mind my asking, Chris, about that book you have? I noticed it yesterday."

After a moment's hesitation, I passed him the novel. "It's a children's book. By Lazarus Took. His last book, I think. I haven't been able to find out too much about it."

He turned the book over in his hands, examining it carefully. "*To the Four Directions*," he read slowly. "I'm not familiar with this one."

"That's part of what brought me here."

"It's really quite lovely," he said, holding the book up to the light. "The symbols on the cover—is this a magical book?"

I started to say yes reflexively, thinking of David, but then I realized what he was asking. "No, it's just a novel."

"Ah," he said, looking at it even more closely.

"Do you recognize the symbols?" I asked, clutching at the faintest of hopes.

"I'm not sure," he said thoughtfully. "Are they important?"

I shook my head. "No, I was just curious."

"This really is quite lovely. I don't suppose—" He looked at me. "This would make a splendid addition to the library," he said. His expression, the sheer covetousness that came over his face, left me feeling uneasy. It was the same look that Tony Markus had had in the restaurant. "Once you're finished with it, of course. I'm sure that the trustees would make a very good offer. If you were inclined to part with it."

The thought of the book being in this library, open to study by anyone with even a passing interest in its powers, filled me with horror. I had seen what Lazarus Took had done with this spell—the thought of someone else getting their hands on it was too much to bear.

"I'll certainly consider it," I said placatingly. "But it actually belongs to my son, and I don't think he'd part with it." Hoping that enough of a sense of "if it were up to me" came across to soothe any ruffled feathers.

"Of course, sir," Ernest said, nodding. "But if I might give you a card . . . In case anything changes."

"Sure," I said. "Thanks." I was unaccountably relieved when he handed the book back to me.

Turning again to the boxes and the desk, I deflated. How could I expect to get through nine more boxes in the hours left to me? Especially not knowing what I was looking for.

Especially feeling as crappy as I did.

The key, I figured, was to not allow myself to get distracted. No matter how fascinating the papers, I needed to focus on finding the lexicon.

Rather than continuing to work backwards, I started with the earliest box, marked "Juvenalia." There wasn't much there beyond some old stories, some letters, most of them between him and Cora, some clippings of newspaper columns that he had written as a young man, and a battered notebook in which he had written his thoughts on books he had read.

"Everybody's a critic," I muttered, dropping the book back into the box and pushing the lid down.

One down. I glanced at my watch—less than fifteen minutes.

The next few boxes were much the same. As documented in a succession of notebooks, Took's reading became decidedly more esoteric, with responses to Yeats's magical writings, to Madame Blavartsky and the Spiritualists. There was an exchange of letters between Took and William Thorne, regarding the young man's admission to the Order of the Golden Sunset. A yellow slip of paper with the library's letterhead gave notice that the first letter of that exchange—from Thorne—had been removed from the archive and was on display in the gallery upstairs.

By noon I was pleased with the progress I had made: four boxes in a little more than two hours.

I was also starting to sweat out the booze, and the room was growing warmer. I needed a break. A walk outside. A cigarette. A coffee.

On my return I attacked the boxes with a renewed vigour. I wished I could take more time—there was a wealth of fascinating material, from a journal documenting Took's involvement with Thorne to the letters chronicling the schism that had led to the formation of the Brotherhood of the Stone. Took's growing interest in magic was captured in a series of notebooks, all of them so densely written the pages were nearly black. But nothing that resembled a guide to ritual. Nothing that looked like a lexicon.

I put the books back into the box. Less than three hours left.

A knock at the door, and a key in the lock.

"Chris," Ernest said, and I was surprised by the sound of my first name in his voice. "I know that you're quite busy, and that your time is limited, but I thought this might be of interest."

He was carrying a brown leather book, which he passed to me.

It was smaller than a paperback, the leather soft and flexible. There was no writing on the spine, nothing on the front cover save a single symbol: the magical eight-pointed star that appeared on the cover of *To the Four Directions*, nestled within the outline of the sun, rendered in a Renaissance style.

"What is this?" I asked, flipping through the pages. The book was full of drawings—symbols and sketches—and handwritten text, mostly English, but with words and phrases thrown in, in Latin and other languages I didn't recognize.

I tried to hold my hands steady.

"It's called *The Language of Sighs*," Ernest said. "It's the . . . handbook, I suppose, of the Brotherhood of the Stone, the group that Lazarus Took formed after leaving the Golden Sunset. That," he said, gesturing at the cover, "is their symbol."

"Where did you get it?" I asked, turning to the title page. "The Language of Sighs" was written in a florid copperplate hand, with the line "as annotated by the Exulted Master of the Stone" below in smaller, slightly less ornate writing. A hand-drawn rendition of the crest from the front cover occupied the bottom third of the page. Everything on the title page—I flipped through the book again—no, everything in the book was written in a deep brown ink, all by hand.

"It was in one of the displays upstairs," Ernest said carefully. "Documenting the splintering of the Golden Dawn and tracing some of the later groups and movements that grew out of it. That"—he pointed at the "as annotated by" line—"is the name that's on all of the material from the Brotherhood of the Stone. It's probably what Lazarus Took called himself during his rituals.

"It's all handwritten," I said, turning to the first page of text.

"Most of the handbooks were," Ernest said. "Especially for the smaller orders. The Brotherhood and groups like it were very private.

Very insular. They weren't looking for new members, so there was no need to publish their 'sacred learning' the way Crowley did with *The Book of the Law*. This would have been strictly for their personal use."

Like creating spells to trap little boys.

I flipped farther into the book: every page was full, right to the end. The careful, precise script never faltered, never gave way to even a hint of sloppiness or fatigue. It made me think of hand-lettered bibles from the Middle Ages, every page a small work of art.

"I know it's probably not much use to you or what you're working on, but I thought you might like to see it. Given the symbols used on the cover of that novel especially." He looked at the book, sitting so innocently on the desk.

I tried to contain my excitement. "No, it's great. Thank you. It'll make for good background material."

"Then I'll leave it here with you," he said, turning back toward the door.

I sat down at the desk and laid the book carefully in front of me. My hands were shaking so badly I had to take a few deep breaths before I took my cell phone out of my pocket. Opening the book to the first page of writing, I held it wide with two fingers as I steadied my phone above it. I focused the image on the screen to take in a single page, then carefully pressed down on the shutter button. Shifting to the next page, I repeated the process, and quickly e-mailed both images.

Then I called Sarah and Nora.

"Did you find it?" Sarah asked excitedly.

"I'm not sure," I said. "That's what I need you to tell me. Check the pictures that I just e-mailed, let me know if I'm on the right track."

"Okay," she said. "Do you want to stay on the line?"

I glanced at the door, knowing that it could open at any time. I didn't want Ernest to catch me with my phone. He hadn't asked for it, but if he knew I was taking photographs . . .

"No, call me back."

She hung up without saying goodbye. I set the phone to vibrate and tucked it into my pocket.

The waiting was agony. I tried to read some of *The Language of*

Sighs, but I was lost after only a few words. I danced my fingers on the desk. This had to be it. It *had* to be.

I picked up the phone as soon as it started to buzz.

"Is this it?" I asked. "Is it the lexicon?" I bit my lip.

"It looks like it," Sarah said. "We'll be able to work with it."

The relief washed over me like a wave.

"It's a bit grainy when I blow it up. But I can read it."

It took almost an hour to photograph and e-mail the handbook. I started with the front cover, not wanting to take anything for granted, then shot every page, studying each image in the screen of my phone before sending it to her.

I cc'd each image to my own e-mail, as a backup. Better safe than sorry.

A couple of minutes after sending the picture of the back cover, I called Sarah.

"How do those look?" I asked.

"Good," she said. "Now we just need the book. When do you fly in?"

"Tomorrow. In the afternoon."

"We'll see you tomorrow, then."

My first impulse was to grab my stuff and get out of the library as quickly as I could. I had the information I needed. But instead, I went back to one of the boxes from the day before and pulled out the scrapbook, going through the articles one last time. I didn't think that I had missed anything, but in light of Nora's theory I read the articles about Pilbream and "the accident" with a more cynical eye.

I couldn't get over the sheer maliciousness, the scale of Took's planning, the amount of thought that had gone into building Took's trap. Pilbream's accident had occurred in 1946—that meant that Took had been working on the spell before that, for who knows how long. And the book wasn't published until 1951—after he had died.

Was this whole thing Took's revenge on the world that had driven him from his home, from his country, a lingering curse that would ensure his power lived on so long as his book continued to be read?

And wasn't that what every writer wanted? Immortality?

"There are three kinds of stones," the magus explained as they walked the quiet trail back to the camp. "The vast majority of stones have absolutely no magical properties whatsoever. Almost every stone one sees in one's lifetime is in this first group—it's virtually impossible for someone not trained, or naturally gifted, to simply happen upon a magical stone. It occurs so rarely that when it does, it is the stuff of legend."

David nodded, thinking about all the beaches he had walked, all the stones that he had skipped.

"Of the magical stones, some are inherently magical. They have their own powers, their own strengths, which they confer upon their possessor. There are defensive stones, which protect their wearers, and healing stones, which can care for the fallen. These stones are powerful in and of themselves: it requires no special skill to wield them."

They had slowed in their walk back to the camp, giving the magus time to speak.

"The other type of stone, like the one I wear, has no inherent power of its own, but it can be used to focus and to magnify the strengths of the one who holds it. Its powers are therefore twice-limited, by the holder's abilities, and by the natural properties of the stone itself, its physical form, its purity."

"So without the stone, you don't have any powers?" David asked.

"My strengths"—the magus was taking great care with his words—"would be substantially reduced, which is why I keep it close."

"Does the captain know about your powers?"

"I would wager that the captain has heard the stories of the Brotherhood. Every child does. But I suspect that he believes those stories to be just that—stories. Legends. Nursery tales." The magus smiled. "To him, I am little more than an old man, too comfortable with his books to have much impact on the world."

David was surprised to hear the magus add, "And that is not a bad thing."

"What do you mean?"

Be careful, David.

The magus took a deep breath. "The captain is a man of action, a soldier, utterly loyal, utterly reliable. He answers not to his heart, nor to his conscience, but only to the Queen. It is best that he think that any abilities of the Brotherhood are strictly the stuff of legend."

It took David a moment to work the magus's words around in his mind. "You're talking about the attack on the Berok camp. If Captain Bream had known of your powers, he would have ordered you—"

"That, and other matters. The captain and I have a slightly different understanding of our present endeavour. To him, it is a matter of retrieving the Sunstone, and returning with it to the Queen. All other concerns are secondary."

"And you?"

"My responsibility is you, Dafyd. I am here to ensure that you succeed in your quest to retrieve the Sunstone, but also to ensure your survival and return to Colcott. Should you fail, even if we succeed in retrieving the stone, I shall have failed in my duties."

"I don't understand," David said. "I know that the book says that I'm the only one who can retrieve the Stone, but after that . . . why is it so important that I return to Colcott alive?"

Not that that's something to complain about.

"It is so written," the magus said. "And I have been so commanded."

With a turn of the trail David saw that they were upon the camp.

"No more of this," the magus said quietly. "For your sake and mine."

They walked the rest of the way in silence. Captain Bream barely glanced up at their return.

☙ ❧

Marci was already at a table when I got to the bar. She waved to me as I came in, beckoned me over.

I wasn't looking for her. Not really.

But I was strangely glad to see her. The hours that I had spent with her over the previous couple of days had been a welcome respite.

She smiled at me as I sat down across from her.

"I guess we're both done early today," she said, glancing at her watch. It was barely five.

"At least we beat the rush."

"And I managed to get us a table."

Something about the way she spoke that sentence, the way "us" seemed to be subtly underlined.

When I asked Marci about her day, she shrugged off the question. "Productive," she said.

"Ah." I leaned back as the waitress set a drink in front of me. "I see."

"And yours?"

"The same, actually. Mixed. I made some headway. Then had some setbacks." I wanted to tell her everything, but that, of course, would make me sound like a lunatic.

"To decidedly mixed days," she said, lifting her glass.

I toasted her across the table.

Her eyes glittered.

"So when do you fly out?" Marci asked.

I had hit that point of drunkenness when everything seemed freighted with significance, touched by an almost unbearable beauty. I watched the way she dabbed her napkin to the corner of her lips, the way she cleared her throat, the way the napkin started to unfold itself after she set it down on her plate. Blossoming.

Then I noticed she was looking at me and I realized that I hadn't answered her. "Seven-thirty," I said. "I figure I need to leave for the airport around five. International flight. Customs. Immigration. All that stuff."

"Right, right." She toyed with the stem of her wineglass. "So it's your last night in the big city."

I nodded.

"And you're wasting it with me."

I shrugged. "What was I gonna do, spend the time packing?"

"Hey, the world's your oyster, right? Sky's the limit."

"I suppose."

"Listen," she said, her voice dropping as she leaned across the table.

"What?" I asked, leaning forward to meet her, maintaining the jocular tone of the conversation.

"What room are you in?"

"2316," I said. "Why?" The air seemed to crackle around us.

"Because I'm going to go up to my room and freshen up and in about fifteen minutes I'm going to come down to your room. I've got a nice bottle of wine that I got from one of my Japanese investors that I really don't want to have to carry home." She left the words lying there on the table as she leaned back in her chair, watching me.

I had no idea how to respond.

"Or you could spend the time packing."

※ ※

Just past dawn the next morning, the captain mustered his men.

"Search carefully," he said. "Every stone, every bush. Stay in sight of the man nearest you. By sundown, I want not a footfall of this forest left unseen."

"Captain," one of the men said, to David's surprise. It was the first time he had heard a guardsman respond to one of the captain's orders with anything other than a grunted "Hai" of agreement.

The captain looked surprised as well. "A question?"

The man seemed suddenly wary in light of the captain's stare. "What are we looking for, sir?"

The captain was almost smirking as he turned to the magus. "Loren?"

The magus cleared his throat. "There is nothing in the books or on the map to indicate what, precisely, we are looking for." The men muttered and groaned. "No clues, or mentions of trickery, which leads me to believe that it will be something fairly apparent when you find it."

"Is that clear, then?" the captain said. "We don't know what we're looking for, but we'll know it when we find it."

David winced at the men's laughter. It was a sound he had heard all too often.

The magus didn't even seem to notice.

The captain stayed at the camp as the men dispersed into the forest. David rose to follow them.

"Not you," the captain said. "You need to stay here, so you're close when the men find . . ." He looked cuttingly at the magus, who was also staying behind. "If they're even looking in the right place."

The magus didn't say anything.

David spent the morning in camp, waiting in silence. With the arrival of every soldier who returned, he expected to hear, "We've found it." But they brought only news of more forest searched to no avail. Every report darkened the captain's face and mood.

By the early afternoon, David was almost as frustrated as the captain.

"We'll give it the day," the captain said, his voice ringing with authority. "The men will search till sundown."

"And then what?" the magus asked.

"We'll burn it to the ground."

He had spoken so matter-of-factly that David wasn't sure at first if he had heard him correctly.

"What?" the magus gasped.

"I'll send men up and down the trail to cut firebreaks, then we'll put this whole stretch"—he gestured with his hand—"to the torch."

David stared at him in horror. He had seen photographs and news footage of forest fires, had driven through the charred remains of one with his mother and father. The thought of doing something like that deliberately—

He'll do anything to find the Sunstone, Matt said. *Like Loren said, everything else is secondary.*

"But you don't know," the magus was saying. "You would risk destroying—"

"There's no risk," the captain said coldly. "Do you honestly think your esteemed forebear would have entrusted the Stone to something that wouldn't survive a fire? These forests have burned before. They'll certainly burn again."

The magus was speechless.

"It *is* a stone we're looking for. Even if we have to shift through the coals, we'll find it."

I WOKE TO THE RINGING of the telephone with no idea where I was. There had been bells in my dream, so I had no idea how many times the phone had rung.

When I opened my eyes the light rushed in with a sudden burst of pain, a crushing pressure like my head might explode.

"Jesus."

I rolled toward the sound, and knocked the receiver off the phone on the night table.

"*Good morning,*" said the cold electronic voice. "This *is your wake-up call. The time is four o'clock.*"

I couldn't remember putting in a request for a wake-up call. I couldn't remember much of anything. Considering the way my head was feeling, that probably shouldn't have come as too much of a surprise.

All of the lights in the room were on: the lamps by the bed and on the desk, light spilling out from the bathroom door. I closed my eyes as I clattered the phone back into the cradle, then opened them again, hoping I would get used to it. No, just as bad.

And it only got worse as I swung my legs off the bed. The pain radiated out from the base of my skull, agony rippling through my head, down my spine.

Jesus, I'd felt bad before, but—

I barely made it to the bathroom before I started throwing up, clutching the cold edge of the toilet bowl for dear life as each heave brought a new wave of unimaginable pain, prismatic beads of colour drifting across my vision. I continued for what felt like several minutes, until there was nothing left to bring up, until it felt like my head was going to collapse inward with the pressure. My throat and sinuses burned.

I slumped against the door frame, closing my eyes, willing my stomach to settle. The headache had receded somewhat, enough that I didn't have to bite back a scream whenever I blinked. I stood up carefully, bracing myself on the bathroom counter, and glanced down at my clothes: they seemed to have escaped the worst of it, but I shucked them off anyway. Better safe than sorry.

It didn't even occur to me until I had spent a full minute under the spray, concentrating the heat and pressure at the node of pain at the back of my neck: I had been dressed when I woke up.

I soaped and washed quickly, minimizing my movements, wishing I could recall what had happened last night.

I remembered coming up from the bar, rushing into the bathroom to have a sixty-second shower, brushing my teeth. Marci had arrived, wine bottle and glasses in hand, showing them off with a "ta-da" in the doorway. She opened the wine and poured the glasses as I walked slowly around the room, finally sitting down on the foot of the bed. Giving her space. Not crowding her.

I turned off the shower and draped myself in a towel, drying my hair, trying to think.

I remembered her crossing the room toward me, the light dim, kicking off her shoes partway. She had passed me a glass of wine.

"To your last night in the big city," she had said.

I opened the bathroom door, shivering as the air-conditioning rushed in.

The bed was still made, the bedspread rumpled on one side where I had awoken, but aside from that, it looked like the maid had been in.

What the hell?

I remembered the toast, the two of us draining our glasses. I had gestured for her to sit next to me on the end of the bed, and she had done so, half turning toward me, one leg coming up. I remembered reaching out, touching her leg, just below the knee, the smile on her face.

But the room bore no sign that she had ever been there.

What had happened?

And then my eyes fell on the clock-radio: 4:33.

"Shit," I muttered, adrenaline rushing in, almost cutting through the headache. I was supposed to leave for the airport in twenty-five minutes, and I still hadn't packed.

I hurried around the room, dressing quickly in clean clothes and throwing the worn ones into my suitcase. I unplugged my laptop, gathered its cords and works and packed it all into the leather case.

The telephone rang at 4:50: the front desk calling to tell me that the car I had booked was waiting for me on 42nd Street.

I crammed the papers from the desktop into another pocket, chaos as time-saver. I barely remembered to grab the clothes from the bathroom floor. I brushed my teeth, trying to purge the horrible taste in my mouth.

Standing back, I surveyed the room. It was 5:11, and everything was packed. My suitcase and laptop were waiting by the door. I slipped into my shoes and pulled my jacket off the back of the chair and put it on, unconsciously checking for my wallet.

My shoulder bag had been hung over the back of the chair under my jacket. As I prepared to sling it over my shoulder, I knew immediately that something was wrong. The bag was too light. I had been carrying it for days: I knew what it was supposed to feel like.

I opened it on the desk, checking things off a mental list. My passport was there. My notebook. My pen case. My e-ticket.

But there was no sign of *To the Four Directions*.

David's book was gone.

PART FOUR

I

IT WAS ALMOST FOUR HOURS LATER, the sun hanging low in the sky, before one of the men returned to camp, a proud smile on his sweat-dampened face.

"Captain Bream," he said, slightly out of breath. "Sir, I think I've found it."

A vague look of displeasure flashed across the captain's features. David glanced at the magus, wondering if he too had seen it.

❧ ❧

Tony Markus tapped his fingers idly on the base of his keyboard. It looked, he hoped, like he was working.

He had spent the last two days waiting, jumping every time the phone rang, expecting it to be either his uncle or someone from Venture Construction, telling him that the job was done. But he hadn't had any word whatsoever.

He knew better than to worry. These people were professionals.

Still, he was a worrier by nature. Would they break into Knox's hotel room, or pay a maid to let them in? That would be the easiest way: no fuss, no muss. But what if the book wasn't in the room? It would be just like Knox to carry it around with him everywhere.

Maybe a mugging, then. That would work. Make it look like a cash grab, maybe rough him up a little. That thought made Markus smile—he liked the idea of Chris Knox being roughed up a little. Or a lot. Wipe that smug look off his face.

His telephone rang and he answered it quickly.

"Tony, there's someone to see you at reception."

"Thanks, Sue," he said, standing up. "I'll be right there."

The reception desk was on the next floor up. When he got there, Sue cocked her head toward the tall brunette standing in the corner. The woman was looking at the framed reviews and awards that lined the walls.

He cleared his throat and surreptitiously wiped his damp palm on his pant leg. "I'm Tony Markus," he said, extending his hand.

She continued to let her gaze take in the walls of the reception area. "I never knew that books were such a big deal," she said, almost to herself.

He faked a chuckle. "I guess to some people they are." He lowered his hand, starting to feel like an idiot.

"This is from your uncle," she said, passing him an unmarked, padded envelope. It was heavy, and he smiled as he curled his fingers around the familiar thickness of a book.

"He says that he never knew books were such a big deal, either."

⌖ ⌖

"You seem to be growing very close to the magus."

For a moment David didn't realize that the captain was talking to him. His tone of voice was too warm, stripped of the sternness David had become accustomed to. Looking around the clearing, David realized they were alone.

"What do you mean?"

The captain was using a crust of flatbread to mop up the juice on his tin plate. One of the men had pit-roasted several rabbits that he had caught that morning, and everyone had eaten very well. Even David, who had initially felt sickened at the thought of eating a bunny, had accepted a second portion.

The captain noted David's eyes darting around the clearing. "He's with the men." He took a bite of the bread, chewing noisily.

David nodded, wondering why the magus hadn't taken him along.

The captain misunderstood the look on David's face. "You are right to be concerned. He and his kind," he growled, "they are not to be trusted. The Brotherhood. On the surface they seem to be harmless old men. It is an image that they have fostered, a way of disguising their true power."

"Power?" David asked, leaning forward, the image of the magus and the bear vibrant in his mind.

The captain nodded. "They've built a veritable empire within the kingdom itself through their dissembling, their words. They can make anyone believe anything they wish."

There was something about the captain's voice that made David dare to ask, "Even the Queen?"

The captain was quiet for a moment.

"You had best be careful how much faith you put in that man and his words. The Brotherhood has their own designs on the Sunstone. It was at their instigation that this quest was undertaken. And you and I are merely the means by which they might have the Stone back in their possession."

David didn't know what to think. "What should I do?"

The captain set down his plate. "Don't *do* anything. Just continue as you have been, but be aware of what he is, and who he represents. Trust none of what you hear, and less of what you see. Do you understand?" The captain rose to his feet.

"I think so," David said hesitantly.

"Good," the captain said. "And remember that I am here. My only goal is to find that Sunstone, and to protect you. If trouble comes, look to me."

࿇

I passed out on the plane, a fractured sleep perpetually wavering between unconsciousness and uneasy wakefulness, slipping in and out of fragmented dreams to the rhythm of coffee carts and stewardesses interrupting.

I don't know what Marci had slipped into my drink, but the dreams were awful: visions of pursuit, the unshakable sense of failure, of loss. Somewhere over the Rockies I dreamed that David had died, and that it had been my fault. I had no idea what I had done, or hadn't done, to cause his death, but I was holding his limp body in my arms, his smooth, pale face gone still and lifeless. I snapped awake, on the verge of tears.

It was clear that Marci had stolen the book, and that Tony Markus probably had it by now. One day I practically have to pry it out of his hands at lunch, and the next day a beautiful woman sits down beside me and introduces herself. I should have known that something wasn't right. Things like that don't happen to me.

I was such an idiot.

The plane landed in Victoria shortly after noon. The sleep had burned off most of the headache, but it was all I could do to drag myself to the baggage carousel.

I made a couple of phone calls as I waited for my suitcase. Jacqui first, telling her I had arrived. Then Tony Markus.

Straight to voice mail.

"Tony, hi, it's Chris Knox," I said after the beep, forcing calm joviality into my voice. "I'm sorry we didn't get another chance to get together while I was in town, but my time got away from me. I'm headed for home now. Why don't you give me a ring tomorrow and we can figure out how to proceed from here. Thanks, Tony. I'll talk to you soon."

The forced good cheer made my face ache.

🙠 🙢

The night had seemed like it might never end.

You have to sleep, Matt said, at various points, as the trees creaked in the dark forest.

David knew that Matt was right, and there was nothing he would have liked more, but sleep wasn't coming.

And it got worse. As David dragged himself through the camp in the pale light of the morning, his body heavy and uncooperative, he began to feel a tightening ache in the back of his head, behind his ears, a dull throbbing that was difficult to ignore.

Shortly after dawn, he left camp with Bream, the magus, and several soldiers.

The woods were deep and glossy with the night's dew, birds singing and chirping overhead, as they pushed their way through the underbrush and down the trail, moving in the direction of the river.

"It's not much farther," the magus said. He was walking two strides behind the captain, just ahead of David.

That's not too comforting, Matt said.

David agreed. The farther they walked, the more his dread grew, a sickly combination of fear and anticipation settling low in his belly. When they reached the river's edge, his clothes were soaked from the leaves and the long grass, chilling him even more.

This was a tributary to the mighty Col, which they had followed during their first few days. Slower moving and narrow, the tributary's waters fed into the Col more than a day's ride downstream from the Rainbow Canyon.

The magus must have seen him looking at the water. "The Brotherhood has always held rivers sacred," he explained. "Water is one of the elemental forces, powerful yet yielding, finding strength in its seeming weakness."

The captain snorted, but the magus ignored him.

"Water will always break around a stone," he continued. "On the face of it, it is the earth that endures, that stands fast while the water surrenders. But over time, the water will wear away the stone. There is little that can resist its power. The Order is drawn to rivers. Nowhere is the power of water more in evidence than at a river's edge, as the water shapes the very land around it. That's why the temples and the schools and the shrines are always built at a river's edge. Like this one."

He had stopped moving at the shore, not far from the rise of a gentle, mossy hillock.

David looked around. He was expecting some sort of building, something like a church or a memorial, but he saw nothing of the sort. Just the forest behind him, the river beside him, and the small hill on the shore.

"There," the magus said, pointing at the hillock. "That's what we've been looking for."

David looked intently at the rise.

"The land has started to claim back its own. It has, after all, been a thousand years. Come."

David followed him around the side of the hill closest to the river.

"You see?" the magus said, pointing.

There was a slight indentation in the bed of moss covering the hill. The moss had been cut away from the smooth green surface to reveal a heavy, metal door. Etched into it was the symbol of the Sunstone.

"I never would have found this," David muttered.

"Nor would most," the magus said, glancing toward the captain, who was still around the curve of the hill. "Thankfully," he continued, his voice now little more than a whisper, as if he did not wish to be overheard, "the young soldier assigned to this area has a brother in the Order. He was familiar enough with the stories to pay special attention to the river's edge, and clever enough to recognize the hillock for what it was." He took another glance at the captain. "We are truly blessed in this discovery. As if we are being guided by forces greater than we can understand."

"Dafyd," the captain called. "We should get underway."

෨ ෩

I took the stairs to the front porch slowly and knocked lightly on the door. Even my knuckles ached.

I could hear Jacqui's footsteps inside. She opened the door cautiously, peering out, then swung it wide when she saw it was me.

"Since when do you knock?" she asked, a smile breaking across her face.

She threw herself into my arms, embracing me tightly. I moved my hands uncertainly up to her back, no longer familiar with even the simplest of things: how to enter my own house, how to greet my wife.

"I'm glad you're back," she whispered.

"Me too," I said, feeling myself relax, soften in her arms, despite everything.

She pulled away from me gently, and took my hand. "Come on in," she said, pulling me. "David will be so happy to see you."

I followed her into the house.

"Look who's home, Davy," she announced in an aggressively cheerful voice as we walked into the living room.

I almost expected him to answer, and it was a shock to see him again as he'd become, after having only memories for so long. I had put out of my mind the way his head lolled, his neck loose, the flat pallor of his eyes, the way his hands jumped with spasms.

He was sitting up in a bright, cold hospital bed that had appeared in the living room. He was facing the television, which was playing the *Teen Titans*, but it was obvious that he wasn't actually watching.

"Your dad's home," she said, more quietly this time, as I stepped toward him.

"Hey, sport," I said, touching his shoulder, flashing back for an instant to my dream on the plane. "I missed you while I was gone."

He probably had no idea that I had been gone at all.

Jacqui's smile narrowed. Her face was care-worn.

"You got him dressed." I hadn't noticed it right away, but he was wearing jogging pants and a T-shirt.

She nodded. "That's one of our goals for every day. To get him dressed, get him fed, make sure he gets some exercise. We've already had our walk around the block this morning, haven't we?" Pitching the question to David's unhearing ears. "I couldn't bear having him in a hospital gown all the time. It made him seem too much like a patient."

I nodded. Seeing him dressed in his own clothes made him seem a bit more like our old David.

"And the bed?"

"It's just a temporary thing."

I wondered how many other parents had used those exact words for a piece of hospital equipment that eventually became part of their lives. "We've been working on the stairs. It's not going to be too long before he's able to sleep in his room."

I had been holding his hand, feeling it pulse in mine. "Is his temperature . . ."

"He's still got that same fever. He's hovering, 100, 100.5. It's not dangerous, but the doctors are watching it. And his hands"—we both looked down—"the spasming seems to be getting a bit more severe. The doctors don't know what's causing it. And he's starting to have small seizures in the night."

I'm so sorry, David.

"Of course, they don't know what's causing any of it." Her smile twisted in on itself. "It's so hard, Chris. I get him dressed, I prop him in front of the TV." Her voice was jagged. "Sure, he walks, he helps me dress and undress him, we go to the bathroom together, but whatever was there, whatever made him . . . *him*, it isn't there anymore."

My knees buckled and I stumbled over to the couch, falling into it as tears started to come. If only she knew how right she was.

She came over and sat down next to me, and we held each other awkwardly as we cried.

"It'll be better," she said. "Now that you're here. We can take turns. We can make it work." Trying to convince herself. "Something'll happen. Something'll give."

I couldn't tell her that I had figured it all out, come up with a way to help David, only to lose our only chance. She still had hope, however small.

"I'm sorry," I gasped. It was all I could say.

"We're a hell of a pair, aren't we?" she said.

I choked back a tearful chuckle. "That we are," I said.

I held her for a long time, trying not to think about what the future held for us, about how I had screwed up, the way a bedtime story had cost us everything.

And then I saw it, right there in front of me, half obscured by two magazines, but right there. If I hadn't been stuporous from whatever Marci had given me, I would have remembered sooner.

On the coffee table there was a rough stack of photocopied pages more than an inch thick: the copy of *To the Four Directions* I had made before I left for New York.

⁂

David studied the markings cut deep into the metal door. Captain Bream had come around the hill to the magus, and the two stood a short distance behind him; the soldiers who had accompanied them stood watch on the other side of the hill.

"Can you open it?" the captain asked sharply. "I can have one of the men bring round a horse to pull it open."

"I think I can do it," David said, looking into the cut-away edges. Sure enough, there was a handprint carved into the stone wall on each side of the door.

And, again as at the cave in the canyon, it took only the slightest pressure from his hands, which fit firmly into the stone handprints, to trigger the ancient mechanism.

The metal door opened with a sound like that of a seal breaking. David stepped back as a gust of fetid, swampy air rushed through the widening entrance.

Both the captain and the magus wrinkled their faces in distaste.

This smells worse than the cave in the Rainbow Canyon, Matt said.

David stepped back from the door and took a deep breath to calm himself. The weight of the leather bag that the magus had brought, packed with everything that had come out of the first cave—the stone and the map, the sack of mysterious red sand—hung heavy on his shoulder.

David was grateful for its weight: it kept him anchored, focused, when all he wanted to do was run.

"You'll want a torch," the captain said.

"I think . . ." David began, stepping into the doorway. "Yes." He wiggled a torch free of the bracket on the wall. "Someone already thought of that."

He fumbled with the tie to the small leather bag of matches attached to the handle of the torch. Striking the match on the wall of the alcove, he touched it to the sticky torchhead and smiled as it burst to life.

"Well," he said, shifting from foot to foot.

The captain took a step forward, his hand falling to the hilt of his sword. "I'm coming with you."

The magus laid a hand on the captain's arm. "You can't."

The captain jerked his arm away and looked at the old man as if he had just slapped him. "We have no idea what dangers await him in there."

"We *do* know," the magus replied, "that the prophecies require the one chosen to face alone whatever awaits him. It is up to Dafyd now." He looked at David for emphasis.

The captain was silent. He let his hand fall away from the hilt of his sword.

David turned quickly and stepped into the darkness.

⤛ ⤜

Sarah was waiting for me. I had suggested to Jacqui that we should get something from Chinatown for dinner, and offered to pick it up. Alchemy was closed by the time I got there, but Sarah unlocked the door before I had a chance to knock, and led me through the dim store.

I had spent the afternoon with Jacqui and David. She was eager to demonstrate the simple activities they had been working on while I was gone.

"Are you ready for another walk?" she asked him quietly before taking his hand in hers.

At her touch David swung his legs over the side of the bed and slid down.

I followed them out the front door, down the porch steps and through the yard. It was a terrible sight. His halting, shuffling gait, his stiff legs, the lurch in his movements.

"He's doing so well, isn't he?" Jacqui said over her shoulder as I followed a few steps behind.

The sunlight had caught her hair, and for a moment I had a vision of the future: Jacqui white-haired and aging, her face wrinkled but still beautiful, leading our son, forty or fifty years old, on his daily walk through the neighbourhood. Caring for him like a toddler for the rest of his days, making arrangements for his care after we were gone.

"He's doing great."

In the kitchen behind Alchemy, Nora pulled me in for a rough hug and a dry kiss on the cheek.

"I'm glad you're back safely," she said, turning back to the table.

"It was only New York," I said as I took my bag off my shoulder.

She shook her head. "I've been reading through these," she said, touching a stack of papers on the table in front of her: the photos I had taken of the lexicon, blown up to eight-and-a-half by eleven. "This is a dark, dark mind you're dealing with."

I glanced at Sarah as I sat down. "Took's been dead for more than fifty years."

"That doesn't matter. This"—Nora touched the pages again—"does not bode well for anyone who comes in contact with it. Merely possessing that book is more than enough to draw dark forces against you."

"I don't have the book."

"What?" they both said.

"It was stolen," I said. "Last night. In New York." It was hard to believe it had only been the previous night. It seemed like another lifetime.

I gave them a brief account of my time in New York, from my lunch with Tony Markus to my days at the library and my conversations with Ernest. I left out any mention of Marci, except to say, "The book was stolen from my hotel room last night."

"Chris," Sarah said. "Without the book we can't—"

Her mother cut her off. "Wait, this is important. You think it's this editor who has taken it."

"I think so," I said, suddenly wary in the bright focus of her eyes. "He was desperate to get his hands on it."

"And you're sure"—she stressed the word—"that it couldn't have been anyone from the library?"

"Pretty sure," I said cautiously. "They didn't even know about the book until yesterday morning, and by then . . ." I couldn't explain why I could rule out the Hunter Barlow's involvement without telling them about Marci. "I don't think it could have been them," I finished, more weakly than I would have liked.

Nora bit her lip and looked away. "And this editor, he doesn't have any magical training?"

"I . . . I really doubt—"

"Chris, this is important. If that book were to fall into the hands of even a novice magician, the damage—"

"I don't think he has any magical training," I said. "He just seemed like he was desperate for his next best-seller." Precisely the reason I had contacted him in the first place.

"Chris," Sarah said. "The lexicon is useless without the spell."

"I do have this." I reached into my bag and dropped the photocopy of *To the Four Directions* onto the table. "I made it before I went to New York, so Jacqui could read it to David while I was gone."

"Well, it doesn't address the problem of the actual book being out there . . ." Sarah said as she started to flip through the pages.

I turned to Nora. "The photos turned out okay?" I asked. "You're able to read them all right?"

She nodded. "I almost wish I couldn't." She looked down at the top photograph. "The man behind these words was a very dark individual. Angry. Violent. Devoted to the pursuit of power. If he wasn't evil, he was as close as anyone I've ever encountered."

"You can tell all of that from a dictionary?" I asked.

Sarah had stopped glancing through the photocopies. "It's a matter of tone and emphasis. You know words. Well, the symbols are like words. Sometimes they have multiple meanings. Denotations and connotations." She glanced down at the top image. "Took has accentuated the negative aspects of each sign to draw out the darker elements. He's reduced an active symbolic language to its blackest, most dangerous . . ."

She trailed off as she realized that Sarah was looking at us, her face drawn and tight.

"What is it?" Nora asked.

"It's not going to work," Sarah said quietly, biting her lower lip.

I felt like I was going to pass out. "What?"

She passed the photocopy of the novel's cover to her mother. Nora held the page up, looked at it for a moment, then lowered it to the table.

"I'm sorry, Chris," she said, sadness verging on despair. She slid the paper toward me.

It took me several seconds to see what was wrong.

"Shit," I muttered, letting the paper fall to the table. All of the symbols on the cover were blurred, as if the book had moved while it was being copied. Or the symbols themselves had.

"Some magical elements, especially if a spell is active," Sarah said haltingly, "they're resistant to mechanical reproduction."

I could make out most of the detail in the large Sunstone symbol, if I squinted.

The smaller symbols around the edges of the cover, though, were lost, shapeless stretched blobs without shape or definition.

☙ ❧

This smells like a swamp, David thought.

He stopped just inside the doorway. The flickering torch lit a small vestibule. At its far end, he saw a narrow stairway, identical to the one in the Rainbow Canyon.

Here we go again, Matt muttered.

David could hear the faintest hint of fear in the other boy's words. The last time Matt had gone down a staircase like this, he had died.

Of course, Dafyd had died too.

David lifted the torch high enough to illuminate the top three stairs. Taking a deep breath, though, he gagged.

"Dafyd?"

David jumped at the sound of the magus's voice. He had forgotten that the captain and the magus were standing just outside.

"It's just a little stuffy in here."

"Is it safe to go on?" the captain asked.

David wasn't sure how to answer. The air stank, and left a sour thickness at the back of his throat.

If there wasn't enough oxygen, the torch would go out, Matt reassured him.

"I should be fine so long as the torch stays lit," he said. "If it goes out, I'll come back."

Running.

☙ ❧

"That took longer than I expected," Jacqui said, when I arrived back at the house with the Chinese food. I had been gone more than an hour, and I had to remind myself that it was just an observation, not a criticism.

"It was busy," I said, setting the food on the coffee table. "Wednesday night. Who would have guessed?"

We ate in the family room, sitting on the couch across from David's bed, hunched over our plates. Neither of us said much of anything.

Jacqui had given him dinner while I was gone, but she fed him a little from her plate.

When we were finished, leftovers in the fridge, Jacqui asked, "Do you want to help me get David ready for bed?"

"Sure," I said. "I should know what's what."

She looked at me for a long moment. "Well, the first thing we have to do is take him to the bathroom . . ."

Toilet. Teeth. Face washed. Then back into the living room for a new diaper, a clean set of pyjamas. It seemed to take forever, even the simplest of actions a complicated series of steps. I guarded my reaction every moment. Jacqui was so proud of him for being able to brush his own teeth, with only a little help. I smiled in all the right places.

This is my life now.

"And now it's storytime," she said, picking up the photocopy of *To the Four Directions* from the coffee table where I had set it down under the bag of Chinese food.

She held the book out to me. "Would you like to do the honours?"

I knew the significance of the gesture. Jacqui was acknowledging my craziness, what little she knew of it, and accepting it. But the sight of the book was almost enough to make me break down again.

I tried to smile. "Why don't you?" I pantomimed a cigarette. "I'm gonna go out to the porch."

It was still early, barely eight o'clock, and there were a lot of people on the street. I raised my hand at the middle-aged gay couple taking their evening constitutional with their small black dog, and tried to ignore the skateboard kids rattling up the middle of the road. Life went on, the way it always did, our small tragedy not even registering on the face of the world.

Jacqui came out behind me and touched me on the shoulder. I didn't turn to look at her, afraid of what my face might reveal.

"That was quick," I said.

"I'm trying not to read too much each night," she said. "We're getting close to the end of the book."

I winced.

"You must be exhausted," she said, her hand still light on my back.

"I am," I said. "I should probably head for bed." The thought of going to my apartment, of being alone again, filled me with a cold horror, but I couldn't just stand there, saying as little as possible to Jacqui, not wanting to risk the truth coming out.

"You don't have to go, you know," she said, almost in a whisper. "You could stay here."

I had waited so long to hear those words.

"No," I said, shaking my head. "No, I can't."

It was hard enough to be in the house with her and David, everything a reminder of how I had failed them.

"Chris—"

"I can't," I repeated, starting down the steps, flicking my cigarette butt in the general direction of the street.

"Chris," she said, in a different tone. "What happened in New York?"

I stopped. There it was: the question, blunt and unadorned, hanging in the air between us. There was no way for me to dodge it, and if I answered it, I would have to lie. Again.

"I'm sorry," I said, starting down the walk. "I have to go to bed. I'm dead on my feet."

* * *

The stairs were slick underfoot. David went slowly, checking his balance with every halting step. He didn't want to have to grab at the walls to catch himself: they were covered with a slimy green coating of algae.

"This is gross," he muttered, keeping to the middle of the staircase. He checked the torch often, vigilant for the slightest hint of the flame sputtering. "The other cave, there was a river running through it, lots of water, but nothing like this."

Maybe something went wrong with this cave.

"Gafilair doesn't seem to have made many mistakes."

It's a thousand years old. And you know what the magus said about water.

They descended in silence for several minutes.

We're well under the level of the river now, Matt said. *It's getting wetter.*

He was right: David's feet were splashing and water was trickling down the walls.

"I've got a bad feeling about this," he murmured, remembering the water in the cavern at Rainbow Canyon.

At least you can still breath, Matt said, drawing David's eye back to the torch. It still burned strongly.

"Small comfort," David said, then stopped. "We're here."

The bottom of the staircase widened into a small, square room. If he had stretched his arms out to his sides, he would have been able to just touch both of the slimy walls with the tips of his fingers.

Not that he was inclined to try.

On the opposite side of the room was another metal door, with the familiar symbol of the Sunstone etched into it just below David's eye level.

He stepped toward the door for a closer look. This Sunstone was different: a hand-shape had been carved into the centre of the stone.

Jeez, I wonder what we should do with that.

"Could you please stop . . ."

Sorry, Matt said. *I make jokes when I'm nervous.*

"I'm scared too," David said. "Do you think that this"—he looked at the palm-print on the door—"would open for just anyone? Anyone whose hand fit, I mean."

No, Matt said simply, as if there were no question in his mind. *These doors were made for you to open. Just like everything else. This is all about you.*

David had come up with the same answer, but it only led to another question. "Why me? Why build a quest and a prophecy out of the son of a tavern owner?"

That's the way these stories are, Matt said. *There's always some farm boy or peasant pulled into a magical quest. It's just the way it works.*

"Like Luke Skywalker," David said.

Who?

David felt a sharp pang. Of course Matt probably wouldn't know Luke Skywalker. Had the first *Star Wars* movie even been released when—

"Sorry," he said, trying to cut off the flow of thoughts.

That's—

Before Matt could reply—perhaps to keep him from replying—David stepped to the door and pressed his hand into the carved metal. He heard a click, the sound of a lock being released, and the door swung open with a groan.

The air that came out of the room made him retch. It was thick with rot and decay, and felt almost warm on his face. He noticed another smell, something sharp. It was familiar, but he couldn't quite recognize it.

I don't like this.

Standing outside the room, David shifted from foot to foot, passing the torch between his hands. He almost convinced himself that he was just waiting for the foul air to clear.

David.

"Okay," he muttered. "First things first." He clenched his hand tightly around the handle of the torch.

David—

"We'll just take a look, see what we're dealing with."

David, that smell—

He pushed the torch into the doorway, hoping to get a better look. The torchhead crackled, and the room exploded.

II

I POURED MYSELF A CUP of coffee and walked back to the desk, lighting a cigarette as I opened up my in-box. The morning sun was bright through the window, and I drew the curtains. Last night had been a brutal night of terrifying dreams.

The top message header read Re: Interview Request.

Mr. Knox—

Thank you for your note; my apologies for taking so long in responding to you. This is a busy time for the Foundation and for our fund-raising, in anticipation of some of the projects we fund each summer (like Camp Dream, a summer camp for children with brain injuries).

Thank you for your interest in a story about the Foundation's work. So far, there has been very little coverage of the Foundation in Canadian newspapers, and it would be most appreciated if that were to change.

While I don't wish to take too much of your article's interest off the Foundation itself, I do agree that some information regarding the roots of the organization, in part what happened with Matthew, would help to put a human face on the cost of these injuries.

Therefore I would certainly be open to a short interview. Please call me directly to set that up, at the number below.

Thank you again for your interest. I look forward to talking with you.

Carol Corvin

I closed the message without writing down any of the contact information—there was no point. Two weeks ago, anything Carol Corvin could have told me about her son's injuries would have been another piece of the puzzle.

But now it didn't matter: I knew what the puzzle looked like, and it would never be solved.

⤞ ⤝

It took a long time for David to get to his feet again after the explosion. He stood up slowly, wincing at the pain in his back where he had fallen against the edge of the stairs.

I was trying to tell you, Matt said. *That smell—it was some sort of gas.*

He took one step toward the doorway. "Oh my God," he said. Before him was the most beautiful, the most terrifying thing he had ever seen.

The very air in the next room seemed to be on fire, ribbons and rivulets of orange flame shimmering and dancing, moving almost as if they were alive. It reminded him of the night his father had woken him and bundled him onto the front porch, pointing to the sky where curtains of light seemed to waver and dance. The heat now coming from the doorway was overpowering, but the flames showed no indication of spilling into the antechamber.

I think it's methane, Matt explained. *From the rotting plants and the slime.*

"No, I think somebody did this on purpose," David said. "Look."

The flames in the air were starting to fade as he watched, retreating to the centre of the room, losing the intensity of their colour. In the dying light of the flaming air, the symbol of the Sunstone was plainly visible, carved into the floor of the chamber in deep channels. Flames rose from the outer circle, low enough to step over, but from the sun at the centre of the room burst a pale orange tower of flame almost as tall as David.

And as the flames extinguished in the rest of the room, leaving only a smell of ash, the fires of the Sunstone showed no sign of fading.

David slumped in the doorway.

He did it on purpose.

"Yeah," David agreed. "Gafilair designed it like this. Someone would open the door with the torch he left, which would light the gases, which would light the symbol."

Not someone, Matt said. *You.*

He gazed into the flames. They seemed to be growing higher.

"I'm pretty sick of it being all about me," he said. He felt so tired, so cold. All he wanted to do was wake up in his own bed, and find out that all of this had been a dream. Back with his mom and dad.

It's a test, Matt said.

"I know it's a test. I'm sick of all these tests. I just want to get the Stone and go home."

No, Matt said. *It's not a test like that. It's not that the book wants you to fail at finding the Stone.* He struggled to find the words. *They want you to get the Stone. It's the only way to get to a happy ending. It's not so much a test as it is a . . . a trial. It's a way for you to demonstrate your worthiness.*

David wished he could see the other boy, read the expression on his face. "What?"

You're the hero of the story, right? That means you have to get the Stone. But because you're the hero, you're the one who does get it. It's already been decided. You already have everything you need to get the Stone.

David tried to wrap his mind around what the other boy was saying. "So because this is all about me, I'll get the Stone, simple as that?"

We just have to figure out how you do it.

➳ ➳

When I let myself into the house, David's sheets were peeled back and the living room was empty.

"Hello," I called out.

"We're in the bathroom," Jacqui replied.

I was bracing myself to find David slouched on the toilet again as I came around the corner, and was pleasantly surprised to see him in the bathtub instead.

And even more surprised to see that he was smiling.

"We decided it was time for a bath," Jacqui said. She was wearing jogging pants and a T-shirt one size too big, her hair pulled back in a loose ponytail.

"I think he likes it."

"He *does* like it," she said, turning back to him. "Don't you? And watch this." Dipping one hand into the soapy water she pushed a small wave toward him, and his smile broadened.

I sank to my knees beside her, alongside the bathtub. "When did all that start?" I asked, feeling like my heart might break.

"When he came home." She shrugged. "He just really likes the bath, I guess."

I dipped my hand into the tub and pushed some water toward him, watched him smile. I did it over and over again, waiting for him to burst into a giggle, the way he had when he was a baby, but he didn't. Just that wide smile.

"So does he play for a while?"

"Oh, we've already had plenty of playtime," she said. "We were just getting ready to wash up when you came in."

"I'll do that," I said, reaching for the cloth.

She looked at me, then passed me the cloth. "Are you sure you remember how?" she teased gently as she stood up and slipped behind me.

"I think I remember," I said. I dipped the cloth into the bathwater.

Jacqui let her hand linger on my shoulder for a moment.

Washing him, the cloth gliding over his pale, slick skin, I couldn't help but be reminded of bathing him as a baby. He was bigger now, but there were still the same fingers and toes to be washed between, the same ears to get behind, the same bum to scrub.

It almost made me feel happy, to be that close to him again, to be the father he needed. Someone to rinse him off and help him to his feet as the tub drained, someone to pat him dry with a fluffy warm towel as he stood there.

"I laid out some clothes for him on his bed," Jacqui said.

"That's gonna be a long walk," I said. "Are you ready to walk all the way to the living room?" I wrapped the towel around him as best I could, then I took his right hand and lifted it gently. He carefully stepped one foot over the side and planted it on the floor before lifting the other out of the tub.

I led him into the living room, and sat on the couch while Jacqui finished drying and dressing him.

"Are you hungry?" she asked. She peeled a banana and broke it into smaller chunks, placing them one at a time into his hand. He never looked at her, but when he felt the banana in his hand he would raise it carefully, haltingly, toward his mouth and put the whole piece in, smearing it into the corners of his lips. He chewed impassively, without any change in his expression, no hint of pleasure or distaste. When the banana was done, Jacqui handed him a sippy cup.

"So are you feeling a little better?" she asked. "With a good night's sleep under your belt?"

"A bit," I lied, watching David's hands. The sleep hadn't helped. It was bathing David, washing him and drying him, that was allowing me to feel even half-human again.

She picked up her coffee cup from the table and took a small sip, staring into its depths. When she looked back at me, she asked, "So what happened in New York?"

I shook my head.

"I know something happened," she said. "I don't think I've ever seen you like you were last night. You looked like you were going to snap."

She wasn't far off.

"I can't," I said, finally. "You wouldn't—"

"There's nothing you could have done that I wouldn't understand, Chris." The look on her face was pretty convincing, though I knew otherwise. "Did you sleep with someone?"

"I didn't sleep with anyone," I said, recognizing the inherent falsehood underlying my words. I would have.

"Then what?" she asked. "You can tell me."

I sighed. My chase was over; she might as well know why I was licking my wounds.

"Okay," I said, still not sure if this was a good idea. "But you have to hear me out. The whole story. All right?"

She nodded, but there was a slight darkening of her eyes, a wariness.

I leaned forward, put my elbows on my knees. "Have you ever experienced anything that you couldn't explain?" I began. "Something that you knew was true, but there was no way to make rational sense of it?"

She looked at me sympathetically, and for a moment it seemed like she might answer, that we might find common ground. But she said, "This is about that book, isn't it?"

I already wanted to take it back, to have kept my surly silence. "Yes," I said. "It's about the book."

She didn't say anything else, just lifted her hand to indicate that I should go on.

It was easier to tell her everything, from my first suspicions about the book to my fumbling attempts to research it on the Internet to meeting Nora and Sarah. That was when she stood up and started walking slowly around the room, her arms folded tightly across her chest.

Her back was to me when I told her about meeting Marci in the bar, but she didn't seem to react. Not the way she did when I told her about spending two days in the Hunter Barlow library and about everything I had found there, tightening her grip around the rail of David's bed.

She leaned over David's bed for the last part of the story, about Marci that last night, about meeting her back in my room, about her drugging me and stealing the book. I couldn't face her as I told her about that, staring holes into the coffee table instead.

She kept her silence for the longest time, and when I finally looked up she was staring at me, her face hard, impassive. "Is that it?" she asked, her voice cold.

"Yes," I said quietly. "That's everything that happened."

"No," she said, standing partway behind the chair, her hand on its back. "I mean, *is that it*? Are you done with that goddamn book?"

"I knew I shouldn't have said anything. I knew you wouldn't understand."

"Chris, I understand," she said. "Something terrible has happened, and it's easier for you to disappear into some"—she looked for the right word—"fairy tale, rather than facing up to the reality that's around you. I understand that. I'd like to lose myself in a fairy tale, too, but I don't have the luxury of a trip to New York to indulge myself. I was here, looking after our son, while you were spending your days in an old library and picking up women in bars."

"I didn't—"

"And you know what's almost as crazy as you and this damn book? It's the fact that I don't care that you picked up some strange woman. Fine. More power to you." Something in her tone, though, didn't ring true. "But this, all this nonsense about the book, and magic, it's got to stop. It's got to stop *now*." Her expression was livid, and she couldn't even look at me now, staring instead out the window behind me.

"The book's gone," I said weakly.

"Thank God for that," she said. "Now maybe things can go back to normal around here."

"No," I almost shouted. She looked up at me sharply, as if unable to believe that the word had come out of my mouth. "We can't 'get back to normal.'" I gestured at David, who hadn't even flinched as our voices were raised around him. "Does he seem 'normal' to you?"

"At least he's real," she spat back, her eyes burning.

"You've seen it, though. You know that reading to him from that book soothes him, keeps him from having seizures."

"There are *countless* possible explanations for that. Maybe he's comforted by hearing the last story he was reading. Maybe he does hear it, but he can't express that to us. Maybe—"

"Countless *lousy* explanations," I said, my voice falling, "and you won't even consider the possibility that I'm right. You won't even consider what I've found. About Pilbream. About that little boy in Seattle. Doesn't that—?"

"I have to live in the real world, Chris. Someone has to be here, taking care of our son, while you go off on these tangents. Someone has to be *here*, Chris. And whether you're in New York or upstairs, you're just not."

⇜ ⇝

David stepped through the doorway. The room was no bigger than his living room at home, the walls black where the explosion had charred the slime. The heat from the flames at the centre of the floor was almost unbearable.

We're going to have to figure it out pretty quick, before this place turns into an oven.

"Yeah."

He looked around the room, peering into the corners, trying to find anyplace the Stone might have been hidden.

You know where it is.

David looked at the burning symbol in the middle of the room, reluctant to accept what he knew to be true. The Sunstone had to be there, hidden in the flames somewhere.

"So do you think we should just wait?" he asked. "It can't burn forever, right?"

It can if this chamber is built on some sort of underground deposit, Matt said. *There's no other fuel for the flames.*

Matt was right: there was no wood or anything in the symbols carved into the floor. The flames seemed to be dancing in the air. Like the gas fireplace in their living room back home. "Yeah," he said. "That's exactly the sort of thing Gafilair would do. Have me start a fire that I can't put out, that I have to get through to get the Sunstone. Which," he added, for Matt's benefit, "we all know that I'm destined to get." As he spoke the words, that niggling thought came back, that sense that there was something wrong with the reasoning.

Right.

"So all we have to do is use what we have." He took another look around the chamber for something to put out the flames.

Exactly.

"Except—" The room was completely empty. No hidden nooks, no shadowy corners. No handprints on the walls. And the flames were getting higher. "We don't have anything."

There has to be a way for you to get the Stone, Matt said, his voice growing desperate as the temperature rose.

And then something clicked within David. He'd been looking at the question all wrong, trying to figure out how to extinguish the flames. Putting out the fire wasn't the issue—the main thing was to get the Stone.

Where are you going? Matt called as David stumbled toward the doorway to the antechamber, pulling the strap of the bag over his head as he went.

Outside the door it was cooler, but only slightly. David fell to his knees and fumbled with the buckle of the bag, frantically searching through its contents. The map. The canister. The Stone. There!

He pulled out the small bag that had been in the canister, remembering the cool, numbing feel of the red sand as he had rubbed it between his thumb and forefinger.

"You might be right," he muttered, pulling at the tie. "About me having everything that I need."

He tugged at the leather thong, which had been knotted and wasn't coming loose. The knife that Loren had given him cut through the leather with ease.

Careful not to spill any, he poured a small amount of the red sand into the palm of his hand. The moment it touched bare skin, David could feel the cold, like a cough candy in his mouth. It wasn't sand, though. More like a powdery clay that dissolved in the sweat of his palm, producing a scarlet, sticky mud.

Without hesitating, David began to rub the mud into his face, slathering it on thick. The shock of the cold took his breath away, but he kept rubbing, adding more of the clay to his hands when they started to get dry.

Make sure you get your neck, Matt advised. *And your ears. And right around your eyes.*

"This had better work," he said, spreading the mud, shivering.

It will, Matt said. *It has to.*

There it was again, that sense that there was something wrong with Matt's theory. David pushed the thought out of his mind. One thing at a time.

Any exposed skin . . . Matt urged.

David frantically smeared the mud over his forearms, up to his sleeves, then around his fingers and thumbs, adding more mud until he was coated.

He tried shaking the bag out over his palm again, but nothing came out.

"I hope there was enough," he said, dropping the leather bag on the floor as he stood up.

Don't waste any time, Matt advised. *We don't know how long that mud will protect you.*

The fire had risen almost to the ceiling, a roaring white-orange jet of light and heat. The air felt like it was singeing his legs and chest, his throat, his lungs; anywhere that the mud covered felt cool.

"So far so good."

He fought against ebbing waves of heat to cross the room, stepping high over the band of flames that formed the outer ring of the Sunstone symbol.

Within the ring of fire, the heat was making it nearly impossible to breathe. Smoke started to curl off his clothes.

It's not smoke, Matt said. *It's steam. It's your sweat, evaporating.*

The heat was sapping what little strength he had left.

I don't know how much longer I can stay in here, he thought to Matt, keeping his mouth tightly closed.

You're almost there.

David dropped to his knees in front of the pillar of flame. It made a roaring noise, like a plane taking off. He could feel a hot sizzling around his head as his hair started to singe.

His eyes stung as he peered into the base of the flame. He forced himself not to close them; he had to be sure . . .

Yes! There it was! Another silver disk, another red stone, slightly higher than the level of the floor, plainly visible just under the bottom edge of the flame.

It should be cooler there, Matt said. *It takes the right mix of oxygen to burn, so the gas is too concentrated under there to burn . . .*

Matt, David said inside his head. *I think I figured it out.*

David, just get the Stone.

That's the thing, he thought, and even thinking the words was almost too much for him. *About your theory. About the happy ending. About me having to get the Stone.*

David, you don't have much time.

His hand was shaking as he reached toward the clear space, just over the silver disk.

See, I think maybe you're wrong. About it being . . . about it being inevitable . . . that there's a happy ending.

His next breath felt like a jet of flame to his lungs.

David . . .

He lowered his hand, almost touching the silver. *Because the last time I did this, I died.*

⁓ ⁓

I sat at my desk for a long time with my eyes closed, trying in vain to undo the last hour. I shouldn't have said anything more about the book.

Mea culpa. Again.

I picked up my notebook, bulging from use, then threw it back down on the desk without opening it.

Carol Corvin's e-mail was open on my laptop when I booted up; I looked at it blankly for a moment, and I felt something shift within me.

This wasn't about me and my failings: this was about David, about making him whole again, about doing anything in my power to save my son. Whatever it cost me.

Carol Corvin was the founder and chair of a foundation responsible for millions of dollars in research into childhood brain injuries every year. She'd been living with a child in David's condition for almost thirty years. She was certainly someone I should talk to.

I picked up my notebook and wrote down her name and phone number. Then I flipped back through the pages until I got to Tony Markus's contact information. I dialled his direct number.

Voice mail again. I took a deep breath and said, "This is for David" out loud as his outgoing message played.

"Tony, it's Chris Knox calling. I've left a couple of messages but I haven't heard back from you. I know that you've got the book. I know you've got it, and I don't really care—you're welcome to it. Davis & Keelor can do what it wants with the book—I've got no claim on it. I just—I really need to talk to you. This is going to sound crazy, but I think the book has done something to my son, and I need to see it, to borrow it for a couple of days to see, to see if I can undo it. Like I said,

I know that sounds crazy, but if you could just call me, please, I can explain."

I left my number and hung up the phone. I'd probably never hear from him, but maybe coming clean would work. I had nothing more to lose. If I could just talk to him . . .

I dialled the next number down the list.

"Good afternoon, Davis & Keelor, how may I direct your call?"

"Can I speak to Tony Markus, please?"

"I'm sorry. Mr. Markus is out of the office today."

"Is there any way to get hold of him? My name is Christopher Knox and I'm working on a project with him."

"I can put you through to a department assistant, Mr. Knox," she said. "One moment."

I waited as the line went quiet, then gave my explanation again to the chipper-voiced woman who picked up.

"I've already left him a couple of voice mails," I continued.

"I don't have any way to reach him except for his cell phone or e-mail," she said.

"It's very important."

"I'm sorry, sir, he's—"

"Can you tell me when he'll be back?"

She named a date, a Monday, a week-and-a-half away.

"That's too long," I said. "I really need to get hold of him."

"I'm sure he'll call you as soon as he has a chance. Would you like me to connect you to his voice mail here?" Genuinely trying to be help-ful. "He said he would be checking it while he was in Oregon." She pronounced the second *o* heavily, the way people from the East Coast always did.

"No, thank you," I stammered. "I'll keep trying him on his cell." I hung up as quickly as I could.

Oregon. He was going to meet with Cat, and bring her the book as a show of good faith, an unexpected gift to sweeten the deal.

Oregon.

Portland was only a ferry trip and a few hours away.

David braced himself as he reached under the tower of flame, squinting against the roar and heat. He half expected to watch his hand sizzle, expected to hear himself screaming.

Almost there.

David could barely breathe as he watched his fingers, coated in red mud, reach toward the silver disk, remembering last time what had come next—

That didn't happen to you, Matt said. *That happened to Dafyd.*

With one final stretch he touched the top of the Stone. He closed his eyes completely, waiting for the crackle of energy, the sharp punch to the chest.

But none of that happened.

Instead, under the pressure of his hand, the Stone descended almost an inch, settling with a resounding thunk. All flames in the room guttered and died. The air was cooler instantly.

He drew a full breath for what felt like the first time in an eternity, and smiled.

You see? Matt said.

"See what?" David asked, revelling in the fact that he was still alive.

It wasn't a trap.

"Right," David said, not sure where the other boy was going with this.

No one else has made it this far. Everything has changed.

"It's a book," David said. "How can everything change?"

That's what I'm trying to tell you. Yes, we're in the world that Lazarus created, but you're not one of his characters. He doesn't control you. And that changes everything.

"I'm not so sure."

Think about it. What book for an eleven-year-old boy would have the heroes butchering a group of people in their sleep? If this was a typical book, you and Captain Bream would be bonding. He'd be showing you how to use a sword. Hell, it would probably turn out that he was Dafyd's father.

"But because I'm here, everything is different."

Exactly.

"So I could just walk away," David said, considering the possibility. "I could sneak away in the middle of the night, keep away from all this." He looked around the room, his gaze returning to the Stone, now almost level with the chamber floor. "Forget that I even heard of the Sunstone . . ."

But . . . Matt said slowly.

"But if I ever want to see my family again, I have to get through to the end. I have to get the Sunstone." His heart sank.

And even then . . .

"I know," he said sadly. "It's only a guess."

Right.

Shifting carefully, he leaned over to take a closer look at the Stone and its silver disk. They were almost identical to the ones he had found in the canyon.

David touched it carefully with his fingertip to see if it would move; it didn't.

"I'm guessing I have to unscrew it," he said, bending close to look. Yes. There was a narrow groove around the edges of the disk, just big enough for his fingertips.

Be careful, Matt said. *Last time we nearly drowned.*

"I know," he said, reaching down to grip the edges of the disk. "But it's not like I have any choice."

At least he's consistent, Matt muttered. *Gafilair. Lazarus Took. Whichever.*

David twisted the disk, trying to force it to the left. When it finally gave, a hissing noise filled the air.

"Oh shit," he said.

It's gas, Matt said. *When you pushed the Stone down it must have sealed it off. And now you broke the seal.*

David unscrewed the disk as quickly as he could. He could feel the gas as it rushed past his hand, his face.

It's not just here. It's all around the room.

Hisses echoed around the chamber, as if the cave were suddenly filled with dozens of snakes.

Hurry, Matt urged as David twisted the canister around and around. It was taking too long.

The air was growing thick, and David was beginning to get dizzy. He took a chance and stopped unscrewing, pulling instead.

"Got it!" he said as he yanked the silver canister out of the floor. There was a hint of resistance—

David!

—and a rasping noise as the last inch of the cylinder came free from the floor. David knew the sound immediately, had heard it dozens of times in his life—the rasp of flint against metal, the thick sound of a spark, like from his father's Zippo lighter—

🙢 🙢

The more I thought about it, the more sense it made. I would drive down to Oregon, maybe stopping to "interview" Carol Corvin on the way, and arrange to meet with Cat. I wouldn't tell her why I wanted to talk to her, but by the time I got there she would probably have met with Tony, so she would have some idea.

And I'd beg.

I looked at David in front of the television, his shapeless posture, his jerky hands. Jacqui had gone out, making some excuse about errands, leaving me with my son.

Oh yes, I'd beg. Anything. For David.

Now I just needed a car.

I was surprised when Dale didn't answer his cell phone—usually he picked it up on the first ring.

"Dale, it's me," I said into the silence of his voice mail. "Listen, gimme a call. I need to talk to you. I've got a huge favour to ask."

I hung up and started to go through my notebook, checking for things that I might need: Cat Took's telephone number, her mailing address. Where was Belden, Oregon?

"Are you gonna be all all right for a second by yourself, sport?" I asked David, leaning low to his ear. "I just need to run upstairs real quick."

It felt awful to leave him, even just to go up to my apartment to grab my laptop.

Back in the house, I read through all of the e-mails I had sent over the past few weeks, mining them for anything of value now that I had a better idea of what was going on.

I tried Dale again—still no answer. He was probably showing clients around a house and had his phone turned off.

I typed "Belden, Oregon" into Google. The first result was the website of an Oregon historical society, which made passing reference to Belden in a list of Oregon ghost towns.

Ghost town?

The next page had a few more details.

"The town of Belden, on the North Coast between Seaside and Cannon Beach, was once a thriving community, based on the profitable lumber industry, and included its own mill and deep water harbour with housing and services for those employed by both. This attempt to carve out a niche in the shadow of Astoria, only a few miles north and already established as a major shipping and lumber centre, was doomed to failure. Following the closure of the mill in 1911, most residents left town . . ."

I backed up and added "map" to the words "Belden, Oregon" in the search box, but it brought up no results.

So, after leaving England in disgrace, Lazarus Took and his wife settled on the Oregon Coast in a town that didn't appear on any maps. A town that had all but died forty years before.

Perfect for someone on the run.

I was relieved that the town was on the North Coast—very close. Just an hour or so away from Portland. And even if I couldn't find it on a map, Cat Took would be able to give me directions.

I tried Dale again. No luck.

I was at a loss: I had been counting on him.

That left me with only one option.

"Hey, Davy," I said, "Do you wanna go for a ride in the van?"

⤛ ⤜

David dropped to the floor as the gas exploded, pressing himself flat and clutching the canister to his chest as a ball of fire roiled above him.

The gas is lighter than the air . . . Matt began to explain, but stopped.

The fire might have been hovering above him, but the flames were consuming all the oxygen in the room.

David gasped for breath.

Crawl, Matt cried.

His elbows and knees scraped over the rough stone as he dragged himself across the room. The moat of flames ringing the symbol of the Sunstone had reignited, creating a wall of flame between him and the door.

Go! Matt screamed. *Roll!*

David swung around, covered his face with his free hand, and rolled through the flames. He felt an instant of pain as he crossed the burning moat, a jagged rush of heat on his back and side like someone slapping a sunburn. When he was through he kept rolling, sure that his clothes were on fire. *Stop, drop and roll,* he thought. *Stop, drop and roll.*

Several feet away, the door to the chamber was swinging shut.

Run!

David got to his feet and ran, as low as he could, for the doorway, driven by the sight of the antechamber disappearing as the door slowly closed. He tried to focus on moving his legs, tried to ignore the pain as his hair burned, as the fire caught his clothes, twisting them into ropes of flame.

He fell to the hard ground of the antechamber just as the door slammed shut behind him, and kept rolling and writhing, slapping at his smouldering scalp. The flames died, but the burning kept digging deeper and deeper into his back.

He drew cooler air into his lungs in great gulps, savouring the swampy, subterranean stink of it. He was alive!

You've got to run, David, Matt urged him. *You've got to get to the water. You're cooking—*

He took the stairs two at a time, half closing his eyes against the burning in his chest. He ran, half blind up the stairway, and he didn't stop at the entry chamber. He burst through the door in the side of the hill, dropping the canister to the ground as he shouldered past Captain Bream and down the short slope to the river. Once he was in the water to his knees, he let himself collapse, let the water close over him like the safe chill of the grave.

David sat silently beside me at Nora and Sarah's kitchen table as I told them of my plan to go down to Oregon and beg Cat Took for a chance to borrow the book.

Nora nodded attentively as I spoke, but Sarah was distracted by David.

Her expressions as we had come into the store had said it all: surprise when she saw me, brief curiosity when she saw I wasn't alone, a brightening smile when she realized who David must be, and then a falling look of such sadness, such sympathy, that I wanted to say something to console her.

She had looked at me and nodded. "I'll put the sign up."

We found Nora sitting at the kitchen table, doing a puzzle in the morning paper.

She stood up slowly and before I could say anything, she took David's hand. "You must be David," she said, looking into his eyes. "Your father has told us so much about you."

For a moment it looked like his eyes met hers, but that was probably wishful thinking on my part.

"Where are you, David?" she asked in a low voice. "I can almost see you in there. Almost. So close, but worlds away."

Under Sarah's tender care David ate two oatmeal cookies while I talked to Nora. She broke each cookie in half, and placed each half in his hand separately, holding the glass of milk for him to drink.

When I finished outlining the broad strokes of my plan to go to Oregon, Nora was silent for several seconds.

"Of course you'll be careful," she said.

I nodded. "I'm just going to talk to the granddaughter. She doesn't know what the book can do."

"That's a silly thing to assume, Chris. And dangerous."

Sarah looked up at her mother's tone.

"Magic runs deep, Chris. It runs in the blood. You're assuming that this woman doesn't have anything to do with that part of her grandparents' life, based on a couple of e-mails."

Nothing in Cat's e-mails had indicated that she had the slightest first-hand knowledge of magic. "I'll be careful," I said nonetheless.

"What will you do if the book's not there?" Nora asked. "What if this editor just shows her the book, then takes it back to New York with him?"

"I thought of that," I said slowly. "I'm not sure there's anything I can do to prevent that."

"You could call her," Sarah said.

"And tell her what?"

She shrugged. "The truth. Part of it. You could tell her that you found a copy of her grandfather's last book, and that it had been stolen from you in New York. You could tell her that you know that Tony Markus is coming to see her, but that you need to talk to her about the book and that you're on your way and maybe she could hang onto it."

I was speechless.

"Honesty can work too."

Her mother smiled.

She turned back toward David. "So you're going on a little trip with your dad."

Her words brought me up short. My confusion must have been evident in my face.

"He's got to go with you, Chris," she said carefully. "With time running out, David needs to be where the book is."

⁂

"Try to stay calm," the magus said comfortingly. "It'll be over soon."

David, his face buried in a heavy blanket thrown over the soft grass, screamed as the old man tore another strip of cloth out of his back.

"That's almost the last of it," the magus said, dropping another chunk of charred fabric onto the ground.

Captain Bream and Loren had waded in almost to their waists to reach him in the river. He would have been perfectly happy to just lie in the water and let it float him away.

"The cloth burned into your flesh," the magus had said, once they had him ashore. "I'll have to get it all cleaned out before I can treat the burn. I'm sorry," he added. "This will hurt. You'll want to brace yourself."

David could feel the pinch as the magus took hold of the fabric and the flesh. Then the sudden tug, the sensation of tearing, of his own skin being flayed from him—

Then everything went black.

PART FIVE

I

DESPITE THE LATE MORNING HEAT, the sun high over the trail, David huddled under his blanket, clinging gingerly to the reins. He was thankful that his horse seemed to know its place, matching its gait to that of Captain Bream's mount a short distance ahead.

He was dimly aware of the magus coming alongside him, looking at him with concern. "How are your burns?" the old man asked.

"Better," David said, the first words he had spoken that day. The magus's salves and herbs had quenched the pain in his back, numbing it and calming it. His only awareness of the burn was a stiffness when he shifted and turned, a binding around his sides like his clothes were too tight.

That, and the cool of the air on his head, burned and hairless.

The magus nodded. "It takes the body a long time to recover from injuries like those you suffered, even with the help of a healer greater than I. And your burns were severe . . ."

David let the old man talk, let him think that he understood. The truth was, his burns weren't bothering him much at all. It was the cold that he was struggling with, the chill that had set in his bones in the Rainbow Canyon and had been worsening ever since.

It can't be much longer now, Matt said.

That's what I thought yesterday, David thought bitterly. *All of that, and it's another stupid map. Another ride. Every time I think I'm getting close, it turns out to be another dead end.*

When Captain Bream had opened the canister at the fireside the night before, gently tipping a rolled scroll into his hand, David almost wept.

"So you figured out the map?" David asked, attempting to shift the old man's attention.

The magus continued staring at him. "We think so," he said, and David was keenly aware of just how carefully he was choosing his words. "According to the legend, we're to go to Lake Abislot."

"Is that far?"

"Probably three days' ride. We'll follow the river south for another few hours, then cross at Osham's Bridge. The lake is to the west." He looked at the sky, as if orienting himself.

"So three days."

"And we'll see what we find." There was something odd about the magus's voice.

"No." The old man seemed to be trying to convince himself. "The legend was very clear. Lake Abislot."

"Loren?"

The magus sighed. "The map itself isn't especially clear. The river is clearly marked, as is the crossing, and the lake itself. But there are other forms and shapes, mountains and rivers, that are out of place." He dismissed his concerns with a wave of his hand. "Nonetheless, we know our destination. That much *is* clear."

"Three days," David muttered.

☙ ❧

Once I had made the decision to bring David with me, it hadn't taken long to pack, leave a vaguely worded note for Jacqui, and get out of the house. The fates were with us: we drove right onto the ferry without having to line up.

I made a couple of phone calls from the main deck of the *Spirit of Vancouver Island*, balancing my notebook on my knee as I dialled.

The first was to Carol Corvin.

I cleared my throat as the phone rang, and someone picked up and said hello.

"Carol Corvin, please."

"Speaking," she said.

"I'm sorry." Suddenly flummoxed. "I was expecting to get a

receptionist."

"No, this is my home number."

I had thought she'd be someone matronly, someone who sounded like old money. This voice was down-to-earth, cheerful.

"And you are?" she prompted.

"It's Chris Knox calling. From Victoria."

A family of three were walking by us on the outside ferry deck, the pigtailed little girl picking her nose. When she saw David, staring sightlessly out of the seat next to the window, she tugged wordlessly on her mother's arm. They slowed as the mother looked at David, then at me, giving me a wrinkled look of sympathy as they passed.

"The reporter."

"Yes. About the interview."

"I'm afraid time's a little tight right now."

"Actually, I was wondering about tomorrow. I'm going to be passing through Seattle, so I thought we might meet for coffee, if that works."

"How about in the afternoon? Say, around two?"

I hadn't realized just much tension I'd been feeling until she said yes and I felt it release, all at once. "I think that'll work."

I had expected her to suggest a coffee shop or a restaurant, but instead she gave me her home address.

"That way you'll be able to meet Matthew as well."

I looked over at David. "That sounds good."

The next call was to the Hyatt in Bellevue, where we had stayed before.

Traffic was light on the highway toward the border, so I didn't have too long to fret. Having heard about custody cases I worried that we might have a problem at Customs and Immigration, but the guard seemed satisfied when I told him that David's mother was in Seattle on business and we were meeting her down there for a family weekend. He didn't ask to see the supporting letter from David's mom, the one that I had faked her signature on.

He even told us to have fun.

Just before eight I pulled off at a rest area and dug into my laptop bag for the photocopied pages of *To the Four Directions*. I turned on the dome light and in that busy parking lot, crowded with campers and trucks, I started to read.

It took most of two pages before David's hands stilled, before his eyes came to rest. I read a bit further, just to be sure, but I forced myself to cut it off between paragraphs, to conserve the remaining words.

"I think that's enough for tonight," I whispered, tucking the book back into my bag.

David, of course, didn't say anything.

This had better be worth it, Tony Markus thought to himself as he signed the charge slip at the front desk of the Hotel Vintage Park in downtown Portland. He was hard-pressed, however, to think of anything that might make up for the hellish travel day he had just had.

He was dialling for room service practically before the bellman had left his room. A rare steak and a couple of servings of *frites* was exactly what he needed. Screw the salad—he was away from home; it didn't count.

Leaning back on the bed, he kicked off his shoes and dialled the number programmed into his cell.

"Cat, it's Tony Markus."

"I take it this means you survived your flight?" It always sounded like she was flirting with him. Something about her voice.

"Just barely," he said, making it sound like a big joke.

"So where's the company putting you up?"

"The Hotel Vintage Park. Right downtown." He had led her to believe, in his last four phone calls, that D&K was sending him out to the coast with the sole purpose of meeting with her.

"That's all right."

He looked around the room for the first time: it was, in fact, more than all right.

"I was wondering when we might be able to meet," he said. Might as well cut right to the chase. "If you give me directions, I can—"

"Actually," she said, "it turns out I have to be in Portland tomorrow for an appointment. Maybe we could meet there instead. Dinner, maybe?

I think the restaurant in your hotel is supposed to be quite good."

"That's what I've heard," he lied. All he knew about the hotel's restaurant was that he had stood in front of it while the valet took his bags out of the trunk.

He hung up the phone after they had agreed to meet there at five-thirty. He lay back in the bed, taking pleasure in stretching his toes, in doing slow loops with his head, loosening up his neck.

He was interrupted by a knock on the door and a voice saying, "Room Service." He practically bounced off the bed.

Things were starting to look up.

☙ ❧

David lost track of how many days they had been riding. It didn't matter: the landscape changed around him again, but all he did was follow the horse in front of him, keep his eyes low, his mouth shut, mile after mile.

Then, abruptly, the forest around the trail broke apart to reveal the shore of a huge lake. His horse waded in, bending his head to drink. Far to his left, the blue water seemed to meet the green of densely forested hills almost at the horizon; down the shore to his right, he could see the narrow mouth of a river, and more trees, more hills. Directly across from him, a small island, little more than a gently rounded hill, seemed to float on the surface of the still blue water.

"Lake Abislot," the magus said, as if it could possibly be anything else.

David huddled in his blanket, shivering despite the heat of the afternoon. His head throbbed with a dull power that made his jaw ache, and he felt utterly spent.

Do you think you're sick? Matt had asked early that morning as they were riding away from the night's camp.

I think I'm dying, he had replied, finally putting into words what he had been feeling since before he had brought back the second canister.

Is it your burns? Matt asked, his voice sharp with concern. *You should have the magus look at them.*

It's not the burns, he said flatly.

But if they're infected—

It's not the burns, he snapped. *It's all this.* He looked around at the guardsmen on horseback, the forest, the imaginary world in which he was trapped. *It's being here. It's killing me.*

He had expected Matt to contradict him, to argue with his conclusion.

But he hadn't.

And Matt hadn't spoken since.

The magus dismounted with a flurry of robes and stepped to the water's edge. "Well," he said slowly. "It seems we have quite a task ahead of us."

One of the guardsmen moved into the shallows and reached for the reins of David's horse.

"The men will take the horses," the captain said, "and make camp farther down the shore, so we're not so exposed to the trail. We"—he locked eyes with the magus—"are going to take another look at that map."

David's first step down from his horse sent a punishing wave of pain up through his body. He walked out of the water and huddled on the grassy verge above the beach.

The magus sat down next to David and unrolled the map. The symbol of the Sunstone hung over a confusing welter of lines.

"As you can see," the magus began, "the trail is easy to follow. There's Osham's Bridge, and we followed this line, which brought us here." He poked his finger at the spot where the trail intersected with the shores of the lake. Written in the space above it, in now familiar script, was the word *Abislot.*

"So we know we're at the right place," David said quietly. He was having trouble focusing on the map.

"We know we're at the right lake," the captain said bitterly. He was standing next to David, looking out at the water. "But as you can see—" He swept his arm to encompass its length. "That doesn't really help us."

"So there's nothing here?" David said. "No clues, no markings, nothing to tell us where we're supposed to look?"

The captain shook his head. "Not unless you can see something that I can't."

David picked up the map.

"Be careful," the magus cautioned. "The vellum is very thin. It's a wonder it has survived as long as it has."

David held it gingerly as he settled it onto his lap. "This is what you were talking about," he said, pointing at the busy confluence of lines in the middle of the lake on the vellum, lines that seemed to have no relationship to the rest of the map.

The magus nodded. "I don't know what they indicate, or what they might represent," he said. "The other maps were so clear, so direct. This—" He traced his finger along a line that ran above the outline of the lake, curving toward the Sunstone symbol, then falling away. "There's no river of that size to the west of Lake Abislot. Not one that I've ever heard of, at any rate."

"So right now," David said, looking up from the map to the lake and the mountains, "we're looking west?"

The magus nodded. "Due west."

He looked down at the map again, back at the line curving under the Sunstone. "And there's no river here," he said, pointing at the line. "Not that . . ."

David nodded, but he wasn't really listening. Instead, he was feeling the thinness of the vellum between his thumb and forefinger, remembering the moment when the captain had first unrolled the scroll the night before, the way the firelight had shone through it.

He looked up at the lake again, the stretch of beach, the icy-looking blue water, the island and the mountains behind.

"I think I've got it," he said.

II

When I woke the next morning, the sunlight was spilling white through the sheers on the windows and the whole hotel room seemed to glow. A small seizure had woken us up in the middle of the night, but David seemed fine now. Or what passed for fine.

"Good morning," I said, my voice still thick from sleep. "Did you have a good sleep?"

I would have given anything for him to answer me. Instead, I snuggled myself into his silence, sliding one arm under his pillow and head, the other over him, pulling myself close. I rested there for a long time, drifting in and out of sleep, warm in the smell and heat of him.

It took me quite a while to get us both ready to go, to get him down to the garage and buckled into the van. I almost forgot my notebook, tucking it into my pocket with my cell phone as an afterthought.

꙳ ꙳

David hadn't risen from his spot on the grass all afternoon, shivering as the hot sun passed high overhead. The captain and the magus checked on him regularly while the guardsmen set up camp.

As the sun started to sink over the western shore of the lake, they both joined David where he waited. They sat close on either side of him, trying to share his perspective on the vista before them.

"I hope you're right about this," the captain grunted.

I hope so too, Matt muttered, his first words all afternoon.

David didn't say anything, just held the map loosely in his lap.

After another few minutes, the magus asked, "What are you expecting to see?"

"Do you see those rocks?" He pointed to a rounded outcropping of rock just off the shore to their left. "What you were saying about water, and about time," he said to the magus. "A thousand years ago, those rocks were probably a different shape, right?"

"Yes," the magus said uncertainly.

"But they still would have been there. And this shoreline, it's probably changed some over that time, but it's still mostly the same. So that island"—he pointed across the water—"that's been there, pretty much unchanged, for the past thousand years too, right?"

"Dafyd, what's this about?" the captain asked impatiently.

"This map," he said, lifting the vellum off his lap. "It works."

"But those markings don't resemble anything I can see," the captain said. "There's no territory I know near here that matches that map."

Glancing at the sky, David nodded. "That depends how you look at it." He lifted the map in front of them, pulling it wide, up to the landscape, blocking their view of the lake. "Here," he said to the captain, shifting the map his way slightly. "Hold this."

The captain took one end of the vellum, pulling it a little.

They could clearly see the fiery orb of the setting sun through the vellum. It penetrated the symbol of the Sunstone, the printed sun shining now with the force of the real sun behind it, glowing like a ruby.

"Almost," David said, glancing to his left. In the waning light of the sunset, he could just make out the shape of the half-submerged rocks through the vellum.

"Here." He reached out and moved the captain's hand. "A little lower. A little farther your way."

"Take care, Dafyd," the magus said.

"That's it," he said, as the rocks at the lake's edge fit, almost perfectly, into a jagged outline on the lower left side of the map.

"Now my end," he said, shifting his end of the map a little lower. He felt a surge of triumph.

"There. Do you see it?"

It took them a moment, but then the magus gasped and the captain said, "By the Gods . . ."

David's heart thrummed.

"Look," David said. "The rocks are here." He pointed to the jagged scrawl, and through the vellum at the rocks they outlined. "Which means this is the shoreline." He traced a long, wavy line that ran the width of the map, one that roughly matched the line of the water's edge that they could see in the sunset light through the vellum.

It's a transparency! Matt said, delighted. *Like for an overhead projector.*

"Now look." He drew their attention to where the sun was perfectly centred on the Sunstone. "Everything has to line up for the map to work. You see? The rocks are here, to make sure the map is in the right position. You match the shoreline and the sun to make sure that everything is centred."

"Which means this"—the magus pointed to the curving line, which everyone had assumed was an unknown river—"is the island."

They could see the vague shape of the island through the vellum, its darkness outlined by the sunset behind it.

"Right," David said. "Which means *this* is where we need to go." He pointed at the spot where, in their original view of the map, the trail intersected with the lake's shore, the two lines forming an X. That spot, on the new map clearly marked a location on the lower half of the island, at the bottom of the hill, close to the shoreline.

He couldn't help smiling, especially when the magus broke into a grin himself. "That's it, Dafyd! You did it!"

The captain, however, was silent. David watched him for some reaction as he traced the lines on the map with his eyes, finally staring at the X on the island's shore.

Then he nodded, and stood.

David waited for the captain's praise, some acknowledgement that he had been right.

The captain said only, "We're going to need a boat."

≈

After breakfast at Denny's, I drove us to the Barnes and Noble near the hotel. We spent most of our time in the Children's Section, where I read David the backs and jackets of anything that looked interesting.

"We should pick out your next book," I told him. "We're just about done what we're reading now."

Hoping that there would be a "next book."

We spent a little time in the local interest section, and I ended up taking a still-wrapped road atlas of the Pacific Northwest off the shelf and tucking it under my arm.

"We should get going," I said, glancing at my watch. "It might take us a while to find this place."

Our slow trajectory toward the cash desks took us past the Fantasy–Science Fiction section.

"Hey," I said, suddenly inspired. "Let's go this way."

As we walked down the row of shelves, I followed the alphabet with my eyes.

I picked a thick hardcover off one of the lower shelves, surprised by how heavy it was.

"How about this?" I asked David, holding the book up toward him. "*The Lord of the Rings*?" He didn't react. "I think you're probably ready for it now."

⇗ ⇖

The captain had sent his two fastest riders back to Osham's Bridge, with uncomplicated orders: "Procure a boat. The King's name has little currency in these parts, so buy, beg, borrow or steal, but don't come back without one."

The men had set off at full gallop into the dark. They returned at midday, two days later, at a more restrained pace, one of them towing a cart which carried a small rowboat.

"That looks almost watertight," the captain said. His words were scornful, but it was clear from his tone that he was pleased: the men must have ridden hard to be back so soon.

He beckoned others over to untie the boat and take it down to the water's edge.

I don't like the look of this, Matt said, as they dropped the boat into the water.

It isn't sinking, David thought, watching the boat. *It seems to be floating all right.*

No, Matt said. *Look how big it is.*

Matt was right—it was tiny.

Barely big enough for two.

The men spent several minutes checking the boat—tapping the hull with oars, climbing in and pushing off from shore, paddling a short distance down the lake. Even with only one person in it, the boat sat low in the water, but when the guardsmen pulled it back up to the beach the boards were mostly dry.

With a curt nod, the captain pronounced her seaworthy.

"All right," he said, taking the oars from the guardsman and looking at David. "Are you ready?"

"Now?"

"Assuming you'd prefer to make it back before nightfall."

David stepped warily toward the boat. One of the guardsmen eased it back into shallow water, holding it steady while David climbed in and struggled to balance as he stepped toward the small bench at the bow.

When he had settled, and pulled the blanket tight around his shoulders, he saw the magus approaching the beach. He had almost reached the boat when the captain stepped in front of him, blocking his path. "The boat will only carry two."

The magus glanced at David. "I need to be there," he protested. "What if—?"

"If the boat sinks?" the captain said. "I'm sure Dafyd will be able to manage. He's done fine on his own so far."

David winced at the words, and the magus backed away. He clearly had no hope of changing the captain's mind.

"We'll be back soon," the captain said, stepping into the water. "And if we encounter a problem that's truly insurmountable, I'll row back and bring you over."

※ ※

It took us a couple of wrong turns, a couple of stops to consult the road atlas, but I eventually got us into Carol Corvin's neighbourhood. It was a nest of winding streets and tree-lined cul-de-sacs built on the side of a hill. The houses got bigger as we followed the street upward, the hedges taller, the cars nicer in the driveways.

"This," I said to David, "would be how the other half lives."

We were pretty close to the top when I turned into the Corvins' crescent. As best I could tell, the address she had given me belonged to the biggest house on the block, near the end of the street. The house was concealed by a tall hedge trimmed into sharp right angles.

I checked the address a final time and tucked my notebook into my pocket. David had escaped breakfast largely unscathed, save for a dark drop of syrup that I figured no one would notice on the front of his shirt.

"We want you looking your best," I said, wetting a tissue with my tongue and rubbing at the corners of his mouth.

I hadn't told Carol that I was bringing David with me, but I needn't have worried. As she opened the front door and I began to introduce myself, she looked past me and stepped toward David.

"And who do we have here?" She crouched slightly to bring herself down to David's level. "My name is Carol," she said, reaching out and taking his right hand. "What's your name?"

"He doesn't talk," I said sheepishly. "His name is David. He's my son."

"Well, I'm pleased to meet you, David." She released his hand and it fell slowly back to his side as she turned to me. "And you must be Christopher Knox."

"I am," I said, shaking her hand. "I'm sorry . . ." I glanced at David. "I wasn't planning to bring my son, but something came up."

"That's all right," she said warmly, looking at David again. "Would you like to come in?"

The house was a reflection of her: there was money there, and an unmistakable style, but it was restrained, intimate. Human-scale. It put me at ease, despite everything.

She led us through the foyer and into a room with a couple of couches and a big-screen TV.

"Why don't you have a seat?" she said. "I'm not surprised you brought your son, Mr. Knox."

"Chris," I said. She wasn't sitting yet, so I remained standing. "Why?"

She waved to me to sit down. "I've found that some journalists become aware of the foundation and its work for personal reasons." She looked at David again. "It doesn't usually come up right away—" She smiled. "But eventually it comes out that they have a son or a daughter or a niece or a nephew or a family friend. If you don't mind my asking, what happened to David?"

I was surprised by her directness, but Carol had spent several decades confronting the hard reality.

"The doctors aren't sure, actually."

She nodded thoughtfully. "Was there an accident?"

"No, it was . . ." I struggled for the word. "Spontaneous."

She smiled, focused on David. "All right," she said. And then, as if remembering, "Can I get you gentlemen something to drink?"

"Oh no, that's not—"

"I'm going to get myself a glass of lemonade. It's just as easy to carry three as it is to carry one."

I smiled. "Lemonade would be very nice. Thank you."

As she left the room, I put my hand on David's leg, sighing heavily in relief. "I think she likes you, sport," I said, squeezing gently.

I don't know what I was hoping to get out of my conversation with Carol Corvin. Mostly, I think I was there to be in contact with someone whose life had been changed by the book, whether she was aware of it or not.

A minute later she swept back into the room with a tray of drinks. "I took the liberty," she said, setting a tall sippy cup on the table in front of David.

"Thank you," I said.

"It's part of the routine."

"You have a lovely home," I said.

She looked around as if she hadn't noticed until I had brought it to her attention. "The unanticipated trajectory of random numbers, Brent likes to call it."

"I'm sorry?"

She laughed at my confusion. "Brent, my husband, is a mathematician.

When we bought this place, one of his first comments was that there would have been no way to anticipate us living like this, no matter what variables you put into the equation. Math geek humility, I think."

"I'm sorry," I said, shaking my head. "I still don't really get it."

"I would be concerned if you had."

I smiled.

"The whole time Brent was in school we had a pretty clear track in mind: he'd get his doctorate, then get a job at a university and teach, and then we'd retire." She shrugged and sat down. "The only variables were where he would teach, where we would live, that sort of thing." She took a sip of her lemonade. "And then, when he was in the process of applying for teaching jobs, he took a position with a company that was just starting up. He said he figured he'd try it for a few years, and who was I to say no? He'd worked so hard, he deserved a chance to do what he wanted for a while."

I nodded.

"Of course," she said smiling, "that company was Microsoft, so he never did take any teaching jobs. More than thirty years now."

I tried to figure out the dates. "Thirty years? He must have been there almost from the beginning."

"Almost," she said. "He wasn't one of the very first, but pretty close. Close enough for all of this." She gestured at our surroundings. "Close enough for the foundation."

"Brent's making more than we ever thought he'd make. Beyond our wildest dreams, as a matter of fact. So I started the foundation as a way of making some of that money do some good. We've been funding summer camps and special shuttles so people with neurological conditions can get to medical appointments. We've got treatment bursaries established, so that people can travel to specialists if necessary. We've been helping fund some significant research. Oh—" She stopped suddenly. "That reminds me," she said, looking at her watch and standing up. "Matthew is probably up from his nap. Would you mind if he joined us?"

I stood up reflexively, because she had. "No, of course not."

"I'll be back in a sec. You sit. Enjoy your lemonade."

I helped David take a drink, unable to keep myself from expecting a reaction—a smacking of his lips, a wrinkling of his face at the sourness, some comment—that just didn't come.

"And here we are," Carol said from the foyer, and then they were coming through the door.

Matthew was in his late thirties or early forties. He would have been a handsome man, I thought, if not for Lazarus Took; his body was soft and gangly, though not fat. He was dressed in loose-fitting grey jogging pants and a tent-like black T-shirt. His face was soft and doughy, and seemed somehow fallen in on itself, completely expressionless. Carol was leading him by one hand. His other hung at his side, limp and motionless.

No clenching.

And his eyes were dead, motionless and dark.

"This is Matthew," Carol said proudly. "And Matthew, this is Christopher and his son David."

Was this what the future looked like?

"Would you like to sit next to David?" Carol asked her son. "I'm sure there's room."

I shuffled over to make space. The two boys sat side by side, distorted reflections of one another, staring straight ahead at the opposite wall.

"So . . ." I cleared my throat, still not entirely comfortable with her level of candour. "What happened . . .?"

"What happened with Matthew?" She picked up my question with an understanding smile.

"Yes."

"Well, I guess it was a spontaneous occurrence, too. The doctors never could diagnose his condition—that's one of the reasons I started the foundation, so that someday there might be some answers to those questions." She nodded. "As to Matthew, though"—she shrugged—"one minute he was reading and the next—"

I seized the moment. "He had a seizure."

"Yes." She looked at me curiously. "We've kept that information private, and I would appreciate—"

"Mrs. Corvin." I leaned forward, closer to her. "That's what happened to David. One minute he was reading, and the next he was in convulsions."

She had leaned back in her chair. "Carol," she said weakly. "Call me Carol."

"Carol." I decided to play all my cards. "Do you remember what Matthew was reading when he had the attack?"

She shook her head. "That was thirty years ago. He was always reading . . ."

"Does a novel called *To the Four Directions* sound familiar? By Lazarus Took?"

"Maybe," she said, but then she shrugged it off. "What difference does it make?"

"Mrs. Corvin, Carol, please, just—" I was aware that I was starting to sound like I was crazed. "Please, humour me. Was it an old book? Brown leather?"

She was nodding slowly as I described it. "With some sort of symbol on the front," she said carefully, trying to remember.

"That's it," I said. "That's the one."

"What one?" she asked sharply.

I took a deep breath. "Carol, David and Matthew were reading the same book when their seizures started. Not just the same book, the very same copy."

"That's not—"

I pulled the photocopy paper out of my pocket. Unfolding it, I passed it to her. "Does that look familiar?" I asked.

She looked at the page, at her son's name, photocopied from the inside cover of *To the Four Directions*, and put her hand to her mouth.

"That's how I found you," I confessed. "I went online to find out who Matthew Corvin was, what might have happened to him, and I came across the foundation."

Her face was pale. "That's Matthew's writing," she said.

"I know it is. In the same book he was reading when he had his first seizure. I don't think that's a coincidence."

"So you think the book had something to do with it?" she asked, staring at the page.

"I'm sure of it."

"Okay," she said, taking a deep breath.

"Okay?"

"Let's take a look at it," she said, her voice strangely calm. "I can get on the phone to one of the local labs, they can test it for mould and spores, toxins in the paper or the binding, psychoactive agents . . ." She was watching me, and she stopped. "What?"

"I don't have it. The book. It was stolen from me, a couple of nights ago in New York."

"You don't have it."

"That's actually why David and I are here. We're on our way to Oregon—we're trying to find it."

"We could do blood tests, then. They could check both boys' blood, compare them, look for contaminants . . ." Carol Corvin was clearly a force to be reckoned with, a woman used to getting things done.

"Sure," I said slowly. "We could do that. But, Carol . . ."

Something in my voice must have registered, because she turned to me, actually listening, rather than mentally calculating her next half-dozen steps.

"I don't think the tests are going to find anything."

She shook her head. "Why not?"

"David's been tested. For everything. I think—" I took a deep breath. "I think it's the book itself."

She looked at me blankly.

"It sounds crazy," I said, forestalling her objections, "but I think something happened to both of our sons while they were reading. *Because* of what they were reading. I think that the book itself—"

"You think *words* did this?"

I hesitated a moment, then nodded.

"Well, that's ridiculous," she said, leaning back in her chair, pulling as far back from me as she could. "Look, if you find this book, we'll run some—"

And then she stopped.

"Oh my God," she murmured.

I glanced over my shoulder to see what she was looking at.

It was the boys. I felt a leap of emotion in my throat, threatening to choke me, felt Carol's hand at my shoulder, clutching, as if she couldn't trust herself alone to see what she was seeing.

It had been only a few weeks since my son had last moved of his own accord; for Matthew Corvin, it had been three decades.

But as Carol and I had been talking, Matthew and David had turned on the couch to face each other, their faces only inches apart, their eyes not only open but focused. Seeing. Looking at one another. Their expressions were still mostly flat, but there was something there in both, some faint hint of emotion that I couldn't quite identify.

"Oh my God," Carol said again in a whisper, her fingers digging into my shoulder. "It's like they know each other."

That was it: recognition. They knew each other, these two boys, though there was more than thirty years between them, though they had never actually met.

In this world, I thought.

Carol drew in a sharp breath that seemed almost a sob as Matthew slowly lifted his hand and, reaching out, laid it across David's, squeezing it gently.

⤜ ⤛

David didn't volunteer to help the captain row. The way he was feeling, he knew he would be of no use. Instead, he huddled in the stern, wrapped in his blanket, watching the boat break the clear, implacable surface of the water.

The captain wiped his hand across his brow. He was sweating. The sun was high overhead. David knew, rationally, that there was heat beating down on his face, but it seemed distant, almost an abstraction against the deep cold that he was feeling.

It's almost over, Matt said. *You'll be home soon.*

We don't know that. David's thoughts were slow and dark.

But once you get to the end of the story—

If *I get to the end of the story.*

You will, he urged. *You will.*

I don't know, he thought. *Have you ever read a story where the hero keeps getting weaker and weaker?*

Frodo, Matt said. *In Lord of the Rings.*

David shook his head and stared down into the water. *I haven't read that.*

You're not dying, David. You just have to get to the end of the story, bring the Sunstone back to the Queen, and—

And what? What then? We've been thinking that that's the end. But what if it's not? What if there's no magical release? What if it keeps going on and on, with me stuck here forever? Or what if, when the story ends, it all just stops? What then?

Matt didn't say anything. The only sound was the captain paddling, the splash of the water, and his grunts and groans. David watched him as he worked, the heavy muscles of his arms, the cords of his neck, the tight mask of determination.

I'm not getting out of this alive.

༄ ༄

Tony Markus made a point of arriving at the restaurant more than ten minutes early. To arrive any later risked being the second person to arrive, thereby putting himself at a disadvantage by giving whoever he was meeting—in this case, Cat Took—the upper hand, primacy of place, all that Sun Tzu *Art of War* shit.

Besides, all he had to do was ride the elevator down six floors, step through the hotel's front door and turn left. Except that as he turned, he almost ran into a woman standing outside the restaurant doors.

"I'm sorry," he said, keeping a careful hold on the bag from Powell's City of Books that he had tucked under his arm.

"Mr. Markus?" the woman said, extending her hand. "I'm Cat Took."

He took her hand, hoping that his wasn't too sweaty, and cursed himself for not getting to the restaurant earlier. "Nice to meet you," he said, as warmly as he could muster.

It wasn't difficult: Cat Took was a pretty woman, not yet thirty, with long dark hair and glowing skin, the sort of look that seemed to come from equal parts outdoor exercise and flakey New Age thinking. Vegetarianism, probably. "How did you know . . .?"

When she smiled, her teeth were bright. "I looked you up," she said. "So I'd know who to look for. The miracle of Google. A single girl's best friend."

"This is starting to feel like a blind date," Markus said, shifting a little. He hadn't expected her to be so pretty, so small and trim, so obviously comfortable in her dark jeans and black top, a large silver medallion hanging just at the neckline. Oh yes, he'd have to be careful in his negotiations, careful not to give too much up. It was easy when it was some crotchety Upper West Side academic, or some overwhelmed first-timer, desperate to get into print. With a woman like Cat Took, he'd have to be very careful indeed.

Still, it was going to be very nice to have her to look at over dinner.

~ ~

We didn't stay too long with Carol and Matthew after the boys began to look at each other. Carol and I watched in silence as, gradually, their faces lost what little animation they had temporarily claimed, returning to their previous slackness almost in unison. Matthew's eyes had started to darken as David's began to flicker, as his hands began to jerk.

When I looked away from the boys, Carol was staring at me.

"What just happened?" she asked, her voice rough, her eyes shining.

"I don't know."

"Matthew hasn't . . . It's been thirty years." She paused. "You think this has something to do with that book," she said, and for a moment she sounded like Jacqui. Not quite openly derisive, but dubious.

"I think so, yes."

"So what are you going to do with this book, if you find it?"

It was the question I had been hoping that she wouldn't ask; I didn't have an answer that would satisfy her. "I'll have to see," I said haltingly. "If there's anything in it that might reverse the effect that it had on Matthew and David."

"Like a magic spell?" she asked.

When I didn't say anything in response, she shook her head. "You know how ridiculous that makes you sound, don't you?"

"I've been hearing that a lot."

"I bet."

Standing up and edging past me to her son, she laid a hand on his forehead. "He looks warm," she said.

I leaned away, giving her space.

"If this works . . ." she said after a moment, so quietly I assumed she was talking to Matthew.

When she didn't continue, I said, "I'm sorry?"

"If this works," she said, still looking away from me, "what do you think is going to happen? To David, I mean."

The question stopped me. I had been blithely assuming that once the spell was broken David would return to normal. Hearing the question put so plainly, though, it occurred to me, for the first time, that David's injuries might be permanent.

"I don't know," I said carefully.

David and I managed to not get too lost on the way back to the hotel, stopping at a drive-thru to pick up an early dinner.

"We'll have a little picnic in the room," I told David as I tucked the bag in at his feet, but I was keenly aware of how forced the lightness in my voice sounded: I kept seeing Carol's face in my mind, the way the tiniest bit of hope, hope in something that she couldn't even bring herself to believe in, had shattered almost three decades of positive thinking and coping.

Once we were in the room, I led David to the easy chair and sat him down. "We're gonna need some extra towels," I said as I picked up the hotel phone and pushed the button for housekeeping.

Once I had made the request, I took a large towel from the bathroom. "Ta-da!" I said as I snapped it open and let it fall to the carpet. I set the bag at its centre.

"Instant picnic," I said to David as I guided him to a sitting position at the edge of the towel. I sat down across from him, close enough that I would be able to help him eat. "Let's see what we've got here," I said, opening the bag and starting to pull food from it.

I was interrupted by a knock on the door.

"And that'll be someone with the towels," I said, continuing the conversation as I stood up. "Cause somebody I know is going to have a bath tonight."

I crossed the room and opened the door, expecting to see a maid or someone from the desk. It never occurred to me to check the peephole.

Jacqui was standing in the doorway, keys in one hand, a look of cold curiosity on her face.

"So," she said. "Do you want to tell me just what the hell you're doing in Seattle?"

I could think of nothing else to say: "We're having a picnic. Do you want to come in?"

The boat ran up the shallows with a grinding of wood on gravel. David climbed carefully over the bow, splashing as he stepped to the shore.

The captain hopped out of the boat and pulled it high onto the small beach by the guy line. He rubbed his hands against the front of his pants. His face was sweaty, and for the first time since David had known him, the captain was out of breath.

"That was farther than it looked," he said, staring across the lake to where they had started out more than an hour before. "But then, distances over water are always deceptive, yes?"

David just nodded. It wasn't that he didn't want to participate in the captain's sudden, and not-quite-convincing show of camaraderie; he truly had nothing to say.

The captain looked at him a moment, but turned away when he didn't reply.

"I wish they had brought a bigger boat," he said, scanning the forested slope that loomed just beyond the beach.

"Why?" David asked, finding a seat on a driftwood log partway up the beach.

"It would be nice to have my men here," he said. "It would save us time searching."

David nodded. He knew that he should get up, but he couldn't bring himself to move. Or speak.

"On the other hand . . . " the captain said, pointing toward the brush.

Farther up the beach, at the point where the gravel gave way to underbrush, David saw a small building. The stone walls, thick with ivy, blended into the forest. There was no hiding the door, though: it seemed to glow, even in the shade, the Sunstone symbol etched deep into the metal.

Tony Markus and Cat Took wasted no time in ordering drinks once they had been seated.

"I'm glad we were able to get a table," Tony said, trying to fill the silence. "I didn't know if I should call down for a reservation."

"It's pretty early," she said. "It probably won't get busy for another couple of hours."

As she spoke, he watched the light from the candles play across her face. Her skin was so smooth, so clear, and she didn't seem to be wearing any makeup whatsoever.

"So what did you do with your day in Portland?" she asked. "I see you went to Powell's." She gestured at the bag he had set on the edge of the table.

"I did," he said, then stopped. He wouldn't mention that the highlight of his day had been a lacklustre massage but a very happy ending from a girl named Angi. "Actually, I spent most of the day there, wandering the aisles, spending too much money." He gestured toward the bag himself. Probably best to come across as a dedicated bibliophile, really show her how much a labour of love publishing was for him. Whatever story worked best.

"So what did you buy?"

"Actually," he said, grateful for the opening. "This isn't something I bought at Powell's. This—" He passed her the bag. "Is why I flew out here." She hesitated, holding the bag in her hands. "Go ahead, open it."

He was almost shaking with anticipation as she slid the book out.

The symbols on the cover caught the light of the candles, seemed to glow.

It took a moment for it to register, but her eyes widened, her mouth dropping open. "Oh," she said, glancing at him, then at the book, then back at him.

"I believe," he said smugly, "that this is your grandfather's last book. And, if all goes well, the centrepiece of our plans to get his work the attention it so richly deserves." Always a place for a little genuflecting.

"But where . . .?"

"I found it a while ago," he said.

"This is wonderful," she said, holding the book before her like some sort of holy object.

He smiled. "Well, I hope we can see to it that it brings as much joy to other readers as it has brought to you." God, sometimes the words that came out of his mouth made him sick. Why couldn't he just say, "Sign on the line and we'll all make a lot of money"? Wouldn't that be easier?

"Oh, Tony." She jumped up from the table and before he knew it she was kissing his face, her arms around his neck. "Thank you. Thank you for doing this, for my grandfather. He'd be so happy."

After cleaning up the take-out containers, I sat down in the easy chair, listening to the faint sounds of splashing and Jacqui's soft voice through the wall, trying not to envision the conversation that awaited on the far side of David's bedtime ritual.

When she'd gotten him settled in bed, she asked, "Where's the book?" The words looked like they filled her mouth with poison.

I picked up the papers from the desk and extended them toward her.

"Don't you want to?" she asked.

"I'm going downstairs for a bit." I grabbed my jacket from the back of the desk chair and got out of the room as quickly as I could.

On the corner outside the hotel, my hands were shaking so bad it took me a second try to get my cigarette fully lit. The sidewalks were crowded: it was Friday night. People were going out for dinner, or to a movie, families and friends and people on dates.

For a moment, I considered running. I probably had everything I needed in my pockets: notebook, cell phone, cigarettes. Keys. I could just go down to the parkade and be gone, back on the I–5 headed south before she even knew it.

I stepped back to let a large group pass on the sidewalk, a wall of laughter and scrubbed skin, aftershave and perfume, then butted out my cigarette under my heel and walked slowly back into the hotel, steeling myself.

When I got to the room, Jacqui was sitting in the desk chair, holding my notebook in her lap. She had turned off the bedside lamp closest to David so the room was dim, with only pools of faint light.

"So is this it?" she said, holding up my notebook. "Is this where I'm going to find out what's going through your head? What could possibly drive a man to kidnap his own son and flee the country?"

"I told you," I said quietly, sitting on the end of the bed near David's feet.

"But what about this?" she asked, gesturing at the hotel room around her. "Why are you here, Chris? Of all places?"

"I told you about Matthew Corvin. He wrote his name in the book in 1976. Well, I met him today. Sort of. I met his mother. Because Matthew has been catatonic since 1976. Thirty years. He collapsed reading *that* book. God, Jacqui, can't you see—"

She was shaking her head. I doubt she was even hearing what I was saying.

"I know what you're thinking. Trust me—I thought it too. For a long time. But . . . dammit, watching David, watching him be fed and taken to the bathroom and put to bed like he's an infant . . . If there's any chance that any of this is real, I can't ignore it. I have to do something."

"Chris—"

"I can get it back, Jacqui," I said, raising my voice. "I know where it is. I can get it back—borrow it long enough that Nora and Sarah can try to figure out what to do. That's what I'm doing here. The book's in Oregon, on the coast. I can get it back."

She had looked away, setting my notebook on the desk next to my laptop, maintaining an air of deliberate control.

"I have to do something."

"Including kidnapping your own son," she said slowly. "How did you get across the border?"

"I told the guard that you were already down here," I said. "For work. I said that we were meeting you."

"That easy," she muttered.

"How did you find us so quickly?"

"Bank card," she said. "I looked it up online. You took some money out in Bellingham last night, and we always stay here when we come down to Seattle, so I thought I'd try here first." She shrugged. "Christopher Knox. Two nights. You're going to have to try harder if you don't want people to find you."

"I wasn't hiding," I said. "I'm not running. I just have to—"

She cut me off with a wry smile.

"Did you know that this"—she looked at the bed, at the notebook on the desk—"is the most involved you've ever been in David's life?"

"That's not true," I said. "I'm there for him every day."

She laughed a little uncomfortably. "In a way," she said, picking up the notebook again, "this kind of gives me hope. I mean, aside from it being completely crazy."

I smiled warily.

She picked the keys up from the desk. "I'm gonna go down and grab my bag out of the car. Dale's car," she added. "He lent it to me." She stopped. "Is that okay? If I bring my stuff up here? I don't want to presume."

Tony Markus made a show of ordering the most expensive bottle of champagne the restaurant carried. "To celebrate," he told Cat, who was still aglow with the discovery of her grandfather's last book.

"To Lazarus Took," he offered by way of a toast.

"To the beginning of a beautiful relationship," she replied, clinking her glass delicately against his.

Her eyes seemed to follow him with a mix of adoration and appraisal that he hadn't, to be perfectly honest, encountered all that often in his life. And that was just fine with him.

The champagne went down quickly, and Tony ordered a bottle of red wine to accompany their dinner. He felt a bit awkward about having ordered a bloody steak when she ordered a salad, but she didn't seem fazed by it, and he let himself fall comfortably into the role of mighty hunter, powerful alpha male to this girl's innocent naïf.

And she was a girl, no question. She had a girlish enthusiasm for life, her hours spent walking in the woods near her home, getting closer to nature; her trips to large outdoor concerts where she could "float away on all the music and the people and the good vibes, you know?"; her "deep" interest in philosophy and alternative ways of looking at the world, "you know?"

"Did you go to school for that?" he asked to keep the conversation going as he finished his steak.

She looked at him like it was a ridiculous question. "Are you serious?" She shook her head, her hair tumbling and swaying. "I've never gone to school. Not university. I figure there's nothing they could teach me that I couldn't figure out for myself, you know? Or with some books, right?"

He nodded as she started talking about Taoism, about how the secrets of the universe could be revealed with nothing more than a copy of Lao Tzu and a night spent on the beach, listening to the waves crash and recede. From there she went on to talk about Buddhism, about the hidden teachings of the early church. Tony didn't even try to follow what she was saying, content to watch the gentle rise and fall of her breasts under her shirt as the steady warmth of the wine and the food rose within him.

"You're quite the free spirit," he said when she was finally silent.

She smiled, showing those pretty white teeth again. "Don't you think that everyone should be?"

"I suppose," he said, draining his wineglass, then realizing sadly that the bottle was also empty.

"No, really," she said, reaching across the table and laying her hand over his. "I mean, why do you think people drink so much? It's not like it's being used for its ritual, sacramental purposes."

"No," he said guardedly. Her hand was so soft, so warm.

"No," she echoed emphatically. "It's so they can cut loose those shackles, so they can shake themselves free of all the expectations and restrictions that society heaps on them, even if it's only for a little while."

She squeezed his hand gently, and he could feel it, like a convulsive ripple of electricity, through his whole body.

"I mean, look at us," she said. "We're sitting here, we've had a good meal, we've had some good wine, and there's this, this energy that's passing between us."

Tony had to stop himself from flinching.

"You can feel it too, right? I felt it when I first met you. But we've been sitting here all this time trying to pretend that we're not feeling it, trying to deny the fundamental truth of our bodies wanting to be together, and it's all because of society. All those rules about how you have to pretend that you're not feeling what you're feeling, how you have to be polite and distant and detached, when what you really want to be doing . . ."

Tony watched the words hanging in the air, wondering how he should finish the sentence that she had left there.

"I mean, what would it take for us to shake off these old rules, these old roles? Some cataclysm? The news that we only had one hour left to live? Why can't it be something simpler? Something natural?" She slipped her hand away from his and started to rise to her feet. The air between them was charged with the energy that she had been talking about. "I mean, what if all it took was me standing up. And walking over to you." She edged around the table. "And kissing you?" Putting one hand gently on each of his cheeks, she brought her mouth to his, her lips cool and tasting of wine, her tongue darting against his mouth. He could feel the heat from her, and he brought his hands lightly up to her hips.

"Do you think it would take any more than that?" she asked, mere inches from his face. "For us to put aside all those rules and expectations?"

She kissed him again, before he could answer.

⤜ ⤛

"That was easy," the captain said as they stood in front of the small stone building on the shore of the island.

Easy for him, maybe.

David agreed: the clues in the map had been difficult to work out, and without them they would still be on the shore, looking in vain for a building that they would never find.

Not to mention almost drowning, almost burning to death, the chills, the pounding in his head.

"Are you ready?" the captain asked.

Looking at the building, David thought of what the magus had told him about the Brotherhood and their beliefs. The building was in a perfect location, a place of power near the water, and where the symbol on the door would catch the first rays of the rising sun every morning.

He suppressed a shiver as he thought about going inside. What would be waiting for him? What traps?

The captain was waiting for an answer.

David coughed. "I suppose," he said quietly.

He shrugged off the blanket, letting it fall to the ground as he stepped toward the door.

The captain remained in place, his face hard and expressionless.

There were no handprints on the sidewalls of the doorway, as he had expected, but there was a faint handprint etched in the centre of the Sunstone itself.

He took a deep breath before he reached out and fit his hand into place.

He turned his wrist and tried to rotate his hand to the right. The metal plate at the centre of the Sunstone followed his motion, turning easily.

David bit his lip.

The plate turned a quarter-turn before David felt a moment of resistance. There was a click, and the door moved.

He pushed lightly, and the door swung silently open, without any hesitation whatsoever, an effortless glide.

Somehow, Tony Markus managed to unlock the door to his hotel room while still kissing Cat Took. He slammed it behind them, tossed the book onto the desk, then fell with her onto the bed. Cat's breath was coming in short puffs of passionate intensity. Her hands were on his chest, fumbling with the buttons to his shirt, then tugging it free from his belt.

He couldn't decide where to touch her first. He slid one hand up her side, cupped her breast tentatively, and she made a small squeaking noise in the back of her throat. He ran his hand down her back, over her ass, and she pushed herself into him, grinding against his body. She slid her hand into the open front of his shirt, onto his bare skin, and he moaned at her touch.

They wrestled there for a long time, wriggling and thrashing, her mostly atop him. And then she pulled away.

"Oh God," she muttered, her eyes half closed, her hair dishevelled.

"I know," he said, breathless, his hands again on her hips, but heavy this time, exerting a force to pull her closer to him again.

"That's what it feels like to break some of those shackles," she said, grinning. She sounded out of it, drunk on wine and passion.

"I feel the same way."

She giggled.

"Just a second," she said, rolling away from him and grabbing her purse from the floor. "I have to—" She pointed at the bathroom. "I'll be back in a sec." She turned on the light. "Why don't you"—she gestured at his open shirt—"get rid of some of those clothes before I get back." She smiled a coy, dirty smile that made his cock throb, and then she closed the bathroom door.

"Oh," she called out. "Why don't you find some music or something on the TV, so we don't disturb the neighbours."

He could hear the water running in the bathroom. "Oh fuck, oh fuck," he muttered, not able to believe what was happening. Maybe there was something to this West-Coast, tree-worshipping thing after all.

He tugged off his clothes and scurried over to the door and flipped the dead bolt into place. He thought of calling down to have more champagne sent up, but there would be time for that later—probably best not having to worry about waiting for someone to come knocking at the door at this point.

At this point!

Markus felt giddy as he scanned through the TV channels, eventually settling on some music station—nothing like this had ever happened to him before. It wasn't quite a barroom pickup, but it was close. He just hoped that it wasn't going to end up as a one-night stand; already he was thinking about ways he could get accounting to foot the bill for more trips out here, or to bring her to New York: editorial meetings, publicity, lunches . . . the possibilities were nearly endless.

Excitedly, he pulled the covers of the bed back, preparing a soft nest to crawl into as soon as she came out of the bathroom.

And then—the sound of the toilet flushing.

He hurried back around to the end of the bed so he would be close when she came out of the bathroom. For the briefest of moments he felt a little embarrassed about how he looked—his hanging gut, his pudgy legs—but he decided that it didn't really matter. She clearly liked him, and it was obvious that she wasn't the sort of person to get hung up on appearances.

He opened his arms as she opened the bathroom door.

She was still dressed. Her face was set, without a trace of the heady, drunk feeling they had been sharing a few minutes before.

His arms fell.

"What—?" he said, stumbling in surprise when he saw the gun in her hand, watched her bring it up and, without a moment's hesitation, fire.

While Jacqui was down in the garage getting her bag from Dale's car, I dialled Cat Took's number on my cell phone.

The phone rang three times before she picked up.

"Cat? It's Christopher Knox calling."

"Mr. Knox," she said. "From Victoria." Her voice was low, but touched with a youthful quality, and the faintest sound of pleasure, as if she was glad to hear from me.

"Yes, from Victoria." I stopped myself. "Actually, I'm just outside of Seattle right now."

"Seattle?" There was a hollow clarity to the line: a cell phone, probably.

I looked over at David, asleep on the bed. "I'm on a bit of a vacation with my family."

"That's lovely."

"It is," I said. "We thought we'd get away for a few days, make a long weekend of it, maybe head down to the Oregon Coast for a couple of nights."

"You'll be right in my neck of the woods."

"That's why I'm calling, actually. I thought that while we were in the area . . . Would you have time to get a cup of coffee or something?" I quickly calculated what the next day might look like, driving times and possibilities. "Maybe tomorrow afternoon?"

"I'm sorry," she said. "Tomorrow afternoon's not good for me."

My heart sank.

"But what about Sunday?"

"That would be terrific."

"Good," she said. "Where are you staying down here?"

I hadn't thought that far ahead. "I think we're just going to find a place once we get there. There are a lot of motels in Seaside."

"That there are," she said. "There's also a coffee shop . . ."

I flipped open my notebook as she gave me directions. We settled on four o'clock.

"How will I recognize you?"

She laughed, a surprisingly delicate sound. "This is starting to sound like a blind date," she said. "Let's see. I'll wear a purple scarf."

"And I'll—"

"I'll recognize you, Mr. Knox." When I didn't say anything, she added, "I found some publicity photos of you on the Internet."

Of course. "Well, add a decade or so to those and there I am."

"I'll do that," she said. "And I guess I'll see—"

"Cat, do you mind if I ask you a question?"

"You *are* a journalist," she said. "It would be out of character if you didn't."

"I was just wondering if you had been contacted by anyone from Davis & Keelor, in New York."

"Someone named Terry or Tony called me a week or so ago."

"Tony Markus?"

"That sounds right. Why do you ask?"

I forced myself not to panic. "But you haven't spoken to him in the last couple of days?"

"No, no," she said thoughtfully. "It was definitely before last weekend."

"That's good," I said, more to myself than to her.

"Is there something going on, Christopher?"

"Sort of," I said. "I'll explain more when I see you on Sunday, but until then, if you wouldn't mind, could you please let me know if he tries to get in touch with you? It's very important."

"It sounds like it," she said. "There isn't anything else you can tell me?"

"He has something of mine," I said, remembering Sarah's comments about honesty, going further out on a limb than I had expected. "Something that once belonged to your grandfather. A book. I was going to return it to you, to the estate, on this trip, but he . . . well, how he got it is a long story. Just, if he gives you anything, could you please hang onto it?"

"This is growing rather more cryptic by the moment," she said.

"I know, and I'm sorry about that."

"I'll let you know if he calls again," she said.

"Thank you," I said, practically shaking with relief.

"I do want to hear this story," she said, almost warningly.

"Sunday afternoon."

"I'll see you then." There was a click as the line disconnected.

≋ ≋

David waited a moment in the doorway of the stone building on the beach, looking into the small room.

"There has to be more to it than this," he said, taking a step forward, as if that might reveal something that he hadn't noticed.

The room was rectangular, and small enough to be lit entirely by the daylight coming through the open door. The walls were plain stone, smooth. There were no other doorways, no stairways, no marks on the wall or carved symbols.

There was only a stack of smoothly cut stone blocks, rising to his waist, standing in the middle of the room.

An altar.

And on top of it a gold chest that caught the sunlight and seemed to magnify it, burning with a silent, undeniable force.

David entered the room and stopped, waiting for something to happen, some trick or trap.

"Why are you delaying?" the captain asked from outside the door. "Is something wrong?"

David took another look around the room, but there was nothing he could imagine posing a threat. Nothing he could see, at least.

"No," he said. "It looks safe."

"Then get the Stone and let's get out of here," the captain said.

David hesitated, still not sure.

"Come on," the captain urged.

It's not like you have a choice, Matt said.

That's true, he thought, as he crossed the room to the altar. He didn't have a choice about any of this.

The gold chest was about the size of his mother's jewellery box, with the symbol of the Sunstone carved into its lid. A ruby was set in the middle of the symbol. No handprints, no clues, no secret locks—just a beautiful box with a lid.

David looked around the room as he opened the box. No flames, no flood.

So far.

Inside was a brown leather bag, still soft despite its age. As he lifted it out, his fingers brushed against something underneath it: a small book, bound in the same colour of leather, with the outline of the Sunstone on the cover.

That looks like—

Matt's thoughts were cut off by the sound of the captain's voice.

"Do you have it?"

Hardly able to breathe, David struggled to untie the knot closing the leather bag. The shape felt right. The weight felt right. If he could just get this knot untied . . .

This is it, Matt thought excitedly. *This is it.*

When the knot came loose, he reached into the bag and pulled out an amulet on a long, heavy chain. The pendant was thick, gold, and when he turned it over, he saw it was set with a large, blood-red stone.

There was no doubt in his mind: after all the narrow escapes and false hopes, all the pain, he was holding the Sunstone.

The ruby seemed to drink in the light, gleaming and growing warm in his hand. Warm! Just holding the Stone, he could feel heat moving through his body, a warmth that he had thought he would never feel again.

He felt light and suddenly at ease. He'd done it! And now the Stone was doing its work, healing him, body and soul.

As the warmth rushed through him, he felt something else: a sense of weightlessness, of moving out of himself. He blinked several times, and each time he closed his eyes, the world changed around him. One moment he was standing in the room on the island, holding the Sunstone; the next, he was in a warm bed, and he could faintly hear the sound of his parents' voices.

"Is that it?" the captain called out.

For a long moment, David couldn't speak, overcome by the warmth, the power, the strange sensations coming from the Stone. There was magic here, no doubt, and he soaked it up like a dry patch of earth soaks up a rain.

"Dafyd?" he heard the captain, as if from a great distance. "What's happening?"

"I've got it," he called, reluctant to break the spell. He could hear the shaking in his voice. "I've got the Sunstone."

As he turned toward the door to show the captain the prize they had won, he felt the cold tip of the man's sword against his chest, over his heart.

David froze in place. "Captain. We have to—"

"*We* don't have to do anything. You found the Stone. Your Queen will be grateful. But your part in this is done. Now put the Stone back in the bag and give it to me." He spoke these last words through clenched teeth.

David, give it to him, Matt urged. *He'll kill you.*

David looked at the captain's face, felt the Stone heavy in his hand. The man's eyes were dark, and so focused they seemed to bore into him. His jaw was hard, unmoving, his determination clear and grim.

He's going to kill me anyway, David thought.

But maybe—

"Give me the Stone," the captain said again, pressing the tip of his sword through the fabric of David's shirt.

David could feel the cold steel against his chest for an instant before his skin gave way with a burst of pain. "All right, all right," he shouted, stepping back slightly as he felt his own warm blood running down his stomach. "Here." He held out the Stone.

Captain Bream shook his head. "That's not mine to hold," he said. "Put it in the bag."

David moved slowly, deliberately, not making any sudden movements that might startle or anger the captain.

When he held out the leather pouch, the captain snatched it away.

You had no choice, Matt said.

The captain lowered his sword slightly as he tucked the bag into a small pocket near his belt.

"So what happens to me?" David asked quietly, watching the tip of the sword, now in line with his belly.

The captain shook his head. "We've got what we came for," he said, his voice cold.

It looked like he shrugged, but his motions were too fast for David to follow: the captain stepping forward, a crunching noise just over his left ear, a flash of light and pain, and everything went dark.

⇾ ⇽

Cat Took had turned the television down when her phone started to ring; as she hung up, she turned it off altogether. There was no need for its noise now; there was nothing left to conceal.

She left Tony Markus's body where it had fallen, face-up on the bed, his expression frozen in surprise, the almost perfect circle of his mouth matching the smaller circle of the bullet hole in the centre of his forehead. He had fallen without a sound, the bed shuddering under the sudden force of his weight.

She had already tucked the gun back into her purse. So heavy in the hand, so concentrated in its force, and yet so easily gone from her sight again. It was as if she had called a terrible creature into being for its one purpose, then allowed it to dissipate back into the ether once she was done with it.

In the bathroom, she splashed some cold water on her face and patted it dry. She reapplied her lipstick, erasing the memories of the repulsive man's mouth on her own. She touched her hair.

Pretty as a picture, she thought to herself.

She used her purple scarf to wipe off the doorknobs, the faucets and the buttons on the front of the TV that she had touched. She was confident that she hadn't touched anything else, but she wasn't overly concerned: even if she had left a fingerprint or two, there was nothing in any database to match them against.

The last thing she did before leaving the room was to cross to the desk and pick up the book that he had tossed so carelessly there when they got to the room. She held it carefully, tenderly, with an intimacy like that of a lover.

"Hello, Lazarus," she said. "Back again."

⚜ ⚜

If you hadn't given him the Stone, he would have killed you and taken it.

Given the situation, David didn't find the words comforting.

"Instead," he said. "He left me here."

They were sitting on the beach, at the edge of the lake, as darkness came.

Alive is better than dead, Matt said.

"Sorry."

They sat in silence for a long while. The water lapped at the rocks near their feet and the breeze rustled in the trees behind them.

"So what now?" David asked.

I don't know, Matt said, and David thought he could hear a helplessness, a sadness that he had never detected before in his friend's voice. *This doesn't fit.*

Reaching forward, David cupped a handful of the cold lake-water and dabbed lightly at the lump where the captain had hit him with the hilt of his sword. Good, it was starting to scab up. So was the small cut on his chest.

"What doesn't fit?"

I never told you, he said. *I always . . . I read the last page of a book first.*

"You read the last page first?" David almost laughed, thinking of what his father would have said about that.

I can't stand the suspense, he said, sounding embarrassed.

"So *To the Four Directions* has a happy ending?"

That's why I was so sure that everything was going to be okay, he said. *Matthias—Dafyd—was this huge hero, and there was a parade and a carriage and Arian . . .*

"But you said that me being here changed everything."

I thought that was just little things. I didn't think . . . I mean, the book's already been written, right?

David sighed. "Does this look like a book to you?" he asked, gazing out at the lake. "This is it," he said slowly, feeling a part of himself deflate with every word. "This isn't a book. Not anymore. It's a world. My world, now." The truth hung in the cool air, the implications still echoing in his head. "I'm never gonna see my mom and dad again. There's no happy ending, no 'you'll make it through to that end because that's what happens in the book.' There's just—" He picked up a handful of gravel and threw it into the water. "Just this. This island. This beach."

And whatever you do.

He looked out at the water.

"I'm going to die here," he said, his voice breaking. "I'm never going home."

You might not have to wait that long . . .

David rose to his feet.

Look, he said, as if David wasn't seeing through the same pair of eyes. *There's a light.*

There was nowhere to hide. The only thing more daunting than hiding in the small building where he had found the Sunstone was the idea of running into the dark woods.

"Who do you think it is?" he asked, touching his ankle, making sure that the knife was still there.

We'll find out soon enough.

David didn't become frightened as the minutes passed, as the light grew larger, as the boat came into view. So much had happened to him, he was content to just watch and wait. As the faint sound of oars on the water reached his ears, David pulled the knife from its sheath and held it in his lap.

Not long now, Matt said.

"No, not long."

He stood up when the boat was close enough for him to see the figure of the old man, paddling hard toward him. David held the knife loosely in his right hand, sure to be standing straight and tall as the light fell across him.

"Dafyd!" the magus cried out when he saw him, but David stood stock-still, not allowing the slightest hint of emotion to touch his face.

The old man dug his oars harder into the water, driving the boat onto the beach. Before it had even come to rest, he was clambering over the gunwale, opening his arms.

"Oh, Dafyd," the old man said. "Thanks be that you're alive. I didn't dare hope—"

David took a step back from the old man and raised the knife between them. "Stay back," he said, hoping his voice sounded firm.

"You're hurt," he said, trying to reach the wound on the side of the boy's head.

David stepped back again, bobbing his head to avoid the man's touch.

"The captain did that to you?"

"Loren,"—David pointed the knife at the man's chest—"what the hell is going on?"

The magus seemed confused.

Maybe it's the knife, Matt guessed.

David ignored the voice in his head, and focused on the magus's face.

"The captain came back alone and ordered the men to break camp." He shook his head. "I knew it was a mistake when the two of you set out alone, but I could do nothing . . ."

David wasn't used to seeing the magus so rattled. The blade wavered. "What did the captain say?"

"He didn't *say* anything," the magus said. "Not about you. He told the men that they were going to ride hard, through the night if they had to. That they were going home. The men cheered when they heard that."

David could picture the scene, could imagine the joy he'd have felt to learn that he was going home.

"When I asked him what had happened on the island, he said that your part in this was done, that you wouldn't be returning to Colcott with us. And when he said 'us,' he looked at me and said, 'And that goes for you as well, Magus.'"

The knife point dipped. "He left you?"

The magus nodded. "With enough food for a couple of days, and the slowest of the horses. And the boat," he said, indicating it with his hand.

"And you came to rescue me," David said slowly.

"I would not have put it past the captain to kill you once he had the Stone," the magus said. "But I hoped that he had only abandoned you on this shore, the way he had so quickly abandoned me."

David lowered the knife to his side. "I'm glad you came," he said, trying to keep the relief he was feeling from dissolving into tears.

"I swore an oath to protect you," the magus said firmly, "and to help you to the fullest of my ability to recover the Sunstone."

"Not necessarily in that order," he muttered.

"No," the magus said. "In precisely that order. That is where the captain and I differed: he wanted the Stone for his Queen, regardless of the cost. The oath I swore, though, was to protect you, to ensure your return. Even at the cost of my own life."

"At least it didn't come to that," David said, hoping for humour to fill the air as he tried to make sense of what he was hearing, to make it fit with the events of the journey.

"It might still," the magus said gravely.

"Why? What do you mean?"

"We're not finished," the old man said. "We haven't much time, and we must get back to the castle before the captain. There are steps that must be taken—"

"But you said the captain only left you with one horse."

"We won't be riding." The magus gave a meaningful glance behind him.

"The boat?" David asked.

The magus nodded. "It's four days hard riding back to Colcott, maybe five, though I have learned not to underestimate the captain. By boat, we should take no longer than three. Getting to the river's mouth at the north end of the lake will be the hardest part."

To his surprise, David was nodding. "Then we should get—"

The magus lifted one hand. "We have a little time," he said. "I took the liberty of adding a tincture to the drinking water as the men were breaking camp." A smile cracked through his silver beard.

"You poisoned them?" His hand tightened again around the knife.

The magus shook his head. "I'm shamed that you would think me capable of cold-blooded murder after all this time. No, not poison. But they will sleep very well. Irresistibly."

David's grin matched that of the old man. "That was clever," he said.

The magus shrugged. "These arms are not as suited for rowing as they once were. And you're not apt to be much help."

"No, I can row," David said.

He looked at David with sudden curiosity. "The last time I saw you, you could barely hold your own weight," he said warily.

David nodded. "I'm feeling much better," he said.

"You touched the Stone, didn't you?"

"Yes," David said. "Why? Is that—?"

"No. No, that's fine. That's just fine." A smile broadened his face as he fell silent.

David waited a few moments for him to say something. He didn't. "I suppose we should go."

The magus nodded. "Yes, we should. But there's one thing I want to do first."

PART SIX

DAVID GRUNTED AS HE DUG the oars into the water, a small sound of exertion that echoed across the dark, silent river.

The magus, sitting on the small bench across from him, looked up at David from the book in his hands. The lantern was at his back, lighting both their way and his pages, but making it difficult for David to read his expression.

"Are you tiring?" he asked, his voice warm with concern.

"No," David said, to his own surprise. He had enjoyed the past few hours, feeling the pleasant ache in his arms and the tightness in his back. "This morning I couldn't have lifted one of these oars," he said, digging in again. "Let alone actually rowed."

The magus nodded. "Such are the powers of the Stone, it seems."

Don't say too much, Matt said. *You still can't be sure of him.*

"Is that what it says in the book?" David asked, looking at the volume the old man was holding. It was the book from the bottom of the gold chest.

The magus had asked David to show him the small building, 'the last of the hidden places', before they left the island.

"It was really that simple?" the magus had asked, standing outside the stone building, holding the lamp high to illuminate the doorway. "It was only a matter of walking through the door?"

"The trick was getting here, I guess."

"No," the magus said. "The key was proving yourself."

David tried to push Matt's comments about his being tested to the back of his mind.

The magus stopped before the chest and lowered himself to one knee. Bowing his head, he reached into his robes and clasped his amulet with his left hand, his mouth moving slightly.

David turned away, giving the man a moment of privacy, turning back only when he heard the rustle of his robes.

"This place," the magus said slowly. "It is one of the holiest sites of our faith, only rumoured to exist, until now. I feel . . ." He stopped, trying to find the right word. "Humbled to be here, to be the first of our brotherhood inside these walls. Until this moment, no one knew if Gafilair had succeeded in concealing the stone. To see this place, to know that he succeeded . . ."

David waited a moment, then asked, "If he succeeded, why didn't he return to the kingdom?"

The magus took a long time to answer. "He disappeared to keep his secret. To keep all of this safe and hidden, for you."

"I'm not sure what you mean."

"The Brotherhood is sworn in our duty and loyal, absolutely, to the King. Had Gafilair returned, and had the King changed his mind, he would have been honour-bound to reveal the place where the Stone had been concealed. Had *any* king asked, the Order would have had no choice but to reveal the truth, had they known. The only way a secret lasts for a millennium is if there is no one to tell it."

The enormity of what the magus was saying washed over David. "He sacrificed himself to protect the secret."

"To protect the Stone. And to protect the kingdom from those who might misuse it."

The words chilled him. "What is Captain Bream going to do with it?" he asked, afraid to hear the answer.

"He's going to give it to the Queen."

"Wasn't that the whole point of this trip? To bring the Stone back to the Queen?"

The magus looked at him sadly. "No. That was the captain's goal, his orders from the Queen. But so long as the King lives, my loyalty, and the loyalty of the Order, is to him."

"But the Queen said she wanted the Stone to heal the king."

The magus nodded gravely. "Yes, she did say that."

David waited for him to say something more, but the magus was looking down at the book, flipping carefully through the pages, filled with the brown ink of the first magus, now familiar from the maps and clues.

Leaning back on his bench, David lifted the oars from the water, letting the boat move with the current as he watched the old man.

"The book doesn't say much about the properties of the Stone itself," the magus said. "It's a diary, mostly. An account of Gafilair's travels in his quest to conceal the Stone. A description of the magics he used to build the chambers, the traps. 'The trials,' as he called them."

David snorted, thinking back to the trials, tasting the river water in his lungs, feeling the burns on his back. But he sensed an opportunity to ask the question that had been bothering him since they had left the stone chamber hours before.

"If the Queen doesn't want the Stone to heal the King, then why does she want it?"

"Perhaps the Queen really does want to heal the King," the magus said reluctantly, as if he would have preferred not to talk about it. "But you felt the Stone's power. If she were able to use that power, to tap into the force of the Stone, the kingdom would be hers."

David shook his head. "But, isn't the kingdom already hers?"

The magus shook his head. "She rules in the King's stead, and in the King's name. Her power is borrowed from him. If he dies, the crown should pass to the next in the line, not to her. But with there being no prince, with the Stone the Queen could claim rightful dominion."

꙰ ꙰

It took a long time to build up the courage, but in the parking lot of the motel in Seaside, I couldn't really put it off any longer.

"Do you want your own room? I asked Jacqui.

"I don't think so," she said, looking out her window.

After checking us in, I hefted the bags out of the back of the van while Jacqui helped David out of his seat. In the bright afternoon sun I was struck by how pale they both looked.

We had all had a rough night: David had had two small seizures between midnight and four, and Jacqui and I had sat up with him until we were sure he was calmed.

"It's getting worse again," Jacqui had said. "I wonder if it's travelling, or . . ."

I hadn't mentioned the book, the precious few pages that remained.

She must have felt me looking at her, because she glanced at me quizzically. I tried to smile, tried to be reassuring, but I don't think either of us believed it.

I shut the van door, and the three of us walked slowly into the motel.

⤙ ⤚

They traded their positions in the boat again just as the sun was rising. The magus picked up the oars as David slumped onto the bench in the stern. David watched as the old man drew the oars through the water.

"Thanks," he said quietly.

The magus just nodded.

During his shifts with the oars, David had pulled blindly into the darkness as the magus slept. Now, with the sun rising, he was able to watch the banks of the river sliding past in the soft morning light. If the speed with which objects and landmarks disappeared behind them was any indication, they were making good time, the force of the river's current rushing them home.

Home . . .

The constant scrolling of the shoreline and the motion of the boat were almost hypnotic, lulling, and David noticed now, for the first time, just how tired he was. It was not that sickly feeling of weakness and decline but an honest desire for sleep.

Bracing himself on the gunwale, he slid onto the bottom of the boat, his back against the bench.

The magus smiled. "Rest well, Dafyd," he said.

David nodded slowly, dopily. He could feel himself slipping away, drifting quickly into sleep. His eyelids hung heavily, every blink slower than the last, and he breathed deeply of the morning air.

He jerked upright, his eyes flashing open. "Do you smell that?"

He needn't have asked: the magus was letting the oars drag in the water as he surveyed the banks of the river around them.

"Smoke," the magus said.

🙠 🙢

I stood on the balcony smoking while Jacqui got David ready for bed. I held the photocopied book loosely in my left hand. As she washed his face, brushed his teeth, got him into a new diaper, I stared out over the parking lot, trying to forestall the inevitability of what was going to happen next.

This was it; two lowly pages left. Not only did I not know what finishing the book would do to David, I wasn't even sure if there were enough words left to soothe him to sleep one last time.

The glass door slid open with a rumble that shook the small balcony. "He's all tucked in," she said. "Are you ready?"

I nodded, and flicked my cigarette butt into the parking lot. "Yup," I said, thinking of Gary Cooper in *High Noon*.

She touched my arm as I came through the door, enough to tell me that she was at least aware of the stakes, even if she didn't believe in them herself.

Jacqui had moved the desk chair close to the bed, close to David. "So are you ready for this?" I asked him as I sat down. "Ready to see what happens to our brave hero at the end?"

Jacqui sat down in the easy chair near the patio door, almost behind me.

"Okay," I said, trying to calm myself, steady my voice.

I began, and kept one eye on him as I read, watching his eyes, his hands.

After a full page, nothing had changed. I glanced over at Jacqui, who was watching from the easy chair.

Halfway down the next page, he was still clenching, eyes still flickering. And I was running out of words.

I forced myself to slow my voice even further.

There. His eyelids sinking shut, the contractions of his hands slowing. I exhaled a breath I hadn't known I was holding.

"The end."

My hands shook as I set the papers down on the bed next to me. I stood up slowly and kissed David gently on the forehead. "I love you, Davy," I whispered. "Sleep well."

I have never meant those words as much as I did right then.

I went out to the balcony thinking that I wanted to smoke, but I ended up just leaning on the railing, looking into the dark.

I didn't hear Jacqui come out, didn't even know she was there until she slid her arms around me from behind, embracing me, leaning her cheek against my back between my shoulder blades.

"He's going to be all right," she said.

"Maybe." I couldn't keep the doubt out of my voice.

"No, this will work out. One way or another."

I turned around into her embrace, and, her head resting on my chest, brought my arms around her.

She had always been good at talking me through my doubts, but it had been a long time since she had done so. I craned my neck and kissed the top of her head. "I know you don't really believe in any—"

"No," she said, looking me in the eye. "But you do."

I smiled.

"I mean it," she said. "You're a pretty smart guy, Chris. And if you believe something, there's probably a good reason to take it seriously."

I pulled her closer, not wanting to risk saying anything.

"We should go in," she whispered sometime later, her voice tinged with regret. "For when David . . ."

Not *in case* David had a seizure, but *when*.

"Yeah," I said, disentangling myself from her. "Do you mind if I . . ." I mimed a smoking gesture.

She shook her head, her hair bouncing. "I'll be inside."

She closed the door behind herself as I lit a cigarette. She didn't draw the curtains, and I watched her moving through the room, checking on David and moving bags and all the minutiae of just another evening. I was struck by how beautiful she was, how genuine and unaffected. How lucky a man would be who got to spend his life with a woman like her. And how stupid he would have to be to fuck it all up.

I crushed out the cigarette butt and went inside.

They saw the camp a few moments later, the low smoky fire close to the eastern bank of the river.

The magus pulled the oars against their direction, slowing their progress as much as possible.

"It's them?" David whispered, leaning over the gunwale. "Captain Bream and the men?"

"They made it farther than I thought they would," the magus said quietly, watching the plume of smoke as they approached. "But I don't understand . . ."

"Why would they build a fire?" David asked, thinking the same thing. "Out in the open like that? They're heading north, so they have to be concerned with Berok scouts and patrols. Why would they—?"

"Get down, David," the magus said, his voice flat and urgent. He himself ducked low to the boards.

David dropped below the gunwale, looking at the man questioningly.

"Archers," he said simply.

"But I thought you had drugged them—put something in the water?"

"I did."

David peered over the gunwale. With no one at the oars, they were drifting toward the shore. "I don't see any archers," he said, realizing as soon as he spoke the words just how stupid a thing it had been to say. Of course he wouldn't see any sign of archers. Not until an arrow buried itself in his throat.

Ducking, David turned to the magus. "So what do we do?"

"Best to just let the boat drift past. If the archers open fire, we might gain some little protection from the hull." He tapped the wood lightly with his knuckles.

David snuck another glance. The current was bringing them perilously close to the land; at any moment he expected to hear the whistle of arrows in flight.

And then the camp came into clear view. Almost without thinking, David struggled past the magus and grasped the oars.

"What are you doing?" the magus asked.

"It's Captain Bream."

"Get down!" the magus said.

"Do you have a weapon?" David asked, comforted only slightly by the awareness of the knife at his ankle.

"I have—"

"Right. Of course you do. You might want to be ready, just in case." David drew hard on one oar to turn the boat toward the camp. "We're going ashore."

"What?" the magus gasped. "David, it could be a trap."

"I don't think so," he said, rowing toward the small beach. "Look."

The camp had been set in a small clearing. The fire was smoky and weak. Around it, several of the guardsmen lay scattered where they had fallen, twisted heaps of uniform against the scrub brush and gravel.

"Are they dead?" David asked, glancing at the magus.

"They shouldn't be," the old man said. "Dafyd, you're being headstrong."

David had been watching the men since they had come into sight, his eyes darting between the bodies, watching for any signs of movement. "I guess we'll find out," he said as the boat scraped the river bottom. As soon as it stopped he leapt over the gunwale, pulling his blade into his hand.

He stood in the shallows, feet apart, watching the camp as the magus pulled the boat higher onto the beach. He could feel the blood in his veins, every sense aware, tuned to the slightest movement, the smallest warning sign. But there was nothing.

"It's not a trap," he said softly, not lowering his blade or relaxing his stance.

"No," the magus agreed, still wary. "It seems safe." He was clutching his amulet with his left hand, his right extended before him.

"You should check the men," David said, turning to him. The magus didn't move. "I want to be sure they're alive. Or if they need help. I don't want any of them to be hurt because of what Captain Bream did."

The magus hesitated another moment, and David couldn't read his expression, but he turned away and went to the closest man, lying next to the dying fire.

"I knew you'd come."

The captain's voice, rough and weak, seemed to echo through the clearing. David jumped, startled, and turned to the man slumped against a rock close to the water's edge.

"Finish the job," he rasped.

David was shocked by how the captain had changed. His face was pale and damp with sweat, his eyes wide and bloodshot against the white of his skin. His lips were dry, his head weaving and bobbing as if his neck were too weak to support it. His hand rested limply on the hilt of his sword across his lap, the front of his tunic stained with vomit.

"Magus. Not to be trusted," he said, a thin rictus of a smile crossing his lips as if pleased that his suspicions had been confirmed. "Knew it from the start."

David stopped in front of the captain, far enough away to be safe. "He's not the one who left a boy to die on a deserted island."

The captain head lolled. "Mercy," he said. "Should have killed you then."

With what seemed like the last of his strength, the captain swept his arm, gesturing around the clearing. "Poisoned. All of them. I figured it out. Too late. Tried to bring it up. Too late. Dying."

"You're not dying," the magus said, stepping up beside David. "None of you is dying. It was just a tincture to make you sleep."

"So the men will live?" David asked, not sure why he found the thought so comforting.

"They're fine," he said. "They'll have sore heads when they wake up, but no worse than after a night in the tavern."

"Betrayed," the captain said, his voice hoarse.

"You're one to talk about betrayal," David snapped.

"I stayed true. To my Queen. To the very end."

His head dipped heavily before he straightened and stared straight at David. "No. Not true. Not quite." He smiled, a horrible expression that bared his teeth. "Let you live," he said. "Mistake." His hand flopped off his sword. "My men. The cost of my disloyalty."

As David was trying to process the words, the magus took a step forward.

"Disloyalty? The Queen told you to kill the boy?"

"I swore," the captain said, trying to pull himself farther up against the rock. "The boy can never return. I swore. Moment of weakness."

"Mercy," David said, correcting him.

"Mercy is weakness," the captain said, before his head fell forward again.

David and the magus waited, but this time he didn't move. The only sound was his ragged breath.

"Even after trying to purge the tinctures, he'll sleep for hours," the magus said, after waiting a few moments. "Enough for us to get safely downriver."

"With the Stone," David said, stepping closer to the captain. He kicked the sword off the captain's lap. "If the Queen wants the Stone badly enough to kill for it," he said, leaning over the captain. "Then it's probably best we don't just give it to her."

Where did that come from? Matt asked, but David ignored him.

"A wise course of action," the magus said.

"He probably kept it close," David said, reaching into the open front of the captain's tunic.

As his fingers touched the softness of the leather sack, the captain jerked and his fingers closed tightly around David's wrist, pulling him off balance with a surprising strength.

"Not yours, boy," he muttered.

David was close enough to feel the man's fetid, sweet breath on his face.

David pulled his hand away. At first, the captain held fast, but his grip released with David's second tug, and he pulled the small leather sack away from the captain. He stepped out of reach, extending his knife.

"I have more right to this than you do."

The captain's eyes turned up until all David could see were whites. He didn't move again, though they waited several minutes, smoke from the dying fire drifting around them.

"He will hunt you down," the magus said, finally. "Captain Bream is not a man to forget an enemy. Or to forgive."

David remembered the Berok bodies in the dirt, the metallic smell of blood in the air.

He's right, Matt said.

"Nobody would have to know," the magus said simply.

David looked down at the unconscious man, slumped against the rock. "I would know," he said, slipping the knife into the sheath and tucking the Stone into his tunic. It felt warm against his skin.

※ ※

Despite the blue sky and the bright sun there was a chill to the air on the beach and a breeze coming off the water. We were already too far from the hotel for me to go back for my jacket.

"Are you sure?" Jacqui asked again, as I rubbed my hands on my upper arms, which were crossed over my chest.

I shook my head. "I'm fine."

Truth is, I was better than fine.

We were just strolling down the shore, moving slowly for David, well away from the crowds, probably miles from the hotel.

But it was the fact that it was the three of us, just walking, that made the day feel so special.

The day hadn't started out well.

David had had another rough night—three seizures after I had finished the book. His worst night since he had come out of the hospital. Jacqui handled the first two with the cool control I had come to expect from her.

With the third seizure, I was in motion before I even realized that I was awake, before Jacqui had turned the light on. Suddenly I was down on the floor where we had made a bed for David. He was strong, and I whispered soothing words to him as his body surged and snapped with a mechanical, electrical force, coiling and uncoiling.

I noticed Jacqui looking down at me, her face pale from sleep. "Go back to sleep," I whispered. "I've got him."

She looked at me for a long moment, then lowered her head back to the pillow, still facing us, her eyes watching, then slowly closing.

As he calmed, I took him into my arms, rocking gently back and forth, murmuring to him, my voice pitched low and soft. I kept thinking, *If we make it through this . . . if we make it through this . . .*

I waited until his breathing had slowed before I lowered him back to the pillow, untangling his legs from the covers and smoothing them over him.

Standing up slowly, I paced in place to burn off the pins and needles in my legs. According to the digital clock on the bedside table, it was 5:47. I had slept in.

I turned off the bedside lamp. Jacqui moaned and shifted in her sleep. In the sudden darkness, the patio door was a rectangle of pale blue-grey, shrouded by the curtains. I settled into the easy chair, pulling my jacket off the back of the desk chair and draping it over myself.

There I sat in the slow-dissolving dark, listening to my family sleep.

When I woke with a start, momentarily not sure of where I was, the clock on the bedside table read 10:17. Jacqui was smiling at me, her eyes dark and shining in the soft light, still nestled into the pillow.

"You never used to hear him at night," she said. "He'd be crying and you'd sleep right through it."

"You were nursing," I said. "I didn't really feel equipped." It felt like nostalgia, not like she was accusing me of anything.

She smiled. "I'd be worrying about him waking the neighbours and you'd be there, snoring away."

"That was a long time ago."

"Not that long." She shifted under the covers. "You're not writing," she said, matter-of-factly.

I shook my head. "No. It just doesn't seem that important right now."

Her response surprised me. "That's too bad."

I was speechless.

"I hope that's not a permanent change," she said. "That would . . . that would be a shame."

We were slow to get moving. I made a pot of coffee while Jacqui showered and brought in the copy of that morning's *Oregonian* from outside our door, laying it face up on the desk so she would see it when she came out of the bathroom. Jacqui, who normally avoided the newspaper when we were at home, loved to read the local paper when we were travelling.

I changed into fresh clothes and ran a comb through my hair. I figured I'd have a chance to shower sometime before my meeting with Cat.

Jacqui stopped me at the door as we were heading out for breakfast—David was already standing out in the hall. "Are you sure you don't want your jacket?"

I glanced back into the room, thinking about the way the sun had felt on my shoulders as I smoked on the balcony. "No, I'll be fine."

After having breakfast at the café where I would be meeting Cat later, we started walking up the boardwalk. It wasn't quite as excessive as Coney Island or Venice Beach, but it had some of the same carnival feel to it. Even on a supposedly quiet weekend in early June the boardwalk was packed with people, the air heavy with the smell of hot dogs and cotton candy.

We took it slow, content to drift along, Jacqui and me holding David's hands between us, pointing things out as we passed. The tide was coming in, and a cool breeze skated along its surface, riffling the sand, bringing up gooseflesh on my arms.

The crowds thinned out as the boardwalk became a sidewalk along the upper edge of the beach. We turned onto the beach, continuing our slow amble in the fine sand.

David had always been impossible to contain whenever we went to a beach, racing to the water's edge to play games with the incoming waves, dropping to the sand to examine castles left behind, relics from children earlier in the day, or to start building his own, or just exploring every nook and cranny, every shell and piece of seaweed.

To see him there, in that bright afternoon light, walking an unflagging straight line, his footprints perfectly uniform and regular behind him, cut through me like the wind.

Jacqui was obviously feeling the same way.

I tried to look at her, but she had turned, perhaps deliberately, to gaze out at the water, her hair playing softly around her face. I wanted to freeze the moment, of her looking away, unreadable. It touched me with a sadness I did not fully understand.

It all came down to this, today. There was nothing left to read, no more forestalling the inevitable. Whatever was going to happen would happen soon. How would David fare tonight, now that the book was done? I thought of Matthew Corvin, and the lines of care on Carol's face. Was that the future? Or would Cat Took be able to help?

We walked up the beach in silence, our steps slow, falling a little behind our beautiful boy, watching him in the sun. Jacqui's fingers slid between mine.

Somehow, the hours slipped away.

"Shit," I muttered as I glanced at my watch. It was already 3:37.

"Late?" Jacqui asked.

"A little," I said, starting to panic. "I have to—"

She smiled. "You go," she said. "We'll take our time back."

I wasn't sure if I'd even be able to make it back to the restaurant in twenty minutes, never mind get the shower I had been planning, or take some time to collect my thoughts and plan my strategy. "I'll meet you at the hotel?"

"That sounds good," she said. Her smile grew strained. "Bring good news."

"I will," I said. "I'll see you later, sport," I called up the beach after David.

He was still walking.

⸎ ⸎

"Not much longer now," the magus whispered, his voice barely audible over the creaking of the oars and the waves buffeting the side of the boat.

David was lying as flat as he could against the hull, covered by the blanket that the captain had left him, and by the magus's cloak. He had almost laughed, about an hour before, to see the old man in just his grey tunic and trousers. The magus had seemed practically naked, tiny and grey. Like a mouse.

They had been rowing two full days, through the bright of the sun and the dark of the waning moon, taking turns at the oars. The distance had passed more quickly than the magus had anticipated, and despite his exhaustion David felt his spirits lifting as the landscape took on the familiar, lush green of the coast. He almost wept when he sniffed a trace of the sea on the breeze.

"None will stop or question a magus," Loren had explained at their last landfall, home now so close that David could almost taste it.

He wondered where this familiarity, this desperate yearning for a place he had never seen, was coming from.

It's Dafyd, Matt guessed. *You're in his body—they're his memories. His emotions.*

That makes sense, he thought. *But then—*

". . . but a boy who was last seen riding off with a company of the King's Men will draw undue . . ." the magus was saying.

David shook his head, trying to catch up. "Are we going to the abbey?" he asked, hoping that the magus hadn't already discussed this.

"Perhaps," he said. "I'm concerned, though, that the Queen might have observers in place, in the event that her plan went somehow awry."

"Because that's where you would most likely go, if you had the Stone."

"Which means it's the one place we cannot go," the magus concluded. He was silent, thoughtful.

"We could go to the tavern," David said quietly, tentatively making the suggestion as an image of Arian flashed through his mind, a sudden yearning tugging at his heart. David tried to shake off the sudden onrush of emotion.

Dafyd is coming home, Matt said quietly. *Maybe he's getting stronger. His thoughts coming more to the surface.*

David tried not to think about the possibility, about what it might mean when Dafyd was home. Would his memories, his feelings, his life, crowd out David's?

"Isn't that where Captain Bream found you?" the magus asked.

David nodded. "So the Queen will think we would never go back there."

"Nonetheless, they are probably watching it."

"There are ways in where we won't be seen," he said, surprised at the words coming from his lips.

The magus thought for a moment. "It's likely no more dangerous than any other place we might hide ourselves. And we can send someone to the abbey to alert them of our return."

David felt like cheering.

They had agreed that David would hide while they were still on the water, and lead once they reached the streets of Colcott.

The longer he spent on the cold boards, though, the less agreeable David found the arrangement.

"Not much longer now," the magus whispered. "We're almost across the channel."

David wanted nothing more than to pull off the cloak covering him, to sit up and watch the crossing. That sight, of the castle dominating the sky, growing larger and larger as he approached, was one of his favourite sights in the world.

Dafyd is getting stronger, David said, trying to separate himself from the memories that were crashing into his own.

It's natural that Dafyd's memories would be stronger about this place, Matt said. *When you were out there in the wilderness . . . he had no experience of those places.*

Maybe . . . David said. *But does that mean that I'm getting weaker?*

The closer they drew to the castle, the less he thought about his mother and father, his house, Liam, Nolan. Instead, he found himself thinking about seeing the tavern again, his mother, Tamas. Arian.

What happens if Dafyd comes back and I just fade away, once the story ends?

Matt had no answer, and in the silence David felt crushed by his fears, the dread he had been able to push down in the headlong rush through the past few days. He reached for the lump of the amulet inside his tunic, wrapping his fingers around its comforting shape and warmth as he pulled his knees closer to his chest.

"Stay still," the magus hissed. "We are nearing the wharf, and there are two guardsmen there."

David pressed himself flat against the bottom of the boat as he felt it slow in the water. He could almost hear the drag of the oars.

"Good evening, gentlemen," the magus said, his voice loud and strong.

"What business do you have at this hour, greybeard?" asked a voice, muffled to David's ears where he huddled under the cloak and blanket.

"Is that what guards are being taught these days?" the magus said. "To show such disrespect to one of the brethren?"

"I . . . I was . . ." The voice faltered.

"He meant no disrespect, sir," came another voice, rushed and conciliatory.

"Whether he meant it or not," the magus said, "the disrespect was there and plain." David could hear the anger, the threat, in the old man's voice. "This is your first posting, is it not? Weeks out of the academy and assigned to the townside dock in the dead of night?"

"Yes, sir."

"Would you like it to be your last?" the magus said, his tone threatening. "One word from the abbey and you'll both be shovelling dung in the stables, alongside your captain, who has obviously taken too light a hand with your training."

David thought suddenly of Tamas, and of how the worst punishment the magus could threaten these men with was a fact of life for his friend.

"Is that what you want?"

"No, sir," both men snapped in crisp, martial harmony.

"Then I would suggest you keep a civil tongue, and show the proper respect."

"Yes, sir."

And then the boat was in motion again, sliding silently through the water.

"We're almost through the outer wall," the magus muttered. To anyone still watching, he would have seemed to be talking to himself.

David waited until the boat came to a stop and swayed under him as the magus stepped out. The scrape of a rope. The shudder as the boat bounced against a rock wall.

A moment later, the magus spoke. "There's a door on the far side of the wharf . . ."

David was already in motion, throwing off the cloak and blanket and clambering out of the boat, shuffling across the wharf, keeping low.

He waited silently in the darkened entry of the tunnel to the streets above as the magus slowly and calmly reached into the boat for his cloak, and spent several too-long moments fixing it around himself. The wharves—a huge, cavelike room of arched stone, lit with a multitude of torches and crowded with small boats rocking gently on the water—were empty, but David was keenly attuned to the silence, fearful of the sound of steps or voices.

The magus reached into the boat again for the book, straightening his robes as if he had not a care in the world, before ambling casually toward the doorway where David waited.

"I wanted to be sure that we don't have any eyes upon us," he explained as they started down the stone corridor, his voice pitched low.

"The guardsmen, you mean?"

"Them. Someone else. Who knows? Better to be safe."

They hurried upward through the tunnels that ran from the wharves to the city above. It was a maze, but David—Dafyd—knew the way. As they rounded each corner, he reflexively lowered his head in case there was someone there.

As they neared the street level, they started to pass other people in the corridors. He recognized the fat, stumbling butcher, his face florid and his eyes glazed with drink, his hand wandering freely on the body of a girl Dafyd had seen in the tavern on numerous occasions.

"Good evening," the magus said as they passed in the narrow tunnel.

The butcher grunted.

"I would guess that they had spent the evening at your mother's," the magus said, once the couple was out of earshot.

"Just another night at the Mermaid," David said, realizing that he had no idea what night of the week it was.

"Which means we must be getting close."

And sure enough, the next turning brought them to a doorway opening onto a narrow street not far from the tavern. The air was cool and smelled of smoke and the sea, garbage and people. David felt his heart leap in his chest.

Dafyd's heart. Dafyd's chest.

Cat Took was waiting for me outside the restaurant. I wouldn't have known it was her, but she was holding a copy of *Shining Swords and Steel* against her chest. For some reason, I wasn't expecting her to be quite so young. Or attractive.

I extended my hand as I stepped toward her. "Cat Took?"

She smiled and shook my hand. "Christopher Knox."

"Sorry about . . . this," I said, trying to gesture at myself, aware of the choppy, broken quality of my voice. I had run the last couple of blocks. "We were taking . . . a walk on the beach . . . and time got away from us."

"That's all right," she said, smiling warmly. "You're on vacation. You shouldn't have to rush around to talk about old books, of all things." She glanced leadingly at the door.

"Of course." I held the door for her, and followed her into the restaurant.

I sat down across from her, trying to keep from looking at the silver chain that disappeared behind the V of her neckline as she sat down.

"So are you enjoying your vacation, then?" she asked, as we waited to be served. Her voice was touched with the faintest hint of an English accent.

"I am, actually," I said. But that immediately felt wrong to say. "Well . . . "

The waitress arrived. I ordered a coffee and instinctively reached for my jacket pocket.

"Shit," I muttered, before I could stop myself. No jacket.

"What?" Her smile creased into a look of concern.

"Sorry," I said, shaking my head and feeling stupid. "I don't have my notebook."

"Is that a problem?" she asked, her smile returning.

"No, no. I should be fine." Forcing a brave face, not wanting to let on just how out-of-sorts I was suddenly feeling. I carried my notebook with me everywhere—to not have it for this meeting felt like I was missing a limb.

The waitress brought our coffees, and the action of adding cream and sugar, which I normally didn't take, helped conceal just how flustered I was feeling.

"So," she said, and I realized that she had been watching me, her eyes green and wide. "You were going to tell me why you weren't having a good vacation with your family."

"Right," I said, and in the moment it seemed that the question provided a good opening. "Well, my son's been quite ill over the last few weeks."

"Oh no," she said, her face full of concern. "What is it?"

"The doctors aren't sure. He's been having seizures."

"Is it epilepsy?"

I shook my head. "No. Not that we know of. He's actually—" I was surprised at how hard it was to talk about. "He's catatonic. He has been for several weeks now."

"That's terrible," she said, leaning across the table and laying her hand over mine.

I was surprised, and had to resist the impulse to pull my hand away.

"What happened? How did it start?"

I took a sip of my coffee, bracing myself. "Actually, that's what I wanted to talk to you about."

"Me?" she said, touching her chest at a point just below where the silver chain disappeared. "Why me?"

I took a deep breath. "This is going to sound crazy," I said, wishing there were some other way to start. "But I think it might have something to do with your grandfather."

"Lazarus?"

"David was reading one of your grandfather's books when the first seizure hit. A book called *To the Four Directions*."

"That's not one of my grandfather's books."

I nodded. "That's why I got in touch with you, asking if you knew of any other books that Lazarus had written."

"But he didn't."

"I'm pretty sure he did," I said, as calmly as I could. "I haven't been able to find anything in any of the databases or online, but it reads like your grandfather's writing."

"You read it?"

I nodded. "I think your grandfather wrote it after he left England, and had it published here in a very limited edition. In fact, I wouldn't be surprised if there was only a single copy ever printed."

"But what does that have to do with your son's . . . condition?"

"I think . . ." I shifted in my seat: this wasn't going to give me a whole lot of credibility. "I think there's a spell on the book," I said, watching her face drop. "I think the book was designed as a trap. A way of . . . capturing its readers."

"But you read it."

"Yeah."

"And nothing happened to you."

I stopped myself for a moment, not sure how much I should tell her, how much detail she would be able to stand before she thought I was completely crazy. Finally, though, I decided it was best to tell her everything.

"No," I said. "I think that's how the spell was designed. Most people, reading it, wouldn't be affected at all. But some—boys, boys of a certain age—meet the criteria and . . ." I lifted my hand helplessly.

She pursed her lips thoughtfully, and spent a long moment stirring her coffee.

"It sounds like you've done a lot of research on this, Chris," she said finally. "And maybe had some help. Unless you're familiar with magic yourself."

"No, no," I said quickly. "Just what I read in books. I met some people in Victoria who were able to help me figure all this out."

I was amazed at how calmly she was taking this all in.

"You don't seem too surprised to hear this," I said. "I thought you'd call me crazy."

"No, I don't think you're crazy," she said, and it felt like a weight was suddenly lifted from me.. "I'm not under any illusions about my grandfather, Chris. I know what he was interested in, the type of magic that he worked with. Judging from some of the things I've seen in the archives, no, I don't think you're crazy at all."

My first thought was of the stacks of boxes in the small office at the Hunter Barlow library, but then I recalled her mentioning papers she had at her house.

"There's stuff . . . material . . . like this in Lazarus's papers?" I asked, hope rising within me.

She nodded. "A lot of it. I haven't been able to get through most of it, to be perfectly honest. It doesn't make a great deal of sense to me. But there's lots of magical stuff in there. It looks like that's what he focused on after he left England. That's why I was so surprised to hear that you had a book from him that I hadn't seen: I didn't think he was doing any writing at that time. But if it was for a spell . . ." She shrugged. "Wait—is this the book you mentioned on the phone? When you asked me about the editor from New York?"

I nodded.

"So you don't have it?"

I deflated. The fact that I didn't have the book was my whole reason for meeting with her, but hearing it confirmed in her voice was hard.

"No, I don't have it," I said. "That's actually why I wanted to meet with you." As her eyebrows lifted, I told her about Tony Markus: about how my attempt to get information on Took had only served to stoke his interest in the book; about how I suspected him of engineering its theft, in hope of her allowing him to publish it. "I thought you would have heard from him by now."

"Well, he did call me a few days ago, wondering if he could talk to me while he was in Oregon, but I had no idea." She looked at me with a directness that I could almost feel. "So what can I do?" she asked. "What do you want me to say when he calls?"

There was a warmth and resolve in her eyes that made me glad that she was on my side.

≫ ≪

As David led the magus toward the Mermaid, they kept close to the walls, in the shadows, silent, as occasional drunks staggered across narrow stone walkways. At one point, they crossed the path of two patrolling guardsmen, several buildings away, but David led them into a narrow alley where they crouched, watching the men pass.

"We'll stay to the alleys now," David said, leading the magus deeper into the darkness. "There are bound to be more people around the closer we get to the Mermaid."

The back alleys of the inner city were a maze of brick walls and garbage, muck underfoot and stink in the air. There were no lamps or torches, but David had no need of light, leading them confidently, instinctively, through a series of sharp turns and obtuse angles. His feet—Dafyd's feet—knew where to go, and David did not resist.

He slowed slightly as he passed the spot where he and Tamas had beaten Zekariah and Jarrett. The spot where this whole thing had started.

That's where the book *started,* Matt said.

Matt was right, but there was more to Dafyd's presence now than simply what was in the book. Dafyd's memories ran too deep, his emotions too strong, to have lived only a fictional life. David was remembering things that the book had never hinted at—the way the other kids used to chase Dafyd, throwing rocks at him; the way he had cried softly in his bed at night, missing the father he had never known. These memories were real.

Another few turns brought them out of the alley near the wall of the small yard behind the tavern.

"The gate will be locked," David whispered. "So we'll have to go over." He looked at the magus. "It's not that high."

The magus scowled. "Do I look to be concerned about the height of that wall?"

David grinned and, tucking his toe into a familiar indentation between two stones, heaved himself over, disappearing into the darkness.

Moments later there was a scream, cut off in mid-breath, and the sound of shattering glass.

≈ ≈

Jacqui and David took their time walking back to the hotel, holding hands and letting the tidal pull of the crowds carry them along the sidewalk. As they passed the restaurant, she slowed their pace, glancing through the windows. Chris was sitting near the back, his face almost hidden by the head of the woman to whom he was talking. Cat Took.

Jacqui considered stopping, interrupting the meeting to join them, but she decided against it. Instead, they returned to the hotel to wait.

She got David's shoes off and got him settled on the bed, turning the TV on at a low volume before collapsing into the desk chair. The walk on the beach, all that fresh air, had left her feeling exhilarated and pleasantly tired.

She reached for the copy of that morning's *Oregonian*. Chris had left it for her on top of his laptop, where she would find it easily. Oddly considerate, for him, but completely in keeping with how he had been acting in the past few days.

She found a strange pleasure in reading the news from a different city, a different country: new scandals, different civic issues, different names. Different, but so familiar.

She stopped at the top story on page A3, almost choking on her breath.

NEW YORK EDITOR IDENTIFIED IN HOTEL MURDER
The body found in a guest room of the Hotel Vintage Park late Thursday has been identified as that of 32-year-old Anthony Markus, an editor at Davis & Keelor Publishers. Markus, who was killed with a single gunshot wound to the head, was, according to his New York office, in Portland for both meetings and personal time. Police do not currently have a suspect, although in the hours prior to the murder Markus was reportedly seen dining with an unidentified woman.

Jacqui reread the article, trying to glean any details that might lurk below the surface of the words, then dropped the paper to the floor. She paced the room in a haze of disbelief, trying to talk herself out of her certainty. It could be someone else with the same name. Another New York editor with the same name. From the same publisher. In Portland at the same time . . . No, it had to be him.

Which meant . . .

. . . dining with an unidentified woman . . .

She picked up the hotel phone and dialled Chris's cell. She couldn't be sure that the woman seen with Markus before his death was Cat Took, but she had to warn—

She jumped as a telephone rang right next to her. Chris's ring. Muffled. Chris's phone, tucked into the pocket of his jacket, still hung over the back of the desk chair.

☙ ❧

David pulled away from Tamas as the magus rose over the wall, hanging silently in the air a moment before stepping to the thin top of the bricks, his left hand tight around his amulet, his right hand extended toward the yard. His face was knit with determination.

"It's all right," David said to the magus in a hoarse whisper, stepping between the old man and his friend. "It's Tamas."

The magus's face remained set for a moment, then seemed to fill in with relief. But he did not release the amulet.

Tamas stood wide-eyed in the dim light of the yard, broken crockery and spilled ale at his feet, gaping soundlessly at the sight of the old man who had floated to the top of the wall. It was the second most amazing thing he had seen in the past few moments, following the sudden return of his friend.

"The stableboy?" the magus asked, teetering on the wall.

Tamas nodded silently, then stopped and shook his head. "Yes. No. I mean, I was, but—"

"Lower your voice," the magus ordered. "Unless you want the whole of the guard here."

Tamas's mouth snapped shut.

"And now . . ." The magus looked around himself warily, as if suddenly aware of his delicate position. "If one of you wouldn't mind helping an old man down."

After a good deal of fumbling and groaning, he was back on solid ground, and the three of them huddled close in the shadows.

"I can't believe you're here," Tamas sputtered, reaching out for Dafyd again, touching his arm to reassure himself that his eyes weren't deceiving him.

David's heart was still racing from both the shock of almost falling over the other boy, and the unexpected pleasure of finding his friend. "Why are you out here?" he asked.

"I've been helping your mother," Tamas said, almost uncomfortably.

"Really?" David said. "But you and my mother don't—"

"What happened at the stables, Tamas?" the magus interrupted.

It took Tamas a moment to shift his attention from Dafyd. "The master told me not to come back."

David shook his head. "And my mother?"

Tamas smiled awkwardly. "She told me that if I was going to spend all my time here, I might as well make myself useful. Emptying piss-pots. Throwing out drunks. Breaking up fights." He shrugged.

"All the things I used to do," David muttered, then he thought of what Tamas had said. "'All your time here'? You were waiting for me?"

"Of course I was," he said sharply. "We all were."

He seemed genuinely surprised when David pulled him into his arms for another long embrace. "You never gave up on me," he whispered into his friend's ear.

"Never," Tamas said, in a voice that sounded close to tears. Then he stepped back from David, wiping his face, trying to look strong.

A tumult of feelings was rising in David: Dafyd's feelings, thoughts, memories, pushing against his own. He looked toward the light in the window. "Are they in there?" he asked, stepping toward the door. "Let's—"

Tamas reached out and grabbed David's arm, held him back. "Dafyd, don't—"

David shrugged off his friend's grasp. "Let me—"

"Dafyd," the magus said warningly, as David reached for the door.

"Dafyd, stop," Tamas said forcefully.

David stopped. He had never before heard such a tone from his friend.

"There are guardsmen inside," Tamas explained. "Two of them. By the front door."

David looked at the magus, who was studying Tamas with fresh curiosity, and a small smile.

Tamas saw him looking too. "I'm not stupid. You came in the back because you're trying to avoid being seen."

David nodded. Perhaps he hadn't given Tamas enough credit.

"How long have the guardsmen been there?" the magus asked.

"Since we opened this afternoon."

"Is today the first day they've been here?"

"No, gods no. There have been guardsmen here since the day you were arrested, Dafyd. They just sit, watch."

David nodded. "The Queen said she would—"

The magus cut David off. "Have you seen other guards nearby? Perhaps watching the tavern when it's not open?"

Tamas thought for a moment. "I don't think so," he said. "The patrols are more frequent, but I haven't seen anyone watching the place."

"And you'd notice if there were," the magus said thoughtfully. "The guardsmen wouldn't conceal themselves."

When David looked at Tamas, his friend was grinning widely at him. "Your mother is going to be so happy. And Arian . . ."

David felt a rush of warmth at the sound of the girl's name.

"We'll need to wait," the magus cautioned.

"I can bring them out here," Tamas said. "Away from the guards."

The magus shook his head. "The guards would notice immediately that something was amiss. No, it's better that we wait, until they have left of their own accord. We can't give them any reason to suspect anything," he said, his voice becoming stern. "Do you understand that, Tamas?"

He nodded.

"Just go about your work as if nothing has happened."

❧ ❧

Cat listened intently as I told her about Tony Markus and what I guessed would be his plans for the book he had stolen from me.

"I certainly don't want to interfere with the re-publication of your grandfather's work," I stressed. "I think that would be a great thing. But I'm not sure that the last book should ever be published."

"No, of course not," she said. "You think that it might have the same effect on other children?"

"I think it already has." I told her about Matthew Corvin and his mother's foundation. She held her coffee cup with both hands, considering.

"You've certainly done a lot of research," she said when I finished. "Do you have any idea what you'll do if you can't get your hands on the book?"

I must have had a horrified look on my face, because she hurried to clarify. "Oh no. No, the moment Tony Markus contacts me again, I'll let you know. You can keep the book, for all I care." She seemed to almost shudder in distaste. "I certainly don't want it." She set her coffee cup down and leaned across the table toward me. "What I mean is, what will you do if we don't hear from him? Especially with your son getting worse."

"I don't know," I confessed. "This might really be our last chance."

"Could your friends, the witches . . .?"

"They can't do anything without the book. They've got the lexicon—"

"The lexicon?" Her eyes widened.

"It's a sort of a dictionary, I guess. I was able to get them a copy of it from that library in New York."

"They might be able to come up with a counter," she said slowly, thinking to herself. "If they've got the lexicon."

"But without the book . . ."

"They probably wouldn't be able to break the curse itself, but they might be able to come up with something to counter its effects on your son."

"Do you think so?" I asked. It was something that I hadn't thought of, a slim ray of hope under a door that I had thought locked for good.

"Well, I don't know a lot about this," she said, leaning back. "Just what I read in Lazarus's papers. I'm sure they'd want to try, especially with David getting sicker."

She was right: I could picture Sarah and Nora in the kitchen, poring over the pages I had sent, trying to do anything to help my son.

"Of course, if we had the book . . ."

I nodded. "I'm sure he'll be in touch."

She smiled. "I'm sure he will be too," she said, still thoughtful. "He seems like the sort. Still, though, I wonder . . ."

I waited a moment. "Yes?"

"I wonder if there's anything in Lazarus's study that would be helpful. Something that might help your friends." She sat forward again. "Do you want to take a look? I can't promise anything."

Her offer left me momentarily speechless. "I . . . I'd like to."

She smiled. "Don't get your hopes up," she said. "The place is a mess, and I have no idea even where to start."

"No, that's fine." The thought of standing in Took's office, of looking through his last papers, filled me with conflicting emotions. Despite everything he had done, the suffering he had inflicted on David and Matthew and who knows how many other children, part of me was thrilled at the prospect of being in his office. "When can I come?"

She glanced at her watch. "How about right now?"

I thought of David and Jacqui, probably waiting for me back in the hotel room. "What about tomorrow? First thing?"

Her face pinched. "Actually, tomorrow's bad. Is there a problem with going now? I can drive."

I nodded slowly. "Sure," I said. "That sounds fine."

She squeezed my hand and smiled, clearly pleased with my agreement. "You can call your wife, let her know what's going on. That you've been taken home by a ravishing young woman."

Her eyes were laughing, and I couldn't help but smile.

☞ ☜

Sitting in the shadows under the window ledge, David and Loren waited. The sound of the Mermaid, a muted burble of voices that reminded David of the river, washed over them.

Time passed sluggishly, and it was all David could do to resist the potent force of Dafyd's emotions, his almost irresistible desire to rush into the tavern and find his mother and Arian, no matter the guardsmen, no matter the cost.

He's getting stronger, isn't he? Matt asked.

David didn't answer. He was keeping his attention focused firmly on the pool of light that the window cast on the stone yard, the small spray of broken crockery from Tamas's mug, the way the sharp edges and spilled ale caught the light.

"My mother would have his hide for that," he said quietly. David hadn't known that he was going to say the words, could only listen as they came, unexpectedly, out of his own mouth.

"What?" the magus asked.

He gestured at the shattered crockery "Bad enough that he was out here sneaking a drink when he was working, but to break one of the mugs . . ." He shook his head. "Better it be broken by someone with money enough to pay for its replacement. He'll be hearing about that."

"I expect she'll be quite understanding about the loss of a single flagon, under the circumstances."

It wasn't much longer before there was a change in the sounds coming from the tavern, the laughter replaced with a slightly stronger, louder muttering and a loud, collective cry.

"That'll be last bell, then," David said. "My mother will be standing on a bar stool, telling the men it's time to drink up and get back to their wives, and the women back to their husbands, and that they should try to get it right this time."

"Your mother is a formidable woman."

"She had to be, to come so far on her own. One of the only taverns inside the walls . . ."

"And now a son who will either be a hero or be hanged in the square at dawn, depending upon how events unfold."

David glanced at the magus, hoping he was joking. He wasn't.

"We'll give it a little longer," David said. "Give Tamas a chance to deal with any stragglers."

Some time later the kitchen door creaked partway open and Tamas looked out into the darkness. As he scanned the yard without seeing them, his face fell, as if his worst fears had come to pass. When David reached over and touched his leg, Tamas jumped.

"Gods, Dafyd," he muttered. "You'd scare me to death if you could."

"It's a good thing you weren't carrying a flagon this time," David said as he stood up. "She'd have your hide for sure."

He squeezed his friend's shoulder as he slipped in through the kitchen doorway. The magus followed closely.

"Is everyone gone?" the magus asked, as Tamas closed and bolted the door behind them.

"Yes," Tamas said. "It was agony waiting for last bell and rounding them up, but there was no way to suggest to your mother that she might want to close early."

"And the guardsmen?" the magus asked.

"I checked out front as I was locking up. No sign of anyone lurking around."

"Still," the magus said. "We should probably stay back here."

Tamas nodded. "I'll get them," he said, stepping into the tavern.

David could hear his friend's voice faintly through the wall as the magus lowered himself slowly onto a stool. Tamas's voice grew louder, more insistent, and then he heard his mother's voice, gaining in volume as she neared the door.

". . . swear to the gods, Tamas, this had better be something bloody important to interrupt me when I'm counting out. I'm going to have to start all over—"

She gasped as she entered the kitchen. She was wiping her hands on her apron, and when she saw her son she froze, her expression one of stunned disbelief that dissolved into tears as she whispered, "Dafyd?"

He nodded, unable to speak, his eyes brimming. And then she was across the room, her arms around him tight, pulling him close into the yeasty, beery, sweet smell of her.

"Oh, Dafyd," she gasped. "I knew you'd come home. I just knew it."

And Dafyd cried, because he had been convinced that he would never see her again.

And David cried, certain now that this was as close as he himself would ever come to being home.

᠁ ᠁

Jacqui was practically dragging David up the street, clutching at his hand, urging him to walk faster than he usually did. She kept glancing between him, a half-step behind her, and the intersection in the distance, the corner where the restaurant was.

"Come on," she muttered, trying not to take out her frustration on her son, but wanting nothing more than to break into a run.

Tony Markus had been the last one to have that book, and now he was dead. And now Chris was with Cat Took, probably the "unidentified woman" that Markus had been seen with before he died.

She cursed herself as she tugged at David's hand: he was shambling along beside her as fast as he could.

She tried to think of what she would say, how she could interrupt their meeting without alerting Cat Took.

It would be easy, she thought. She'd introduce herself and David. She'd linger until she was invited to sit down, and she'd smile and join them, and then at the earliest opportunity she'd tell Chris that they had to go.

She was breathing heavily with the effort of pulling David along, but it was just a block away. A half-block . . .

She pushed open the door, and felt her knees buckle.

The booth where Chris had been sitting with Cat Took was empty, a few bills tucked under one of the abandoned coffee cups.

≈

Mareigh clung to him tightly, squeezing him so he couldn't breathe, then leaned him back to take a look, still holding his arms. "You look awful," she said, reaching up to touch the lump at the side of his mostly bare head. "What have they done to you?"

"It's a long story," he said, embarrassed by her attention.

"You look like you haven't eaten in a week, for starters," she said.

"It's close to that."

"Well," she said, stepping away from him. "We'll see to that. Arian," she called, turning.

But the girl was already standing in the doorway. She was so pale, so delicate, she seemed almost like an apparition, like an errant breeze might blow her away. When their eyes met, she appeared to solidify, a tearful smile breaking on her face.

He stepped toward her as she moved toward him, and they met in the middle of the room. They didn't touch, the very air between them alive with things yet unsaid. They stood like that for a long moment, just looking at each other, not speaking, not needing to speak.

"Well," said Mareigh—and the spell was broken. "I was going to ask you to prepare some food."

David started, as if he had been caught in a dream, looking out through someone else's eyes.

"Yes, ma'am," Arian said crisply, turning away.

"You, sit." She gestured toward the table, then stopped, as if noticing the old man for the first time.

"Hello, Loren," she said slowly, unsteadily.

The magus smiled and rose slowly to his feet. "Well met again, Mareigh," he said, bowing his head slightly, his voice full and formal. "It has been a long time."

Mareigh glanced at David, then back at the magus, looking puzzled to find the old man in her kitchen. "Very near a lifetime," she said hesitatingly.

"Indeed."

"So do I have you to thank for drawing my son into this?" Her voice wasn't angry, but there was a cutting edge to it, an undertone of warning.

"My apologies, Mareigh," he said, lowering his head again. "I am but a humble servant."

She snorted out a disbelieving laugh. "So you've always said." She looked at him for a long moment, as if expecting him to speak. When he didn't she gestured at the table. "Sit, sit. Everyone sit." She looked at her son. "Practically starving to death, you must be," she said.

"Actually, I wonder if I might impose upon your girl," the magus said, as David was pulling out a chair for Arian. "For a small favour."

David glanced at him sharply.

"Do you know the abbey?" the magus asked Arian.

The girl looked at him curiously. "Of course," she said cautiously.

Everyone knew where the abbey was.

"Might I impose upon you to deliver a message there? Neither Dafyd nor I can be seen delivering it, and I'm afraid Tamas is also too familiar a face." He reached into his robes and withdrew a folded piece of vellum, sealed with a dot of red wax. "Which, unfortunately, leaves only you." He extended the note toward her. "If you would be so kind?"

Her hand was shaking slightly as she took the message from the magus. "Who should I deliver it to?"

"Ask at the gates for Brother Maximus," he said, smiling encouragingly. "Tell them that you have been sent by Brother Loren, and that you bear a message of the utmost importance."

She looked down uncertainly at the note in her hand.

"When did you find time to write that?" David asked. The only time the magus had been out of his sight in the past few days had been while he slept and the old man rowed.

The magus half turned to him. "I've carried that with me since the day we left," he explained.

"You knew?" David gasped. "All along you knew that Captain Bream—"

The magus cut him off with a glare.

"What about Captain Bream?" his mother asked, setting mugs of ale in front of them.

"It's nothing," the magus said placatingly.

His tone was so smooth, so comforting, that David knew his mother would see through it immediately. To his surprise, though, she said nothing, only turning back to the counter for mugs for Tamas and herself.

"I'll keep yours waiting," she said to Arian. "For when you get back."

Arian took another look at the note in her hands, at the red wax seal. "Yes, ma'am," she said, the decision to accept the errand made for her.

As she passed behind David's chair, he felt her fingers brush against the back of his neck.

"I think I'm just about done with that girl," his mother said as the door shut behind Arian. "I'm not even sure why I keep her around." She was still at the counter, cutting meat from a large joint. "I'm fully capable of running the place myself. Did it for years . . ."

She seemed to be talking to herself, but David could feel every word twisting his belly. Dafyd wasn't liking this.

"And it's not as if she's a great help," she continued as she carried a tray of meat and cheese to the table. "With all the mooning over the shore boys that she does."

She set the tray on the table, then looked at David. The air hung heavy for a moment, then everyone began to laugh. Everyone except David.

She ran her hand gingerly over his bare head. "Best not to make jokes," she said. "Someone takes that one a little seriously."

Cat Took drove with both hands on the wheel, her gaze fixed ahead on a series of increasingly narrower roads. She kept off the highway altogether, her route taking us first through several small, weather-beaten subdivisions outside the gaudy heart of Seaside, then onto a winding country road that offered occasional glimpses of the ocean as the car steadily climbed along the coast.

"So you grew up around here?" I asked.

"I've been here my whole life," she said, watching the road.

The trees, dark and lush from the fine mist that clung to them, pressed in on both sides, as if someone had cut the smallest possible path through the forest.

"Did you go to school in Seaside?"

"My mother taught me at home, actually," she said.

"All the way out here?"

"It's not that far," she said, turning onto a gravel path barely wide enough to accommodate even her little Volkswagen. It rumbled and shuddered on the rough surface.

"So it was just you and your mother?"

"Lazarus chose this house because of this forest," she said, ignoring my question. "I think he liked the fact that it was so secluded, so surrounded by nature. And I think he liked the irony of it."

"The irony?"

"The man who owned it before, who built it, owned one of the biggest lumber companies in the state."

"A logger baron."

"Right. Only he refused to allow any logging within sight of his house. He said that he valued nature too much to have it decimated around him."

That struck me as precisely the sort of irony Lazarus Took would have appreciated.

As she spoke, the road widened and the shuddering of the car ceased as the tires gripped paving stones. The house itself appeared with a breathtaking suddenness—with a flash of unexpected sunlight, we emerged into a huge circular driveway.

"Wow," I muttered, unable to help myself.

"Yeah," she said, pulling close to the front steps of the house. "That's what everyone says."

It wasn't the stately manor that I imagined Took owning in England, but it seemed a close cousin. The brown stone walls stretched three stories high, broken with mullioned windows, grown over in places with ivy. The windows were dark. The building seemed wilfully imposed upon the landscape.

"You can't see it from here," Cat said, turning off the engine. "But there's a tower around the front, overlooking the ocean."

"Let me guess."

"Yes, that's where Lazarus's study is."

Of course.

As I climbed out of the car, I was shocked by the sudden cold in the shadow of the house. The ocean rumbled nearby.

I followed her up the wide staircase and through the heavy front doors, noticing only as I passed under them the words etched above the entry:

RAVEN'S MOOR.

～ ～

"So," his mother said, in a tone he recognized well. "Is one of you going to tell me just what in the name of the gods happened? You're taken by the King's Men, then you stumble back in here a month later in the dead of night, no word—"

"A month?" David gasped. "That's how long we've been gone?

His mother looked at him as if he might be an idiot. "Almost five weeks."

He knew that she must be right, but all the days and all the nights, the riding, the rowing—they had all blended together.

"Where have you been in that time?" she asked, first glaring at the magus, then setting her eyes on David, as if daring one of them to answer her.

David was about to speak, but the magus shook his head slightly as he raised his ale to his lips, a tiny gesture that Mareigh missed.

"That, dear Mareigh," said the magus, wiping his mouth, "is a very long story, and one which we'll have time to tell soon. But right now—"

"Don't you try to work that gilded tongue on me again, Loren," she said, her voice icy, threatening. "It worked once. It won't again."

"You don't seem to have suffered," he said, his voice now matching hers in strength.

"You would be best not to tell me what I have or have not suffered."

Tamas glanced at David, looking for some explanation. David had none.

Clearly there's some history, Matt said.

David was startled. With the flood of Dafyd's memories and emotions, it was almost as if Matthew had been swept away, or drowned out, for most of the day. David found it comforting to hear his voice.

Clearly, David thought.

"And now you're back here and I find it's you who is responsible for taking my son, bringing him back home half-dead—"

"Mareigh, I'm—"

"I've a mind to—"

"Mareigh—"

"Mother," David said sharply, his voice cutting into the air between them. "It wasn't his fault. It was the—"

The magus slammed his mug on the table, but the word was already spoken.

"—Queen."

Mareigh pulled her lips between her teeth, her eyes narrowing as she looked at the magus.

"The *Queen?*" she asked, her voice dripping with venom.

At that moment, there was a loud whistle from just outside the back door, and an answering whistle from the front of the tavern.

"Dafyd," the magus cried out, jumping up from his chair.

A large log bashed the back door open. Two guardsmen dropped it to the floor and drew their swords. Another crash from the next room as more guardsmen came through the tavern's front door.

"They're back here!" one of the men in the kitchen called.

Guardsmen rushed in from the tavern, dispersing around the edges of the kitchen, swords drawn, encircling them like fish in a net.

David reached carefully toward the knife in his boot, but the magus warned him off with a glance.

"Well," said a voice approaching through the tavern. "What have we here?"

As Captain Bream stepped into the kitchen, David marvelled at the change that had come over the man. When he had first seen him in the tavern yard the captain had been a towering figure of strength and command. Powerful in everything he said and did.

The captain who entered the kitchen now was diminished, pale and drawn.

Not weak, though, Matt said. *Still strong enough to drive that sword through you.*

The captain advanced on David, his teeth bared in a feral grin. The point of his sword came to rest on exactly the same spot it had pierced in the chamber of the Sunstone.

"I warned you," he said, his voice barely above a whisper. "I warned you of the cost of mercy. And now you'll pay that. In spades." He pressed the tip of the sword through David's shirt and the blade sliced through the thick fabric, breaking the skin with ease.

"Stop," David's mother cried out, pushing between them.

The captain rounded on Mareigh, slapping her so hard with his gloved hand that she spun and stumbled to the floor.

"Don't—" David said, desperate to protect her, stopped only by the cold steel of the sword against his chest.

"Or what, whoreson?" the captain spat. "You've done your worst. You had me in your power and you stayed your hand. Now it's my turn." He held David's eye, neither of them flinching, neither of them blinking.

The sword-tip drove deeper into David's chest. David flinched, but he did not look away.

"Captain?" one of the men said. Then, after a moment, he repeated, carefully, "Captain?"

Bream flinched. "What?" he snapped.

"The Queen," the man said, sounding uncomfortable.

"Don't tell me about the Queen."

The man tightened his lips and took a step back.

It was enough for the magus, however. "So the Queen wants us alive," he said, moving toward the captain.

"The Queen just wants the Stone," he said, his attention wavering between David and the magus.

David saw the opportunity that Loren had provided him and took a half-step back, away from Bream's blade. The front of his shirt was wet and warm with his own blood.

"I could bring her your heads at the end of a pike and she would be more than pleased."

"I don't think that's true," the magus said. "I think she gave you explicit orders that we were to be brought to her unharmed." Something flickered in the captain's eyes. "And you know how the Queen treats those who disobey her orders."

"As you will soon know first-hand," the captain said.

"I expect I shall."

David released the breath that he had been holding. This was probably only a momentary reprieve, but it was better than being slaughtered in his mother's kitchen.

The magus extended his hands. "And will you be binding us to take us to the Queen?"

David didn't understand: with his hands tied, the magus would be helpless, unable to draw on his powers.

The captain looked at him scornfully. "I don't think that will be necessary," he said. "Your herbs will do you no good now."

Then David caught a hint of a smile, little more than a twitch in the corners of the magus's mouth.

"Let's go," the captain barked to his men. "Take the prisoners."

"All of them, sir?"

The captain looked at Mareigh, and at Tamas, sitting white-faced at the table. "No, leave these two."

The captain's eyes met Mareigh's.

"But make sure they know we were here," he said coldly.

He pushed David roughly by the shoulder, guiding him through the doorway into the tavern. As they followed, the men responded like animals in a burst of concentrated fury, attacking the tavern, overturning tables, smashing chairs and glasses. David could hear Mareigh crying out from the kitchen, but there was nothing he could do.

"That's enough," the captain said after a minute. "Let's go."

Not a piece of furniture remained whole, the floor scattered with chunks of wood and shards of glass. Mareigh gasped as she came through the door, but when the captain looked at her she kept her face expressionless.

"To the Queen?" the magus asked.

"Of course to the Queen," he snapped. "Who else?"

"Perhaps the King might have an interest in this."

Mareigh stiffened.

"The King has no interest in you whatsoever," he said, his voice flat. "Your time as his trusted adviser is clearly at an end."

The captain shoved him forward, driving them into the night.

⚶

The hotel elevator seemed to take forever. Jacqui paced as she waited. Maybe he was just upstairs, waiting for them to get back.

If not, she could call the police. That would probably be the best thing . . . Call the police? And tell them what? That her husband had been kidnapped? But he hadn't been. Not really. And he'd only been gone for a few minutes.

She could tell them about Tony Markus, and the book . . . But she would sound like Chris, ranting and crazy.

Her heart fell as she opened the door to the empty hotel room.

"Damn it," she muttered in the doorway, pulling David close.

She led him into the room and sat down next to him at the foot of the bed. She couldn't go to the police. And she had no way of getting in touch with Chris, with his cell phone still in his jacket pocket.

His phone.

She didn't draw breath as she started to rifle through his jacket pockets. Notebook. Pens. Spare pack of cigarettes. Wallet. She found his cell phone in the left inner pocket. She sat back down on the foot of the bed and started to scroll down his contacts.

It took her several minutes to work through the list, having to press at each cryptic nickname to figure out who he meant: Big Dick was Chris's shorthand for his Canadian editor, Richard; Roger Dodger was how he referred to his agent—former agent; John Castille was the name that Chris had used for Dale in *Coastal Drift*. There were a bunch of others, publicists and newspaper contacts most likely.

She found Cat near the bottom of the list, under "Took Exec." Executor? She took a deep breath as she pressed the button for details, hoping against hope.

But no. There was no address, just her phone number. She had no idea what she was going to say, but she pushed the Send button.

"The AT&T Wireless customer you are trying to reach . . ."

"Damn it."

She looked at David, still sitting at the end of the bed, his feet together, his back straight, staring into the mirror on the opposite wall, his reflection staring back at him.

"What are we going to do, David?" she asked.

She put the phone back into Chris's jacket. When her fingers brushed against the notebook again, she pulled it out.

On the front cover, Chris had written "Lazarus Took" with a silver pen, the way he labelled all his notebooks. The words were neat and regular, unlike most of his writing. Her hands shook as she slipped off the elastic closure and began flipping through the pages.

"Ha."

Close to the front of the book, in spidery black fountain pen ink, was a page titled "Cat Took." Chris had added under her name, at various times, "webmaster," "Executor," "Granddaughter," then her e-mail address and her cell phone number, each on a separate line.

And last, her address.

⌲⌲

The streets of Colcott were cool and silent. The moon hung high over the walls. The sharp snap of the soldiers' boots echoed in the still air.

The men marched in unison, staring straight ahead as they cut through alleys and lanes, retracing the route that had brought Dafyd to the castle the first time.

"This is awfully familiar," David muttered, and the magus glanced at him sharply.

"Watch what you say," the old man said, darting his eyes to the guards around them.

"Does that mean you have a plan?" David whispered, keeping his voice as low as he could manage.

The magus shook his head almost imperceptibly. "No. No plan." David could barely hear him. "Things are unfolding unexpectedly . . ."

"Then what was all that back at the tavern?" he asked, thinking of the magus offering his hands to be bound, and his mention of the King.

"When it comes time," the magus said, "one must play all the cards in one's hand."

⌲⌲

The rooms of Raven's Moor were dark, and it was difficult to distinguish any details as Cat led me through the house toward the tower.

I wanted to slow down, to look around. I couldn't help myself—I knew that he had been dead for more than half a century, but I wanted to spend some time in the rooms that Lazarus Took had inhabited, just looking. Remembering him as the writer I had loved, once.

"It's right through here," Cat said, leading me into a huge, old kitchen, then to a narrow staircase on the other side.

"He wanted to keep his private rooms away from the rest of the house," she said as we started up the dim stairs. "He needed the quiet for his work."

I could relate.

The top of the stairs widened into a spacious office. I had to catch my breath: the room was lined with bookshelves, crammed to bursting with leatherbound volumes. The tables and the leather chair were stacked with papers and more books. A large, ornately finished oak desk dominated the room, with a leather chair behind it, and a closed door behind that.

"This is it," Cat said, sweeping her arm to take in the whole room, from the shelves and desk to the high windows and the door leading out to the balcony, overlooking the Pacific. "The scene of the crime."

Her voice was playful, but her words were jarring: being here, in the most private of his places, I could picture Lazarus Took pacing the floor, letting the view of the trees and the ocean distract him while he was trying to write. I could picture him reading in the chair, holding his book with one hand, a glass of brandy in the other. Or behind the desk, his pen flying over the pages of a notebook.

I was picturing myself, really, imagining myself living and working in this room.

I took a step past Cat.

"I think you'll find everything you need in here," she said. "It's as he left it. I couldn't bring myself to clean it up."

I nodded appreciatively.

"I'm going to find the cordless so you can call your wife," she said, turning away. "Take a look around."

I was surprised, first, by how comfortable the study seemed. I had expected a palpable sense of menace, of cruelty, but I felt nothing of the sort. Just a writer's room, a place of creativity and contemplation. There was a pipe rack on the desk, and I imagined that I could still smell traces of sweet tobacco in the air.

I looked across the bookshelves, but I didn't find what I'd expected. No magical texts. Instead, the shelves were packed tight with volumes of philosophy, Victorian children's books and early editions of the classics that would likely be worth a fortune to a collector. There was no dust on the books or the shelves, or anywhere in the room for that matter. Cat might have been reluctant to move anything, but she kept it clean.

I turned toward the window. This wasn't the room of an evil man. There had to be somewhere else in the house, a ritual room, a place where Took could shake off his disguise, his respectability. I considered the door behind the desk. It made sense: behind the facade of gentility, I'd find the real Lazarus Took.

I pushed the chair aside so I could get to the door. I jiggled the knob, only to find it locked.

There had to be a key. He'd have kept it somewhere close, out of sight but convenient.

I reached for the main drawer of the desk, but before I could open it, my breath stopped fast in my throat.

There, centred on the blotter, was a copy of *To the Four Directions*, as if Took had been looking at it the last time he had sat here.

The upper right corner was dinged.

"Oh, Jesus," I muttered, feeling suddenly like I was going to be sick. My hands were shaking as I reached for the book . . . as I opened the front cover . . .

"Oh, Jesus."

Matthew Corvin, Seattle, 1976

I dropped the cover closed.

I didn't even want to think about her motivations, what game she was playing. I just had to grab the book and get out, before she came back.

"Oh, Chris," Cat said, almost flirtatiously, "you should see yourself."

Caught.

She was standing at the top of the stairs. In her right hand she held a gun, levelled at my chest. The black hole of the barrel gaped hungrily.

"Going somewhere?" she asked.

Mareigh watched through the front doorway of the tavern as the guards disappeared up the narrow street, torches held high against the midnight black. The door lay in splinters at her feet.

She watched until they passed out of sight before she turned back inside. She ignored the destruction that the men had left in their wake: there would be time to clean later. Time to repair. But not now.

She almost bumped into Tamas when she entered the kitchen. He jumped back before he realized it was her. The boy was drawn and pale, his face twisted in anguish.

"Oh gods, Mareigh," he choked, looking around the tavern behind her.

She could see the little boy inside his young man's body, the boy she had known almost his whole life.

"What did they do?"

She shook her head. "Nothing that can't be undone."

"I'm sorry, Mareigh," he said tearfully. "I could have . . ."

"Don't be an idiot," she said, but her voice was gentle. "There's nothing you could have done that wouldn't have ended with them taking Dafyd anyway, and leaving you dead."

He looked like she had slapped him, the words that she had intended to comfort him having precisely the opposite effect. "I could have tried."

"Go home," she said, fighting the urge to cup his cheek in her hand. "See to your mother. It's best you keep your distance from all this, for her sake."

He looked crestfallen, defeated. "He's going to be okay, isn't he?" he asked, in the voice of that little boy.

"Of course he will," she lied.

❧ ❦

Jacqui forced herself to drive slowly along the winding backroads outside Seaside. She knew she was going south toward Cannon Beach, but out here the roads were largely unmarked, and she had already taken a wrong turn, requiring a lengthy backtrack.

She had Chris's road atlas spread open on the passenger seat, with David buckled into the back. Every few minutes she would ease the van onto the shoulder and double-check the thin blue lines to reassure herself that she was on the right route, silently cursing the time it was costing her.

With the sun going down, the trees along the sides of the road cast shadows that plunged the road ahead into almost complete darkness. She clenched the fingers of both hands tight around the steering wheel and craned forward. She let the van slow as she followed the turns of the narrow road, barely more than a path worn through the forest. She didn't let herself worry about what she would do when she got to the house: she just had to find it.

One step at a time.

≈ ≈

Mareigh pulled the stool from beside her bed over to the cupboard. Balancing on one foot, she stretched her arms deep into the highest shelf. Her fingers searched blindly for a moment before they brushed against the smooth corner. Stretching a little farther, she managed to grip the box and pull it free.

She had screamed at him when he tried to give it to her. Had told him that she would never use it, that as far as she was concerned, he was already dead to her. Her soldier. Her hero. Riding away from her. She had made a mistake, and would accept and deal with the consequences.

As the memories came back to her, thoughts that she had suppressed for almost two decades, she stepped down and set the box on the bed.

It was a plain wooden box. It wasn't even locked—there was no use in securing things that she didn't care about.

"But there has to be something I can do?" he had pleaded, uncomfortable in his sudden powerlessness.

"Yes," she said, her right hand cradling, unconsciously, the small swell of her belly. Something that would make a difference to her, that would enable a life for her and for their unborn child. For a mother to raise a child alone meant destitution; this, at least, would address a few concerns.

When she told him what she wanted, he stared disbelievingly at her for a moment, then burst into laughter.

"A tavern?" he said. "I would give you anything in the world, and all you want is a tavern?"

"A tavern is a life. My life. Our child's future."

Her hand shook now as she opened the box.

He had eventually agreed. "Is there nothing else?"

Oh, there was so much else she had wanted, but those things were not hers to have, and she knew better than to even mention them.

When she shook her head, he reached into the pocket of his tunic. "I understand why you have asked for what you have. But there will come a day when you may require something else. For yourself. Or for our child."

"There won't."

He withdrew an envelope and held it out to her. "If that day should ever arrive, come to me. Bring this letter"—he'd placed it in her hand—"and this." He twisted the large signet ring off his finger. When she tried to wave it away, he pressed it on her. "You are carrying my child," he said, in a voice of exquisite pain and sadness.

She took the ring and the letter, and put them into the box that same day. And later, when she and Dafyd, then weeks old and still hungry at the breast, had moved across the channel from Colcott Town to the city inside the walls, from the scullery of the inn to the tavern that bore the name she had given it, she put the box on the highest shelf and tried to forget about it.

"If there is anything I can do . . ."

Yes. Yes, darling, there is.

⪻ ⪼

"How did you get this?" I gestured at the book on the desk.

"It always comes back," Cat said. "It's part of the charm." She smiled. "Well, *a* charm, actually. A homing spell, you might say. This time it happened exactly the way you thought it would, Chris. Tony Markus called me, saying that we needed to talk about Lazarus's 'legacy,' as he called it. And here we are."

I could barely speak. "He just . . . gave it to you?" And I knew, even as I formed the words, that this wasn't what had happened.

She smiled even more widely, baring her teeth. "Eventually."

The coldness of her voice was almost enough to take the legs out from under me.

"So you know," I said. "You knew about this all the time?"

"Of course I did, Chris." She looked at the book. "It's mine."

"But did you . . . Did you know what it did? What it would do to my son?"

She entered the room, holding the gun casually, as if without a care. The barrel, however, never wavered.

"Let me take it," I said, grasping at the last strands of hope. "Let me just borrow it. I'll take it home, and let my friends look at it, and I'll bring it right back. I swear. I'll drive it back down myself." My voice was growing ragged, desperate. Pleading.

"Why would I let you do that?" she asked.

"To save my son."

She took another step toward me. "And undo all the hard work I put into this?"

"What?" I had to brace myself against the desk.

"Did you really think that Lazarus Took could have done something like this?" she asked, pointing at the book. "Please. Lazarus was a second-rate dabbler, at best. He had a few charms, and a knack for separating people from their money, but really he was little better than those pathetic kitchen witches of yours, with their praising of the goddess"—she made the word sound like a sneer—"and their crystals." The stone that Nora had given me still hung on the leather thong under my shirt. "Lazarus couldn't have cast a spell like that if his life depended on it."

She took another step forward, so only the desk separated us. She leaned forward, her smile so wide and close that, for a moment, I thought she might sink her teeth into me.

"It was mine," she said plainly, almost laughing as she watched my expression.

"But that's impossible," I said, turning it over in my mind. Even if she had faked the publication date inside the book, she was clearly younger than Matthew Corvin—she wouldn't have been born at the time the book had claimed him.

She bobbed her head girlishly. "I've already told you everything you need to know, Chris. For someone who seems to have all the answers, you're not very good at putting things together, are you. Tell me, didn't it strike you as odd that there wasn't any mention whatsoever of children in anything you read about Lazarus Took? No mention of family in the papers at the Hunter Barlow? Didn't that ever occur to you?"

I hadn't even noticed it. No children meant no grandchildren . . .

The only possible explanation was growing within me with a sickly power. She must have seen it on my face.

"I even told you," she said, clearly relishing the moment, "back in that very first e-mail, who I was."

I thought back, trying to ignore the undeniable presence of the gun, trying to visualize the e-mail.

C. Agatha Took. But please call me Cat.

"Cat Took," I muttered. "Cora Agatha Took?" My mind rebelled at the thought, buzzing hysterically.

"In the flesh," she said, turning a little, showing herself off. "And quite nice flesh it is, too, don't you think? Your friend Tony Markus certainly thought so. Poor man. All those hopes and dreams and . . ." She jerked the gun in her hand. "Bang."

I flinched, and she laughed.

"You must be—"

"I celebrated my hundredth birthday last year," she said. "Well, it was a quiet celebration. Just the two of us."

Two of us? I shook my head, still trying to understand what she was telling me. This couldn't be Cora Took—Cat looked like she was in her mid-twenties, at the oldest.

"How?"

She rolled her eyes in mock exasperation. "You're holding the answer, Chris."

She extended her hand for the book.

※ ※

The Queen was sitting on her throne at the far end of the marble hall, wearing a gown so colourful it might have been made of peacock feathers, her pale face flat and expressionless.

David hesitated a few steps away from her, his feet refusing to take him any closer. It lasted only for an instant, but it was too much for the captain, who shoved him forward with a blow that took his breath away. He stumbled, catching himself before he fell to the tiles.

"Kneel before the Queen," the captain snarled, pushing down on his shoulder. David's knee hit the tiles hard, and he winced.

"You are right to fear me," the Queen said.

David didn't speak, but stared down at the floor, anything to avoid looking her in the eye.

"You may rise," the Queen said, her voice cold.

The captain pulled at David's shirt, hauling him to his feet.

The magus was slower in rising.

After several moments of silence, David couldn't fight the impulse and he glanced at the Queen, only to find her staring back at him.

"I believe you have something that belongs to me." She extended her hand.

Something in her voice . . .

David had to force himself not to reach into his tunic and hand her the Stone. The power of her gaze was almost impossible to resist. More than that: he *wanted* to give it to her. He could feel the urging in his muscles. The thought of just handing it to her, of seeing her smile of satisfaction. He wanted so badly to please her. Just hand it over. The fight for the Sunstone had nothing to do with him anyway. Just hand it over. He could save himself.

He reached up—

The magus stepped forward. "Your Majesty."

"You dare speak in my presence?" the Queen roared.

As her attention shifted to the magus, David felt an easing in his mind, a quieting of the imploring voice.

The Queen turned her head slightly, and the captain slapped the old man across the face so hard that he stumbled to one side. He didn't fall, however, and pulled himself to his full height.

"I stand before you, one of the Brotherhood, the keepers of the Stone, sworn in allegiance to the kings of Colcott." His voice was unflinching. "It is my right and obligation to speak."

"In the absence of the King, your allegiance is to me," the Queen said, almost dismissively. "The Stone—"

"The Stone is in our keeping. And the King is not absent," the old man said, his voice growing stronger. "He is here. Still the rightful heir, and the rightful owner of the Stone." As he spoke, he lifted his hand to his chest as if scratching himself unconsciously.

"The Stone belongs to the one who holds it," she said, rising slightly, coiling herself, turning her attention back to David. "Dafyd, give it to me."

She seemed to have two voices: the one which he heard her speak, and a low, insinuating whisper that echoed in his skull: *Give her the stone. Give her the stone.*

"Dafyd," the magus said. "Don't listen to her. Don't—"

David raised his hand to his tunic, slipped it into the opening.

Give her the stone.

His fingers curled around the leather bag, feeling the warmth there.

"Dafyd!" The magus barked his name in a commanding tone that drowned out the Queen's voice in his head.

David dropped his hand, turned to look at the old man.

The magus was facing him, his right hand extended, his left hand tight around his amulet.

"You fool," the Queen cried at Captain Bream. "He has a moonstone!"

As the captain lunged, David could hear the magus's voice inside his head. *Run*, it said. *Run to the King.*

David didn't hesitate. As the captain reached out for the magus, David spun away and raced toward the curtain behind the dais.

"Get the boy!" the Queen screamed. "Get him!"

His feet slipped on the slick tiles, but he found his balance. He could hear the captain behind him, too close. Too fast for him to outrun.

He pushed the curtain aside, throwing himself into the King's chamber. He had just long enough to see the King on the bed, his haggard, shrunken face looking at him in surprise, before the captain tackled him to the floor.

David's face crashed into the tile. His nose snapped, his mouth filled with blood. He tried to drag himself forward, coughing, but the captain held him fast. He could feel the man's hands tearing at his clothes, ripping his tunic open.

"I've got it," he cried out, standing up, holding the small leather bag high in the air.

The Queen swooped into the room and snatched it from his hand, as David spat blood onto the cold grey tile.

≫ ≪

Jacqui had been driving so long she had started to think that she was lost. Hopelessness threatened to overshadow her urgency. But when the narrow road widened into a circular driveway, she knew that this had to be the right place. The house before her was a stone monstrosity that seemed to jut out of the darkness. A red VW sat parked in front of the steps.

She pulled in behind the car and turned off the engine. "I'll be right back," she said to David. "Okay? I'm just gonna see if anybody's home."

She took care on the steps, half shrouded in shadow. The last thing she wanted to do was fall and break her neck.

Glancing back at the van from the porch, she couldn't make out David in the dark. She turned toward the doors, which were faced with frosted glass.

Taking a deep breath, she knocked.

She waited, listening for any hint of motion inside. She still had no idea what she would say to the woman when she opened the door. One step at a time.

No one appeared. She knocked again, louder this time, bruising her knuckles against the wood.

Still nothing.

"Damn it," she muttered, before pounding on the door with the side of her fist, calling out, "Hello? Hello? Is anybody there?"

She tried the door: locked.

Chris was obviously inside the house, but David was in the van and couldn't be left for long. What was she supposed to do?

She pulled off her sweater. The sea air chilled her bare arms as she folded the sweater in half, forming a thick pad which she held against

the glass near the doorknob. Holding it with one hand, she brought up
the other elbow and smashed it, several times, against the window. She
didn't stop until she felt the sweater starting to fall inward, heard the
tinkling of glass on the floor inside the house.

She punched the rest of the glass away and reached in, turning the
bolt on the lock.

With one look back at David, Jacqui opened the door.

※ ※

A row of guards stood at the castle gate as Mareigh approached. Flames
leapt so high from the torches in the walls that it was almost as bright
as day.

Her heart was racing, but she didn't even slow down.

"Which one of you is the captain?" she asked, stopping in front of
them.

"Ma'am," one man said, stepping forward. "The gates are closed."

"Are you the captain?" she asked. Just her luck: someone she had
never served in the tavern.

"Yes, ma'am," he said, standing there stiff-backed.

"I need to see the King," she said, fighting the quaver she could feel
in her throat.

"That's impossible," the captain said, his hand moving to the hilt
of his sword.

He stopped himself when she held up her left hand, the signet glit-
tering on her ring finger, catching the torchlight like a small ember.

"I have come to see the King," she said, extending the ring toward
the captain as she drew the letter, still sealed with the royal crest, from
her blouse.

"He's been expecting me."

※ ※

Reflexively I clutched the book close to my chest and took two steps
backward. "You did this," I said. "You did this to David. To all those
other children."

"Wouldn't you?" Cora asked, withdrawing her outstretched hand.

"If it meant that you could live forever? Eternal youth, with none of that Greek-myth be-careful-what-you-wish-for crap? Forever young, forever beautiful? Who wouldn't want that?"

I threw my head back, trying to stave off the flow of tears that threatened. I looked away from her, around the room where Lazarus Took had spent the last years of his life, reading and writing.

"I should have known," I said. "I should have known it wasn't him."

"It was his idea," she said, and I looked back at her, at her wide eyes and the dark barrel of the gun. "Well, sort of. Lazarus always said he wanted to write something that would make him immortal. Something that people would remember." She shrugged. "That was one of the things he did, one of his little gifts. He wrote those books." She said it as if this left a sour taste in her mouth. "Those little spells that captured his readers, that pulled them into the story. Well, not literally." She smiled again. "That part was my idea."

She took a step to one side, starting to edge around the desk. I took a step in the opposite direction, trying to keep as much distance between us as possible, as if the width of a stride would protect me against a bullet.

"Lazarus was a dabbler," she continued. "Reading cards and writing those books. Oh, he was a grand performer when he needed to be, but he didn't know anything about real magic."

"But you did."

She nodded. "It's in my blood, you see. Everything that you read about those old magicians, it's always about the men. The almighty William Thorne. The evil Lazarus Took. But the real power, that came from the women. It always has. When they arrested Thorne, they thought they were rescuing my mother, that this poor, innocent, virginal girl had fallen under the devil's spell, and that, praise the Lord, they had rescued her before he had a chance to defile her." She spat out a laugh. "Little did they know that it was her hand on the blade that cut the throats for the ritual sacrifices. That it was her body that was the font of what little power Thorne ever had."

"Your mother? Thorne?"

She nodded. "He was never the same after she was gone. He spent the rest of his life chased by the police, writing his ridiculous books, building up his legend, while my mother disappeared into the darkness of history with her child."

"You? You're Thorne's—?"

"I'm my mother's daughter," she snapped. "And that's all that matters. She taught me everything she knew, showed me how to awaken the power within me, to harness the power of those around me."

"Lazarus." I took another step away and she took a step closer.

"He had some power," she conceded. "But he'd never have been able to use it on his own. I showed him some tricks, let him shine like a beacon, drawing people to us. People and their power."

"And their money."

She waved the comment away. "Money's of little concern. There's nothing you can buy that people won't willingly give."

"Or that you can't take," I said, thinking of the book in my hand, of Tony Markus.

"If something was meant to be mine, what difference does it make how I came by it?"

"But you're killing my son." As I spoke the words, I felt my fear vying with a sudden flash of anger.

"So?" she said. "I needed him, to keep me alive. Do you spare a thought for the pig on your plate as you tear into its flesh?"

I lowered my head, unable to look at her any longer.

"You poor, poor man," she said, condescension dripping from every word. "You came here thinking that I would help you, that you could count on the poor, sweet, naive girl, when all along . . ."

She made another movement toward me, and I backed into the doorknob: there was nowhere left for me to retreat.

"When I came in, you seemed awfully interested in seeing what was behind that door. The key's in the desk."

I didn't move.

She waved the gun between me and the desk. "Go on," she said. "Satisfy your curiosity. No secrets between us now."

I still didn't move. Paralyzed by fear, by the horror of what she had done.

"Open the door, Chris," she said coldly, her voice cutting the air between us. "You might as well. You've got absolutely nothing left to lose."

I stepped to the desk and pulled open the drawer, watching her closely. I glanced down to see a brass key in the tray alongside two fountain pens.

"So what are you going to do to me?" I asked, looking up again.

"Well, first," she said, taking another step toward me, so close now she could have reached out and taken the book. "We're going to take a look at what's behind door number two." She gestured with the gun. "And then we're going to go out on the balcony and you're going to take a dive onto the rocks."

I gasped.

"And then I'm going to call the police and tell them how I tried to stop you, but you were so overcome with grief about your son that you couldn't go on. Inconsolable. I'll cry and I'll heave my breasts and the police will feel so sorry for me it'll never occur to them to look for any other possibility."

"I won't do it."

She looked at me as if I were a misbehaving child, and she spoke to me the same way. "In that case, I'll shoot you in the head. There are dozens of ways to make a body disappear." She shrugged as if it made no difference to her. "So why don't you open that door." She spoke the last three words in a low, almost guttural voice, a command that I was powerless to resist.

I slowly fit the key into the lock.

The tumblers opened with a heavy click.

I glanced at her, and she nodded.

"Go ahead."

I turned the knob, and pushed the door open.

"Oh God," I muttered.

"I suppose I should make the introductions. Chris Knox, this is Lazarus Took."

As David struggled to his feet, he felt the magus's hand on his arm, helping him rise. "I'm sorry," he sputtered, spitting out another mouthful of blood. "I tried."

The magus shook his head. "It's enough," he said. "It will have to be."

The captain pushed past David, reaching for Loren's neck. He grabbed him around the throat, dragging him down.

"I should kill you now," he snarled, his face red and damp.

"Captain," came a hoarse whisper from the bed. "Let him free." The King's voice was weak, but his tone brooked no argument. "You do not want to incur the wrath of the Brotherhood."

Bream held the magus by the throat as he turned to the Queen. She appeared to consider for a moment, then nodded.

As the captain dropped the magus to the floor like a heap of grey laundry, the Queen untied the thong closing the leather sack.

Jacqui stood for several seconds in the doorway, listening, expecting someone to come running at the sound of her breaking into the house. A single lamp burned on the table in the foyer before her. When no one came, she stepped inside, leaving the door open.

In the lamplight she could see a staircase, but it was pitch dark at the top. The same for a doorway to her right: dark and silent. She turned to the left, where a light was on in what looked to be a small sitting room.

She walked through it and into a kitchen. And through the next door saw a narrow staircase.

She took the steps carefully, planting her feet softly on each in order to prevent any creaking. From the landing halfway up she could hear the faint sound of voices coming from above. Voices that became clearer as she climbed: a woman's voice, mostly. And then a man's. Chris's voice.

But she had never heard him sound like he did right now.

She peered over the top stair into what looked like an office; she could see a desk, and the back of a woman standing next to it. She was speaking to someone hidden behind the frame of a doorway behind the desk.

Pushing down her fear, Jacqui climbed the last few steps and pressed herself against the wall outside the office.

⇜ ⇝

Mareigh had to trot to keep up with the captain of the watch as he led her through the wide halls of the castle. She clutched the letter tightly.

She had been inside the castle only once, years ago. Like everyone else in the walled city, and many of the people from the shore, she had gathered in the large square to watch the new King's coronation, late the same afternoon that had seen the passing of his father, the old king.

He had looked every bit the prince regent that day. The way the sun caught his eyes had made his hair look like a river of gold over his shoulders. He wore a simple white tunic as he walked the length of the yard, two steps behind the Master of the Stone, the senior member of the Brotherhood.

Behind the prince strode his two closest friends, the men who had been at his side at the Battle of Deren Plain. Paul Bream, who had been named captain upon his return from the war, marched proudly in full dress, the sunlight sparkling off the crest on his chest. Loren, however, looked the same as he always did, older than Bream and the prince, but looking older still in the grey robes of his order. While Bream stared straight ahead, the magus seemed distracted, glancing furtively about as if looking for someone.

When he saw Mareigh in the front row of the gathered crowd, he stopped searching. He smiled at her, a sad, understanding smile, then turned away.

The prince had passed near her that afternoon, almost close enough to touch, but he hadn't seen her, his eyes fixed forward, head high, unwavering on that day that had mixed tragedy and jubilation. His jaw was set, but she could see the puffiness around his eyes—he had been crying, and she alone of all the hundreds gathered was able to recognize it.

She watched as he knelt before the empty throne, and heard him swear the oath to the country, and to the Stone which was its symbol, its very source. And then the Master lowered the thin gold crown to rest on his head, draped his shoulders with the blood-red cape.

When he rose to his feet and turned to face the people gathered—his people, now—she couldn't help herself, lowering her head so her tears fell to the ground. She knew that she wasn't alone, that many others within the crowd were weeping, but none, she knew, for the same reason.

That was the last time she had seen him. She had refused to attend the ceremony marking the Royal Wedding, the King's arrival home with his new Berok wife. She was, she explained to people, far too busy, trying to establish the Mermaid's Rest with a little boy underfoot.

"It's not much farther, ma'am," the captain of the watch said, leading her around a corner.

She bit her lip and tightened her fingers around the letter, praying that she wouldn't be too late.

≈ ≈

Cora prodded me through the door with the barrel of her gun. I stepped into the room, reeling from a foul smell of rot and decay.

It was an octagonal room, cold, stone. A candle guttered in a nook carved into each wall, the flames casting a dancing light around the small space.

"What have you done?" I said hoarsely.

Painted on the floor in rusty tones was a perfect circle, equidistant to the edges of the octagon. Inside the circle were the same symbols as on the cover of the book. The same pattern was painted on the ceiling.

At the centre of the circle on the floor was a bed, barely big enough for the man who lay in it.

"Lazarus, honey, this is Chris Knox. He's a big fan. He's read all your books."

I barely recognized the shape on the bed as a man. He was wizened almost to the point of desiccation, his skin stretched tight over his bones. He looked mummified. Skeletal.

And then he opened his eyes.

"He's alive," I gasped, the bile filling my throat.

"What?" she said. "Did you think I was making the introductions for dramatic effect?"

"But how . . .?" I took another few steps into the room, toward the bed.

"It was necessary," she said, as if that phrase were enough to excuse everything. "I couldn't write the book myself, and the spell that he wove with the words was enough to . . ." She gestured with the gun. "Well, you can see."

I did see. "The book is keeping him alive as well." Clutching it closer to my chest, I moved closer to the bed.

"More or less. Once I realized I couldn't do it without him, I made him part of it. All this—" She gestured at the symbols on the floor and the ceiling. "That's all mine. Well"—she smirked—"*his*."

What I had thought was brown paint used to craft the symbols was actually blood. Took's blood.

With a groan, Took turned himself in the bed, pushed himself up slowly to a sitting position. As the covers fell away, I retched: his skin was grey, covered with oozing sores, caked with mustard-coloured pus. As he moved, the stench in the room became unbearable.

"He's a prisoner," I said.

"He's a conduit," she said. "These symbols and glyphs, they focus the power of the book—"

"The souls of the children."

"Through him and his story, and into me," she said, with a feral smile.

I took another step toward the bed, around the end of it now. I shifted the book, holding it close to my heart. The beginning of a plan was coming to me.

"So this is how you treat the man you claimed to love?"

Step one—keep her talking.

She rolled her eyes. "Love. Love had nothing to do with it. We both went into this relationship knowing what we were looking for. Power. Magic. Renown. And that's exactly what we got." She too stepped closer to the bed, leaning over to meet Took's eye. "As long as we both shall live, right, darling?"

I took advantage of the momentary wavering of her attention to take two quick steps along the bed, tucking myself in close beside him, putting him between me and the gun. I crouched slightly, reaching into my pocket, disgusted with myself for hiding behind the body of a suffering man.

"Oh, very clever, Chris," she said. "You think I won't just come around the bed? How long do you think you can hide there?"

"Long enough," I said, "to do this." With my left hand I held the book by one cover and let it fall open, allowing the pages to fan free. I struck my Zippo with my right thumb, bringing the flame toward the open pages.

"What are you doing?" she cried, her voice betraying her surprise. Lazarus's eyes flashed in the firelight.

"Don't come any closer," I said. I held the book near my body, keeping the flame close to the pages.

"You don't want to do that," she said. She was coming around the bed, the gun in plain view again.

"This is keeping you alive, right? Either you let me go, or . . ." I teased the lighter close enough to singe the edges of the pages.

"Right now it's keeping your son alive, too," she said. "Is that what you want?" She took another step toward me.

I moved around the bed, behind her husband again.

"Do you want to be the one to kill your son? Because that's his soul you're holding there."

I looked down at the book again, at the flames playing near the dry paper. I wanted to do the right thing. I wanted to be part of the greater good, to protect future children from this woman, no matter the cost to myself.

"You're a terrible bluffer, Chris."

I dropped my lighter, heard it hit the stone floor.

Looking at the book, the charred edges, the unscathed leather, I realized that I was crying.

"That's better," she said, back in control. "Now why don't you put that down, before you do something you'll really regret."

I didn't have any choice—there was nothing else to do but drop the book on the bed beside Lazarus Took.

As I watched it fall toward the stained sheets, I heard Jacqui call from the direction of the doorway, "Chris, don't!"

I looked up in time to see her face, to see her reaching out toward me, before Cora turned and fired the pistol. The shot blossomed red in the centre of Jacqui's chest, the force of it throwing her backwards with a sickening thud on the stone floor.

David wiped the blood from his face with the back of his hand as the magus rose slowly to his feet, rubbing his bruised throat.

Both of them were watching the Queen.

She untied the thongs holding the bag closed with a look of barely contained excitement, then opened the mouth of the bag and poured the Stone into her hand.

Her smile widened, a dark, bitter maw. "It's mine!" she cried triumphantly. She raised the Stone high in one hand, extending her other hand toward David. She muttered a few words in a language he didn't understand, and then—

Nothing.

She frowned, a sharp line crossing the centre of her forehead and between her eyes. She shifted her grip on the Stone, flexed the fingers of her right hand toward David.

And again, nothing happened.

She lowered the Stone, staring at the markings on its surface, then glared at David. "What have you done?" she demanded.

A wheezing, gasping sound came from the bed, barely recognizable as laughter. The King's laughter. His eyes were pressed tightly shut, his mouth wide, his head thrown back.

"You?" the Queen snarled, rounding on him. "What did you do?"

The magus spoke. "The King did nothing, My Lady," he said.

She stormed toward the bed. "Then why doesn't it work?" she shrieked.

"Because the Stone is not yours," the magus said, no satisfaction in his voice. "It belongs to the rightful rulers of Colcott."

"But I am the Queen," she thundered.

"And the King is still the King," the magus said.

"Then let the King be no more," she cried, reaching for the sword in the captain's belt. With a single motion she drew it, turned, and drove the point deep into the King's chest. The wound gushed blood onto the bedsheets, the King's head snapping forward with the ferocity of the blow.

"My Lady—" the captain gasped, but he was interrupted by a voice from the doorway.

"Dafyd!"

David turned. His mother. Dafyd's mother. Her hands pressed to her mouth, face twisted in anguish.

Mareigh rushed into the room, not toward her son but to the side of the man dying in the bed, the King of Colcott, the only man she had ever loved. "Oh gods," she cried, leaning over him. "Oh gods, Dafyd, what did they—?"

"Who are you?" the Queen commanded, heaving the sword from the King's chest.

Mareigh turned at the sound of her voice, her face stained with tears, her eyes flickering between the Queen's cold gaze and the bloodstained sword in her hand.

"You?" she whispered.

"Me," the Queen said, as she thrust the sword into Mareigh's chest.

"Mother!" Dafyd cried out.

David felt the full force of the other boy's will spill free of whatever had been holding it back, the sheer power of his thoughts, his emotions, his memories and his anguish, pushing David out, forcing him loose of the body he had begun to feel was his own.

With a sudden shock, David jerked, just once, his body snapping against the seat belt.

The world came dizzyingly back into focus. It was like waking from a dream.

With a cautious, shaking hand, he reached for the buckle, pressing the button to release himself.

As he opened the van door, he heard a sound, faint, like a firecracker, borne on the sea wind.

"Mom!" He ran toward the dark house.

My heart surged in my throat as Jacqui fell to the floor. I called her name, and started to step forward. The room lurched around me.

"Don't move," Cora Took said, swinging the barrel of the gun back toward me.

The stone floor seemed to move under my feet. My vision swam, and I stumbled, putting my hand down on the bed to keep from falling.

"Jacqui," I whispered.

"Mother!" Dafyd cried out, running to the bed and falling to his knees.

Mareigh had fallen on her side across the foot of the bed. He turned her gently onto her back. Her eyes were open, her face a mask of pain, her hands clutching the wound as it billowed blood from just below her ribs.

"Leave her!" the Queen commanded.

"Dafyd," she whispered.

Dafyd looked at her, his eyes blurring, his stomach lurching as the room seemed to shift and move around him.

The door swung open at David's touch, and as he stepped into Lazarus Took's house his feet felt unsteady under him. He had difficulty walking. Not surprising, considering how long it had been since he had used this body, since he had moved his own legs, walked with his own feet.

He turned to the left, the way he knew, somehow, that his mother had gone.

"Mom," he said breathlessly, moving through the shadowed rooms.

"Your pretty wife?" Cora asked, her tone mawkish for a moment before the gun wavered in her hand. Her eyes darted around the room, and she stumbled, as if trying to keep her footing on a moving boat.

It was all I could do to hold onto the bed and not fall. I tried to focus on the gun, watching as it lurched and bobbed in her hand, but I couldn't. Cat seemed to shift in and out of focus, not blurring, exactly, but fading somehow, the barrel stretching and bending, then snapping back into sharp clarity.

The Queen glanced around the King's bedchamber, and Dafyd followed her eyes. The stone walls seemed to curve, bulging outward, then twisting the other way, pulling away from the room. The floor followed the motion of the walls, sometimes stretching, sometimes rippling.

She turned sharply toward the magus. "Stop this," she sneered, letting the point of the sword sag.

The magus, however, looked as confused as she did.

She dropped the sword to the floor with a clatter, raising her right hand toward the old man, the Sunstone still clutched in her left. "I command you," she began, then stumbled as the floor moved under her.

As he started to climb the stairs on the far side of the kitchen, David realized that his legs weren't the problem. The house seemed to be moving around him, the steps like Jell-O under his feet, shimmering and bouncing.

Matt, he whispered urgently, inside his mind. *What is this? What's going on?*

He stopped halfway up the stairs. Matt didn't answer, and there was no sense of him inside David anymore, no niggling presence in his thoughts.

He took the last stairs more slowly, trying to stay quiet. He tried to push down the fear he was feeling, tried to ignore the fact that, for the first time in as long as he could remember, he was completely alone.

Cora looked at the desiccated body on the bed. "Lazarus," she hissed. "What is happening?"

I glanced down at the old man, looking for the same answers. He didn't have any. His eyes were filled with fear.

I was dizzy, the room seeming to spin, the walls seeming to breathe. I could hear my breath, taste bitterness in the back of my mouth.

I had to close my eyes against the nausea.

As the Queen stumbled, the captain stepped behind her, his body rocking with the motion of the room. He didn't try to fight it, just rode the movement as he reached for his bloodied sword.

Dafyd flinched and pulled his mother close to him, his stomach pushing up toward his mouth as he watched the Queen's hand, waiting for the crackle of power he knew was to come.

David would have known it was a writer's study even if he hadn't known the first thing about Lazarus Took. It looked like his father's office, in a way, with a chair for reading and a desk and—

He had to blink, shake his head. For a moment, the room had seemed to shift somehow, the desk replaced by a flickering image—thrones. A tapestry behind them.

He blinked again and the study was the way it had been: a heavy wooden desk, an open door behind it, voices rising from inside. The air, though, the air seemed thick, gelatinous somehow, and moving through the room felt almost like swimming. He had to fight his way forward, his body seeming to pull and stretch with every motion.

He blinked—

I opened my eyes, hoping that the nausea had passed, then closed them again as quickly as I could. What I had seen, it couldn't be real.

The Queen lowered her hand. "You lied," she screamed at the magus. Her mouth seemed to stretch and pull, as if it were melting. "You told me it would work."

The magus was pale, and unsteady on his feet, his hands extended to keep his balance. "No," he said, his voice rough. "I said it would only work for the true steward, the rightful heir."

The Queen whirled toward Dafyd. "You."

—and when he opened his eyes again, David was in the throne room in Colcott, the two thrones on the dais a short distance away. He shifted his direction slightly to go around the dais—

blink

—desk, to get to the doorway—

blink

—the tapestry behind the thrones. He could hear voices. They were all familiar, but too distorted to make out what they were saying, like he was hearing an echo.

I struggled to rise to my feet.

Reality was coming apart at the seams. The house was shaking now, our every motion slow and distorted. I could barely see, images flickering past like a film caught in a projector, twisting and doubling over one another. Two beds, two old men, two women, each pair seeming to occupy the same space, and no space at all.

Cora lowered her gun. "What . . .?"

The room lurched again, and I lost my balance.

The Queen's face seemed to melt from her bones. "You." She pointed at him. "Her . . ."

Dafyd glanced toward the magus, who nodded slowly.

"That whore," she spat.

Mareigh's body jerked in Dafyd's arms. There was a sound like a cough, or a sharp laugh. When he looked down at her, blood trickled from her lips.

"You knew all along," the Queen accused Loren.

He nodded. "He was my oldest friend. My Lord. My King. When he summoned me . . ."

A look of dawning horror and understanding seemed to rise in the Queen's face.

"He told me he was being poisoned. That the Queen was killing him, just slowly enough to gain control over the kingdom before he died. I did not want to believe him, but I made plans with him. And then the handmaiden was poisoned . . . Why did you kill the girl?"

The Queen looked scornfully at the magus. "I needed to get you out of the castle. My brother had men waiting on the road. What matters the life of a servant?"

As Dafyd glanced between the Queen and the magus, trying to

follow what was going on, the room shifted again. Everything flickered like torchlight.

"So you went to your books, your prophecies . . ." the Queen continued, lurching with the room.

The magus shook his head. "King Dafyd and I made up the prophecies about the chosen one, to allay your suspicions. There were no prophecies, no mystical signs. We knew where the heir was. We had known his entire life."

A bubble of heat formed in Dafyd's chest, building, until it seemed to burst, a sob racking him. The King . . . his father. He glanced up, toward the body on the bed, then down again at his mother's face, bloody and slack.

"The only prophecy was that of the Stone. And as you see, the boy has more than proven himself. He is the true heir. The true steward of Colcott."

A steely calm seemed to come over the Queen, a resolve that was terrifying in its simplicity. "Ah well," she said. "Easy enough. Kill a king. Kill a prince. A small price to pay."

Her eyes scanned the ground, searching for her dropped sword.

As she turned, Captain Bream brought the blade up, set the point level with the centre of her chest, his eyes focusing on her with a savage intensity. "No, My Lady."

As I caught myself on the edge of the bed, Cora raised the gun again, held it unsteadily toward us. A flicker, and another woman seemed to be standing in her place.

"Make it stop," she cried out, and I couldn't tell who was speaking, and if she was talking to me or to the husk of her husband in the bed.

My head throbbed with a concussive force. I tried to breathe through it, and—

"Mom!" David cried out, pushing through the thick air as he crossed the study to where her body lay in the doorway. He fell to his knees beside her. He didn't know if he should touch her, and all he could do was watch as her chest shuddered, as blood bubbled at her lips. "Mom," he whispered, his voice breaking—

"Mom."

The word echoed through the King's bedchamber like thunder. Dafyd and the Queen both looked to the doorway, where shadows shifted in and out of focus. It seemed like there was a fallen body, there one moment, gone the next, and a small figure bending over it.

David. The voice in Dafyd's head was a desperate shout, and only a moment later he realized that he had cried the name out loud.

I looked up at the sound of David's name, a shout in a young man's voice I didn't recognize. A shadow at the end of the bed, human shaped, turned its head toward the doorway.

I glanced up, and my eyes met David's. He was crouched over Jacqui's body but staring into the room, his eyes seemingly locked on the shadowy figure that had spoken his name.

David's eyes met Dafyd's, and for a moment he couldn't breathe. Two lifetimes of memories seemed to swell inside his head, and he rose slowly to his feet, stepping through the doorway and—

—everything seemed to solidify. The throbbing in my head dissolved, and the room stopped moving, my stomach settling almost instantly.

I rose carefully to my feet, not yet trusting the stability of the floor. "David," I called out, and as he looked up at me, Cora Took whirled toward him, levelling the gun, now solid and unwavering in her grip.

Then she caught sight of two figures who had been behind her, a woman in rich formal dress, and a strong-looking man in some sort of uniform, the tip of his sword almost touching the woman's chest.

The hand holding the gun fell limply to her side.

"Reg?" she said.

As David stepped into the room, Dafyd turned from his mother's limp body and rose slowly to his feet.

They stepped toward each other haltingly, cautiously, each wet with his mother's blood, seeing each other for the first time.

His sword point drifted slightly from the Queen's breast as Bream turned to the sound of a name he had never expected to hear again.

"Cora?" he said, his voice thick with an emotion that Loren had not heard from the man in the more than twenty years he had known him.

Cora's face was wide with wonder.

The captain stepped toward her, his sword lowering.

As he turned, the Queen fumbled at her dress.

The magus cried out, "Bream!" as a knife flashed in the space between the Queen and the soldier.

I looked around the room—rooms. We were still in the room where Cora had imprisoned Lazarus Took, and I could see the circle of his blood, the symbols, on the floor around me. But at the same time, we were in a much larger, older room.

It took me a moment to place it, like something from a dream. It was the King's bedchamber, where Dafyd had gone at the end of the book, where he had used the Sunstone to heal the old man, where he had knelt to be knighted. It was different than I had imagined it, but I knew I was right.

And if this was the King's bedchamber, then . . .

Bream sidestepped the knife almost effortlessly, and turned in the same motion, his sword coming up again and catching the Queen above the neckline of her dress. Her momentum, the thrust that should have been a death-blow to him, instead buried his sword deep in her. There was a crunching sound, a hiss as blood sprayed the captain's face, and her eyes went wide, disbelieving. She fell.

Bream drew the sword from her body, and stepped toward Cora Took.

The magus gestured toward the Queen's body. "Dafyd," he said, "the Stone."

I made a move toward David, toward Jacqui's fallen body, but I was held back by the pinch of cold fingers on my arm.

I turned to the bed. Lazarus Took had pulled himself up, had reached out to stop me.

"Is that . . ." he said in a pained whisper. "Is that your son?"

I nodded, wanting to pull away, wanting to turn from the sight of him, from the sight of the body on the bed next to him, the wizened man with the bloody wound in his chest, the red foam at his lips.

I stopped myself, my thoughts reeling: if that was the King, how had he been wounded? That wasn't in the book. And if that was Dafyd, then the man who had just killed the Queen, the man who looked so familiar . . .

Took's face formed with effort what might almost have been a smile. "Good," he said, releasing my arm.

"Reg," Cora said as he faced her, as if they were the only two people in the room.

"Cora." His voice had lost the hint of sadness.

"I never thought I'd see you again," she said breathlessly.

"After this, you mean?" he said, looking down at himself, at the uniform of the King's Men, at the sword.

She reached out and ran her fingertips along his cheek, smearing the Queen's blood in thin trails. "It's been so long," she said quietly.

Dafyd followed the magus's gaze down to the Queen's body, to where the Sunstone lay just above the wound from Bream's sword.

"Quickly," Loren urged.

Dafyd lunged toward the body and grasped the Stone. Pulling it sharply, he snapped the chain, and the Queen's head bounced against the stone floor with a dull thud.

"I did everything you asked," Bream said.

"I know," Cora said, in the tone one might use to comfort a child. "I'm sorry."

"You told me we would be together."

"Yes," she said, still stroking his face. "I've missed you. It's been so long."

He stiffened at the words. "How long?" he asked, his voice suddenly cold.

Cora took a step back. "It's not—"

"How long?" he asked again, his voice rising.

"Sixty years," I said, advancing a little, hoping to get past them to Jacqui and David.

He turned at the sound of my voice, his sword rising. It was as if he hadn't even known I was there.

"It's been more than sixty years," I said.

"Sixty years," he muttered, rolling the words in his mouth.

Dafyd slipped between Bream and the bed, the chain of the Sunstone dangling from his right hand.

"Sixty years?" Pilbream repeated, turning back toward Cora. "But how? You haven't changed."

She shook her head slightly, suddenly awkward in the face of his questioning eyes.

"That's why she sent you away," I said, taking a half-step forward. Bream cocked his head, listening to me without taking his eyes from Cora. "Why she put you into the book. It was all a spell. To keep her young." I tried to keep my voice from breaking, tried to sound strong, but when I looked toward the doorway, saw Jacqui's body still on the ground, saw David crouching again next to her, touching her gently on the cheek, I cracked. "She didn't care who she hurt."

Her eyes flashed at me, and I retreated back to the bedside.

Dafyd stood beside the bed for a long moment, his fist tight around the Stone. He looked first at the King, his chest shuddering, blood seeping from his wound, soaking the sheets around him. Then he looked at his mother, slumped against the foot of the bed, her face damp, contorted in pain.

"Dafyd," the magus urged him.

He bent toward the King, lowering the Stone to the wound on his chest. When he glanced at Bream, their eyes met, and the soldier nodded, his face showing something that looked like pride.

The Stone began to glow as it neared the wounded man. Dafyd closed his eyes—

—and didn't see the King reach up and grasp his wrist, pushing his hand away.

Dafyd's eyes flashed open.

"Stop," the King muttered, in a voice so weak it was difficult to hear.

Dafyd struggled against his grip, trying to push the Stone back toward him.

"Stop," the King ordered again, and this time his voice resonated with a trace of its former power. "Your mother."

"Your Majesty," Bream said, starting forward.

The magus grasped his shoulder, stopping him.

Tears streamed down Dafyd's face.

The King's grip on Dafyd's hand loosened, and his arm fell heavily to his side. "Your mother . . ."

Dafyd bit his lower lip and rose to his feet. Before he turned away, though, he took the King's hand in his own and squeezed it gently.

"Leave him," the magus said to Bream. "It's what the King wants. It's what he always wanted, to save the woman he loves."

As Dafyd knelt beside his mother, the glow of the Sunstone flickered off her face. Cora Took was standing next to Bream, completely rapt with what she was watching, her gun at her side.

I took a careful step back and glanced at David. He was craning his neck to watch as Dafyd pressed the stone into his mother's wound.

She gasped as the stone touched her, and bucked like David in the midst of a seizure, her body snapping and flailing.

And then the movement stopped, and she opened her eyes.

Dafyd lifted the Stone away.

"Dafyd?" she whispered.

I glanced back at David, wanting to urge him to run, but when I saw the expression on his face, the words died on my lips. His eyes wide, he was watching Dafyd and his mother as they embraced, as the Sunstone fell with a barely perceptible clatter to the floor.

Jacqui.

Cora was still watching Dafyd and his mother.

I took another step back. Neither Cora nor Pilbream seemed to notice.

But Pilbream wasn't looking at Dafyd: he was looking at the wizened, festering body next to the still form of the King.

"Lazarus?" he whispered, his horror plain.

The old man didn't speak: he seemed to radiate weakness and pain, his face contorted in agony, his hand fallen over the book where I had dropped it beside him.

"Lazarus, what has happened to you?"

"He's just an old man now, Reg."

Bream's eyes darted around the room, taking in the sores on Took's body, the symbols written on the floor. He approached the bed and dropped to his knees.

"Lazarus, can you hear me?"

Cora flinched when she noticed me still beside the bed, as if she had forgotten that I was there. Her fingers tensed on the gun, but it remained at her side.

I should have told David to run while she was distracted.

By what seemed to be sheer force of will, the old man lifted his hand from his side and took Pilbream's in his own. Pilbream turned back to Cora. His eyes were bright with tears.

"Did you do this to him?" he asked, his voice low.

"It was all part of the plan," she said, keeping her voice light with affection. She sounded like she had in the coffee shop, when she'd kept me off guard long enough to lure me here.

"What plan?" he said, seething. He lowered Took's hand gently to the bed and stood up.

She took a step back. "The plan we talked about."

He moved toward her, and I could see his fingers tightening on the hilt of his sword. "You told me we would be together. You told me we would go somewhere, and never have to worry about him."

"Yes," she said, taking another step backward.

"You never told me about this." He followed her retreat.

"And what—" she asked, her voice suddenly sharp, "what would you have done differently?"

"I never would have hurt him," he said. "Not after everything he did for me. I would have refused."

She laughed. "You've never said no to me."

His sword flashed.

I didn't think it had even touched her, but seconds later a thin seam opened across her throat, widening as blood spurted from it. She rocked back on her heels, and I expected her to fall.

Instead, a faint glow seemed to come from the centre of her chest, just below the neckline of her blouse, a glow that intensified as I watched until it was almost blindingly bright.

And as quickly as it had opened, the slash across her throat closed, like a zipper shutting. The glow faded, leaving her neck pale and unmarked.

She smiled, and raised the gun.

Pilbream stared at her, not understanding, until she reached with her free hand and drew her pendant out from under her blouse, holding it toward him, toward us. It was an identical match to the Sunstone from the book, the amulet that Dafyd had used to heal his mother.

"I don't die easily, Reg," she said coldly. "Though that did take a lot out of me. Keeping me alive is one thing, but healing me . . ." She looked at the Stone, seeming pleased. "I wasn't sure it would work. This opens new worlds of possibilities. New worlds, Reg. But not for you."

I saw the hole open in his forehead, saw his body snap backward, before I heard the shot, the thunder that seemed to fill the world. It echoed in the room as Pilbream's body crashed to the floor.

"David, run!" I screamed, turning toward the door myself, catching his eye.

Cora Took spun and fired.

The bullet caught me as I began to run, too. It should have hit me in the chest but instead hit me in the left side, just below my ribs. It felt like a punch, and I clutched myself, surprised at the burst of searing pain, the sudden disorientation. Glancing down, I saw my blood pouring out of the hole.

"This is one hell of a mess I'm going to have to clean up, Chris," she said. "First things first, though."

She took off after David.

I tried to go after her. I tried to get my feet to move, but I couldn't.

As I started to fall I caught myself on the edge of Took's bed, leaving bloody red handprints on the grey sheets, slowing myself enough that I slumped to the floor beside Pilbream's body.

I tried to fight, tried in vain to pull myself back to my feet.

"Son?"

The voice was a creaky whisper, and I turned to it. To Took.

"Is that your son?" he asked, a question he had asked minutes before.

I nodded, and the movement made me even dizzier. "Yes," I managed.

"Good," he said. "Lighter."

It didn't make any sense to me. I knew the word. I could picture the lighter in my mind, the engraving. But—

"Lighter," he said again, gesturing toward the floor.

Yes, I had dropped my lighter. It felt like a lifetime ago.

I could barely reach it, but I found its weight in my hand oddly comforting as I traced the letters of my name as if they were the most important thing in the world.

He gestured for it with his hand, and I passed it to him. Over the edge of the bed, I made eye contact with Dafyd and Mareigh. They were crouching behind the bed, clearly hiding, hoping that Cora had forgotten them, as I had.

"Your son?" Took repeated.

"Yes. Yes," I gasped, wondering why it was so important.

And then I knew.

I watched as he picked up *To the Four Directions* with one shaking hand, holding it loosely to fan the pages as he struck the lighter. The paper took a moment to catch, the edges curling in the heat. And then it was burning.

Cora burst back into the room smiling triumphantly, dragging David by the ear like a naughty schoolboy, stepping over Jacqui's body. I thought I heard a groan, faint but unmistakable, and Jacqui's hand lifted slightly.

Still alive.

My head swam: I knew I wasn't going to be able to hold on much longer. Blood pulsed against the hand I had pressed tight over the wound.

"He didn't go too far," she said, her voice crisp and bright. "Didn't want to leave his mommy and daddy."

Oh, David.

"I thought you might want to watch," she said, her lips forming a malicious smile. "Kind of a family reunion."

She lost her balance for a moment: I had thought it was just me, but the room was changing again, shuddering and wavering.

"What . . .?" She saw what Lazarus was doing, saw the flames consuming the pages. "Lazarus!"

"David!" Dafyd called out, rising to his feet. "The amulet!"

But David was already in motion, writhing in her grasp, turning enough to grasp the amulet hanging from around Cora's neck and to pull with all his weight. The chain snapped and he stumbled away as she released her grip, reaching instinctively, but too late to protect it.

The room shook like an earthquake had hit. When I glanced at Dafyd, he seemed to be losing focus, shimmering slightly. He was moving to the end of the bed . . .

"Lazarus!" Cora screamed, his name dissolving into a shriek of pain and confusion.

She was changing, somehow, her body losing its definition. At first I thought it was what was happening to Dafyd and Mareigh, the book in flames, closing on itself, but then I realized: Cora was aging. All of those years, all of the pain and change coming on her at once, her body convulsing, shrinking, crumpling.

As she screamed in rage and fear, she lifted the gun.

I knew what was coming. With my last bit of strength, I pushed myself away from the bed, falling hard on my side.

I couldn't keep track of what was happening anymore. I could hear Cora screaming. I could see Dafyd moving at the foot of the bed.

I heard David calling, "Dad!"

It was so cold. I could feel myself drifting away.

"Chris!" The voice was deep and strong, a boy's. I tried to focus, but Dafyd was rippling, growing shadowy. The book . . . the book must be just about gone.

"Chris!" Dafyd said again. David must have told him my name. "Before it's too late."

I looked down at his hand, at where the Sunstone was glowing, nearing my chest. Even it, though, seemed to be blurring, fading, becoming indistinct. One more thing that would leave this world when the book disappeared.

"Sir!" He wanted me to turn, to give him easier access to my wounds.

"No," I said, holding his hand away, struggling to sit up. "No."

"But there's not much time."

He wasn't expecting me to grab for the Stone. It came loose from his hand.

"David," I called, not sure if I was even making a sound.

He turned to me, his eyes wide, frantic.

"Your mother," I said, holding the stone high. "Your mother." I mustered all my strength. "Catch," I said.

And the last thing I knew was throwing it to my son, watching the Sunstone arc through the air, glinting red, as everything else faded to black.

☙ ❧

In Portland, Oregon, Stephen Griffin woke for the first time since 1952.

In Taos, New Mexico, Dan Santos opened his eyes, waking for the first time since 1963.

John Philips, in Poughkeepsie, New York, awoke after feeling he'd been in another world since 1969.

In Omaha, Nebraska, Stuart Johnson woke from a dream of shadows and stones that he had been trapped in since 1987.

In San Jose, California, Raymond Chan spoke for the first time since 1993, asking his father for a glass of water.

In Liberty, Florida, David Miles, twenty years old, awoke for the first time since 2001.

In Bellevue, Washington, Matthew Corvin opened his eyes.

The room was unfamiliar, but he knew, without knowing how, that he was home.

"Mom?" he called out, testing a voice he hadn't used in more than thirty years. "Mom?"

He heard a scream in the distance, then the sound of feet on stairs.

"Matty?" his mother said as she stepped timidly into the room, her hands clenched in front of her as if to defend herself.

When he smiled at her, she broke, her tears accompanied by huge heaving gasps. She stumbled toward him, toward his bed, and then she was holding him and touching him and tousling his hair.

Home.

"Oh God, Matty," she crooned. "Oh God, baby."

In a stone room, high above the Oregon Coast, Christopher Knox opened his eyes.

The first thing I saw was a shadow. As my vision cleared, that shadow took on shape, took on David's familiar features. He was leaning over me, his face tight with fear, his eyes widening as I smiled.

"Dad!" he said, throwing himself on top of me, hugging me tightly.

I held him close, smelling him, feeling him breathe, listening to him as he cried in my arms. All I could do was say his name.

"Davy," I breathed.

I breathed.

"What happened?" I asked into his hair.

"You died." The voice wasn't his.

Glancing up, I saw Jacqui looking down at me, her face drawn and pale. The front of her shirt was drenched with blood, a ragged hole over the centre of her chest.

"Jacqui." I reached out, weak, shaking. She took my hand. "You're okay."

She nodded, then her own tears came. She let them streak down her cheeks without actually allowing herself to cry.

"We have to get out of here," she said flatly, her eyes flickering somewhere to my right.

As I followed her gaze, I became aware of waves of heat pulsating toward me. Took's bed was on fire.

"Come on," she urged, pulling at my hand.

I braced myself against the floor with my other hand. As I rose stiffly to my knees, I saw a flash of silver on the floor: my lighter. I reached for it, almost falling again as I grabbed it.

I got to my feet, leaning against David. The flames were rising higher from the bed now. Deep within the orange caldera I could vaguely make out the shape of a body under the burning sheet.

I had to turn away: he had saved us all.

Jacqui took my other arm. We staggered slowly toward the door, and as we approached Cora Took's body I pulled David closer, held his face tight to me, hiding the sight of her withered form.

She was just an old woman now, fallen dead to a hard floor.

We didn't stop until we were outside, in the cool dark, the breeze off the water heavy with the smell of the sea, the old trees above us. As I collapsed on the front steps, David looked around in the moonlight.

"This is what it smells like," he said quietly. "Colcott. Not the town, but just outside of it, where the trees start to close around the road."

I looked at him, my son, my boy, come back to us from so, so far away.

The stories he could tell.

"David," I said. I gestured at the stone step beside me, and he sat and snuggled in, still small enough to fit into my embrace. Jacqui sat down beside him, her arm around his shoulders, her hand touching my back.

At first, he didn't want to talk about it, but I had to know what had happened, after. After I was gone.

"At first, when the man on the bed—"

"Lazarus Took," I said.

He just looked at me for a long moment. "When he lit the book on fire, everything started to change. It was like Dafyd and his mother and the magus . . . they were disappearing."

"Back into the book," I said.

"Yeah," he said, shivering a little in the breeze. "And the Sunstone, it was fading too. When I . . ." He glanced at his mother. "When I touched it on Mom, it was like it started to dissolve in my hand. I didn't think it was going to work."

"But it did," I said quietly. My eyes met hers; neither of us looked away.

"Yeah."

It took me a moment; my mind was slow, groggy. "But if the Sunstone disappeared . . ."

He wriggled against me as he reached into his pocket, his elbow jamming into my ribs. When he pulled his hand out, he was holding the Sunstone, the chain dangling between his fingers.

"It was hers," he said. "That woman's." He held the amulet out toward me. "I thought maybe, if the other one worked, this one . . ."

He pushed himself into me as hard as he could. I could feel his back trembling as he cried. Jacqui's arms enwrapped him, and me, from the other side.

We just held him, for a long time.

"We should go," Jacqui said when he began to calm, looking at us, then up at the dark house.

I nodded. "Let's go, sport," I said, squeezing him again for good measure.

"Home?" he asked.

I looked at Jacqui.

"Soon," she said, meeting my eye.

⁂

Arian and Tamas had spent the day carrying armloads of splintered tables and chairs through the kitchen, piling them in the corner of the yard. They had salvaged what they could, Tamas fixing what he was able to, scavenging pieces from furniture that was beyond repair.

The Mermaid's Rest looked almost its old self by the time they were done. There weren't many places for people to sit, and most of the ale was lost, pooled on the floor from smashed kegs—but with no sign of Mareigh, The Mermaid wouldn't be opening its doors that day anyway.

They hadn't spoken much over the day, each of them alone with private thoughts. Once Tamas had told her what had happened after she went to the abbey, Arian had closed down. He had tried to cheer her, telling her, "I am sure he'll return," but neither of them really believed that, and silence seemed a better choice than lies, however comforting they were intended to be.

"So what should we do now?" Tamas asked, leaning against the bar.

She pulled him a flagon of the remaining ale, and set it on the bar next to his elbow.

He looked down at it. "You'll hear about that when Mareigh gets back."

She bit her lip. "I hope so," she said.

"You should have one too."

She shook her head. "Not—" And she stopped herself. "Not while I'm working."

Tamas drank in silence as the sun slid through the front windows, the late afternoon light glowing against the floor.

At first, the sound seemed like distant thunder, a low rumble that they felt more than heard. It took a moment for Tamas to recognize it for what it was.

"Horses," he said, starting for the door, Arian following.

All up the street, people were coming out of their doors, looking up in the direction of the castle as the sound grew louder. When the first of the riders rounded the sharp corner, people reflexively stepped back, giving the mounted guardsmen wide berth as they passed.

Four mounted guards led in full dress, pikes gleaming in the sun. Behind them, four of the Brotherhood, their cloaks rich and silver. Dress robes. Formal.

The guardsmen came to a stop just past the tavern, turning their mounts so they faced the rest of the procession.

Behind the Brotherhood, two men on horseback. One, a member of the Brotherhood, his robes grey and dingy, his beard white.

The other . . .

"Dafyd," Arian whispered, and Tamas had to look twice.

It was his friend, his oldest friend, sitting high on one of the finest mounts he had ever seen. Dafyd was dressed in a simple tunic of deep green, but even from a distance Tamas could see that it was finely made, not the rough work of uniforms and street clothes. The crest of Colcott was embroidered on its front, and matched the amulet that hung from a gold chain around his neck. The gold caught the afternoon light, as did the circlet he wore on his head.

Dafyd stared straight ahead, a grim look on his face. In the weeks he had been gone, Tamas thought, he seemed to have aged years: he looked strong, confident.

As he turned to the doorway, though, he seemed to lose some internal battle for poise, his face breaking into a wide grin.

"By the gods," Tamas muttered.

"His Majesty the King, Dafyd the Second," one of the riders called out, and Tamas and Arian realized they'd best drop to their knees.

Behind Dafyd and the magus, a bright carriage drawn by two horses came to a stop.

Dafyd dismounted easily, almost gracefully, and moved to the door of the carriage before the steward could open it.

When Mareigh stepped out, dressed in finery befitting a lady of the court, Dafyd took her hand and led her toward the doorway.

"That," Mareigh said, looking at the two kneeling figures, "is what I like to see."

Arian glanced up and caught the teasing smile on the woman's lips.

"King Dafyd?" Tamas said, staring at the ground. "What have you done?" He risked a glance up and saw Dafyd smiling at him. When the new King reached out a hand, Tamas took it and allowed himself to be drawn up to his feet, into Dafyd's embrace.

Dafyd whispered in Tamas's ear, "There's someone I want you to meet."

Tamas pulled away from him. "Who?"

Dafyd cocked his head, and one of the lead riders, one of the guardsmen, dismounted and approached.

"This is Captain Knox," he said. "He'll be in charge of your training."

"My . . ." Tamas looked between Dafyd and the soldier as the full weight of the words settled on him. "Tell me you are not joking."

Dafyd smiled. "I am not joking. A king needs a guardsman, someone to advise him, someone to stand alongside him. And I need a friend."

Tamas nodded and grinned, almost bursting with excitement.

"And you," Dafyd said softly, turning to Arian, who did not raise her eyes. "Arian," he said.

She looked up at him.

He extended his hand.

She accepted it, and allowed the new King to help her to her feet.

✿ ✿

I drove back to the hotel at a crawl, leaning forward against the steering wheel, not trusting the roads, not trusting myself.

Jacqui was silent beside me, her face dimly lit by the blue glow of the dashboard. David was in the back, and I caught myself checking him in the mirror, over and over again, needing to reassure myself that he was there, that he was really there.

"Chris," Jacqui said, as the road widened out of the ancient forest. "The police?"

"I don't know," I said. "I think it will take them a while to find . . ." I couldn't bring myself to say the word 'bodies.' I thought about the room and how it had looked as we left. "I think it'll be okay. Lazarus died in his bed. Burned. And Cora . . . I think they'll think she had a heart attack. Maybe she did."

"But the gun?"

I shrugged. There was nothing we could do. There was the gun, and my blood on the floor beside the bed. But there were also all the symbols, and Took's blood, everywhere. It would be a mess to sort out.

"If we're lucky, the whole place will burn down."

I was about to tell her not to worry when my telephone rang, its light flashing from the cup-holder closest to the driver's seat. Jacqui must have brought it with her.

I looked at her, glanced at the clock on the dashboard. Too late for anyone to be calling.

"Hello?" I said, holding the phone carefully, easing off on the gas.

"Chris? It's Carol Corvin." Her voice was measured, as if she were struggling to hold something in. "Is David with you? Is he . . ."

"He's . . . here," I said carefully, well aware of the significance of the word.

"Can you put him on? Matthew—" Her voice broke, and her next words came out in sobs. "Matthew wants to talk to him."

I handed the phone back between the seats. "David," I said gently. "It's for you."

He was slow in taking it from me. In the mirror I could see the confusion in his face, the wariness.

"Hello?" he said tentatively.

Listening, his face broke into a smile, and I could see tears in the corners of his eyes.

I could feel them in mine.

"Chris, what . . .?" Jacqui asked.

I shook my head, and reaching across the space between the seats, took her hand in mine.

ACKNOWLEDGEMENTS

I've been living with *Bedtime Story*—in various forms and stages of development—for more than half a decade now. In that time, I'm sure that errors and mistakes have been made: I'm responsible for those. I cop to it freely.

Those things that went right, though, I owe to a tremendous group of people.

First, to my family, which somehow seems to keep growing: births, marriages, remarriages, domestic arrangements . . . To all the Eddys, the Wiersemas, the Dusmanns, and the various other permutations—I cannot thank you enough.

Special thanks, of course, are due the moms in my life: my mother Helen Eddy, and my mother-in-law June Dusmann. I cannot express my gratitude for the support and their enthusiasm over the years. And to my grandmother, Phyllis Eddy, one of the people I most admire in the world.

To my mind, *Before I Wake* was a story about mothers and daughters; *Bedtime Story* is a novel about fathers and sons. With that in mind, I want to give my deepest thanks to some of the men who have shaped my life. My father, Joe Wiersema, who gave me life and a middle initial, also gave me a love of reading: his were the first "grown-up" books I read, and I never looked back. To say that he has always been one of my biggest supporters would be a grave understatement. My brothers, Dave and Jon, are writ large in my soul. We're not the closest of siblings, but I would die for either of them. My stepfather, Tom Baldwin, is both smart and wise, and makes my mother happy (which is both wise and smart). My father-in-law, Rolf Dusmann, either welcomed me into his family, or tried to scare me out of it, with a white-knuckle Volkswagen ride which haunts my dreams. He still scares the hell out of me, and I love him dearly. My brother-in-law, Terry Dusmann, has always been one of the strongest supporters of my writing, and he vows he's my "one phone call" should I ever get arrested in the GVRD.

And my thanks to one teacher this time, Mr. Siver ("like a diver, not a river"), who on the first day of grade five introduced a classroom of malcontents to the idea of Jungian archetypes. One of us was listening, and it shaped my life.

My life, and writing, have also been shaped by twenty years as a bookseller. I've been blessed to have spent the bulk of that time working for, and with, Mel Bolen and Samantha Holmes, who have been nothing but supportive and encouraging. I go to work, every day, at Bolen Books, with the finest booksellers in the country, and good friends who keep me (relatively) down to earth. Being a bookseller also means being a part of a larger community of like-minded rebels who recognize, and have given their lives to, the written word. B.C. is graced with the best booksellers and sales reps I know, and I am truly blessed to have you all as friends. Thank you, always, for fighting the good fight.

The actual writing of a novel is a long, solitary process. There are a couple of people, though, who provided invaluable assistance during that lonely time. The good doctor—and writer—Kevin Patterson once again offered crucial medical guidance, and my thanks go out to Chris Houston for his invaluable support.

Once the manuscript was off my desk, it went first to three people whose eyes I have come to depend upon: Cori Dusmann, James Grainger, and Colin Holt. Saint Jimmy is the sort of man every writer should be lucky enough to have in his corner: never short of opinions, with a keen eye and a sense of vision (the two should always go hand in hand). Colin has become essential to my survival over the last few years: he not only weighs in on the words, but he has a knack for planning and a pragmatic efficiency that has rescued me more than once.

I'll come back to Cori.

As the manuscript went out into the wider world, it became clear, once again, that I have been fortunate enough to align myself with, frankly, the best in the business. I'm represented by the McDermid Agency, and my thanks go out to Martha Magor, Monica Pacheco, and Chris Bucci. My deepest appreciation, however, I extend to Anne McDermid, who is less an agent than a force of nature.

A special thanks to Lisa and Gregory Thomas-Tench, and the team at Redwerks.org, who are responsible for the redesign of robertjwiersema. com: drinks are definitely owed. And drinks also to Michael Holt, who held my hand through my early forays into the online world, and who has been a rock of support.

The whole team at Random House Canada is also without peer. From people like Karen Blair, who has been one of my biggest supporters from the beginning, to Cassandra Sadek and Julie Forrest in the online department, to Leah Springate, who made *Bedtime Story* a beautiful object, inside and out, I'm really in the best of hands. My thanks go out to Craig Pyette, who edited this book both bravely and skilfully, to my publishers Anne Collins and Marion Garner, and to Louise Dennys. My publicist, Sharon Klein, is simply the best, and, as such, is the only person—other than my grandmother—who gets away with calling me "Robbie." And special thanks to Kendall Anderson, who was there at the beginning, and whose influence carries clearly through these finished pages.

The act of writing acknowledgements like this is something of a double-edged sword: it provides an opportunity to publicly thank the people who have made a difference, but it also underscores just how insufficient words can be.

Nowhere is that more clear than when it comes to Cori and Xander.

Xander is eleven now, the same age as David in this novel (I'll leave the psychological ramifications of that—and so much else—for someone else to decipher), and he inspires and amazes me every single day. He is also supportive, and an earnest champion, and he knows now that dreams come true, but not free.

And Cori. This book, once again, owes everything to her. She is not only a fearsome reader and editor, she is also my inspiration. She is the reason I write, and has been now for more than two decades. These words belong as much to her as they do me. Thank you, Cor. From the bottom of my heart.

I would like to gratefully acknowledge the financial support I received from the Canada Council for the Arts, which assisted immeasurably in the writing of *Bedtime Story*.